END TIME

Daniel Greene

ISBN: 0692489266
ISBN-13: 978-0692489260

To my parents for instilling in me the power to dream.
To Jennifer, for allowing me to never give up that dream.

JOSEPH
Kombarka, Democratic Republic of the Congo

Dr. Joseph Jackowski awoke with a gasp, a breath caught in his chest. His fitful night's sleep broken as if an apparition threw frigid water on his face. He blinked his eyes rapidly. The familiarity of his tent ceiling did little to calm him. The heat of the night washed over him like a thick woolen blanket making him uncomfortable at best. *What was that?*

As if to answer his thoughts, a scream pierced the humid night. He rubbed his eyes and reached for his wire-rimmed glasses, securing them on his face. *Am I dreaming?* The frogs, bugs, and other creatures of the night that screeched, buzzed and flapped endlessly were now quiet, as though they dared not make a sound. He turned his head to the side, listening intently.

Another scream bellowed long and low through the thick nighttime air, making him jump.

"Jesus Christ," he cursed. These were not the screams of pleasure or fear. They were the wails of pain; a person in terrible amounts of pain. The sound punched Joseph's gut, making the hair on his arms stand on edge. He had never heard anything like it, but some deep-rooted primal gene, long dormant in Joseph's line of descendants, whispered to run. Only evil lies ahead.

Joseph contemplated crawling further into his sleeping bag, but knew he couldn't. He had patients to care for in the hospital near the center of Kombarka. If one could call the middle of the village, a center, a few hundred-forest dwellers living near the Congo River was hardly anything to write home about. They were poor people. Sick people. Dying people.

He glanced at the glowing face of his Seiko watch. It read 4:30 a.m. His thin, orange, nylon tent was dark. Lightless in the deep foliage. There were no city lights or lampposts, not even a lantern this far into the jungle. Even the moon hid in the night. He fumbled around for his flashlight, scaring himself as he scratched the tent bottom with his fingernails. *It's only me you oaf. That dumb thing should be somewhere around here*, he thought. His fingers patted down his laptop and pack.

More screams from the village made him slap the ground faster. *What's going on? Rebels? No. There is no gunfire. Unless they were using machetes to hack up the villagers, a much more likely and no less terrible option.* Joseph shuddered, his thin body trembling a bit. Every trip to the bush brought with it a host of dangers, disease, wild animals, poisonous insects, including death at the hands of overzealous rebels of which there were many in the DRC.

The rustling of Agents Reliford and Nixon in the tent next to his confirmed that he wasn't imagining the horrid cries. The screams were not some sort of delusional manifestation brought upon by dehydration or, even worse, the virus that had brought him to this horrible heart of darkness called Kombarka.

The agents were there to provide security, but their presence afforded him no solace from the calls for help below and provided him with no protection from the deadly microbe that had ravaged his patients' bodies. It was unlike any virus he had seen, so he observed only tepidly at a distance.

The symptoms were similar to that of Monkeypox: a rash, swollen lymph nodes, fever, and dysentery. The most notable exception that he discovered within a few days were that the timetables had been more accelerated than any other disease surveillance deployment he had been on for the U.S. Centers for Disease Control and Prevention. It chilled him to the bone, because nothing he had done even remotely slowed down the rapid progression of the disease. The first patient had died early in the night, and he knew it wouldn't be the last.

Joseph pulled on his pants awkwardly in the dark, unable to stand totally upright in his low-hanging tent. He felt for the zipper to his tent. Succeeding, he unzipped it and peered out into the darkness. Countryside dark. The kind of pitch black that can only be found beyond a city's limits. *Wish I could have found that flashlight,* he thought. Ahead he could just make out the large white hospital tent, and to his right he could hardly see the Diplomatic Security Special Agents' matching tent next him, only a faint, orange mound protruding from the dark. They always had to share a tent during disease surveillance expeditions. He was sure the two men loved that.

A mosquito buzzed past his ear. Joseph slapped at the infuriating creature, but was rewarded with only a stinging handprint on the back of his neck. No matter how much of the chemical laden industrial bug spray he put on, they still came for him. He knew that they were attracted to the steroids or cholesterol on the surface of the skin. With his impeccable vegetarian diet he found it hard to believe he emitted such chemicals. *These prehistoric monsters must be immune to modern insect repellent*, he thought, swatting at another winged creature.

Beads of sweat instantly rolled down his back. Joseph listened intently, straining his eyes, but all he heard was the high pitched whining of insects darting in and out around him. A tense nothingness hung in the air.

"Arhhh, Arhhhhhhh," screeched from the hospital tent.

"Oh God!" he said out loud, hurriedly throwing on a white undershirt.

He finally located his elusive flashlight and began to fiddle with it as he walked towards the hospital tent. "Come on work," he pleaded with the non-compliant flashlight. He short stepped toward the hospital tent, trying not to fall or worse break an ankle. A cool hand grabbed him from behind surprising him.

"What?" he gasped, spinning quickly.

"Hold on there, partner. You shouldn't be running around in the dark by yourself," Agent Nixon said, his normally jovial voice tremulous.

Joseph exhaled loudly.

"Jesus. You scared me," he breathed and squinted at the outline of the agent in the dark. He could hardly make out the man's frame, but he sensed that the cocky bastard was smiling in the dark. Nixon was a new member to the embassy security detail and the two men had only met a week ago.

His first impression of the man was less than favorable. Agent Nixon had shown up late for their departure to the field. This wasn't a horrible slight in itself, but the fact that the man had been fraternizing with female members of the embassy staff made it unacceptable.

"Something is going on in the hospital. I must check on the patients," Joseph said, staring at the man impatiently.

"I know Joseph. Let's wait on Agent Drago before we go running off into the night getting ourselves in a lick of trouble," Agent Nixon said. But, despite his continued jest at Agent Reliford's appearance, Nixon sounded tense.

"It is Dr. Jackowski, please, I earned that title. And this is an emergency. People's lives are in danger," Joseph said. He waited, irritably staring at the white

Red Cross hospital tent, crossing and rubbing his arms in an effort to brush away the mosquitos. *In danger from what?* A shadow moved across the tent outlined by the white material making his gut churn. *Something is out here.*

His attention came back to his escort as Agent Reliford and his interpreter Bowali sauntered up from their tents. The contrast between the two was stark: Reliford was tall, white and muscular; Bowali was short, black and thin.

"It seems that we're waiting on you this time, Agent Reliford. Your team has made a habit of being late." He didn't care if he was rude. These agents were getting in the way of his research, something that a man of his caliber had no time for.

"I don't have time to waste waiting on your team to do their job," he added.

"We have a protocol for this type of thing, doctor," Agent Reliford said. He glanced down at Joseph, brow furrowing as he secured a small plastic earpiece around his ear. "We should have already left after the reports we received from the embassy."

Even in the dark, the large man wore his trademark scowl.

"If it's rebels, we'll exfiltrate back to the consulate... Nixon, switch communications to Channel 2."

Joseph looked at him furiously. More seconds escaped into the night. "Are you finished with your lecture?"

Agent Reliford stared through him. "I'm sorry, but your safety is paramount. We are sticking to the book on this one."

The doctor returned his stone-cold gaze, and then averted his eyes. "Fine, but hurry. These people are depending on me. This may be vital to my research."

Ahead of them, a small hovel, cobbled together with a host of random materials, burst into flames. The sudden singular brightness bloomed a miniature sun in the dark.

"Fucking A," Nixon cursed. Shadows moved in and around the hovels, trying to put out the flames.

"I'll make a quick circuit around the village and see if they need help. Nixon, make sure nothing happens to Dr. Jackowski," Reliford said, heading off into the night.

Joseph could taste the smoke in the night air and he breathed it in as he ran to the hospital tent. It stung his eyes and burned his throat. Joseph ripped open the mosquito mesh door and ran straight into a man in dirty, torn clothes. The emaciated man fell backwards clumsily onto the floor. Agent Nixon, a step behind, caught Joseph as he stumbled.

"Gotcha there, boss," he said, straightening Joseph out and mock brushing his shoulder for him.

Joseph waved him off. "Get your hands off me. You scoundrel," He straightened his glasses. "Claude and Jules, what is going o-?"

His local nursing aides were not inside the tent. But others he did not recognize were. They walked around the neat rows of makeshift hospital cots. Most were clustered around the patients still laying in their cots.

"Visiting hours are over," he said, a little more shrilly than he would of liked. "Bowali, make the translation," he said. His translator rapidly made the statement behind him in their native tongue, Lingala. The people did not respond, and he realized that they were dressed in the same soiled clothing as his patients, confusing him. Anyone who contracted the disease was bedridden within days. In fact, most just lay in makeshift cots in their own excrement.

"I... how is this possible?" he asked himself.

He lashed out at a group of people nearby. This was *his* hospital tent.

"What are you doing?" Joseph called out. People shouldn't be in here without his approval. The disease was just too unpredictable. It most likely spread from eating infected meat from the bush, but he couldn't rule out an airborne mutation.

"Joe, what's wrong with them? There's blood all over them," Nixon said, covering his nose.

"That is terrible," Bowali said. "I feel like I'm going to be," Bowali said, bending over to retch.

Agent Nixon was right. Blood covered their faces and hands, sweat staining their dirt-covered clothes. *Could this be a mutation?* He would have to get one of the aides to change out their clothes.

"Cover your mouths," Joseph said, taking a step back.

He took stock of the tent. Almost none of the patients were in their cots. "Bowali, please tell these people to lie back down, and we will get them treatment as soon as possible," he said, trying to control his emotions.

Bowali relayed the message voice shaking. The patients did not respond. They continued to dig at a patient still laying in his cot.

"I said, what are you doing?" Joseph asked loudly, over the muffling of his shirtsleeve. The entire situation went beyond his comprehension.

What is wrong with these people? Delusional manifestations? Had the virus attacked the Labyrinth of the inner ear, affecting the patients' hearing and balance?

A few moments passed, and the patient Joseph had knocked down began to pull himself up off the ground like an old man rising out of bed. Joseph had completely forgotten about the small man amid all the activity.

"Bowali, help him to a cot," he ordered with a wave. His attention wrapped solely around the crowd of people ahead. The crowd of emaciated people clawed the flesh of their victim by the handful, stuffing their faces with it. They mashed their teeth loudly, chewing with their mouths open. An infected woman in a loose gown, blood oozing down the sides of her mouth, pulled on one of the bedridden patient's arms. She pulled in a tug-of-war for the limb until the flesh tore sounding like a linen ripping in two.

He stood still jaw dropping behind his sleeve. Confusion and shock washed over him as crimson fluid sprayed the perpetrator's face and body.

"What the hell?" Agent Nixon swore underneath his breath.

Joseph shouted: "Stop! Stop this nonsense now."

The patients were deaf to Joseph's pleas. Bowali's voice quivered as he translated. His translation jarred the gore-covered patients' attention toward the three newcomers as if they had just noticed them for the first time. They dropped bits and pieces of the man. Awkwardly, the bloodied sick people stumbled forward with arms outstretched, like toddlers reaching for a coveted toy. The faces of his patients entranced him; their pupil-less eyes snow white.

The soft sound of gun metal releasing from hard plastic revealed Agent Nixon's play.

"No, please…" Bowali's terrified voice brought Joseph back to reality.

Bowali grappled with a skinny man, who bent in, his neck reaching in an inhuman stretch, to take a chunk of flesh from Bowali's arm.

"Get back," shouted Agent Nixon. His weapon in one hand, he shoved the patient to the ground with the other.

"Please, you must stop. I can help you," Joseph pleaded. His breath wasted on the blood-covered patients ambling towards him. An all-out panic consumed him. He had come face to face with deadly microbes that could kill a man in a matter of hours; some even faster. But never had he come into contact with murderers. They looked rabid, like deranged barbarous animals.

This can't be happening. It's just a horrible dream. That's it, a nightmare. Joseph held his breath in an attempt to wake up. *It's just a dream. It's just a dream.*

Agent Nixon's voice cut through the craziness of the background. Gunshots exploded in the air. Joseph's eardrums reverberated with high-pitched ringing. Scared shitless, he fell backwards, becoming entangled with an empty cot, now an insurmountable obstacle. Joseph struck the hard dirt floor with a thud and his glasses flew from his face as if they no longer wanted to be there. His breath struggled to reach his lungs, only able to take in the smallest amount of air. His eyes squeezed shut in pain.

After a moment, he slowly opened his eyes. Milky white eyes glared into his, the unblinking and lifeless eyes of a man with a bullet hole in his head. *This can't be happening.* His vision blurred, Joseph groped the earth-packed floor for his glasses.

Any second now the crazed patients would be all over him, biting and chewing him to pieces. He wet himself as two hands slammed into his shoulders and dug into his sweaty skin.

"No, please," he begged, curling into a ball.

A great strength pulled him to his feet. Joseph opened his eyes with hesitation, anticipating a macabre face inching toward his.

"Joseph?" a voice entreated. Agent Nixon stood close to him, his face flush with agitation. "Are you okay? We need to leave."

Nixon's eyes darted back and forth. "I got no comms with Reliford. We are going back to the vehicle."

Nixon stuck his head through the tent door. "I don't know what's going on here, but I don't want to stay around to find out," he said, removing some sort of bullet holder from his gun. The agent looked closely at the bullets before slamming them back in the gun.

Joseph had never understood guns. He turned to study Bowali standing there holding his forearm, a dumbfounded look scrawled across his face. He held his arm close to his body as if he were afraid he was going to lose it, redness seeping between his fingers.

"He bit me. Doctor, he bit me," Bowali said, gritting his teeth.

Joseph snapped back into his role as a man of medicine. Although trauma care wasn't his specialty in the medical community, he had more than enough training. Bowali's hand shook as he removed it from his wound, revealing the imprint of a human bite. Puncture wounds revealed white bone exposed from where the teeth had sawed all the way through the muscle.

"A thorough cleaning, and some stitches and you'll be fine," Joseph said, dismissing the severity of the injury. Although a human bite could carry high quantities of bacteria, Bowali's bite was medically superficial. In their current situation, his bite could be much worse.

His ears still faintly ringing, Joseph said loudly, "Wrap it in this towel. I'll clean it in a moment." He tossed a rag to Bowali, who pressed it into his arm.

Joseph surveyed the blood-spattered room in shock. His research hospital utterly destroyed looking like a horrific slaughterhouse. Bodies were strewn about what should have been a place of healing. "What have you done? You shot these people," he yelled at Nixon, gesturing madly.

"Couldn't you have done anything else?"

"Listen, Joe, I don't know if you saw what those 'people' were doing, but they were gutting that guy," Nixon shouted, his voice rising in a frenzy.

"It doesn't matter. We have a responsibility to help them. It's possible this was only a symptom of the disease. Maybe it could be treated."

Joseph rushed over to the bodies of the fallen patients and began to palpate their carotids for signs of life. He would never be able to save them here. He would most likely be ostracized from his medical community for allowing his patients to be killed. Joseph rolled over the nearest body to examine the wounds. Shredded flesh protruded from the man's wounds like he had eaten an exploding mushroom. *Poor bastard*, Joseph thought. *Well, at least he won't suffer anymore.*

Joseph glanced up as Nixon's radio went off. "This is Reliford… we… oh shit, get back." A loud gunshot boomed, followed by another boom.

Nixon's brow bunched up over his narrow-set eyes as he responded. "Nixon to Reliford. You copy? Over."

Static erupted through the radio as Nixon spoke into his mic again. "Nixon to Reliford. Do you copy? Over." More static reverberated. The tent's eerie silence contrasted with the occasional scream and the slap of running feet from the outside.

"We have to move to the rally point," Nixon said.

Bowali nodded, a terrified look in his eyes. "Yes, we must leave here," he slurred. Joseph glowered at the interpreter who looked like he was about to faint.

"You Agent Nixon are responsible for this. This carnage," Joseph chided. A loud moan resounded from behind Joseph startling him. The patient with the mortal gunshot wounds to the chest pulled himself into a sitting position, a rag doll sitting upright. Blood ran freely from his wounds his body unable to keep it in. Then he stood up as if two bullets hadn't just decimated the organs contained within his puny skeletal body. *This is not possible*, Joseph thought.

With horror in his eyes, Joseph took a few steps back.

"But... but... that's impossible," Joseph whispered. The thunder of gunfire roared through the tent. Finding a place to hide was his only thought.

STEELE
Undisclosed Location

The cabin of the aircraft shook with turbulence, shuddering violently. *Were they using duct tape to keep this thing together?* He took a sideways glance at the man next to him. The suited businessman cast an eye over the cabin nervously, pupils shifting side to side. His hands dug into the armrests, white-knuckled and afraid.

"We're going to be fine," Mark Steele said to the man.

His words seemed to appease the man momentarily. The man closed his eyes and whispered what sounded like the Lord's Prayer over and over. *Jesus. I hope this guy isn't some sort of nut job, EDPs were the worst.*

Steele looked at the passengers around him seated in the plush leather seats of first class. A body filled every seat, four passengers per row split down the middle by a single aisle. A relatively unsuspecting group surrounded him: a host of businessmen; a couple of honeymooners, flight attendants and a few upgrades. One man kept ringing his flight attendant call button, of which the male flight attendant in the galley actively ignored now.

There was nothing of note on the surface, but something wasn't right in the first class cabin. A tension hovered over them that made the hair stand up on the back of his neck. In the industry, they called it a 'sixth sense' or 'intuition.' When something didn't feel right, odds are it wasn't. *Always go with your gut.*

Steele turned his broad frame in his seat, eying the passengers behind him with unsuspecting suspicion. A woman sat stoically behind him. She wore a light tan jacket with a red scarf around her neck. She stared right back at him, her eyes cold and her facial features flat as if waiting to be impressed. He gave her a friendly smile and a nod.

I'll probably have to shoot her. He fingered the course handle of his SIG Sauer P226 .40 caliber pistol wedged inside the front of his pants.

He would have to wait though, until she made the first move. Slouching a bit in his seat, he pulled a magazine from the pocket of the seat back. A couple on the front cover strolled causally through a marketplace on a cobbled city street. *Visit the Cradle of Civilization: Damascus.* He flipped through a few pages trying to ignore the uneasiness winding in his gut.

Why would anyone want to go to Syria? Steele looked back at the cover. The date read October 2010. *No wonder.*

"Hey, look here," he said, showing the magazine to the man next to him. "You ever been to Aleppo, *Bob?*"

The man next to him shook his head no and peered out the window. *Guess he isn't going by Bob today. Oh well. He would probably live.* Steele flipped the page, trying to appear nonchalant. *Some people just couldn't fly.*

The aircraft swung into a nosedive and Steele felt his body slide forward in his seat. Only his seatbelt prevented him from face-planting into the seat in front of him. His stomach rose up into his throat. *Is anyone flying this thing?*

People yelped in surprise. Hands pushed on the seats ahead of them, holding their owners in place. A male flight attendant sat down in a folding jump seat near the cockpit. Steele wasn't that surprised. He had flown more times than he cared to count in the past six years; something his muscular body hid well. Dropping hundreds of feet in the air wasn't unheard of, especially when they hit an air pocket, the equivalent of hitting a pothole in a car.

Ding. The yellow seatbelt light flashed above the galley and the aircraft leveled out again.

"Sorry about that, folks. Just making sure you were still awake," the captain said over the PA system.

A few people laughed out loud. *Bunch of comedians in the group. Its always easier to laugh at the guy in the hot seat.* A man cursed, and a moment later angry footsteps pounded up the aisle.

Steele knew they were coming. He wondered why they had waited so long. Perhaps they were just toying with him. Perhaps not. *The bastards are coming. More than one.*

He tried to get a look back out of the corner of his eye. A body blurred passed him, then another and another. They were eerily quiet until their kicks and fists reverberated off the cockpit door with loud, hollow booms.

"Open the fucking door," one screamed.

Positioning themselves strategically in the aisle, the hijackers pulled out handguns, brandishing them at the passengers in first class. *Glock 9mms.*

"Oh my God," yelled one of the businessmen, half standing in his seat. The thumping of fists on the door continued from the front galley. The honeymooners held each other in terror. *Jesus Christ*, Steele thought. He peered over his shoulder at the shorthaired woman behind him. She still stared straight ahead, not responding to the stimulus of guns. *Unusual.* His heart beat a mile a minute.

"Everyone shut the fuck up," the hijacker yelled, pushing his gun into a female flight attendant's face. He wrapped an arm around her neck, holding the handgun to her head. His bald head poked up over her shoulder. "Hands up," he shouted, spit flying from his goatee lined mouth.

"I'll blow this fucker out of the sky," said another hijacker from near the lavatories in the middle of the cabin. He held something in his hand, wires running under his shirt.

Steele looked at him cautiously. *Really? A half-dozen hijackers with bombs and guns. Christ. What have I gotten myself into?*

Focusing forward once again, he collected himself. He hoped one of his partners was paying attention. Out of his peripherals he barely noticed a fist sailing his way. He half-ducked, catching it off the top of his head covering the side of his face with his arm, ramming a shoulder into the gut of the businessman next to him. *Really Bob? You are in on this too?* The man grunted upon impact with the skin of the aircraft.

Steele shoved his hand down hard onto his gun, drawing it deftly. Keeping the firearm close to his body, he fired two shots into Bob's stomach. The concussions from shooting the gun so close, reverberated over him. Steele ignored the ringing in his ears and leaned across the seat backs, popping the guy wearing the suicide bomb vest with two rounds to the face. He collapsed without a sound.

More gunfire erupted from the front of the cabin, and one of the male flight attendants took down a hijacker at the cockpit door, gun in hand, apron hanging loosely around his neck.

Steele breathed heavily. White smoke filled the cabin and his ears continued to buzz from the gunfire. He scanned for more threats, and it appeared as though all the bad guys were down. He exhaled a bit, momentarily relaxing. A decision he immediately regretted.

A fiery singe of pain raked down his left side. He twisted in his seat. The straight-faced woman behind him swung wildly with a knife that blazed. He dodged her swing, throwing himself backwards into the seat in front of him and put two rounds in her. She writhed in pain and sat still in her seat. *That sneaky bitch.*

"Are we clear?" called a gun-toting flight attendant from the front.

"We're clear," Steele called out taking the skin of the aircraft. The smoke settled in the cabin.

"Okay, everyone out of role," called the instructor.

Steele holstered his gun, showing his hands to the masked instructor wearing a red shirt with an eagled badge on the breast. The man loomed near the back of first class where he observed the entire scenario. He nodded to Steele, prompting him to help Bob up.

"Everyone is clear," the muscled man with the clipboard, yelled out. Steele took in the clean air finally released from the confines of his claustrophobic protective helmet.

"Shit, you almost knocked me out with that sucker punch," Steele said with a smile to the role-player.

Bob returned the smile letting him know there were no hard feelings. "Jesus, what have you been taking, or maybe I am just getting too old for this," he said, rubbing his sternum.

"We sweat more now, so we bleed less later. Besides, how long *have* you been doing this?" Steele said with a laugh.

"I've been helping young bucks like you get ready for the real world for much too long," he said wiping the pink paint off his shirt where Steele had shot him point blank with the simulation rounds.

Steele rounded on the cold-eyed female role-player.

"Claire, I swear to God. Do you not have a soul?"

The short, blonde-haired woman shrugged her shoulders removing her protective mask. "Per our wager, you owe me lunch," she said, lips curving upward.

"I said you'd get lunch if you eliminated me from the scenario. I was still in the fight when Instructor Mitchell called out of role," Steele said, raising a finger in objection.

"No. No. No. You aren't getting out of this that easy. Another few minutes and you would have been down for the count."

"It was merely a flesh wound." He smiled triumphantly.

"Next time then," she said.

"Role-players, take ten. All the agents with me," shouted the chiseled-jawed instructor. He wore a navy blue hat with an American flag stuck to the front. Instructor Mitchell always looked pissed, even when they performed well.

Steele rubbed his side where Claire had taken the stun knife to him. He lifted up his shirt, revealing a nasty red line. The pink skin stung, irritated by the 10,000 volts that had zapped through his flesh during the hijacking scenario. *That wound would have left him in a world of hurt in the sky. Going to have to tighten it up in the field.*

The three Counterterrorism agents gathered outside the simulator; a mock aircraft they used for training.

"Thank God we are done with this training for the year," Blake said, taking off his flight attendant apron.

"Definitely safer in the field," Steele said with a grin, turning in the red gun used to shoot the simulation rounds. Rounds that flew at a slower speed than real rounds with paint filled tips. They stung, often leaving scars when they dug into the flesh. The welts were a painful reminder to check your six, before you made a move.

"Bring it in," Instructor Mitchell said.

He reviewed his clipboard, running a pen down the side, then stopped. "Everything looked pretty good out there until Steele got stabbed," he said, eyeing Steele disapprovingly.

"There's only so much I can do. I stopped two sleepers and the bomb guy."

The other members of the team chuckled. "Let's try and stay alive out there," Mitchell said, glancing back down at his clipboard. His strict scrutiny was cut short by a PA announcement.

"Attention in the office. Agent Steele, please report to Operations," echoed over the loud speakers.

"Saved by the bell," said a honeymooner in disguise, Agent Andrea Carling. She gave him a slight look of contempt. "Probably got busted for something."

"Attention in the office. Agent Carling, please report to Operations," the voice echoed.

"Ha, looks like you're busted too," Steele said.

The short brunette, who couldn't have been more than five feet tall, smiled. "It must be a pay raise if they're calling me. Come on, knuckle-dragger. Let's go see what they want."

"Have fun getting your hands dirty. I'll see you in a couple of weeks,"

Instructor Mitchell added, flipping a page. "We got a special week long course

coming up with the Secret Service on protection details the fifth through the tenth,

then a survival, evasion, resistance, escape course with our Devil Dog buddies at

Quantico on the twelfth, and last but not least, a prisoner transportation course with

U.S. Marshals on the thirteenth."

"Yuck," Blake said.

"It's all part of the job," Mitchell reiterated. "Extradition doesn't work if we

can't move the subjects," he said, showing some teeth in place of a smile. His finger

ran down the clipboard.

"Ah, I almost forgot. After that, I get some alone time with you guys in the

mat room. Andrea, bring your A game. I heard you won that Brazilian jujitsu

tournament last weekend. I want to see what you got," he said, making a fist in the

air.

"That shouldn't be a problem," she said, and Instructor Mitchell dismissed

the agents with a curt nod.

Agents Steele and Carling marched through the facility. Framed pictures

adorned the off-white walls of men and women shooting guns, fighting in hand-to-

hand combat and exercising. They had been on the same squad for more than a year.

They rounded the computer room, a few agents sat in front of screens. Steele saluted

a giant blond man as he hunt-and-pecked his keyboard, his brow furrowed in deep

concentration.

"Jarl, keep up the good work," Steele said.

"Ah, fuck you, Steele," the hulking brute retorted with a glower through his

beard.

"They should really get him a bigger keyboard," Andrea said, grinning.

"I know. No wonder he's angry all the time," Steele said.

They passed a giant Counterterrorism Division seal that hung on the wall; a gold shield emblazoned with a bald eagle, talons gripping a sword soaring above a globe. The Division, as it was called by people in the know, was a joint counterterrorism organization. It existed to defeat all terrorist entities worldwide, and the best personnel from every corner of the government and military belonged to it. Military special operations, CIA, FBI, NSA, even the Treasury Department had personnel in the Division. If you wanted to be on the frontline fight against terrorism, you strove for a position within their ranks.

Steele's team had been re-upping their certification in aviation security and tactics over the last three months. They spent an extensive amount of time training for every plausible 'shit hits the fan' scenario that some twisted mothers could come up with. After 9/11, the Counterterrorism agents were made to certify every three years to ensure they were up to speed with the latest threats and ready to deploy at a moment's notice. It fell in line with being the federal agents who would go anywhere, track anyone and win against all odds.

When the federal government wanted to be eyes on but unseen, it called the CT agents to action. They were tucked away from the public, absconded by layers of bureaucracy. There had been rumors that they existed, but nobody really knew for sure. The internet teemed with conspiracy theories. They were the watchers, silent swords in the darkness, poised ready to strike evildoers worldwide.

Glass doors slid open as they entered Operations. A horseshoe ring of people on computers, all facing a host of wall sized flat-screen TVs. The televisions depicted every event of interest to the Division taking place in real-time.

A heavyset man in business causal attire waved them over from behind a computer screen. He plopped down into his seat and shoved part of a submarine sandwich in his mouth.

"Mika, what have you got for us?" Steele probed. "Better be something good. Last time I had to sit in a safe house near the Chennai airport for three days."

"Sorry pal, nothing I could do on that one, but I hear they have a wonderful curry dish there," Mika said, licking his lips. *Jesus man, you are literally eating,* Steele thought.

He rolled his eyes at Andrea, who laughed under her breath.

Mika squinted over his computer at them. Tossing down his sandwich next to him, he smashed away at his keyboard with a slight frown. "You two picked up a Special Protection Detail coming from Kinshasa," he said, staring at his screen.

"Kinshasa? What's a Kinshasa," Steele asked, running a hand through his thick blond beard.

"Haha. It's the capital of the Democratic Republic of the Congo. Neither democratic nor republic, but most definitely the Congo." Mika chuckled at his own words as his fingertips hummed across the keyboard. Steele was always amazed that a man with his girth could type with such blazing speed using bratwursts for fingers.

Steele gave Andrea a look.

"Do we even go there?" Andrea asked, crossing her arms. She raised her eyebrows at Steele questioning the legality of the operation. Steele shrugged his shoulders. He was used to going to places that he had only read about.

"We do now," Mika said. "Came down this morning. A couple of pen strokes from the President and off we go. Team Lead Wheeler wants you back here by 1700, and make sure Mauser knows, too."

It was already 1300. It figures that they would let him train all day and then give him an extended mission. Steele thanked Mika and walked out with Andrea.

"All right, Andrea. I'm gonna hit the office gym quick and make sure Mauser's awake. He'd probably sleep all day if I let him."

Andrea snorted a laugh. "I think the gym has had enough of you," she said, punching him lightly in the shoulder.

He flexed his bicep, bringing his arm level with his shoulder. "It'll never be enough," he joked in an Austrian accent.

"Don't be late," she called after him. "You know how Wheeler hates it when we're late."

JOSEPH
US Embassy Kinshasa, DRC

Joseph and Nixon barreled up to the embassy gate roughly five hours later in their battered, gore-stained government Tahoe. The embassy was a nondescript, three-story, tan building made of thick concrete. A twelve-foot, cast-iron gate topped with razor wire surrounded the compound along with two guard towers overlooking the street. Sometimes it reminded Joseph of a minimum security detention facility.

A smaller guard shack that housed Congolese soldiers, who assisted the Americans in perimeter security, sat outside the compound near the gate. The embassy, like the rest of the DRC, was a leftover from colonial times.

"Home sweet home," Nixon said, eying the building with bloodshot eyes. Joseph paid him no heed. "State is supposed to be building a new one in the next few years. Update this monolithic prison looking place," Nixon prattled as the guards did their security check.

Two DRC soldiers, slender men in baggy camouflage and AK-47s slung on their backs, rounded the government vehicle with expandable mirrors to detect explosives under the vehicle, while a Marine security guard reviewed their credentials. He scrutinized their vehicle.

"What did you hit, a deer?" the clean-shaven Marine guard with a vanilla Iowa accent asked. He poked at a chunk of pink flesh on the cracked windshield with his finger.

"Please don't touch that, it could be contaminated," Joseph said. The Marine pulled his hand away as if it had been slapped.

"Diseased with what?" the soldier asked, wiping his hand on his pants.

"Monkeypox, Ebola, AIDS, just don't touch anything," Joseph snapped at him.

The soldier gave him a skeptical look and pointed at his clipboard. "There are supposed to be four of you. Where's Agent Reliford and your interpreter, Boo-wally?" the young guard asked, peering into the back of the vehicle.

Joseph leaned over Nixon. "They're dead, and a hell of a lot more people are going to die if you don't let us through."

The Marine visibly gulped. "Let 'em through, Ryan," he shouted, waving his hands.

A couple of hours later, Joseph sat in an embassy conference room. He clasped his hands in his lap. The embassy big wigs sat in front of him. A standard, dark brown, wooden government table, that seemed a bit too wide for the conversation they were having, separated Joseph from Ambassador Brinkley, Dr. Edward Harkin and detachment commander Master Sergeant Snow, head of the Marine contingent stationed at the embassy. Holding the title of commander and being sergeant was not something that happened very often. He was surprised that Regional Security Officer Kline wasn't there. He formed the Post Security Team with Snow. *Must be out sick.*

The conversation was going less well than Joseph expected, and now they all stared at Joseph as if he would be better off in an asylum. Always dressed to impress, Ambassador Brinkley wore a three-piece suit despite the unwavering heat. Brinkley had received his ambassadorship through political appointment, but never failed to make sure people addressed him by his appropriate title, as if he had earned it. Joseph was sure Brinkley had earned it through campaign donations.

Joseph had voted for the President, who then in turn appointed this pretentious jerk. Ambassador Brinkley had a silver streak running through his dark hair and that, combined with his pointy nose and beady eyes, always reminded Joseph of a ferret. The ambassador sat back with his arms crossed, a smug look of disbelief settling in his eyes.

"Let me get this straight. Dead villagers got up and attacked you? This wasn't part of some bizarre bush ritual?" He pulled a piece of paper up in front of his face. "What is it you do out there? Investigate AIDS or something?" The Ambassador continued to glare at Joseph disdainfully, awaiting a response.

"It was Monkeypox, and I am a disease surveillance specialist," Joseph said under his breath, rubbing his bloodshot eyes. "I was on a Monkeypox surveillance deployment. We do this to stay on the forefront of any emerging outbreaks within the country. There were reports of an outbreak in Kombarka, near the Congo River."

How long has it been since I slept?

"*And?*" Brinkley pressed.

"I was observing and treating the people there with the standard Monkeypox medical treatment, and monitoring the effects it was having on the progression of the virus."

"Wait," Brinkley said, shaking his head. "Why should I care about Monkeypox, again?"

Joseph took a deep breath. "Like I said before, Monkeypox in itself is a highly contagious virus. It can be spread from bodily fluids, a bite or from consumption of contaminated meat."

The Ambassador interrupted him again. "Contaminated meat?" Brinkley doubted, looking at Dr. Harkin and Master Sergeant Snow for the social go ahead to blow this entire thing off as some tribal voodoo. "Why would someone eat that?" He leaned back, laughing to himself. "I mean, come on, if these people can't even cook their food, how can we expect to make any headway in business or developing new industry?"

I should have donated more, Joseph thought.

Joseph was tired of giving this cultural lesson on top of answering Brinkley's arrogant questions, but he continued anyway, hoping something would penetrate the man's wavy hairdo.

"It's a common occurrence in the rural communities that run along the Congo River. Think of it as deer or duck hunting back home, except these people trap jungle rodents or animals." The Ambassador sighed. Joseph wanted to snarl, but held it in. He calmed himself and continued.

"The disease that killed these people wasn't Monkeypox. It was something else entirely. It is highly infectious and extremely deadly and we need to get a jump on it before it spreads too far."

Master Sergeant Snow leaned in from across the table. He was more or less the opposite of Brinkley, aside from the fact that they were roughly the same age. Master Sergeant Snow was in his fifties and had the resemblance of a career soldier: crew cut, clean-shaven, an avid follower of a high intensity interval regimen. The only problem with Snow was that he was convinced that the embassy could come under attack at any minute, any day of the week. Joseph had avoided him in cafeteria on many occasions because of his hard grizzled unapproachable look.

"How many rebels were there?" Snow punched out from his emotionless mouth. It was as if he were some sort of robot.

Joseph ground his teeth together. At this rate he would have nubs for teeth by the end of the day. He tried to explain again.

"Sergeant, as far as I know there were no rebels. The people from the village were out of control, murdering each other."

"You're sure?" Snow spat. Joseph almost thought the man was trying to give him an out; a way to save face by admitting some rebel group attacked them.

"This is vital to the security of this embassy and the national security of the United States as a whole," Snow said.

"I can't be sure, Sergeant Snow. It was dark, and people were screaming and shooting." He massaged his temples. An oppressive migraine loomed over him. He hoped to God he hadn't contracted the virus.

Snow leaned back satisfied, displaying neither anger nor happiness, a general air of duty surrounding him. "I have no more questions for the doctor."

The Ambassador reviewed his notes. "What happened after you saw the *dead* people walking? What happened to Agent Reliford?"

Joseph closed his eyes, mentally replaying the flight from Kombarka in his head. Everything had happened so fast. It was a blur of violence.

"As we exited the hospital tent, I saw the village elder having his stomach ripped out by his own teenage daughters; presumably they had been infected with the virus. Agent Nixon pushed me forward and we ran to the SUV. There was smoke in the air and many of the village homes were ablaze, but nothing prepared me for when Agent Nixon flicked on the lights, illuminating a horrifying scene. Bestial," he said, before stopping to collect himself.

The row of embassy leaders stared at him.

"No desensitization classes could have prepared me for this kind of gratuitous violence. People were burning alive, screaming, waving their arms wildly, while others stumbled around, seemingly unconvinced they were alight. Still more villagers lay on the ground, most likely dead. Some crawled, trying to get away from the others. Many appeared to be dismembered; arms, legs, heads gone. I couldn't tell you who belonged to what. Other villagers, whom I deemed 'infected,' moved in small packs from corpse to corpse. After the encounter in the hospital tent, I realized they were consuming the fallen. I believe it is a symptom of the virus infecting the brain and nervous system," he said, shaking his head.

"I've never seen anything like it. They tore pieces of flesh from their victims with their hands and teeth, like they were possessed," he said, bile rising in the back of his throat. *Why would anyone do such a thing?*

"Savages," Ambassador Brinkley muttered, amazed by the animalism of the native population.

Joseph paused and continued his rendition of his nightmare. "We sat in the SUV for a moment in utter shock. Then, one after another, they noticed us. The lights or the engine must have attracted them, but I don't really know. Dozens of them came at us at once. They pounded on the windows with blood-stained fists, attempting to smash their way in." Joseph had shrunk down in his seat that night, trying to get away from the windows.

"I saw a woman shatter her teeth on the window, with no recognition of pain or acknowledgement of what she was doing. I screamed 'Drive.' Bowali cried in the backseat. He kept mumbling and praying. 'Please God. Please God.' Agent Nixon gunned the vehicle into the mass of crazed villagers, bodies thudding off the front grill. It was the most sickening sound I've ever heard. The vehicle rocked as we drove over the bodies. They just threw themselves in front of the Tahoe, fingernails scraping the windows as we drove through them." Joseph stopped as Brinkley raised a hand shaking his head.

"Wait." Brinkley held up a halting hand. "Diplomatic Security Agent Nixon ran over a group of Congolese citizens in a government vehicle?" Brinkley wondered. He waved over an aide and whispered in her ear. The aide scurried from the room.

Master Sergeant Snow appeared amused. The only thing Joseph could fathom he was thinking was that he would have done the same thing in Nixon's position.

"Please get to the part about Agent Reliford. Where is he?" Brinkley asked, taking a quick look down at a very expensive gold watch on his wrist.

"When we reached the edge of the village we saw a man standing with his back turned toward the road. It was Agent Reliford. His clothes were disheveled as if he had been in a fight. We couldn't tell at the time, but he had been infected." *We should have known*, thought Joseph.

"Agent Nixon pulled the SUV alongside him and Bowali opened the door. When he turned toward us, we could see it was too late. His face had been disfigured with multiple horrific human bite marks, and he was bleeding profusely from a severe neck wound to his carotid artery."

Joseph could feel the tears forming at the corner of his eyes as he continued: "Agent Reliford leapt. He leapt so fast and he pulled Bowali from the backseat by his feet. Bowali never really stood a chance. He kicked and screamed, but nothing mattered."

Joseph stopped. The sound of Bowali's screams would never leave him. "Agent Reliford tore him apart with his bloodied fists and then, he bent low ripping out Bowali's tongue with his teeth. There was nothing I could do. Agent Reliford is twice my size."

"How did Agent Reliford die?" Snow asked.

"Agent Nixon shot him," Joseph paused. "He shot him in the head," he finished.

Snow and Brinkley exchanged a glance. "And the local embassy employee, Bowali?" Snow asked.

"He sustained extensive trauma to his face and neck. Nixon gunned the truck, and left him. However, as we drove away, I saw him stand up. I have never seen anything like it," Joseph recalled.

"You left Bowali on the side of the road?" Brinkley questioned.

"Yes, we did," Joseph closed his eyes.

Joseph's supervisor, Dr. Harkin, was his only hope in understanding what had happened. Harkin simply stared at Joseph, wide-eyed behind his black-rimmed glasses.

Joseph was not one to tell tall tales. He believed in science, logic and evidence, and it was incredibly frustrating to have these men, including his mentor, doubt him.

Joseph stared directly at Harkin. *Believe me*, Joseph pleaded with his eyes. Harkin returned his gaze concern written on his intelligent face.

"We're glad you're safe, Joseph. I'm sure the Ambassador will investigate this event thoroughly at a later date," he said.

Joseph rose shakily from his chair, relieved to have the grand inquisition over.

"Wait," Brinkley interrupted, holding up a hand. "How do we know you aren't carrying the disease?" he asked, cut short by gunfire rattling from outside.

Master Sergeant Snow leered past Joseph a slight frown on his statuesque face. He slowly stood up, fully erect, and staring out the window toward the sound of gunfire. "What in God's name? We do not have any 'Reacts' scheduled."

He pointed at another soldier who stood near the door. "I need a full report from Post 1 on what the hell is going on out there," Sergeant Snow ordered.

A Marine raced from the room.

Master Sergeant Snow turned toward the Ambassador, his face slightly perturbed. "Ambassador, we need to implement Evacuation Alpha and get you to a secondary location while we figure out what's happening out there."

The two didn't even bother to dismiss Joseph. They just stormed from the room, a Marine accompanying the pair.

Joseph shuffled together his notes from the table where Dr. Harkin waited. "We should make our way to the emergency rally point. Talk to me, along the way Joseph. What are we dealing with?" Harkin asked as they walked. He was Joseph's senior, and although they shared a mutual respect for one another, Joseph still considered the older colleague a mentor.

Joseph shook his head. "I don't know, Ed. I saw a man with bullet holes the size of half dollars in his chest get up and walk around."

Harkin took him by the shoulder. "Adrenaline could explain it, or maybe he was just a tough son of a bitch. The human body is an amazing system, incredibly resilient, yet so vulnerable at the same time."

No. Adrenaline could not explain this. Neither could toughness. The villagers actions were inhuman. Non-human. Lacking any piece of humanity. Abominations. Corruptions of men.

Joseph's blood rushed to his face. "The man was dead. I checked his pulse and those of the other patients with gunshot wounds and, even if he had somehow been alive, he only weighed about a hundred pounds. That trauma would have ruined him."

"I believe you. But what was it? There must be a scientific explanation as to how this happened."

Joseph racked his memory about all he had observed of the disease. *It had to be some manifestation of the virus, but how?*

Other people walked quickly down the hallway to the emergency rally point.

He closed his eyes as he tried to think. "It's not Monkeypox. At least, not the strain we know. I can't be sure; we just need to do more testing. The only thing I'm sure of is that the virus spread rapidly through oral transmission."

A couple of Marine guards ran down the hallway rifles in hand. This didn't seem like a drill.

"Interesting, the virus is in the saliva, like rabies, Ebola, or Monkeypox. Is it possible that Monkeypox manifested violent tendencies in the patients, causing them to act this way?" Harkin inquired out loud.

Joseph sighed, unable to find the answer. "Maybe it mutated or melded DNA strains with another virus, or somehow changed its DNA pattern. It's not implausible," he said, eying Harkin for confirmation.

Dr. Harkin looked troubled behind his glasses. "Let's get you some rest. I overheard the Ambassador say that when you and the DS agent arrived they went into a code yellow, which is a soft evacuation of the embassy. We'll be back in the U.S. soon, where it's safe."

Joseph felt a little better. Maybe going home for a while was the best option. He could visit his parents for a couple of weeks down in Raleigh. They were his only family.

"All staff please report to the main cafeteria," an announcement boomed. His momentary hope eroded, and an uncontrollable panic set about pummeling his gut, as though his stomach had decided to do continual somersaults.

Harkin looked at Joseph worriedly. "I'd like to see your blood samples when we get a chance. It appears we might get out of here sooner than expected."

Joseph followed his supervisor into the cafeteria as more gunfire echoed from outside.

STEELE
Fairfax, VA

Steele raced home down VA Route 50. Per usual, traffic had already started to pick up in Northern Virginia. He gunned it around a vehicle putting along blocking a lane of traffic. Survival of the fittest on the NoVA roadways. It was the old three o'clock traffic. A seemingly endless stream of people constantly flowing into and out of the District.

His annoyance with his fellow drivers faded quickly when he pulled in front of his gray townhouse and saw her: a beautiful blonde in tight yoga pants, leaving only a little mystery about what lay underneath. She stretched in the front yard, arms extended over her head.

"Gwen," he said, closing the car door with a smile.

She smiled. It was an infectious smile. One couldn't help but fall in love with her. Many previous admirers deeply regretted letting that smile fade from their lives. She bent at the waist, stretching her hamstrings.

"I didn't expect you back so early. I would have waited for you to go running," she said.

He threw his pack over his shoulder, watching as she reached down to the ground toward one leg and then the other.

"I picked up an SPD," he said, embracing her. Special Protection Details were hard to come by, only reserved for the best or well connected, however most of the time it boiled down to babysitting some spoiled politician. The opportunity presented a chance for him to standout a bit to the agency. Check the box on a mission accomplished.

They momentarily locked lips before she quickly pulled away.

"I hate that thing," she complained, rubbing her chin. He laughed at her. His beard always bothered her.

"Listen, it's my baby." He tugged on it a bit. "Do you know how long it took me to perfect this. It's an art." Just a bit shorter than some of his buddies' beards who were special operators, he wore it to cover his identity in foreign countries as well as to blend in where it was customary to have facial hair.

"Where?" she asked, a look of unease registering in her sparkling green eyes.

"Somewhere in Africa," he said. The corners of her mouth drooped making his heart droop a bit. Making her upset was on the bottom of his to-do list.

"The Red Cross International Division is swamped. Africa is going wild right now. We've gotten at least a dozen requests for aid in the last twenty-four hours. I hardly got out of there today. It's unbelievable how bad it is."

He readjusted his bag strap. The danger didn't concern him. Worrying her did.

"At least it's not the Middle East," he said, looking at her hopefully. She hated it the most when he deployed there. He understood. It was one of the more dangerous places he deployed. Too many variables and too many people who were waiting for a chance to stick it to the 'Great Satan.'

"I don't even know if we'll be able to deploy enough resources," she said, trailing off in her own worry.

"Everything will work out," he said reassuringly. He wrapped his arm around her and walked with her to the house.

They went inside, finding their roommate, a reddish-haired man with a grizzled five o'clock shadow in his late-thirties sitting on their couch. He leaned over a disassembled SIG Sauer P226 .40 caliber, vigorously scrubbing the smokey barrel.

"Mauser, what's up, man? Did Ops call you?" Steele asked.

Mauser's anchor-tattooed hand set down the barrel as he turned his attention to the frame of the gun. The muscles in his forearm were lean and sinewy, like they were made with steel suspension cords. Completely consumed by his work, he didn't look up.

"Just polishing up the smoke wagon here before we head out."

"Excellent. Give me a few minutes and I'll be ready to go," he said, hurrying up the stairs.

"Gwen, can you fix up some chow? You know how much I hate airport food," Steele shouted down the stairs. He crossed his fingers as he dug through his clothing drawers. Tense seconds passed.

"Yeah, yeah," she shouted up at him. *Whew*. His gamble could have been perceived in the wrong light with Gwen, but she would always help him out given the chance.

He had met her two years earlier, when they both deployed to New Jersey during Hurricane Sandy. He had been tasked out to assist federal authorities, while she had been stationed with the Red Cross. It had felt like fate, a ray of sunshine amidst a whirlwind of disaster bringing two dedicated public servants together. One who rendered aid like a saint, the other who protected his community like a shepherd his flock. Both unwavering, undeterred, and determined to make a difference. They were a yin and yang of service, both aspects necessary and yet, neither successful without the other.

He gathered handfuls of underwear, socks, shirts and pants; the standard amount of clothing for a few nights. Sometimes when things didn't go according to plans, he could get stuck somewhere. Across the hall, sat his office, a room he had turned into a shrine of duty. A large old wooden table his grandmother had left him sat in the corner, holding all his gear. A faded 'Don't Tread On Me' naval flag hung above the gear table, a prized possession from his father's service to his nation. It hung alongside a painting of several firefighters hoisting the American Flag at Ground Zero, a reminder of Steele's service to his nation. Both he and his father had answered their nation's call to service in its time of need, his father in the Persian Gulf and Steele years after 9/11. Service ran deep in his veins.

Next to the flags sat a picture of his graduating academy class: a dozen agents lined up in their black suits and black ties. Mauser's red head poked up alongside Steele's in the back row, grinning obnoxiously. The academy.

Steele could recall every moment of his first day including how he met Benjamin Mauser. The butterflies danced in his stomach as he stepped into a whitewashed conference room wearing his finest suit. Pictures of agents in plain clothes or in tactical gear lined the room.

His eyes were drawn to a plaque dedicated to the agents who had died in the line of duty. Steele started to count the stars, each gold star representing a fallen agent. Stopping at twenty, he found himself looking for a seat in the midst of soon to be peers.

About twenty-five men and women had clustered in small groups, speaking softly to one another. The candidates had sized one another up, judging each other's worthiness. A couple of guys in the back talked loudly about their previous military exploits. The whole scene reminded him of a grade school bus ride with the cool kids in the back, the nerds up front and nowhere to sit except next to the weird guy in the middle. Steele cut across the row only realizing as he sat down why no one sat by this lone, shaggy-haired recruit.

The only man in the entire group dressed in jeans and a black-and-red sweatshirt bottomed off with sneakers. Steele was beside himself. *Just the kind of person I don't want to be associated with.* Tentatively, he watched the man from the corners of his eyes panicking a bit when the out of policy cadet turned his way. He squirmed under the cadet's gaze. Desperately, Steele thumbed through his paperwork trying not to be noticed. *Please don't make contact.*

The underdressed man leaned over to Steele, reached out a worn callused hand and, with a loud booming voice, said: "Hi. I'm Ben Mauser. It's good to meet *you*." It sounded like Mauser was trying to explain directions to a person who didn't understand English.

Damn. Contact. He politely took Mauser's hand in his and said: "I'm Mark Steele. It's good to meet you."

Steele promptly flipped back open his orientation package, trying to find a way to avoid any continued conversation. *Either this guy hadn't received the memo or he had a big pair to defy dress code on the first day. There's no way this guy is going to be here long.*

Their orientation coordinator shouted from the back of the room cutting Steele's mental critique short. "Attention. Special Agent in Charge on deck."

The cadets stood at attention, or what Steele imagined standing at attention looked like. The Special Agent in Charge, or SAC, strode into the room looking like a million bucks, surveying his new recruits. He marched to the front podium and spun around to judge the eager faces of the would-be CT agents, hands clasped behind his back.

"Sixty percent of cadets fail out of the academy," he paused for emphasis. "Look at the men and women around you." Steele kept his eyes forward. He needn't look further than the man next to him.

"Most of them will not make it. Sixty percent of you do not have what it takes." The SAC's gaze surveyed each recruit in silence, hoping for some form of weakness to pounce upon, exposing the inferior being in his presence. He scanned the recruits and stopped as his eyes fell upon the causally dressed Mauser. The weak link had been identified.

The SAC's eyes widened and then narrowed. "Now, what do we have here? A Freddy Krueger *look-a-like*? You must be the jokester in the group? I've seen your kind before." The SAC floated down the aisle until he stood face to face with Mauser, eyeballing him with severe scrutiny. "I presume you know today's attire is *business*?"

Mauser held his chin level, eyes focused directly at the SAC. "SIR, YES, SIR," he shouted.

"And I presume that you will rectify this situation tomorrow?" the SAC asked, his eyes cutting him down mercilessly.

"Sir, my suitcase was lost in transit, sir. I am told that it will be delivered sometime this afternoon."

The SAC inspected him up and down. "That's great, Krueger. But I can not let this violation of the rules go unaddressed. I mean, if we don't enforce the rules then how do we get you to respect them," Steele smiled. *This guy is going to get kicked on day one. Better his dumb ass than mine.*

"Everyone down into the front leaning rest," the SAC commanded. Steele learned quickly that the front leaning rest was no rest at all, just a different term for the highest point of the push-up position.

Steele's chin hung to his chest. *This guy can't possibly be serious. We are in our primo business suits. Freshly dry cleaned and pressed, our Sunday best. On top of that, we haven't done anything wrong it was only that guy, Mauser. How could the SAC be so unfair?*

As Steele would find out on the double, none of this meant much to the Counterterrorism Division. They would live and die as a unit. None of them were superheroes, or James Bond, this was real life. They had to be tough, smart and watch each other's backs if they wanted to be successful. If one person failed, they all failed.

The recruits clambered onto the floor to perform their pushups, eking out rep after rep as the SAC harangued them on the importance of policy, following the rules, accountability and — most importantly — making the correct decisions under pressure. They groaned as they reached a hundred reps. Luckily, Steele had put himself in an intensive physical training regimen for months prior to his recruitment. The unprepared were easily singled out as their arms gave out.

Beads of sweat ran down Steele's face. He chanced a look over at this character in his sweater, who accepted the punishment in stride with Steele going rep for rep. *There is no way this guy would survive training. He will be one of the many who washed out. He couldn't even get the first day right.*

The SAC had allowed them to *break* in the 'front-leaning rest position. "Welcome to the most specialized counterterrorism agency on the planet. If you can't be smart, then we will make you strong."

Much to Steele's initial dismay; he had been seated next to Mauser for every training event at the academy. As their staff ID numbers were consecutive, the two would not only be partnered up for scenarios, but would sit together during endless hours of classroom training and even bunk together.

The academy had forged a friendship for life. The shittier the experience, the closer it brings men in arms. It taught them to close ranks when things went bad, to rely on one another in the face of danger. As years passed, life bound them together like brothers. Because while one needs a brother to celebrate his victories, one needs him more when the enemy screams for his life. Not merely a sibling of your mother's breast, because that bond sometimes is not enough, but a brother who has tied himself to you through earned respect, shared experience and common cause.

Steele collected his equipment. He carried the standard Counterterrorism agent issued kit laying in neat order, starting with his *Death Dealer*, the SIG Sauer P226 .40 that he placed into an inside the waist leather holster in his pants. He tossed his stainless steel handcuffs, zip ties and his baton into a pocket of his suitcase. He could never fathom why they had issued the agents a baton, aside that it made them seem more like police when in reality, they were anything but.

Next, he flicked open a spring-loaded Benchmade out-the-top blade, closed it and clipped it inside his pants along with a tactical flashlight. He clipped two extra magazines onto his belt and placed one in his ankle magazine holder. *Can't hurt to have that extra mag when everything goes to shit.* This was a common practice among the agents.

Finally, he put his gold-emblazoned tactical badge around his neck. While the badge itself was light, the responsibility weighed heavy, but he had grown accustomed to it and craved it.

The call of duty set him apart from a regular citizen of his great country. It came with massive responsibility. Most people either didn't want the responsibility or couldn't handle it. It was much more convenient for them to think evil didn't exist or could never touch their lives. Steele was a part of the few who formed a thin hard line between order and chaos. He was a shield to the weak. He was a sword to the breasts of evildoers. As a shadow, he stood watch in the night over his people so they may rest unmolested in their beds. If death called his name, he would never fully accept his fate, fighting tooth and nail to the bitter end. For he had sworn an oath, that he would support and defend the Constitution of the United States against all enemies, foreign and domestic. He would uphold the law and bring justice to all those who would do harm to the citizens of the greatest country in the world.

Steele slid the badge underneath his shirt, finishing his preparations as the smell of grilling beef burgers wafted up the stairs. Gwen always made something tasty and decidedly unhealthy for him right before he deployed. He was convinced she was plotting to make him fat. Happy, but fat. He hauled his luggage and pack down the steps.

"So it's burgers and fries?" he asked.

Gwen's red lips curved. "You just remember what you're coming back to," she said, flipping a patty on a warm toasted bun.

"I'll think about it," he teased, not waiting to tear into the burger. He had no problem coming back from missions. By the end of a mission he was so exhausted, that he could hardly drive home.

"You'd better," she called from the kitchen.

"Man, I wish I had something to eat," Mauser prattled, opening the fridge and rummaging around.

Gwen smiled and produced a second and a third plate, setting them down on the kitchen table.

"I wouldn't forget you, Ben," she said. She sat down and took a big bite out of her burger.

"Where does all of that go?" Steele asked.

She smiled. "Some of us actually run. So this is fuel."

After he devoured his meal, he leaned back in his chair ready to burst. *She is definitely a keeper*, he thought. He glanced at Mauser.

"You ready, big fella?" he asked.

"Yes sir. Let's do this," Mauser said. Steele nodded, turning to Gwen. He kissed her. "I'll be okay," he said.

"I know," she replied softly, looking down straightening his shirt.

"That's what all the training's for," he said with a kiss to her cheek. At least, that's what he kept telling himself.

JOSEPH
US Embassy Kinshasa, DRC

Joseph and Harkin entered the main cafeteria, a large room consisting of dozens of oblong tables. Food distribution staff handed out water bottles and snacks. Embassy personnel from all over the building trickled into the room. A large crowd had clustered near the panoramic-style windows overlooking the front courtyard and gate. The muffled cries of children in their mother's arms gave away that the embassy staff's families were also gathering. It was not uncommon for staffers to have their entire families with them abroad, but to have them all in one spot meant something bad was happening.

Joseph caught a kid, sitting nearby, picking his nose while he stared defiantly at Joseph as if he dared him to do something about it. Joseph turned away, slightly repulsed by the wretched little person.

Joseph never had a family of his own, and as he watched the small children squirm and cry in the cafeteria, he didn't regret his choice. The truth was, he was slightly afraid of kids. They seemed so naively bold and they were perpetually dirty, excellent hosts for viruses. *And what do you talk to a kid about anyway? You could never have a conversation about the merits of using cidofovir as opposed to ganciclovir as a primary treatment for cytomegalovirus.* Yet, sometimes when he looked at the families, he yearned to have people around him; his own people.

He placed all of his energy into his work because it could never betray him, but it wasn't that he didn't want somebody of his own to love and hold. He had a love interest, of sorts, back in college. She always badgered him about studying too much. She just didn't understand. In the end, Joseph had ended up alone. He told himself he was better off that way, but he often questioned his own rationale, wondering if maybe he wouldn't be happier with someone else to share his life with.

Joseph joined the cluster of people near the windows. Normally, it was quite a nice view: a few office buildings, and beyond palm trees and green hills, the more attractive part of Kinshasa. Not today, though. Anarchy had exploded all over the streets. The embassy staff murmured to one another in hushed whispers as they gawked behind the safety of their window within their concrete building, surrounded by Marines, fences and barbwire.

People ran amok through the business district. Some fought one another with their bare hands, while others swung machetes with vicious effect. Muffled gunshots accompanied the symphony of chaos like an offbeat snare drum. Wails for help were accented by the calls for mercy and screams of pain. The opera of agony never stopped. New voices would pick up as others faded out, each person below contributing their piece of the destruction song. The most unnerving part were the screams, dampened by the thick embassy glass, but still audible.

Joseph stared at the people dying outside the embassy gates. It made him sick to his stomach, but he couldn't turn away. *There is going to be a long line for therapy after this.* Like a horror film in real time, he knew death stalked them, yet he continued to watch. A man chopped a machete into another's neck, cleaving a jagged wound, his blood spilling in the street. The woman next to him covered her mouth in horror. A man placed a hand over his daughter's eyes turning her away from the ghastly scene.

"Joseph, maybe this isn't a good time. When we get you back home, we will get you to see the department psychologist. Let's take a seat," Harkin said, pulling him back toward the tables like a child.

"Not now, Harkin," Joseph mumbled. He brushed off Harkin's hand. He wanted to see it. It drew him in. Humanity collapsed and he had a front row seat. Joseph stared in silence as the violence continued to unfold in front of him.

Marine guards shot tear gas into the streets the canisters clinking off the pavement. "Please disperse," clamored a megaphone over and over in French and English. Neither the gas nor the warnings seemed to have any impact on the civilians that had crowded around the gate. Arms reached through the gate trying to grasp the soldiers that defended the compound.

The DRC's military detachment to the embassy had abandoned their post, no sign of them remained. A body dangled from the concertina razor wire, blood flowing freely from numerous bullet wounds. Marines scrambled below with their gas masks on. However, their numbers were small compared with the swarms of people outside. *Not enough if they break through. A mere speed bump in the face of a tidal wave of people.*

He glanced over at Deborah, a Foreign Service officer, crying into the sleeve of John, a tall linguist. She bore her face into his arm, terrified. Joseph would never be the rock for someone. He just didn't have the machismo to be considered a pillar of strength in times of danger.

The whispers of alarm grew louder as four more Marine guards rushed towards the gate, lashing out with the butts of their rifles at hands that stretched wantonly for them through the fence.

"Attention," boomed Master Sergeant Snow, his presence startling Joseph.

He had entered the room quietly, flanked on either side by two Marines and two DS agents in civilian clothing covered with tactical vests and Heckler & Koch MP5 9mms. Gas masks hung at their waists.

Snow continued: "As you've been watching outside, things are getting pretty bad. It looks like we have an all-out civil war on our hands. We have currently evacuated the Ambassador to the airport with his detail. We tried to get as many people out as early as possible, but this situation escalated quickly. You will all be evacuated to safety in due time. You have my word that no one will be left behind." His hands clasped behind his back, his stance wide and powerful.

"Things were getting bad" was an understatement. Joseph knew what was happening, but he would never have dared imagine that it could happen so fast. *If these people were infected, the virus must be mutating exponentially. It would be like the small village on the scale of a megacity, with millions of people potentially infected.*

Their prospects were grim, at best. The medical infrastructure of the DRC could never treat a large number of people, and even if they could, they did not have a working treatment. Sweat beaded on Joseph's forehead and his gut churned. He hugged his stomach trying to calm himself.

The staffers had edged their way toward Snow in an effort to glean information. People always wanted to know more, and were ever suspicious of somebody in uniform telling them that everything was fine when they could clearly see that it was not.

"You need to get us out of here," yelled a man from the back of the room.

"Yeah," a few more staffers took up the cause, fists clenched, a people's movement of protest.

Snow raised his hands in defense. "You have my word that you will be safe inside the compound until you can be evacuated. If we rush the evacuation it could be more dangerous for everyone involved. We need everyone to remain calm and to follow our orders. We have a detachment of twenty-five Marines here who have been trained for exactly this type of situation."

"You're supposed to keep us safe," shouted a short heavy-set blonde from the human resources staff. Angry, terrified energy ebbed from the crowd. Joseph felt the herd mentality rising up like spooked gazelle watching the lion, knowing that danger lurked near, but frozen in indecision, not knowing which way to run. It oozed from them, driven by one factor: fear.

Snow curtly nodded no, a short, purposeful head maneuver, and then pierced her with his ice like blue eyes. "*No one* is in immediate danger. Washington knows this is happening. You will *all* be evacuated to a safe location."

The fat woman snapped her mouth closed. Anger settled on her red rotund face.

"I will be filing a complaint against you," she said, trying to get the last word.

"I can't wait," Snow's lip curled into a semi-smile.

Joseph wanted to rip his hair out. *They didn't understand. Snow didn't understand, Harkin didn't understand and Brinkley, that rat bastard, didn't understand. We don't have time. We need to get out of here.*

"What about the airport? You should be taking us there," voiced a portly, bearded man near the front. Joseph had often seen him eating in the cafeteria.

"All I can do is tell you to sit tight," said Snow. He turned abruptly and left the room with his militant entourage.

That's it? Joseph didn't feel any better about the situation. There were too many similarities to Kombarka for it to be a coincidence. The outbreak had spread to the African capital.

He ran toward the Marine Master Sergeant. "Please wait, Sir," Joseph called after him. He reached out and grabbed the hardened soldier by his shirtsleeve.

Snow glared down at his sleeve before prying it from Joseph's grasp. "Yes, doctor? And it's Sergeant; I work for a living," Snow barked, his eyes glaring. This man was a pit bull.

Joseph met his hard gaze as best he could, adjusting his glasses on the bridge of his nose. He looked away before he started speaking. "I. Sorry," he stammered, grimacing from the altercation.

Snow threw daggers with his eyes, waiting.

"Don't let your men be bitten by any of those people out there," Joseph warned. Joseph forced the words out, hurrying while he still had the commander's attention. "That's how it spreads. One infection within this compound and it will spread like wildfire," he said.

Snow fixed him with a gaze so cold it could have frozen the devil himself. "We have it under control, Dr. Jackowski. Good day," he said. Turning, he moved with purpose down the hall.

STEELE
Undisclosed building, VA

Steele and Mauser scanned their ID badges to gain access to the Washington Field Office, a secure facility, before making their way to a small SCIF. The walls were encased in special metal and soundproof doors to block people and devices from eavesdropping. Here, they could discuss and hold classified information, without risk from phones, pagers, and other transmitting devices.

By the time Steele and Mauser arrived, three other agents were already prepping their gear inside. Agent Carling loaded her magazines while she talked with a colossal man, her thumb gliding each round into the magazine with practiced efficiency.

A salt-and-pepper-haired man, in his forties, signed paperwork near the front, his tactical badge clipped on his belt. He checked his watch as the agents walked in and tapped the watch face. Then he held his fingers about an inch apart. *Apparently, Team Leader Wheeler thinks we're cutting it a little close.* Steele pointed accusingly at Mauser and the man went back to his work, shaking his head.

Two unknown suits and the Special Agent in Charge of the Washington Field Office conversed in low tones near the front. Steele eyed them warily. Unknown suits were always a sign of trouble. They could potentially be upper management, swooping into the field office to raise hell about some trivial policy, or maybe trying to make a name for themselves by adding yet another layer of bureaucratic red tape to an already bogged-down system.

Best not worry about things that are out of my control.

Steele and Mauser claimed a table and set out their gear. Wheeler approached them. He was dressed in regular, everyday garb, just like them: jeans, a shirt and a light jacket. A warrior concealed by civilian dressings.

"I need you two to sign this paperwork," he said, dropping a stack on the table in front of them.

"Gotta keep the suits happy." He plopped a pen on top as if he worked in an ice cream shop.

"Jesus, you got something against trees, Wheeler?"

"Where I'm from we could use a little global warming," he said with a chuckle.

"Well, I just don't have time to sign all of these. You're interfering with my Zen time," Mauser said mockingly, hefting the pen. "You know I need at least thirty minutes of zero paperwork before I can start my day."

"Trust me. If there was a way around this, I would be doing it."

"I can think of one way around this. You think we can take him?" Mauser arched an eyebrow in Steele's direction.

Steele cracked his knuckles. "If it means we don't have to sign all these fucking forms, I think it's worth a shot." They all laughed as Wheeler took a step back with a wide grin.

"Wouldn't be work unless bullshit came with it." He turned to Mauser.

"How's my favorite puddle pirate? Been a few months since we've worked together. How's Amanda?" The older man grinned.

"Amanda? I don't recall a Amanda, sir," Mauser said with an evil smile as he scribbled his signature across the paperwork.

"Must be a Kelly or a Sarah in there somewhere?"

"No sir, just flying solo," Mauser retorted, tossing the pen to Steele. He preloaded his handcuffs with a click, click, click.

"And how about our youngest member of our justice league? Captain America himself. How's Gwen?" he inquired.

"We are more like avengers, sir," Mauser said.

Steele shook his head and laughed, not bothering to explain.

"She's good, sir. Doing the usual, saving the world one disaster at a time." Steele knew Wheeler well. Everyone in the service knew, or at least heard of, this man. The legendary 'Captain' Don Wheeler. A veteran of hundreds of deployments and ghost wars that wouldn't be released for public consumption until 2060. Senior CT agent Wheeler had been with the Division long before 9/11. Somalia, Kosovo, Iraq, Afghanistan, Libya and countless others. If someone were declaring war officially or unofficially against the United States, you can bet he'd been there.

"You put a ring on it yet, son?" Wheeler asked.

"Not yet, sir. But she keeps hounding me for it," he replied.

"That she will son. That she will. She will until she's got ya' by the balls, and by then its too late, and you'll have gray hair, a few kids, and a fat belly," Wheeler reminisced.

"Like you," Steele joked.

"Careful there son. I've been offing terrorists since you were in diapers." They laughed.

Andrea hollered at them from across the room. "You better lock that shit up Steele. She has got to be a saint for putting up with your hairy caveman ass. How can she even find you through that thick mane of fur, anyway? If you break her heart, I swear to God." She shook a fist at him.

"All right, everyone calm down. Her hand will be asked for in due time. Everything has to be perfect."

He scratched his signature across a pile of paperwork, acknowledging that he knew the risks of the business. It seemed a little redundant, but they did it before every single mission. If he didn't come home, they could deny he worked for them. Or if he was horribly maimed he couldn't come after them for liabilities. All in the fine print.

Wheeler collected his papers and worked his way back toward the front of the room. Within a moment, he changed the subject.

"Oh, sir. Do you happen to know the score of the Tigers game last night?" Steele asked with mock innocence. The Detroit Tigers had just swept the Minnesota Twins.

"We've only lost a few games. The season's a marathon, not a sprint. I smell a pennant in the near future," Wheeler said defiantly.

Steele chuckled. "Dementia must have set in early with this one," he said to Mauser, slapping him in the chest.

Steele had always thought of Wheeler as a mentor. Wheeler had taken a liking to the mature young agent as soon as he entered the Division straight from college six years prior. Wheeler had made it his duty to teach Steele everything he knew.

"Oh yeah, I almost forgot. Steele come on up here. There is something I need to talk to you about." Mauser gave his friend a wide-eyed look.

"Shut up. I'll be back."

Steele approached Wheeler uninhibited. He trusted this man.

"What's up?" Steele asked.

Wheeler's posture emitted a seriousness that made Steele straighten up. *He can't possibly be mad about the previous exchange.*

"This mission is vital to national security. Where we're headed isn't nice, and we can't accept anything other than success. But I would expect no less from you. This is for real. The big boys are out to play. That's why I've chosen you to be my assistant team leader."

Steele beamed. He had been waiting for this opportunity. The ATL spot usually went to an older, more experienced, agent. This meant Steele never got the opportunity because of his age. But he knew that as long as he stayed locked on, it would happen.

"Now, if you can't handle it, it's okay. No one will think less of you," Wheeler started.

Steele nodded. "No, no, of course I can handle it."

"You know the rules. If I go down, you're in charge. Complete the mission at all costs."

"I got it Cap," Steele said.

"Good, because I picked you all for a reason: you to be my number two; Jarl for his experience in protection details; Andrea for her ability to blend in; and Mauser for his..." Wheeler hesitated, thinking of something to say. "...And Mauser for his charming good looks. I'll let you conduct your checks," he said with a nod, taking his leave.

Steele surveyed his teammates. They were a strong unit. Each could hold his or her own in the shit, but together they were a terrorist's nightmare. Smart, discreet and ready to broach any conflict with speed, surprise and aggression.

Inwardly Steele smiled at Wheeler's choices, as they were almost definitely against the SAC's preferences. Everyone at WFO knew that the SAC didn't get along with Wheeler and would much rather have handpicked his cronies for this priority mission, given the opportunity. Contrary to set standards, favoritism ran deep throughout the government even within the elite Counterterrorism Division.

The SPD must have come down from a department head with a special request for Wheeler to lead it. The longstanding rumor within the Division was that Wheeler previously had a fling with the female Deputy Director back in the day. He vehemently denied the rumor, but his denial made his colleagues even more suspicious.

As a backup to Wheeler, Steele's responsibility was to complete any rudimentary administrative tasks that Wheeler didn't want to do. His duties included ensuring equipment was prepped and ready. It was a pointless job, considering that everyone was squared away and responsible for his or her own equipment, but since the big wigs were in the room, formalities were conducted.

After safety-checking Mauser's gear, Steele walked over to the giant of a man wearing a black compression Under Armor shirt. He had twenty-two inch arms covered in Norse runic inscription tattoos. Two black ravens flew on his arm: one upward and the other downward on either side of a symbol of three interlocking triangles which in turn interlocked on each other. He could have been a fabled Viking warrior like Bjorn Ironside or Ragnar Lothbrok. He towered head and shoulders above everyone else in the room. *Glad this guy is on our team.*

"What's up, Jarl? I thought Chip was rolling out with us?" he said, inspecting the man's gear.

Jarl peered down at Steele through a bushy beard. "Boar tusk," he boomed, placing a meaty paw on Steele's shoulder.

"Boar tusk, friend," Steele repeated.

The term 'boar tusk' had become a greeting between the two men. They would utter to one another like a secret password into their warrior society. Jarl claimed the ancient saying originated from his family's homeland, Sweden.

"It's good to see you, brother. Wheeler say Chip's sick," Jarl said with an accent.

"How's that book I saw you writing earlier coming?" Steele poked at the man.

"You know I hate computers, but my boss keeps making me do action reports," Jarl growled, a scowl settling across his face at the thought of writing more reports.

"I feel ya' man. You have all your mags?" Steele asked, making a mental checklist of everything.

"I brought a couple extra mags for you, little boss," the big man boomed down at him.

"Hopefully we won't need them."

Steele meandered his way over to Agent Carling's table. Her gear was laid out neatly for inspection; organized and tidy, without a single piece an inch out of place. He glanced at her and then back at her gear. Her brown hair hung freely along her shoulders, a small smirk settling on her lips as if she dared him to find a piece missing. She was pretty and the moment you underestimated her she took you out. Andrea was to be the lone female in the group, and it wasn't unusual for females within the Division to work with all-male teams. Former military, especially special forces, dominated their workforce.

"What?" she said, folding her arms across her chest as she glared at him.

"Nothing. I wonder if Wheeler has a back up blade for you."

Anger steamed from her. "No way," she stammered. Andrea shifted her gear from place to place, picking up one piece at a time. She found the blade and pushed the button, revealing a wicked edge.

"Oh, there it is," he said, dodging a swipe.

"Screw you, Steele. Get your eyes checked."

"You're right it is hard to see you all the way down there."

She puffed her chest out. "I'm tall enough to whoop your dumb ass," she said, raising her arms into a striking position.

"Okay, Okay. Simmer down now," he said with a smile.

Close to the same age as Steele, Andrea had always felt like a sister to him.

Steele shoved his hands into his pockets. "You heard from Chip?" he asked, leaning on the desk.

"Nah, I haven't. I overheard Wheeler saying he called in sick at the last minute, and the big bad SAC over there won't bring in a replacement." She rolled her eyes.

"Needs of the mission," Steele snorted. "Don't ask any questions because you won't get no answers. Stick with it."

Despite his joke, it concerned him. "That's not like Chip. I guess we're rolling with a five-man team then."

"I think you mean *five-person* team," she corrected with a smile, extending her baton and swinging it back and forth as if testing to make sure it worked.

Steele took a step back. "Five-person team," he said carefully.

She grunted, closing the expandable baton back down by slamming it vertically onto the floor shrinking it to normal size. "I'm not too worried about it." Andrea stopped talking as the SAC ambled to the front of the room, drawing everyone's attention.

Here we go.

JOSEPH
US Embassy Kinshasa, DRC

Thirty agonizing seconds passed since the last time Joseph had glanced at the mocking white clock on the cafeteria wall. The walls were plain and beige, generating an overall emotionlessness feeling to the room. He had moved over to a chair at a roundtable, away from the window, but it hadn't made him any less anxious. *Is it worse seeing them in the streets or knowing they were out there and ignoring them?*

His insides turned over and over. Waiting was the worst feeling. His leg bounced up and down. A swig from his water bottle did nothing to quench his dry throat and roiling stomach. He wished the cries from outside the embassy would just stop, but they wouldn't.

The crisis outside had gone from bad to worse. The crowd of locals at the gate had thickened and hundreds of people were now pushed up against the fence. Their arms and faces pressed painfully against the iron bars trying to push their way through. The fence held, but it was only a matter of time before it gave way to the mass of humanity on the other side.

Earlier, a few people had tried to climb the fence. One skinny Congolese man in a torn, weathered T-shirt and shorts had almost made it. Joseph had watched as he frantically kicked at the people below him. Just before he made it to the top, a hand caught his foot and pulled him down into the expectant hands of the crowd below. No one else had tried to climb the fence since.

Harkin pulled up a chair, next to Joseph, moving his extra girth with surprising efficiency. "Joseph, how are you holding up?" he asked, hands clasped in front of him like a trusting therapist.

"Okay, I guess. This is madness, Ed. I know it's related to the virus."

Harkin leaned forward. "There's nothing to worry about. All of this is just standard procedure. We both know that since Benghazi, the policy of protecting diplomats from hazardous crowds in consulates or embassies is a top priority. Anything that resembles even a protest like this is viewed as a direct threat, and is treated like a potential terror attack."

Joseph took another drink of his water, swishing it around in his mouth. "It doesn't seem to be going too well." Joseph eyed his colleague.

"I assure you the new Sec State had everything beefed-up. As lead of the scientific mission here, I have to sit on all of embassy operational meetings. We have more embassy guard units and diplomatic security details, and they work closely with intelligence services across the board: CIA, DIA, NGA, NSA and the FBI." Harkin rested a hand on Joseph's shoulder. "It will be fine."

"Well, what about Dr. Gao? And Dr. Nichols? And Dr. Sherman? Where are they?" He hadn't seen the other three members of his team since he had returned.

They had all gone out into the field at about the same time as him. A full deployment of the CDC staff was highly unusual, even for the beginning of the fall rainy season. The rainy season brought with it a surge in the spread of infectious diseases including Monkeypox, but never like this.

Harkin took a deep breath leaning back. "I haven't told you yet, but we lost contact with them two days ago. Best intelligence they've given us is that their communications equipment has gone out. RSO Kline took a detail and went to check it out. As you can see, he hasn't returned either. I'm sorry I didn't tell you earlier. I just thought you had enough on your plate." *Enough on my plate?*

"So they could still be out there and we're just gonna leave them?" Joseph asked, suddenly getting angry. *That could have been me out there.*

"I'm sorry, but my hands are tied. The acting DS agent in charge told me a full investigation's underway."

"Someone help! A doctor, please!" a staffer shouted from the other side of the cafeteria. People huddled around a woman on the ground.

Harkin perked up, but Joseph felt a little like lying down. *Oh God, what now? Surely, this isn't related to the virus. I'm not supposed to be treating people. I am supposed to be researching and studying diseases at a distance.* He wished he had a shell like a hermit crab to crawl into.

Harkin stood up. "I'll take care of it, Joseph. Just relax," he said, waving a hand at Joseph to stay seated and then moving over to help a woman lying on the ground.

Relax? How can I relax? My entire staff is most likely massacred, and the city is boiling over into an all-out riot. Every minute, more and more people crowd the gate. A ticking time bomb. It isn't if; it's when. We need to get out of here now.

Joseph surveyed the room nervously. Harkin attended the sick woman, while others sat around on chairs, on the floor, or sprawled out in various stages of distress. Maybe Joseph should help Harkin; after all, he was a doctor. He stood up, thinking about making his way over. The woman looked as though she was about to throw up. He sat back down. *Harkin could handle it himself.*

Joseph's gaze fell upon a man seated against the cafeteria wall. "Why is this happening?" he said loudly, staring into space.

As if God had answered his prayers, Joseph heard the prominent swoosh, swoosh, swoosh of a helicopter, and the building shuddered as it set down on the rooftop helipad. There was hope. There would always be hope. People glanced up with light in their eyes. They would make it, after all. This disaster would come to an end. The wagons were circled, and now, the cavalry had arrived. People rose up and flooded toward the exit, and Joseph found himself in the middle.

People jostled into the hallway bumping each others shoulders appearing polite but on edge.

"I need everyone to go to the roof in an *orderly* fashion," yelled a helmeted Marine guard in full battle dress. He elbowed open the door to the stairwell, his long gun slung across his body as he directed them.

Blood red flood lights coated the stairwell and dimly lit the way. It was as if the darkness would hide their actions. They ignored the guard's instructions, and as soon as they hit the stairs, they started running in a state of panic. They pushed and shoved, scrambling for position as they sprinted up the stairs. Joseph got caught up in the rush and lost sight of Harkin. Shoulders, arms and hands drove him forward. Soon, he found himself doing the same, as he put a hand into the person's back in front of him, fear in his gut driving him onward. A woman tripped, hands reaching out to brace her fall.

"Someone please help," she cried. No one bothered to give her a second glance.

Joseph couldn't stop. The tide of people swept Joseph up. He made a feeble reach to help her; at least that's what he told himself. The last thing he saw of the woman was her bloodied face, stricken with fear as she tried to use a handrail to pull herself upright.

The rooftop door opened with a bang, and the staffers bolted through. They ran for the helicopter, becoming a frenzied mob.

The only thing that slowed them down were two DS agents in full tactical gear. Vests featuring bullet holders, guns, and cylindrical things hanging from clips. The militant contraptions went beyond Joseph's understanding. He had never even held a gun.

The agents held up their hands. "Stop!" they shouted, attempting to bring order to the mob. Joseph recognized Agent Yang from an earlier deployment.

"Keep your heads down," they yelled over the rotor blades, hands cupped to their mouths.

"Women and children first," shouted the other agent.

"Get in line!" shouted Agent Yang.

One man led his family aboard the aircraft, and then another. The number of seats dwindled rapidly like the worst game of musical chairs he had ever played in his life.

Joseph could feel a swell of panicked energy from the civilians around him. They all wanted to rush on. They didn't want to be left behind like some less vigilant creature of Noah's biblical flood.

They were like animals that had been backed into a corner: shaking with fright, willing to do anything to survive. A staffer in a sports jacket fell forward, knocking into Agent Yang.

Yang tried to block the staffer from entering the helo, and a scuffle ensued.

There was no way everyone could leave on the lone chopper; it was just too full. It would have to go and come back. *It has to come back*, thought Joseph. *Unless I can somehow squeeze to the front.* He turned sideways and weaved his way forward.

"Wait your turn, asshole," shouted a staffer, putting a rough hand on Joseph's shoulder. Joseph wriggled in fear, slipping through the man's hands. Now he had a front row seat to the end of all his hope.

Agent Yang extracted himself from the man's grasp, striking the staffer in the face. "You, stay back," he bellowed, pointing his MP5 submachine gun at the staffer, more out of fear than malice. "This bird's full. The next one'll be here shortly."

The man clutched his face where he had been struck, crinkling in hate. "Fuck you. I want on THIS one," he yelled.

He lunged for Yang's gun and, caught off guard, Yang fell backward, excitedly ripping a few rounds into the crowd before losing his grip on the weapon. The two men rolled around on the ground, fighting for control.

The woman next to Joseph dropped to her knees, holding her stomach. She pulled her hand away from the wound, lips quivering as she stared down at her own blood. Everyone gaped at the woman in silence as she gasped for breath.

"Ahhhh," she wailed in pain bringing a bittersweet drenched hand toward her face. Everyone just stared. Joseph's jaw dropped. The man responsible for their safety had shot one of their own. That was the turning point.

As one, the entire crowd rushed for the helicopter, each individual trying to force his or her way on board. Joseph forced his way around the other agent as he tried to hold people at bay. They formed a school of human fish escaping obstacles in their path. The other agent looked about in panic as the mass of people drove him toward the edge of the helipad. He momentarily maintained his balance as he teetered on the line, but he couldn't hold on.

Joseph knew he would never forget the look in the man's eyes as he toppled over. Pure astonishment. Joseph tried to get inside, but fell victim to the classic case of survival of the fittest. The aggressor would be the victor. Driven by more wild primal rage than Joseph, they swept him to the side.

The pilot saw the rush of people, and took the helicopter airborne. Unwanted passengers clung to whatever they could. They latched on to foot railings, other passengers and side handles. They were ticks on a deer. The pilot struggled to bring the overburdened helicopter more than twenty feet into the air. It hovered spinning around in a circle as he tried to gain control.

Joseph stood to one side, feeling helpless. He was no longer in control of his own fate. His only hope for escape floated above him. The helicopter swerved back and forth as the pilot tried to maneuver the bogged down aircraft. Flying low, it veered towards the airport, shaking off one of the passengers from the foot rail. The man screamed as he plummeted to earth, silenced within seconds as he struck the ground. The unbalanced helo jackknifed to the right at a dangerous angle.

The pilot struggled to keep it straight coming back the other way angling awkwardly. The helicopter wobbled before the rotor blades dug deeply into a white apartment tower. Huge chunks of building sprayed onto the people and streets below. They stared up at the chopper, oblivious to the dangers of the hot metal, rubble and debris that rained death from above. The rioters were drawn to the destruction, ignoring their crushed and maimed allies as they followed the crashing helo. The frame of the helicopter tipped backward out of the building and collided with the street in a fiery mangled mess.

That couldn't have just happened? Smoke and flames erupted from the wreckage. Bodies blanketed the ground around the helicopter like a human patchwork quilt. The loss of life was horrendous.

As if the whole scenario couldn't get any worse, the people still alive on the street below swarmed over the debris. The pilot crawled out and the locals fell upon him like a pack of hyenas. The struggle was over quick. The last Joseph saw of him, he tried to hold his entrails in while the locals pried them from this grasp. They tug-of-warred for his insides. Joseph puked over the side of the helipad. It didn't make him feel any better.

Clearly, the people in the streets were infected with the virus. They were impervious to falling debris. Relentless in their assault upon the living and feeding upon the dead. Joseph hoped for the children's sake that they all died in the crash. He stared vacantly, traumatized by the situation.

The air sucked out of the people around him. Many were crying as they watched the horror below. Joseph didn't know if they were weeping for their friends and family, or because their means of salvation had disappeared in a fiery inferno of flesh and metal.

"There's another helicopter coming, right?" a man asked Joseph. Joseph didn't acknowledge him. He wiped his mouth and continued to watch the grisly scene below with detached interest as the remaining staffers and families slowly retreated inside the embassy. The pain in his gut disappeared and was replaced by a hollow, empty feeling; a feeling of despair. The embassy slowly eroded like a sandcastle of refuge, and the people outside were the waves destroying them piece by piece. It was only a matter of time before it collapsed.

This confirmed what he had known deep down: the virus was unstoppable and that, unchecked, it had spread rapidly among the urban population of Kinshasa.

His distant, dead stare faded upon hearing a familiar voice. "Joseph! Joseph!" Echoed up from the stairwell. The man still couldn't address him properly.

Joseph turned limply. Nixon appeared in the doorway of the stairs dressed in tactical gear, his MP5 dangling from his shoulder.

"I found you," Nixon exclaimed. Gasping for breath, the agent leaned over revealing his emerging bald spot, resting his hands on his knees.

"Phew, that's a lot of stairs," sputtered Nixon. He stretched his back and whistled when he saw the crash. "Was that ours?"

Joseph nodded, his eyes unfocused on the scene below.

Nixon searched clearly looking for someone. "Where are Baxter and Yang? They're supposed to be up here."

Joseph didn't know what to say, so he simply replied: "They're gone."

Nixon gave him a concerned look. "Snow is prepping some vehicles near the garage," he said. Joseph hugged himself. The people from the streets would come for him.

STEELE
Undisclosed building, Virginia

"Men and... ah... woman. You have been hand-selected to cover an SPD from the Democratic Republic of the Congo to the United States. I will let the team leader disseminate the details, but I am here to remind you that we have policies in place for a reason. I would expect you all to follow them to a T," said the Special Agent in Charge, glaring directly at Wheeler.

He glanced over at the other two suits. "That said, you will be traveling with two Agency personnel to Africa, so be on your best behavior."

"Jesus. What are we... fucking kids?" Mauser whispered to Steele.

Steele shook his head and laughed under his breath. This guy would talk down to them any chance he got.

"Upon arrival, you will escort the staff from the U.S. Embassy Kinshasa back to the United States. They are going to be pretty shaken up from their experience, so do your jobs right and get them back home. I'll let our 'comrades' from the intelligence community introduce themselves. Good luck, gentlemen and lady." He snatched up his notes and promptly left the room, not wanting anything to do with them once the formalities were done.

A gray man stepped forward. There was no set look to a CIA officer. They came in all different shapes and sizes. He supposed that, like in his covert line of work, blending in was paramount to success. The taller of the two spooks addressed the team. He had an average build and appeared to be in his early fifties. To Steele, he resembled somebody's slightly awkward uncle; the kind who would drink a few too many beers at Thanksgiving and then tell dirty jokes. He clasped his hands in front of him as he spoke.

"Let me introduce myself. My name's Bill, and this is my colleague Bob. We're going to Kinshasa with you gentlemen and lady. I hope you don't mind us tagging along," he said with a smile.

"This will prove to be an interesting trip. The DRC really is a beautiful country, especially this time of year; plenty of areas to hike and places to eat in the North End."

His gaze at the end showed that he didn't believe the words he spoke. A cold, calculating mind lurked beneath his friendly exterior. "My friend Bob here is going to give you a short briefing on what's happening on the ground in the DRC."

Bob, a shorter version of Bill, made his way to the front of the room. He spoke with a Texan accent: "Hi y'all. Thanks for having us. We're going into a very dangerous region. We have intelligence from the ground that the country is suffering from multiple rebel insurgencies. A bit of a hotspot, but not unsurprising, considering the weakness of their democratic institutions. However, it is concerning to us that all of these factions are active at once. The government is on the verge of collapse. When we land, we'll disembark from the plane and meet with some of our local contacts and try to figure out what is really going on. The embassy is evacuating and should meet ya'll at the airport. They'll be scared, but happy to see you guys. Thank you for your service. If there is anything we can do to help, please let us know." He said this with a small smile.

Steele gave Mauser a quick glance. Mauser gave him an indifferent shoulder, with his best 'whatever they say' face. The counterterrorism agents didn't pose any questions. They had been conditioned over time not to ask them. They were ready for anything and everything. They would treat any threat with extreme prejudice. As long as the staffers were at the airport, they didn't need much more information than that. Wheeler took his turn at the front.

"Hey boss, nice skinny jeans," Andrea said with a shy smile. Wheeler had everyone's respect, but the agents still liked to joke around with one another. It helped to relieve the tension of the job they were about to do.

Wheeler looked down at his pants. "Why thank you, Andrea," he said.

"Are they bedazzled, sir?" Mauser chimed in.

Wheeler broke into a smile. "As a matter of fact, I think they are. I grabbed them from your top drawer on the way out," he said. Everybody burst out laughing.

Steele chuckled. A regular person would have turned red, but Mauser just beamed.

Wheeler continued: "Unsurprisingly, we have no new intelligence from our side of the aisle."

The agents shook their heads in scorn. It wasn't uncommon for them to go on missions where the premise was to be alert, but they received nothing in terms of intelligence. It was like searching for a needle in a haystack, except that at any time the needle could come up behind you and put a bullet in the back of your head.

Wheeler continued his short brief: "This is what I do know. Our mission is to do a special protective detail for some embassy staffers. The embassy is being evacuated due to a probable terror threat in the region. That means nothing happens to these people on the way home. Nothing."

He looked from one to the other, staring each of them in the eyes.

"Everything else is secondary. We will not disembark the aircraft. The staffers should be awaiting our arrival. Our Agency friends will be on *business*, so to speak, so don't blow their cover. We're in it for the long haul. So get some rest on the way over because I need everyone on top of their game for the way back. Jarl and I will be in first; Andrea, you're our sleeper in business class; and Mauser and Steele you're in 'steerage' with the rest of the peasants."

Mauser leaned over to whisper to Steele, "I guess we get to slum it in the back."

Steele nodded. No hot towels or classy nuts for them, but they needed to provide coverage over all the staffers.

Wheeler ignored Mauser and continued: "I'll meet you all at gate D15. No later than 1945, Steele is my secondary on this one." Steele nodded.

"Does anyone have any questions?" He paused. "Good, our end time will be 1830 tomorrow, so tell your significant others not to wait up."

A short time later, Mauser and Steele cruised down VA Route 29 in Mauser's lifted Chevy Silverado. They passed a plethora of reflective glassed buildings belonging to defense contractors, aerospace, IT companies and government agencies. The whole region was filled with them. It was as if they were replicated on a nightly basis. Four squad cars zipped past heading south, as they approached Washington-McCone International Airport.

"Dude, what's that about?" Mauser asked, raising his thick framed Oakley shades and checking his rear-view mirror.

"I don't know. Do you think the donut shop is getting robbed?"

"That's a safe bet. I can't imagine any other reason why those guys would be getting so bent out of shape."

Steele shook his head. He understood the convenience of fast food and food on the go, but food fueled the body. The better quality the fuel, the better the body would run. That's why he didn't understand why people, especially police officers — people who depended on their bodies to run at a high level because their lives depended on it — would decide to run them on garbage.

He scrolled through his contact list until he came across Chip's contact information and hit the call button. "Turn that down," Steele told Mauser. Mauser frowned. "Come on, man, you know 'Die Zombie Die' is one of my favorite jams," he said, begrudgingly complying with Steele's request.

The phone rang and rang, but Chip didn't pick up.

"That redneck can't possibly be sleeping. He knows he's missing out on seeing the motherland, right?" Steele said.

"Well, he's probably out spending time with his family, enjoying his 'sick' leave," Mauser said, messing with the radio.

Thirty minutes later, the pair made their way through the airport on the look out for suspicious activity. If they could handle an incident before they were in the air that would be ideal. Duking it out at thirty thousand feet was a much riskier endeavor.

They walked to the gate in a leisurely fashion. Roller boards squeaked behind them, just like any other day. Travel was work for the men. A family hustled on by, racing to reach their flight on time.

It seemed pretty light for a Friday. The blue shirted security stood around waiting for patrons to pass through their checkpoints. Every day people commute

through airports, and those who travel enough begin to notice trends. As a frequent

traveler, Steele noticed that something about today was off. Friday was a busy day: a

day when people traveled home from business trips. If it was a holiday, add in

families with children and college students. Today just didn't feel right. To Steele, it

felt as though some people were just gone.

He confirmed his hunch when they approached gate D15, and only a dozen

or so people sat around the lobby. "Did we get a gate change or something?" Steele

said aloud.

"I'll check it out," Mauser said, walking over to the gate agent. "This is the

right spot," he said when he returned.

"Either people are much smarter than we are, or they must have watched the

news," Steele said.

"Does that make them smarter? Or does that make them plain crazy?"

Mauser asked.

"I'd have to bet on crazy," Steele said.

"Well what about these poor saps sitting here with us? What does that make

them?"

Steele people watched in a relaxed fashion. A couple of men in tan tactical

pants with matching tan packs sat conversing with their backs to the wall. They were

former military, most likely defense contractors for the government. They could be

potential allies if things went bad, or the worst of enemies if they went bad.

On the other side of them, sat a group of young men and women in a semi-

circle lounging like they were on a school field trip. They were dressed like backpackers, but were clearly going on some sort of humanitarian mission. A shorthaired woman with a bandana around her neck gave Steele a dismissive look. Apparently, he didn't fit her criteria of acceptability. She would sing a different tune if a bad guy pointed a gun at her head and the only thing between her life and death was Steele not missing. He ignored her. He didn't get to pick who he protected, but he would protect her regardless of her color or creed. He wondered if she would do the same for him, or if he was just too different for saving.

He leaned back in his seat and relaxed, but never fully. He was ready to spring into action at a moment's notice.

"I'd have to bet on stupidity," Steele said, after sizing up the other passengers.

"Why's that?" Mauser questioned.

"For two reasons. One, you've got to be kind of dumb if you're going to go over there to risk your neck. Two, you've got to be dumb if you're going over there to risk your neck without a gun," Steele surmised.

"So what's that make us?" Mauser asked.

"That makes us slightly above average," Steele said.

Mauser laughed, shouldering his bag. It was time to go.

Without observing anything noteworthy, the agents boarded the plane. They were taking a Boeing 777 over to Kinshasa. The dual-aisle plane could seat around three hundred people in its current configuration. A few individual pods for passengers decorated the first class cabin, the business class area held individual pods placed closer together, an economy plus segment with extra legroom and economy regular, 'sardine-crammed' seating. Naturally, most seats were the kind where passengers had to practically sit on top of their fellow travelers. Steele often had a hard time staying within the confines of his own seat; just one of the problems resulting from spending a few too many hours eating steak and lifting weights.

The rest of the team had already boarded, congregating in the first-class cabin.

Wheeler called out his orders from just beyond the partition. "I want this plane licked clean of any suspicious items. If it isn't supposed to be here, I want to know about it. That includes Jarl's sister."

Steele laughed. "God, I hope we don't find Jarl's sister on here. Where would she hide?"

"Well, if we haven't found her already, then we are doing a really shitty job searching the plane," Wheeler laughed.

"She can hide in the seat next to me. Just like our Christmas party last year," Mauser said.

Jarl's broad face popped out from behind a lavatory. "I can hear you, shitheads. Mauser you never touched her. None of you will ever touch her," he said, raising a meaty fist at them. "She's an angel," he muttered to himself.

"All right, you two. Finish your checks. Then we can get the chatterboxes on board," Wheeler yelled at them. Steele turned away, shining his tactical light into the corner of the cabin.

They deemed the aircraft safe after a thorough search. They gave the flight crew the go-ahead to enter the plane and begin their preparatory actions for a flight. A host of flight attendants in their blue uniforms, along with a pilot and two copilots entered the aircraft. They talked together loudly as they came aboard.

Daniel Greene

"You would not believe what Caitlyn did to Gina. Seriously, she is such a bitch," a dark-haired flight attendant said, flinging her hair back.

"Doesn't surprise me. That woman's totally out of control," an older blonde said to her colleague.

They breezed past Steele and Mauser, not giving them a second glance. The flight attendants were part of an interesting community, to say the least. Everything was pure drama with them. Steele tried to steer his nose clear of that mess.

As the flight attendants made their safety checks, Wheeler waved Steele over to the cockpit. Hundreds of tiny lights flickered on the control panels. Steele always wondered how the pilots kept all the controls straight. The captain ducked under the doorframe of the cockpit. Wearing a finely pressed white shirt with four gold bars on his shoulder, the distinguished man nodded his graying head to Steele as he approached. "Captain Richards, I'd like you to meet our ATL, Agent Mark Steele. He's my protégé of sorts," Wheeler said.

"It's nice to meet you, Mark," he said with a firm handshake. "Hopefully you haven't taken too much advice from this man here. He was quite the lady's man back in his day."

Steele was confused. He gave Wheeler a questioning eyebrow.

"This old man here?" Steele said, gesturing toward Wheeler.

"Captain Richards used to fly aircraft for the Navy. We're old war buddies."

"Oh, I see. Well then I will have to say he's taught me everything he knows."

Captain Richards laughed. "God help us. If shit hits the fan, just don't miss. Got it?"

"Got it," echoed Steele. *If shit hits the fan, just don't crash the plane.*

"Let's see here," Captain Richards said as he scanned his flight log paperwork. "Looks like, it'll be about ten hours over to Kinshasa. We've got a good tailwind today." This meant it would be an even longer haul on the way back. Everything was a give and take.

Steele's phone buzzed in his pocket. He nodded and politely left the two old friends taking an empty seat.

"Hey babe," he said, smiling.

"Come back," Gwen cooed on the line.

Steele always felt comforted that she wanted him to come home. It was nice to be missed.

"You know that I have to do this. I'll be back in a few days and then we can enjoy the weekend."

He usually had a long weekend after an extended tour of duty to recover from the intense tempo of operations.

"I know, I know. I just have a bad feeling about this trip. Things are bad out there. The news is saying our embassy is under attack."

This concerned Steele, but it wasn't the first time something like this was happening, nor would it be the last.

"Really? That *is* bad."

"Yeah rioting in the streets. It looks dangerous."

"We'll just have to roll with the punches."

They sat in silence for a moment, both of their minds racing over the dire circumstances presented to them. He broke the silence with a faint whisper: "I love you. I'll do anything to get back to you."

"I love you too," she said with a slight quiver in her voice.

"I'll call you on our layover," Steele said. "Bye love." He punched End Call on his cell. Saying goodbye was always the hardest part.

JOSEPH
US Embassy Kinshasa, DRC

Joseph dug through his office. A small, simple room contained only a desk and chair, along with a computer and a filing cabinet. A small window overlooked a storage building that housed food and beverages for the embassy. Since he wasn't leaving anytime soon, he would make sure his things were ready to flee.

He fished out all the notes he had collected on Monkeypox over the past year. Carefully, he placed dozens of blood vials into a small, padded case. The building had begun to heat up, as though someone had turned off the air conditioning. Sweat trickled down his back. He reached over to flick on his light switch. Flick. No lights came on. *Only emergency power must be on.*

While the staff waited for an escort to safety, they set about burning and destroying anything of value, lest it fall into the wrong the hands should the embassy be overrun, as it had been in Tehran in 1979. No one had bothered with Joseph's office yet. Not that the people outside were interested in his research, but even if they were, it was not high on the list of national security priorities. His collections on Monkeypox were shared liberally with the public, as well as the University of Kinshasa School of Public Health. He thought hard, trying to remember everything he would need to take with him. Sweat stung his eyes, causing them to tear up. He plopped down in his chair. He must be ready to run when Nixon came back.

His eyelids dipped low, his body feeling as though it weighed a thousand pounds. Unable to keep his eyes open any longer, Joseph laid his head down on his desk, using his arms as a pillow. Maybe just a quick nap. *I can rest my eyes for just a moment.* Sleep took him quickly.

Bloody faces plagued his dreams. He couldn't escape their greedy hands and gory mouths. Agent Reliford's tooth-gouged face and neck dripping blood loomed close as he grabbed Joseph in a vice-like grip. Joseph twisted out of Reliford's hands, only to be pulled in the direction of Bowali's face, a mangled mess beyond repair. The only distinguishing mark that remained was the small metal crucifix hanging from Bowali's neck.

Reliford and Bowali struggled over Joseph's body. Red hands yanked him side to side in a battle for his limbs. Joseph lacked any control over his body. Now, his patients were there, skinny emaciated Congolese tearing his flesh in revenge for not saving their lives. The charred remains of burnt Marines joined them, skin peeling from their faces like paint off an old weathered barn. His mouth opened as he tried to scream, and the stench of the dead filled his nostrils as their oppressive weight smothered down upon him.

The building shook, rumbling Joseph out of his horrid dream with a cloud of dust. He sat up, attempting to catch his breath, eyes still groggy from his uncomfortable sleep. *How long have I been out? Has another helicopter landed on the roof?* He listened intently but couldn't make out the twirl of the rotor blades.

His window provided him with no view, so he walked into the hallway.

Oh my God.

The remains of one of the guard towers smoldered thick black smoke. Rubble covered the manicured front lawn, along with the remains of three or four Marines - it was hard to tell among the wreckage - one held his face thrashing in the grass.

End Time

He ducked down below the window as another explosion decimated the second tower. The tower blazed into a fiery inferno, flames engulfing the small building. The burning forms of the men inside collapsed onto the ground, smoke rising from their bodies. Joseph put his hands to his head. *There were men in there. Our men. Men that I talk to everyday when I enter the compound.*

An extremely large truck, one that must have survived World War II, rammed through the crowd of people at the gate pushing them to the side like a V-shaped cattle catcher on an old locomotive. The truck didn't stop as it struck the gate. Bodies writhed and squirmed, pinned between the gate and the truck as the vehicle bore them forward into the compound. The truck screeched to a halt, sending the still alive and probably infected people sailing across the embassy lawn. They slowly got to their feet, now with mangled irreparably bent torsos and broken limbs. *Infected.*

Two large army transports followed closely behind the first. Bodies splattered under the large trucks following the carved path of the first. They appeared even older than the original truck; perhaps left over from the Belgian colonial period.

Gunfire sprayed into the people in the streets from the back of the trucks. Guns rattled the bullets point blank into their faces, exploding the heads of the attackers into the street. The scene went beyond horrific. *So much death. When will it end?*

Blood-spattered people climbed onto the back of one of the transports. Bullets punched through their bodies with no effect, spraying their insides all over the other rioters. Some fell down, never to get up again, but many others stood back up with gaping holes in their bodies. Men screamed piteously as they had nowhere to run but were forced to face the jaws of death.

The remaining Marines retreated to the front of the embassy. Using doorways and concrete pillars as cover, they fired at the infected protestors that flooded into the compound from the street. Constant gunfire did nothing to deadened their mad rush. *This fight will be over quickly*, thought Joseph.

The lead transport turfed the once-beautiful lawn as it spun its wheels in reverse speedily backing into place between the compound and the infected. The Marines' stopped firing as the trucks physically blocked the people on the street from entering the compound. Men dressed in faded camouflage hastily replaced the infected.

The Congolese Army had come to rescue them. "The Army," he said aloud affirming his belief. A ragged cheer went up from the begrudged Marines. One Marine strode forward waving at the Congolese soldiers. *The staff could escape in those large trucks.* A glimmer of hope shone through the most depressing of events.

A door swung open on the lead truck and a soldier leaned outside popping a sidearm. The Marine fell backwards clutching his neck. He writhed in pain as Congolese troops jumped down from their trucks, guns blazing, but instead of shooting the infected, they attacked the Marines.

The soldiers bolted toward the main embassy building firing their guns on full auto, spraying bullets everywhere. The glass next to Joseph shattered inward. He fell awkwardly, trying to get out of the way, glass landing all around him.

Joseph crawled back into his office on his hands and knees, hastily shoving thumb drives and more books into his satchel. His hands continued to shake and his heart beat feverishly. The booms of gunfire echoed in the courtyard. Using his hands as earmuffs, he covered his ears and pushed his back against the wall.

Closing his eyes, he prayed for everything to stop. When he opened them, Agent Nixon's beet red face hovered next to him. His mouth moved, but Joseph couldn't make out the words. Nixon's mouth moved furiously and he looked around urgently. The agent hauled him up and pushed him toward his office door.

Joseph tripped as he tried to get to the door, the satchel of materials and briefcase tangled in between his legs an albatross around his neck. His mind ran blank unable to think straight. Like a painting of himself, he froze in time while everything around him moved in fast forward.

Bullet holes drilled through the wall next to him as gunfire banged down the hallway, and Joseph stood frozen in the doorway. *People are shooting at me? How can we escape now that the enemy soldiers were here and the infected loomed at the gate?* Dread settled upon him. Gunfire sang out its staccato tune in one of the stairwells.

Nixon dragged him back inside the office by the collar of his shirt, poking his head out into the hallway and quickly slamming Joseph's office door. "I know that sound anywhere. It's an AK-47, a Kalashnikov," he said.

Joseph didn't want to hear that. "What does that mean?" he asked.

"It means there are men in the building that don't belong," Nixon said, pulling the metal top piece back on his weapon, making a clinking sound. Joseph didn't have any understanding of how guns worked. They made him uneasy, at best, and the fact that there were men in the building that wanted to use them on him, made his bladder want to release.

"Stay quiet," Nixon breathed, holding a shaky finger up to his lips.

Joseph's breath came out raggedly and loudly, with his heartbeat resounding in his head. The silence made his breathing seem all the louder. He knew that the anticipation of what was to come was always worse than the actual act; that fear always made actions so much worse. Joseph couldn't handle the anticipation.

He stood unsteadily and opened the office door.

"What the fuck are you doing?" Agent Nixon called out hoarsely. The agent reached for Joseph, but his hand missed, not quite quick enough to catch him.

Joseph gaped down the hallway, illuminated by red emergency floodlights. A large African man in an officer's uniform strode brazenly down the middle, brandishing a handgun. Rough-looking soldiers in berets flanked him on either side like a gang. Joseph allowed himself to be pulled back into the room, and Nixon quickly closed the door before leaning his back against the wall.

"You idiot. We might have been able to hide," he spat. Nixon glowered at him, daunted by the sequence of bad events. He wiped the matted brown hair sticking to his forehead, resting his gun barrel against it as if he were praying to his gun.

Joseph felt an odd surge of euphoria, as though he were sitting on a cloud; a sense of detachment from the events that were unfolding around him.

Nixon gripped his weapon with fierce hands that were white with the effort. Joseph wondered whether Nixon would fight. He pictured an unimaginable attempt at male bravado ending with Nixon going down in a hail of gunfire. Joseph could never imagine such a thing for himself. Living was just too preferable to death no matter the cause.

The loud, echoing footsteps slowed and stopped. A low-pitched, accented voice echoed down the hall: "Surrender and we will show you mercy. You have five seconds to make up your mind or we will kill you."

Joseph desperately wanted to pass out.

NIXON
US Embassy Kinshasa, DRC

Nixon slid his SIG P229 and MP5 submachine gun into the hallway. He gave Joseph a shoulder squeeze. The doctor looked shell-shocked.

"Just do what they say. Okay, Joe?"

Joseph nodded slowly, his eyes vacant. Nixon knew he couldn't win this fight, and if whoever was in the hallway wanted to kill them they wouldn't have bothered negotiating. At least, he hoped not.

One of his greatest fears was ending up on some jihadi website in an orange jumpsuit reading a script written by an extremist nut job just before they hacked his head off with a machete. He prayed they would just shoot him before it came to that. *Just one of the perks of being an American.*

Quick-booted footsteps raced down the hall. African soldiers rounded the corner with AKs pressed loosely to their shoulders.

"Obtenez sur vos genoux!" the Congolese man screamed. Nixon had no idea what the scrawny man in the ill-fitting, blood-covered fatigues yelled. He resembled a little boy playing dress-up with his dad's clothes.

A couple more AKs were shoved in his face to gain compliance. They didn't even need to bother with Joseph. Nixon held his hands in the air.

"All right guys, take it easy."

"Get down on knees! Get down on knees!" a skinny soldier screamed at him in broken English, with wide yellow-tinted eyes.

Nixon complied. He didn't want to give the man an excuse to shoot him.

"Just take it easy, now," he said as they zip tied his wrists.

The soldier pushed his head. "Ta gueule." The yellow teethed soldier smiled as he shoved a dirty rag into Nixon's mouth. *Did this come off the guy's sweaty ass foot?*

"You like," the soldier mocked. Nixon turned his head away in passive resistance causing the soldier to smack the back of his head.

"Don't be cowboy." The soldier wrapped duct tape around his head. *That's going to be a bitch to take off.* He preferred to keep what hair he had remaining on his head because he wasn't getting any younger.

Nixon and Joseph were shoved along the plain corridor, their footsteps echoing off the tile floors. Gunfire bursts from outside the compound sounded like firecrackers on the Fourth of July. They were driven to the back of the cafeteria, now a detention center. A soldier indicated he wanted them to sit with the rest of the hostages by crosschecking Nixon with his gun across his spine causing Nixon to fall to his knees.

Nixon didn't see Snow among them, which meant he either was dead or still 'in the fight.' Hopefully he waged a one man guerrilla campaign, inside the compound. With Snow free, they still had a fighting chance at rescue, albeit a slim one. Although Master Sergeant Snow wasn't his supervisor, they had worked closely on the Post Security Team while they were running protection details for the Ambassador. If he were still alive, he would be fighting to the last man. *Tough old bastard*, thought Nixon, who had once seen him do a hundred pull-ups in three minutes at the embassy fitness center. That was about ninety-five more than Nixon could do. The man had the tenacity of a terminator and the heart of a commando. He was a total war machine.

Nixon and Joseph sat uncomfortably with their backs against the wall, in a long row of hostages beneath the panoramic window. Nixon struggled with his bonds, the hard plastic ties cutting into his wrists. *Stupid zip ties.* He couldn't move his wrists at all as they were pinned together in a tight embrace.

Nixon racked his brain. There had to be a way out of these things. He thought he had seen an online video on how to break a zip tie, but he couldn't remember how the Internet phenomenon broke free.

A rough-looking soldier glanced his way as he struggled with his ties. They locked eyes briefly. The man's eyes were bloodshot and almost the color of egg yolk. His skin dark like the night. Nixon broke his eyes away, looking deliberately downcast. He made sure to slump down on the wall, his chin tucked low, trying to appear pathetic. To his surprise it came rather easily, given his current state of affairs.

When the guard lost interest, Nixon nudged the doctor with his shoulder, trying to reassure him, but the doctor just gave him a blank stare from behind his glasses. *There's no fight left in this guy. If they'd come here to kill us, they would have done it by now. This isn't Benghazi.*

He tried to get a glimpse out the window. Tough to see because of the angle, it looked as though the heavy truck still blocked the smashed gate entrance. The rat-a-tat-tat of AK-47s sounded off, bodies piling up around the truck. There were no crowd control techniques here, only the brutally effective methods of murderous violence.

The gate. The hostages. It dawned on Nixon. These weren't the actions of an assault; this was an occupation. These men were here to stay.

End Time

The doors to the cafeteria – once a place for people to go for a pleasant social exchange, but now a prison – were thrown open.

The large African officer, who had demanded their surrender earlier, treaded through the door, his tightly laced boots clicking the floor. A few people begged for mercy. Although he wore camouflage, no DRC military insignia decorated his uniform, but these people wouldn't know the difference. *In fact, he isn't wearing any insignia. Just a uniform. Keep it together.*

"Hello, my friends. I am Colonel Jacobin Kosoko." He beamed a sinister white-toothed smile off set by the darkness of his skin. Well over six feet tall and with a good deal of muscle, he wore blood-decorated fatigue pants and jacket, with a black tank top underneath. Gold sunglasses dangled off the front of his shirt. On his hip he wore a Western-style gun belt. A machete handle poked up over his shoulder. *The machete seemed to be the melee weapon of choice for people in this part of the world, and sure enough this big bastard has one. Here we go. Fire up the video cameras. Shit is about to go crazy. Who would he choose to chop up first? The lady crying in front? No, too easy. He would pick one of the toughest ones to pacify the entire group. Standard kidnapping protocol. Kill the most likely to present resistance first.*

Colonel Kosoko knelt down in front of a woman sobbing. "Shhh, you are safe. Everything is fine," he said, brushing a sweaty strand of hair off her cheek. *Judas, he is going to kill her first.* Nixon wrenched his wrists and the zip ties cut him keeping him restrained. He was no hero, but he couldn't sit by while this massacre took place.

Nixon strained his legs upright making his knees feel like they were going to pop. He must do something. *What do I do now?* He let out a muffled cry through his gag trying to look fierce with his hands tied behind his back. He took a step forward getting ready to throw himself at the man. Kosoko didn't even release the woman.

A wood stock cracked into his belly. The air rushed from his lungs and he fell back on his ass. *Its where you belong*, he told himself. The soldier with the yellow eyes stared down at him and Nixon stared up through the eye of a long grey metal AK-47.

"No, no John Wayne," the soldier grinned yellow-stained teeth.

The woman stopped sobbing sniffling back her tears as Kosoko pet her face. "Good. Good my pretty lady," Kosoko said, rising.

Nixon's hope faded as the goateed officer paced in front of him stopping. Looking Nixon in the eyes, he stared with no remorse. Kosoko ruled the roost. The leader of the pack. Nixon bowed his eyes. His pathetic fight lost. *What could he possibly do?*

Kosoko continued to pace. His right cheekbone was sunken in as if it had been broken and never properly fixed. He eyed them all. Kosoko sniffed out the poor in spirit; those who would give him what he wanted.

"There is nothing to fear. I assure you that you are safe for the time being. Please cooperate with myself and my men, and we will have you out of here in no time at all."

Wait a second. Where do I know that name from? Nixon had heard it before. It had come up during some stuffy briefing he had probably nodded off in. *Think. Think. It was during a country briefing. Yes, a country briefing on rebel groups. The caved in side of his face, that was very distinctive. Jacobin. Kosoko. Kosoko, Jacobin. Hmmmm.*

It struck him like a bolt of lightning. Jacobin Kosoko was the military chief of the Free Congolese Brigade, a rebel group based in eastern areas of the DRC. That was it. The Free Congolese Brigade had been added to the State Department's list of Foreign Terrorist Organizations in November 2012 for beheading forty captured DRC soldiers. Kosoko had denied accusations that the Free Congolese Brigade had conducted such heinous crimes, until a video popped up on online showing him hacking off the head of a soldier with three mighty swings. *Three powerful machete swings. Probably with the same damn machete that hung menacingly on his back.*

We're fucked. I tried to stop him. I'm fucked. This was one mean hombre. His faction had broken away from the other political leader, Jean David Kapeni, which had led to tremendous suffering and bloodshed among the local population of the North Kivu province. *He was a long way from there. Kinshasa must be over fifteen hundred miles from North Kivu.*

"But if you do actually resist." He paused as if to mock Nixon in his effort. "Like your Sergeant Snow has, I have no problem feeding you to those who hold no breath outside. Please stand."

"Stand up! Stand up!" shouted a guard, gesturing wildly.

People cried out as the soldiers lashed out with the wooden stocks of their assault rifles.

Nixon helped Joseph up with an elbow. They faced the panoramic window. *Was this it? Was the plan just to capture them and then shoot them in the back? The diplomats of the world's greatest superpower - helpless, and with no aid or succor from their government - were to be executed for the whole world to see.* He had never thought it would be like this. He also never thought he would have to shoot his partner in the head because he was eating their interpreter. Alas, he was not in control of his own fate.

Every second ticked by like an hour. People sobbed in their pathetic line, faces red with pitiful dismay. Nixon would leave them to their last moments, not judging how they spent their last seconds on earth. Nixon steadied his breathing, saying a quick prayer in case the big man upstairs was listening. He tensely awaited the hot rounds from an AK-47 to rip through his back and explode out his front, like mini mushroom clouds of pink mist. Any moment now he would be riddled with bullets executed in a cowardly fashion. Thirty seconds agonizingly ticked by. The air stuck in his chest as if his last breath hid from the outside world. It was as if his body were greedily hoarding the air waiting for the bullets to present the escape route. Cries filled the room. *What were they waiting for?*

Nixon saw them below. A group of Congolese soldiers led a man in Marine Corps Combat Utility Uniform toward the courtyard. He could make out the gray hair and the chevrons on his sleeves. The man marched erect toward the fence with his chin upward unafraid. It was Sergeant Snow; no one else at the embassy was like him. He was alive, and had been captured.

Snow's hands were tied, preventing any sort of aggressive action. "Ah yes. There is your hero, Sergeant Snow," Colonel Kosoko said in his bass voice. "He was a difficult man to capture, but his detainment was inevitable."

The group stopped near the fence. One of the soldiers turned around looking up at Kosoko for approval. *Come on Snow do something.* Kosoko nodded his head giving his men the signal.

"Watch carefully my friends," Kosoko commanded.

Snow wouldn't go down without a fight. Not the old war machine himself. As the soldiers pushed him close to the fence his posture changed dramatically. He dropped his weight low and drove his shoulder up into a rebel soldier, knocking him backward into a truck. The embassy staffers cried out as the battle unfolded. Snow front-kicked the other guard, sending him flying onto the lawn. *Atta' boy, give them hell.*

Snow turned to the fence, scanning for an escape route, but the only reprieve offered were infected hands that reached for him. Their faces pressed through the bars, mouths clamping together like an ocean of land piranhas. He spun away and made a run for the heavy troop transport truck. Two more soldiers emerged on the scene swinging their rifles. Snow juked back and forth bringing the heel of his boot into one of their knees sending the soldier screaming to the ground. *Yes, the war machine strikes again.* Nixon couldn't hide his excitement, standing up on his tip toes to get a better view of the fight.

The remaining militiaman tried to crosscheck Snow in the face with his rifle, but Snow sidestepped the man's attack, crashing the top of his forehead into the soldier's jaw, knocking him out.

Nixon silently cheered him on through his duct-taped mouth. *He had to make it. Someone had to make it. If anybody could get out of this situation it was him. He was a Devil Dog to the core.*

The first soldier recovered, scrambling upright, and Nixon prayed that he would trip or fall or anything. *Please, if there is a God.* His prayer was cut short as the rebel brought the butt of his rifle down in the middle of Snow's shoulder blades, sending him crashing to the ground before he could open the door to the vehicle with his teeth. The grizzled warrior's frame slumped, stunned by the blow. Another soldier grabbed his other arm, and they dragged him over to the fence.

Snow moved slowly as if his feet wouldn't obey his mind, and struggled clumsily against his captors, but he gained no leverage.

He screamed when they forced him into the waiting hands of the infected, and Nixon knew he would never forget it. The piercing wail of a man who was ripped to shreds in mere moments.

Nixon felt like he owed it to the man to watch his last acts here on earth. Most things go out the window when you stare death in the face. A fearless warrior can defeat a hundred enemies and only lose to one, and that will be the one battle no one forgets.

Fingers scratched at him and hands ripped away at his combat uniform. Mouths clamped down on his exposed flesh. Skin from muscle, muscle from bone, bone from ligament and organs from body. The people on the other side literally pulled him through the fence piece by piece. The staffers turned away and Nixon bowed his head as Snow finally disappeared.

The man had fought to the bitter end. Somebody threw up through the gag in his or her mouth and the room began to stink of stomach bile. People sat back down, defeated. There was no reason to look outside any more. The only things that had come from outside were death and more death, and the diplomats were done with hope.

A sense of helplessness washed over the room. A group of people could only take so much. The helicopter crash, the assault, being held hostage, the death of their greatest warrior; each blow knocked the wind from their sails like a sucker punch to the stomach. He felt it too. The weariness of the past few days had been too much.

After thirty seconds, Colonel Kosoko spoke softly and somberly. "I need to speak to one of you who is a doctor."

The blood visibly drained from Joseph's face.

"I know there must be at least one doctor here." Joseph looked terrified, but nodded and stood. *At least Joseph isn't just lying there in fear as the terrorist executes more hostages.*

The commander removed Joseph's gag. "You must be the man I am looking for," Kosoko said, wrapping an arm around Joseph's shoulders. Joseph gave Nixon a backward glance and nodded timidly.

"Yes," he mumbled.

"Very good. No reason to be so down Joseph. You have done a very good thing. You saved everyone from some very unpleasant circumstances."

KOSOKO
US Embassy Kinshasa, DRC

Colonel Jacobin Kosoko pushed the fear-stricken doctor ahead of him into the embassy kitchen. *Why were doctors always so frail? Maybe it had something to do with their immense intelligence. Or perhaps they neglected their bodies as they were so consumed with the knowledge of others.*

A couple of his Free Congolese Brigade guardsmen, each wearing a different colored beret, saluted as he walked by. He guessed the protocol gave them something to hold on to; some semblance of order. At this point, it was about survival, but his survival meant paying lip service to the hierarchy of order he had established. He gave them a quick salute on his way past.

Kosoko had the back kitchen turned into a makeshift field hospital, where a single patient lay. The sight of the patient made fire boil in Kosoko's veins. He pushed the doctor toward the patient.

"Help him."

He pointed at his son, who was a lankier version of himself. Kosoko wanted to shout with rage seeing him lying there strapped to the stainless steel kitchen table; tied down like a dog. His people were not dogs. They were not meant to be bound, muzzled and caged. They were meant to be free and wild. They were the princes of this world.

Kosoko's son Ajani, strained against thick leather belts turned restraints, his feet, hands, head and body pushing against them. Bloody bandages hung limply around his arm and neck. *He deserved better; he deserved life. The American doctor would help him. The Americans had powerful medicines.*

"Remove his gag," Kosoko commanded.

His soldiers gave him a fearful look, contemplating whether his wrath was worth getting close to his sick son.

"Do I not speak plainly? Remove his gag." Kosoko gestured, pointing at his son.

Timid feet shuffled. They had been fighting almost non-stop for days against the demons in human flesh outside. They had seen a number of their brothers torn to pieces. His men were not stupid. They knew a bite from one of the creatures would be their doom.

"Remove his gag or I will remove your hands." His machete scraped free from its sheath. Kosoko could almost hear it cry for insolent blood.

The men hesitantly set about loosening Ajani's gag. One of his men's hands shook, spinelessly trying to loosen the gag without getting close. Ajani pulled hard on his restraint, taking a chunk out of the coward's hand. Blood streamed out of the wound. The soldier fled backwards eying his hand as if it had betrayed him.

Kosoko flexed his hand gripping his machete handle. *Idiot.*

"No, please Colonel. I'll be fin-."

Kosoko cut off his insulting remark by swinging his machete deep into the man's neck. The soldier's eyes widened in shock as his blood spurted forth, free from the confines of his body. Kosoko swung again harder, anger driving him, releasing the soldier's head from his torso.

Weaklings couldn't get anything right. He bent down wiping the blade on the soldier's uniform. *They would all be dead by now if he hadn't led them out.*

Enough of them had already been killed.

He dismissed the other militiaman who was eager to find a task to take him out of sight.

The doctor stood there jaw gaping. "You understand the necessity of such action, do you not?" he said, standing upright sheathing his blade. The doctor nodded dumbly. He swept a hand over Ajani's cool graying forehead not fearing a bite from his son.

"Many of my men have had to be executed in such fashion to contain the spread of the curse."

But, the order doesn't apply to my son. The American doctor would fix Ajani. The Americans had the money, and the money bought the medicine. Americans had medicines to fix every ailment imaginable. They could even cure AIDS.

Kosoko wiped some of the fresh blood off of Ajani's uniform. He still wore his green and black fatigues encrusted in dried flaking blood from when he was infected. No one had been able to change his clothes since then, when the monsters had overrun Kosoko's base.

"Two of our own men did this. They sank their teeth into his forearm and neck, like demons. When they would not release him, I shot them both in the head like rabid dogs. Spineless bastards."

The doctor nodded still standing back from the table.

Ajani had stood there shaking, bleeding profusely. A confused look of betrayal upon his face, as if to say, 'Father, why are you letting them do this to me?' The feral men tried to take him down to the ground with his flesh in their teeth their necks straining for leverage. Their white eyes almost glowed in the dark.

A mournful wail filled the room as if Ajani were trying to speak. Kosoko pet his son's head causing Ajani's milk colored eyes to stare feverishly up at him.

"When was he bitten?"

"Three days ago. My people think it is a curse. My men call them 'dongola misos,' a native Lingala term. Do you know this?"

The doctor looked up from examining his son's chest. "I speak French, but I have an interpreter in the field to translate Lingala."

Kosoko nodded. The doctor was learned in things other than the human body.

"What is a dongola miso?"

"You do not have these in America?" Kosoko was curious of the American culture.

"No, we don't."

"The dongola miso is a monster with scary eyes; at least, that is how the legend goes. My mother would tell me when I was a child that if I didn't go to bed on time they would take me in the night. If she had used these monsters, I would have," he said with a sad grin. *I never imagined them like this as a child.*

The doctor frowned at the story, or perhaps it was at his son.

"How quickly did he succumb to his illness?"

"Within an hour."

The doctor looked like he had choked on something.

"Why do you grimace?" he said confused by this man.

The doctor ran a hand through his long hair.

"I do not understand. You have seen the affliction that plagues my son before?"

"Yes, near the Congo River, but they turned over a period of days not hours." The doctor moved around the table.

"And they acted fearless. Attacking with no regard for their own safety? They were relentless in their assault?" the doctor asked.

Kosoko met the doctor's eyes. "Yes, they did."

Ajani clicked his teeth together fresh blood still on his lips. *Even the bravest man showed some hesitation when staring down the barrel of a gun.*

The doctor gave him a fearful look. He feared the condition that tormented his son. Kosoko did not fear anything, but he feared this. He had seen it, and it corrupted everything it touched. He had lost over half of his command on the thousand-mile journey to Kinshasa.

"So you can fix him then?"

The shaggy haired man looked up through his glasses, hesitating.

"Do you have a son of your own, doctor?" Kosoko asked.

"My name is Dr. Joseph Jackowski. And no I do not have any children." Joseph's eyes cast downward. *My doctor friend is ashamed by his lack of family.*

"Ah, you see. You wouldn't understand unless you had a son of your own. You would understand why I would do anything to help him. Why I would kill anyone to save him. Even you my good doctor. I had others, but he was my only true son. If you value your life, you will help him."

Kosoko watched Joseph, as he checked Ajani's vitals. It was clear that his son was still alive. *Anyone could see that, with or without medical training.* The doctor placed his forefingers on Ajani's wrist and then, shaking his head, he moved

End Time

his fingers to the side of Ajani's neck.

Joseph turned to give Kosoko a sidelong glance with intelligent and frightful eyes, removing his glasses and rubbing his brow.

"There is no way around it. This man is clinically dead."

Kosoko motioned towards Ajani. "That is not true. He walks, he makes noise, and he eats. You said yourself this is a virus. Cure him, or I will feed you to the dongola misos."

Kosoko wiped Ajani's forehead with a wet cloth. Ajani's eyes blinked rapidly and his mouth snapped open and closed. His skin grayed, as if the man already stepped in the grave. *No.*

His beloved son. Kosoko had given everything to Ajani; his only true legacy. One day he too would run the Brigade, acquiring more wealth and power; perhaps even his own country. His son's eyes flickered wildly as Kosoko's hand moved closer.

"He has no heartbeat. He is not breathing. Unfortunately, I know of no cure. Many things could cause such a response. The body can continue to fire neurons through the nervous system after death. I can't explain this disease, but I may be able to figure out how it works given enough time," Joseph told him.

"Figure it out over time? I want you to fix him *now*," Kosoko growled, throwing the cloth. He didn't look at Joseph as he spoke.

"If you cannot help him, then I have no use for you." He snapped his fingers, and his guardsmen grabbed the doctor by the arms.

"Wait, please."

Kosoko signaled for them to take him away.

"Wait, wait," he shouted as they dragged him out of the room.

"Bring his head back without his body. It will provide me with more value than the two pieces together."

Kosoko would trade the American hostages for the medicine, and if they didn't want to trade, he would kill the hostages and wait for his next opportunity.

The doctor stuttered. "If. If you give me some time, I, I can come up with something. I'll start by cleaning his wounds. Yes. That should help. Bring me some bandages."

Kosoko grabbed the doctor by the throat, making the weak man's eyes widen. "You do that, you pathetic little man. Fix him, if you value your life. I know I will make it through this, but it's you I'm not so sure about." He smiled at the shocked doctor. If Kosoko was anything, he was a survivor.

KINNICK
Arlington, VA

The buzzing of his work phone on the nightstand, awoke the Undersecretary of Political Military Affairs, Michael Kinnick. The clock next to his bed read 4:39 a.m.

Kinnick rubbed the sleep from his eyes as the concerned officer at the other end of the line explained the situation. He pressed the end button, sighing heavily. Things had gone from bad to worse.

"What is it, honey?" His wife rolled over in the bed concern for her husband shadowing her voice.

"Nothing, honey. I have to run into work now. It's going to be another long day. I'll give you a ring when I'm on my way home."

She turned over in a docile manner, her dark curls delicately falling on the pillow. "Be careful," she mumbled drifting back into sleep.

Kinnick had been in emergency meetings throughout the previous day. *The situation was bad. Very bad.*

Undersecretary Kinnick threw his phone into a lockbox outside the secure SCIF. He scanned his encrypted badge, as he had done a hundred times before, and entered the conference room.

Nervous eyes watched him as he tossed his jacket onto the back of his chair. His team sat around a long, oval-shaped table.

Everyone avoided his eye contact. Papers shuffled. Somebody coughed nervously. Their body language told him they were skittish, uncomfortable at best.

Kinnick had very little patience for waiting. Ignoring what he considered to be their piss-poor body language, he broke the ice.

"What have you got for me?" He leafed through an intelligence file. He licked his fingers and thumbed through the documents. When no one responded, he looked around the room at his staff of civil servants, military personnel and his personal aide, Jackie. He tried to avoid staring right at her. He received blank stares from the others, while a few gazed intently at the papers in front of them, as if they were some sort of protective shield against their responsibility to assist him.

Yesterday, it was just protests in the streets. *People could always find something to protest against – a movie, a picture in a newspaper. Shit, I could protest about the coffee they served in the cafeteria, not that anyone would listen. It wasn't enough of an injustice to televise, but maybe if I framed it correctly - the possibilities were endless.* He had to constantly remind himself to be cognizant of other people's cultural sensitivities, especially when Americans were in harm's way. The end goal was the safe return of American diplomats from abroad.

He took a deep breath. "Okay, let's start small. Who's responsible for the attack?"

A young intern with gelled hair spoke up from the back, surprising Kinnick. He tried to remember his name; *Hunter or something.*

"The country has been experiencing significant unrest. There are five large unrelated rebel groups, along with a dozen or so insignificant parties. Our best guess is it's one of them."

One of five. Great.

"Okay, has the Congolese government sent us anything from their side?"

Sometimes he had to spoon-feed them until they could get the ball rolling on their own.

Hillary, a civil servant in her thirties showing a bit too much cleavage, said: "I've been trying to contact various government entities there since this came down the pike. I haven't gotten any straight answers. One said it's Muslim rioters in the streets; another said rebels have taken the capital. Still another said a military coup. They stopped answering the phone about four hours ago."

Muslim rioters in the streets? Military coup? Rebels in the capital? All spelled potential disaster. "Hillary, I'm going to need you to confirm the lead that there are Muslim rioters in the streets, *or* that this is in some way connected to al-Qaeda, seeing as ninety-six percent of the DRC's population is Christian."

She gave him a shy nod, which Kinnick ignored. Either way, they had already taken the initiative to evacuate the staff and military units posted at the embassy. Christian or Muslim, if his colleagues were in danger he wanted them out of there.

He nodded at Jackie for another cup of terrible coffee, who hopped to it immediately. She looked a bit bookish, but performed her job adequately.

Kinnick had been in the Air Force for twenty-one years before he crossed over from Department of Defense to Department of State. He had achieved the rank of Colonel, so he was no novice to conflicts in failing states. He had served in Somalia in the nineties before the shit hit the fan in Mogadishu or, as the soldiers had named it, 'the Mog.'

He had switched over to the State Department in 2003, after his country had become embroiled in the affairs of two other conflicts. The differences between the cultures of State and Defense were dynamic, but he had always felt a little more diplomatic than his peers at Defense. It comforted him to know he could open a can of whoop ass on anyone of his staff. He continued to eyeball some of the smartest people he knew. They had the information for him, but he would have to pry it from them piece by piece.

"What do we know for sure, here? Terrorists have overrun our embassy, and there are an unknown number of American hostages. Do they have the Ambassador?"

Kinnick turned toward his most senior analyst expecting to be impressed. "We don't know, sir," Aaron replied.

A lot of good that Ivy League education is doing us now. "Has there been any chatter online from anybody claiming the attack?"

His senior analyst answered again. "No traffic from the usual suspects."

At least he knows what we don't know, which is a hell of a lot. Kinnick massaged his temples. *Its going to be another long day.*

After three hours of bouncing around 'what if' scenarios, a light appeared in the darkness.

"Sir?" A civil servant, he thought her name was Tammy, leaned in and handed him a sheet of paper containing a transcript. Her perfume smelled divine as it tickled his nostrils.

She summarized it for him: "This guy called on the regular line from the embassy. He referred to himself as Colonel Kosoko. At first we thought it was a prank call, but upon further review we think he is credible and part of the rebel group Free Congolese Brigade. It's a militia from the North Kivu province in the DRC."

End Time

What the Hell are they doing so far West?

Tammy had his full attention. She continued, "So get this… he kept talking about some sort of medicine. We have no idea what he's talking about, but he also said he was willing to trade hostages for it."

Kinnick immediately began to exploit the information in his head. He turned to Michelle, one of his intelligence analysts. "I want a full report on these guys: leadership profile, numbers, where they sleep, what they eat and where they shit. And I need it yesterday," Kinnick said firmly.

Michelle nodded, scrambling from her chair to send out feelers to the other intelligence agencies.

An hour later, Jackie set another piping hot cup of coffee in front of Kinnick. He was getting a little jittery from the caffeine, and his head had started to throb. *Maybe some food would help.* He snagged a doughnut from the middle of the table. There were only glazed ones left; none of his favorite powdered sugar variety. *I guess it would do for now.*

He still knew too little about this Jacobin Kosoko and his Free Congolese Brigade. Apparently, Kosoko was the military chief of a rebel group that had broken away from the government. Nobody knew exactly how many men he had under him, or how large a force held the embassy. He would kill for a subject matter expert, but the one person in his department who would know was out sick.

"Somebody get Peter on the phone. Tell him he can't be sick today."

"Michelle, keep reaching out to the intelligence community. Somebody has to know something about this guy. You're doing a great job. Keep it up."

She flashed him a pretty, dimpled smile.

Kinnick sipped his coffee as he reviewed the militia profile. The coffee tasted like ground dirt. The rebels exploited the mineral reserves controlling the region and had been blamed for countless human rights violations. Child soldiers. Systematic rape. Beheadings. He kept skimming the intel report. No obvious al-Qaeda affiliation lurked beneath the surface. The group seemed to be tied to the Hutu-Tutsi conflict, which had affected the DRC as well as neighboring Rwanda and Burundi. Millions of deaths had taken place just over the country's borders.

It appeared that these guys were willing to kill at the drop of a hat. He said a short prayer for the embassy staff.

Kinnick became immersed in his paperwork, and before long he was nodding off.

Suddenly Jackie grabbed his arm, scaring the hell out of him. "Jesus, Jackie," he said, giving her a dirty look. "This better be good."

"The Secretary is on the line. He says it's urgent."

"Good enough."

God, what now? He hurried over and picked up a secure phone in the corner. Jackie followed him still talking.

"No one has been able to get ahold of Peter. No one is answering the phone at his house."

Kinnick covered the mouthpiece. "Keep trying."

"This is Kinnick," he said softly.

"Hello, Undersecretary Kinnick. This is the Secretary." Kinnick wanted to yell at him to get to the point. The man always referred to himself as 'the Secretary' first. *What is the point in having a personal assistant answer the phone for you if people like him were determined to make the same announcement all over again?*

Kinnick humored the man. "It's good to hear from you, sir."

"You know why I'm calling. We're in a real tough spot. We have limited military resources in the region. The DRC hasn't been a major priority in this administration or any of the previous ones. In fact, nobody's really cared much about it since the Belgians left in the fifties. Our rapid deployment forces that cover this area are tied up in other deployments."

"I see, sir." *Someone somewhere had to be available to pull out the embassy staff. This guy can't possibly be telling me that there was no one available to extract his people. I know we have teams in Italy and multiple Marine units in the Horn of Africa. They could drop them in. Shit, it wouldn't take long to get a ship to the coast of the DRC. A week, max. But they didn't have a week.*

"We want this to go away quietly. No Benghazi, no publicity."

"What are you saying?" Kinnick murmured. He didn't like where this was going.

"Apparently, there's some sort of outbreak, a flu or disease or something, and we have a team of doctors being held hostage as part of the embassy staff. This is coming down from the top."

The top top, thought Kinnick. *The only higher rung on this ladder is the President himself.*

"We're going to negotiate with this 'rebel' group and give them what they want. So make the calls and get the operation underway. We've coordinated with the Counterterrorism Division, and they've already deployed a team of CT agents to escort the embassy staff back to the U.S. A couple of CIA officers are headed to the

DRC as well. The problem we have, is that neither of these groups knows about the trade. I suggest you contact them and get them to work out the details. I know we are asking a lot of everyone, but people's lives are at stake. We just don't have the military assets in the region to assist, so we're going to play ball with what we've got. Do you understand?"

Kinnick rubbed his brow. "Yes, I do. We'll move right away."

He hung up the phone and rejoined his staff at the table. *They were officially up shit creek. How am I supposed to make this trade happen when we don't have anything to trade? This is a huge risk, but we're going to have to throw the dice. I have no choice.*

He waved, gaining their attention, hand on hip. "All right, everybody. This guy Jacobin Kosoko wants to make a deal, and the administration wants to move forward with it." His team eyed each other nervously. "I know. I wasn't expecting this either."

The previous administration probably would have gone in with guns blazing. This administration had shown some constraint. Kinnick's job wasn't to question the decision; it was to make sure it happened. They could not afford another Benghazi. It would destroy the administration and make the American people lose faith in their government, more so than they already had.

He knew that if this went bad, it would be one of the worst public relations nightmares in American history. And he knew who would be sitting in the hot seat during that congressional hearing.

"I want to be in touch with this Kosoko fellow, *now*. Yes, call him back. We need to see what we can offer him. Jackie, get me in touch with the Director of the

Central Intelligence Agency and the Director of the Counterterrorism Division. We need to contact their people and get them onboard. Our people are coming home."

KOSOKO
US Embassy Kinshasa, DRC

Kosoko lounged in the Ambassador's office inspecting the man's crystal liquor decanter. Pouring himself a glass of the brown oaky liquid, he stuck a thumb in the spirit and licked it. *Not bad, Ambassador. Not bad.* His situation was favorable at the moment. The American compound was secure. His men had rounded up all the American diplomats, the best hostages in the world, and his soldiers had swept up the rest of the Marine guards.

One of those bastards had fragged a dozen of his men in a stairwell, leaving pieces of the maimed and slain everywhere. It was a mess. Kosoko had wanted him taken alive to be made an example out of, but his men had been a bit overzealous riddling his body with bullets.

He threw his booted feet up onto the Ambassador's desk and lit up a Cuban cigar. *Stupid Americans. If they only knew what they were missing, insisting on an embargo with Cuba. The Cubans truly made the best cigars. The Nicaraguans made good cigars, but nothing beat a Cuban.*

The rich tobacco smoke filled his mouth, and he exhaled a light gray plume. Leaning back in the Ambassador's luxurious maroon chair, he rubbed the soft leather with the palm of his hand. He closed his eyes.

The slums of Kinshasa were a distant memory. A blur of uncertainty in his past. Memories that only brought him pain, but reminders of how far he had come. Kosoko had never known his father. According to his mother, he had died soon after Kosoko's birth. To this day, Kosoko never knew the truth, but it was safe to say that if his father had been alive all this time, he was dead now.

Most of his childhood, he struggled to get enough food in his belly. At the age of twelve and despite his meager efforts to save her, his mother became ill and died. He had no one to turn to. Begging by day, he turned to thievery by night. It was easy to be overlooked in a city with seven million inhabitants where the average income was less than $1.25 per day.

He ran with a pack of thugs as he grew older: other orphans, castaways and abused youth. Being the leader required brutal efficiency, and it grew more natural over time. He constantly had to be the meanest, and the most willing to gamble it all in a heartbeat.

When he turned eighteen, he got caught up in a police shakedown at a local brothel and mouthed off to the wrong officer, who had beaten him within an inch of his life. The police were no more than an armed gang with uniforms; the only difference was they had better weapons. The right side of his face had been broken and healed poorly, leaving him disfigured. He was lucky to be alive. Before he blacked out, he remembered only one thing, the laughing policeman pissing on his battered face, too injured to move out of the way.

Kosoko opened his eyes, running a hand along his scarred face. He gazed around the Ambassador's rich brown mahogany desk, admiring the luxury of the finished wood. A picture of the Ambassador with his family drew his eye, and he smiled as he puffed on his cigar. It was the typical American family. He had seen these families in movies. One son, one daughter and a beautiful wife, sitting on a beach somewhere dressed in white. *Cute daughter*.

He smiled inwardly as he remembered the day when he finally caught up with the officer who had wronged him. The man who brought shame upon him.

It had been a moonless night, and bugs buzzed around the single floodlight outside the officer's home. Kosoko had joined the military and risen to the rank of Colonel. A bribe in the right place could work wonders for a career.

Kosoko and a squad of soldiers surrounded the police officer's front door, and Kosoko kicked the door in himself. The officer pissed himself when Kosoko burst into the room with a squad of troopers at his back. To his superiors it was as an 'antiterrorism' operation.

Kosoko knocked the man's revolver out of his grasp. They quickly corralled the man's screaming family in the one-room apartment. There was nowhere to hide; nowhere to flee to. The officer huddled his arms around his wife and daughter, holding one another sobbing.

"Please, please let my family go. There's money under the floorboard," the police officer said, desperately gesturing toward the corner of the room.

"Shhh." Kosoko pressed a finger to his lips. He crouched down in front of the terrified family, addressing the father.

"Do you remember me?" His lips curved upward in a cruel smile.

Twenty years had taken a toll on the older officer turning his hair almost white.

The aged officer stared up at him through his tears. "I, I, I don't know. Please…"

"Think harder." Kosoko waved his sergeant forward holding a baseball bat.

"I don't know. Please let us go."

"I always loved American baseball." Kosoko gave the bat a test swing.

The man held his wife and daughter close as they wept.

Kosoko knelt down in front of the officer. "Look closely, old man. I used to live in the East End, and you gave me this as a present." Using the bat he touched his crushed face. He stood to his feet, slowly wagging his bat back and forth.

"Baseball is such a beautiful game. So much strategy, and yet an entire game can change with just one swing of the bat."

He swung the bat downward onto the man's knee, exploding his left kneecap with a loud pop. The man screamed, grabbing his destroyed joint.

"Do *you* remember *me*?" Kosoko yelled, using the bat to lift the groveling man's face.

The man sobbed openly. "Yes, yes. The Pink Lounge. I'm so sorry. Please. Let my family go," he cried, holding his ruined knee.

Kosoko moved to the other side of the police officer. He held his bat close, reading the inscription. "A Clarksville Comet. Everyone must have one of these in America. I've never been to this Clarksville, but I imagine it's an amazing place."

The man nodded furiously in agreement. "Yes, of course. Of course it is."

Kosoko smiled. "I'm glad you agree, but I don't think it's going to help, YOU," Kosoko shouted as he brought the bat down onto the man's other knee.

The room filled with a sickening crunch as the polished wood impacted his knee, completely disabling him.

"Now." Kosoko paced forward and backward in front of the man. "You can beg for your life, but will you really want to live after this?"

Kosoko reached down grabbing the officer's wife by her thin wrist. The broken man instantly reached out, begging for her return. Kosoko looked her up and down, smelling her fear; the sweat glistening all over her body.

"She is nice, huh?" His men laughed in the background.

"You want some fun boys?"

His men hooted and hollered from behind. *Entertained men were loyal men.*

"Take her." He shoved her into the eager arms of his sergeant, who handed her back to the men. Crouching down next to the officer, he smiled as he watched his men jockeying for position. They laughed and puffed on cigars as they took turns violating her like a piece of trash. They amused Kosoko.

"She didn't cry out much, did she? Suppose it doesn't matter now does it." The officer sobbed in response.

Once the last man finished, Kosoko drew out his machete and dragged it across her throat. They left her bleeding out in the corner, gasping for air as her lungs filled with blood.

Kosoko watched the officer's face as he held his daughter for the last time. *He must know this is coming.* The old man cried and whispered, "It will be okay. It will be okay."

Kosoko bent down, grabbing the man's daughter by the hair. He ripped the girl from her father's arms, shrieking. Kosoko held her in front of him, dangling her like a rag doll.

"Please. I'll do anything. Please don't harm her. Take me. Kill me." The officer pleaded with his eyes for mercy. "I have money," he added, mumbling the words.

"Do you think I came here for your pathetic stash? Your money means nothing to me." He craved the sweet taste of revenge. He didn't care about this girl;

he cared about the power she held over her father. She was the love of his life. His only living legacy. His child.

Kosoko pinned the girl down with one hand tearing her clothes off. She lay quiet, while the officer begged for him to spare her; to be allowed to die in her place.

"No, no, please stop."

A short time later, Kosoko finished and zipped up his pants. "Now that I have ruined everything you love, you may die."

He granted her father's request by hacking the man's head off with his machete. Revenge tasted as sweet as honey to Kosoko.

His eyes darted over to the secure phone in the Ambassador's office. It sat plainly on his desk; a thick brick of a phone next to the regular one. The Americans had not reached out to him. All this time had passed and they hadn't called him back. He felt it odd for them to be so unconcerned with their building and their precious people. The world had been conditioned to believe that an American life was valued so much higher than everyone else's.

How many people have I seen die during my lifetime? Fifty? A hundred? A thousand? How many people had died in civil war, tribal conflicts and cleansing since Congo's independence? Four million, five million, maybe more. How many news stations covered a murder in my city? None.

That would never happen in America, where every individual was worth so much. Yet he had captured their embassy and no one seemed to care. He had expected more from the 'Land of Plenty.' The Americans would have to be more careful or they would end up like the DRC: corrupt, poor and weak; at least for the majority of the Congolese.

Kosoko chuckled out loud. Americans loved their liberty and their freedom too much for that. It had been totally different when Kosoko and his men defected from the military. *But am I not the same as the Americans? I wanted the freedom and liberty to do as I pleased. In reality, the American dream was about money.* Something Kosoko understood all too well.

Kosoko and his men hadn't been paid for more than a year when they rebelled against the government. He had already set himself up as a criminal kingpin in the province by dominating the diamond exports in the region. This way he didn't have to pay tribute to the corrupt government for his extra-curricular activities. He simply kept everything he made for himself. *That is the American way, right? Create more revenue by cutting out the middleman.*

Kosoko easily convinced his men they would be better off running their own little fiefdom. They turned their backs on the government at the drop of hat. They called themselves the Free Congolese Brigade. They were free men, and they had done well. Now he sat inside the American embassy. He was safe for the time being, but at this point, only one thing scared him, and it - or they - were threatening to fill the courtyard below.

The secure phone rang. Kosoko's mouth slowly curved upward. *So they the Americans have something to say. Choose your words wisely my friends.*

His hand fell hovering above the receiver. He let it ring a few times before he picked up the phone.

"This is Colonel Kosoko."

STEELE
Somewhere over the Atlantic

The flight had been uneventful. A spattering of heads decorated the economy class cabin, most laying unmoving on their headrests asleep. Since the team moved into position for their special protection detail, they were technically off the clock. A boring prospect filled with magazines, tablets and music, but even being off the clock Steele could never really fully relax.

Steele plowed through his *Muscle & Fitness* magazine taking notes on how to perfect his deadlift, and moved on to *The Economist*. Often CT agents worked twenty-four hour days, especially when they deployed on international missions. He used his time to catch up on his reading. Finding a chill song, he opened his magazine.

He perused several articles as he listened. Steele grew bored reading an article about how the U.S. was starting to engage the Afghan Taliban in talks. He turned the page, and browsed an article about how Detroit was bankrupt and unable to pay its city employees. It was so bad the city had stopped turning on street lamps. The Motor City was in rough shape.

Steele had grown up in Bloomfield Hills, a northern Detroit suburb. The suburbs around Detroit were very nice, and as long as the auto industry had thrived, these affluent areas had done the same. When the auto industry collapsed in 2008 and needed a bailout, many people had moved out of state, leaving the region stripped of good paying jobs.

After he left for college, his parents retreated to their second home on the sand dunes of Lake Michigan in an effort to get away from the sink hole of Detroit. They lived in a beautiful log cabin surrounded by deep woods on one side and the lake on the other. Long beautiful beaches stretched either way as far as the eye could see, every inch covered in clean gold sand. Clear fresh water touched the horizon with blue fingers, contrasting and complementing the beach at the same time. It was like living on a privately owned fresh water ocean.

Five hours in, Steele's eyes were dried out and strained from staring at his screen for so long. He stood up, stretched, squeezed some drops in his eyes and joined Mauser, who stood in the back galley with an attractive flight attendant. The frequent globetrotting made hook-ups easy for both groups. Steele had dated one in the past, and decided that once was enough. He smiled as he watched his friend. *You old dog, you.*

"Can I get you anything, sweetheart?" the red-haired pixie cut flight attendant asked.

"Just some coffee, ma'am. Thank you."

She handed Steele his coffee, which he sipped as he listened to Mauser laying it on thick: "Yeah, I remember my first rescue. It was a lady with her baby stranded at sea. Their sailboat capsized, and we arrived too late to save the father."

Mauser shook his head really playing it up."The winds were whipping the helo somethin' fierce. We just couldn't keep the chopper over the wreck. The pilot screamed that it was too rough to go in, but I couldn't let them die. I just couldn't have lived with myself with their deaths on my conscience. So I launched myself from the helicopter door, dropping feet first into the twenty foot crashing waves."

The flight attendant gazed at him, free hand covering her mouth. *Mauser had this one in the bag.* Steele shook his head and looked out the exit door porthole. The vast dark ocean sprawled out beneath him. At thirty-five thousand feet it was possible to make out tiny ships and, on closer inspection, itty-bitty white caps.

Steele had been returning home with Jarl from an international mission, tracking a Hezbollah cell, when a crazed passenger tried to pry open the emergency exit door. It was just the kind of thing they didn't want to deal with when they were trying to get back home.

"I, I, I...I have to get out of here," the man yelled, standing in his seat. The balding passenger, in a sweat stained business suit with a loosened tie, leapt from his seat and sprinted up to the front galley.

Steele made eye contact with Jarl, who's lip curled upward on his face. Steele almost laughed aloud at his partner's expression, but held it together.

It wasn't humanly possible for the man to open the door mid-flight. The pressurization in the passenger cabin made it an impossible feat. Steele sat calm in his seat observing the man break bad. A man who was about to have a very bad day. The psychotic businessman shoved a flight attendant to the ground and threw all his weight into the aircraft door lever.

It always seemed to Steele that if you wanted to see peoples' IQs drop forty points, the best way was to hand them a boarding pass. Instant lobotomy.

This guy is in for a world of hurt. Unsuccessful at prying open the door, the man once again threw his weight onto the lever, trying to force the door open. *This has gone on long enough.* With a flick of his wrist he unbelted himself and moved with speed to the front galley.

"Don't move," Steele shouted.

The crazed passenger looked right through him with a thousand-yard stare, heaving even harder on the door.

Jarl effectively covered Steele's back while he worked. Contact and cover rules. With his height, Jarl had excellent vision over the cabin, making it easy for Steele to work without interference from other passengers or potential hostiles. Steele almost felt bad for anyone who tried to get past him.

Cornered, the crazed man took a wild swing at Steele. Steele saw it coming from a mile away and deflected the punch with a bent elbow and followed with a quick jab to the nose. The nose pushed inward rewarding Steele with a sharp crack. Smoothly, he transitioned into an arm-bar using the perpetrator's shoulder joint to take him to the ground.

"Ooh, my nose. I have to...get..." the deranged man whimpered.

"It's all right, buddy, just take it easy." Steele swept the perp's arm behind his back, placing a knee on the man's lower back and neck to maintain control. Once Steele had gained control of the man's other hand, he quickly pulled out his cuffs. Click. Click. Steel bracelets on.

Hauling the man to his feet, he checked on the flight attendant.

"Flight Attendant, are you okay?"

The older wrinkled woman smiled faintly. "Yes, thank you." She rubbed her elbow where she had fallen.

"Good. Will you let the Captain know we took care of the issue?"

"Yes. Thank God you were here," she said, picking up the galley phone.

"Anytime, ma'am." Steele pushed the perpetrator in front of him.

To the applause of the other passengers, Steele placed the panic-stricken man into a seat.

"Jarl, would you like to do the honors?"

"Fine. As long as he stops crying."

The man continued to whine in his seat. Jarl wasn't one for open displays of emotion. He leaned over, a frown covering his broad face.

"You be quiet. NOW," he growled. The man had bowed his head in defeat. *Just another day in paradise.*

His mind returning to the present, Steele listened to Mauser finishing his story about his rescue. The story had won over plenty of females to Mauser's cause and Steele was pretty sure he could recite it in time word for word.

"The ocean roared around us as waves crashed down. The baby screamed bloody murder, but I kept us afloat. Baby in one arm and mother in the other, I kicked and drove all the way to the chopper basket. They both survived. I received the Coast Guard Cross, and became the child's godfather at his christening. Little Lucy calls me Uncle Ben, now. It's the least I could do for the family." He finished by breathing on his nails and brushing them off on his shirt.

Her name tag read Crystal. Pinned above her name tag was a flight attendant union pin. "You just take this and call me when we get back. I'd love to grab a drink with you and hear more about your rescues," she said, a mischievous smile spreading across her red lips.

"You got it, babe," Mauser said, tucking the number into his jeans as if he were going to lose the small piece of paper.

"I've got to hand out this water, but I'll talk to you later," she said, moseying down the aisle hips swaying.

"You're disgusting," Steele said, shaking his head.

"She could be the one."

"Yeah, one of the many."

"Come on man, you know they're the bane of my existence."

Choppy air rocked the cabin up and down. "Another five hours to go," Steele lamented.

"I'd better catch some sleep then." Mauser eyed his seat from the galley.

"Yeah, yeah. I'll take first watch." Steele settled into his seat wishing it didn't feel like his back was supported by a piece of cardboard.

An hour later, Steele sat playing a turn-based strategy game on his iPad. He just couldn't conquer all of North America. *Damn green armies. They are like a never-ending horde.* He had a weird feeling that someone watched him. Steele perused the little mounds of heads sprinkled throughout coach. Nobody eyed him with malice.

Something in the back of his skull made him uneasy as if someone were sneaking up on him. Out of the far reaches of his peripheral vision he could see a man standing almost behind him.

It startled him at first, and the man reached out to grab him. Steele spun and immediately recognized the graying man as Wheeler.

His presence was still concerning to Steele. Only an issue of serious magnitude would bring the TL to the back of economy.

Wheeler motioned him to the back galley, his face grave. "We need to talk. Just got word from the Operations Center that our marching orders have changed."

End Time

They couldn't have changed too much. We'll still be sitting on a plane at thirty-six thousand feet for the next few hours.

"What's going on?"

Wheeler leaned in close. "It looks like we're still going to pick up the staffers, but they're being held hostage by some sort of terrorist group."

At the mention of the word "terrorist," Steele looked around at the handful of passengers scattered about economy.

"A terrorist? AQIM? Al-Shabaab? Boko?" He wanted to know what they were up against. Any little bit of intelligence increased their chances of succeeding.

Wheeler frowned slightly. "I don't know. Or more likely, they didn't say. But either way, be ready for anything. Operations also relayed a message to those spooks. Then they started requesting med kits, so there must be wounded."

This could be bad.

Wheeler continued. "There are some doctors in the group that have been designated priority status. The government must want these guys back real bad." He peered over Steele's shoulder.

Steele still absorbed the information. "Why are these doctors so important?"

Wheeler shrugged, sipping his coffee. "Beats me. All I know is that they take the highest priority over everything else out there. No one else matters. When we land back at McCone, there'll be an armed escort for the docs."

"I got it. Make sure the guys with MD after their names arrive safely," Steele said with a mock salute.

Wheeler gestured with his thumb over at Mauser. "Will you let sleeping beauty know that Jarl and myself will be running close security for the trip home?"

Steele smiled. "It's about time he woke up, anyhow." He chucked his empty Styrofoam coffee cup at Mauser's head.

Mauser shot out of his seat, hands in a striking stance.

"Who goes th--?" He looked around sheepishly when he realized no one was there. After a few confused seconds, he zeroed in on the culprit, who sat back down, laughing.

"I know where you live, asshole."

KOSOKO
Kinshasa International Airport, DRC

Twisting the steering wheel, Kosoko swerved around a stranded vehicle, crushing the bodies of the afflicted with his heavy transport vehicle. The bodies thudded off the sturdy steel front as even more shades roamed out of the reach of the truck's lights.

A dongola miso clambered onto the hood, fingers hooked around the top. He was a poor bastard, clothes ragged and worn; the left side of his face was all exposed bone and tendon, making him a dead bastard. Its milky eyes stared knowingly, but somehow unknowingly, straight at him. Clawing the windshield in a futile attempt to reach Kosoko, Kosoko leaned out the window and fired his .45 caliber revolver into the head of a monster. The body limply rolled to the side of the road after the man's brain exploded out the back of his head. Sporadic gunfire came from the back of the flatbed truck.

That was close, I'm going to have to go faster. The truck's speed had dropped too low. He gassed the pedal, edging the speedometer around forty kilometers per hour. Any slower, and sometimes the stronger monsters could cling on.

Kosoko's lips drew tight across his mouth. The Americans had made the deal. All he had to do was make it to the airport in one piece. They were flying in a plane with the special medicine on board for Ajani. Provided they kept their word. *If they back out on the agreement, the hostages have more than the dongola misos to worry about.*

128

As he turned onto Airport Road, dozens of bloodied people clustering at the airport gate spun toward the truck. The Kinshasa Airport gate crumpled as Kosoko floored the truck through bodies and gate alike rocketing onto the airfield. It wasn't made to resist a vehicle; it was merely there to keep people out. Lazy guards normally lounged nearby, but they had either run or died, as the booth sat empty.

Kosoko barreled into the secure part of the airport. Nothing moved here. No people. No planes. No dongola misos, but that would change. Only a single terminal sat unmolested. It was a thick, concrete, faded yellow building. Built by the Belgians in the forties, Kosoko was convinced it hadn't been upgraded since. Floodlights illuminated the sky above the entrance to the terminal, but no one moved outside.

He checked his side mirror. The plagued shadows poured through the gate behind the transport. He didn't have much time before the dongola misos caught up with the trucks. Most of them were slow, walking speed tops, but some seemed to be a bit faster, depending on their injuries. It was far more of a curse than a virus. Dead that were not allowed to rest.

Where are those damn Americans? No one awaited his arrival. He saw no plane with U.S. markings. *What should I expect, them to roll out the red carpet after I kidnapped their people? I almost wish it was a trap. Fighting would be preferable to being hung out to dry.*

He momentarily considered trying to fly one of the abandoned planes to escape. Some lay dark and dormant, forgotten skeletal remains in their hangers. *No, I can't fly these machines.* He slammed on the brakes.

They must have backed out. Those bastards should have come. They would lose a great number of their people today. It would become a day of infamy for them.

End Time

I will be vilified for it, but in reality, it was their failure for not holding up their end of the bargain. One way or another, Americans always pay.

He rested his head on the large black steering wheel. The heavy dud-dud-dud of gunfire banged from the back of his truck into the endless night. *The dongola misos will be here soon.*

Perhaps the Yankees were late, and he could hold up in the terminal. Kosoko wanted to howl with rage. *Too many options and none of them were any good.*

"Come Dikembe."

Kosoko hopped down from the driver's seat marching to the rear. Shadows trudged toward him in a never ending onslaught. He didn't have any time.

"You, come here." An older gentleman with black glasses stared back at him lacking awareness of his fate.

"Get down here, now." Kosoko grabbed him by his shirt ripping him down to the pavement from the flat bed.

"I am a doctor, please," the man pleaded. No one stood up for him or cried out in protest. Compliance was easy when dealing with mere sheep.

Drawing his long barreled revolver, he aimed at the doctor's head. The doctor covered his face with his hands. *This man does not understand the necessity of his sacrifice.*

"What do I need two doctors for anyway?"

Gun smoke drifted from his barrel and the doctor held his leg. *The monsters were drawn to the living.* The dongola misos moaned in reply as if Kosoko had rung a dinner bell.

The doctor pushed onto his wounded leg.

"You shot me. You devil." He grimaced.

"Let's move," Kosoko barked at his men and they saddled back up.

"Don't look so happy, Dikembe. That could have been you. Keep your eyes open for the Americans." Dikembe visibly gulped peering feverishly around the airfield in apparent usefulness. His men and the hostages alike were thankful he hadn't left them for dead.

Kosoko glanced in his side mirror as he drove away from the injured doctor. Dragging himself back toward the vehicles, Kosoko was almost impressed by the doctor's willingness to live on. His struggle, however, was short-lived, as the dongola misos caught him after a few steps. They took him down like a lion would a gazelle with hands that dug into his skin like claws. Tearing into his flesh in a wild manner, they ripped the meat from his bones with greedy hands.

Dikembe grabbed his sleeve frantically. "Colonel, Colonel, over there," he pointed toward a hangar by the air fuel depot.

"We are in luck," Kosoko laughed, pressing the gas pedal flat and the truck hesitated waiting to lurch forward for a moment. Knowing that people must have fallen in the back and not caring, he drove the truck right into the hanger and pulled it alongside the aircraft.

Two white men in their fifties stood near the tail of the aircraft wearing smart blazers. One held a nondescript gray case. *Not very official looking: there are no biohazard symbols or special markings that I would expect on a case that held such powerful medicine.*

Kosoko called out to his remaining followers, pointing at them in turn:

"You, watch our backs. You, make sure the hostages don't get away. And you two, come with me." He jumped down, approaching the men with an urgent confidence.

Only a handful of his men remained. The escape from the embassy had been messy. Negotiation was his only option now, and Kosoko wouldn't take no for an answer.

He glared at the two men. A stand off of wills. The taller of the two men, who must be the CIA agents he had been told to meet, broke the silence first.

"Jacobin, is it? I'm Bill, and I'm here to make a trade with you."

"We have no time for pleasantries old man, even now, they come," Kosoko hissed. The CIA agent didn't appear hard pressed for time.

"Who is coming?" Bill exchanged a glance with his shorter comrade.

"The dongola misos, but it doesn't matter," Kosoko waved him off. "What do you have to trade?" He lifted his chin upward as if he dared them to deny him of what was his.

Bill slapped the case onto a maintenance cart and flipped the latch open. "Here you go. There's an antidote for your son in this case. We just need you to release the hostages before we give it to you."

Kosoko didn't move his eyes from the two men. He weighed them. *The case doesn't look official. How can I trust the word of an American pig?*

"How do I know you speak true?" he asked, not expecting a honest answer. He waved to Dikembe. "Bring me the young doctor, Joseph. Administer the antidote to my son."

Turning back to face the two agents, Kosoko added: "If it doesn't work," he said as he quickly drew his sidearm, pointing it at CIA Bill. He felt like an old west gunslinger getting the jump on them. It was the O.K. Corral and he was the famous Wyatt Earp. "You will die first."

Cold recognition slid over the tall agent's face and he slowly put his hands up. "Now, take it easy Jacobin. The antidote is going to take some time to work. We have assurances from our top medical professionals in America that this will cure him."

Dikembe shoved the doctor forward, cutting his zip ties with a knife. Joseph rubbed his wrists. *Weakling.* His men carried over Ajani, strapped to a stretcher, and laid him on the ground in between the two parties. Joseph knelt near Ajani, rummaged through the medical case, and pulled out a vial and a syringe. He gave a nervous glance back at Kosoko.

"Hurry up, Dr. Joseph. Our time is short."

Joseph nodded in acceptance.

Ajani clapped his teeth together as Joseph neared him. *I will let Ajani feed on the doctor first if the medicine doesn't work, after I deal with the corrupt Americans.*

Joseph slipped the syringe into Ajani's arm, emptying the contents. Ajani squirmed against his restraints. His condition remained unchanged. His son continued to strain against his bondage. The doctor carefully checked Ajani's pulse, shaking his head, and then stood up abashed.

"Ajani?" Kosoko muttered. "Is he better?" The doctor held his gaze for a moment then turned away. Fear.

Kosoko was so immersed in his son's treatment that he didn't hear the approaching monsters. Gunfire rocketed from behind, and Kosoko twisted as a man wearing an orange airport vest sank his teeth into Dikembe's neck. His comrade tried

to push the man away, and as he did the dongola miso brought half his neck with

him. Blood spurted in rhythm with the Dikembe's dying heartbeat. *Damn it Dikembe.*

The hostages screamed and cursed as the front of the diseased pack made

their way toward the truck. Distracted by the death of his man, Kosoko turned back

toward the agents. *I have been deceived. They must die.*

The agents reached under their coats drawing guns. Blackened steel barrels

eyed him with malice. Time slipped into slow motion. Kosoko drove his shoulder

into the ground as bullets melted through the soldiers on either side of him. Lying on

his side, he leveled his aim at the shorter agent. He caught the man dead to rights,

staring dumbfounded at his weapon as he pulled the trigger, nothing happening. *A*

weapon malfunction. Perfect.

Kosoko squeezed the trigger of his six-shooter hand-cannon. The agent

staggered backwards, his hands holding his chest. CIA Bill went down under AK-47

fire as one of Kosoko's soldiers fired from the window of the truck. Gunfire spewed

from the plane door, and Kosoko's man in the truck fell silent. There must be more

of them onboard the aircraft, but he didn't have time to worry about that. The cursed

surrounded him.

The dongola misos wandered into the hanger haphazardly. Zeroing his

sights, he shot a woman with gnawed stumps for arms, wearing a toga-style dress,

through the forehead. He capped another monster realizing the futility of his

struggle. *I have only one shot to leave here alive and wreak havoc upon the*

Americans. Especially Joseph, that sniveling useless doctor.

Kosoko crawled on all fours over fallen bodies like an animal. He stopped when he came across a slain Congolese soldier bullet wounds decorating his body like bleeding nighttime stars. Glassy white eyes stared up at Kosoko. Rushing he stripped off the dead man's jacket. *It is covered in blood, but it would do. Everyone is covered in blood.* Donning the folded green beret shoved in the soldier's belt, he stood. *It will be enough.*

He ran to the truck holding the hostages, yanking the hatch open.

"To the plane, now." Ushering them out, he helped them down. "You are free. I am here to help." He kept his head low, as the Americans scrambled out the back without a second glance, bolting toward the jetway stairs. *I will blend in with the Americans as they escape. Surely, a nation founded by immigrants wouldn't reject a military refugee trying to escape his collapsing country?*

A monster wearing a soccer jersey grabbed his arm, and he shoved him down onto the cement.

"Move." The Americans continued to scurry. He aimed his pistol at the dead man, but before he could shoot a sharp pain seared through his calf muscle.

Infuriated, he gaped down, cocking his pistol. Ajani practically grinned as he chewed gluttonously, staring with dim white eyes. Having broken free of his restraints, he had crawled all the way across the hanger floor, still attached to his stretcher, to bite his father. Kosoko growled and kicked his son away with a heavy boot. Betrayed by his own flesh, he limped to the airliner.

JOSEPH
Kinshasa International Airport, DRC

Joseph covered his head as bullets whizzed back and forth between the rebels and the Americans. The living dead were overwhelming the remaining rebels. Both Americans took rounds to the chest and the dead were already making their way toward the newly fallen. A man in a soldier's uniform unloaded the hostages. The embassy staffers clambered out of the trucks. *The Congolese military finally made an appearance.* Joseph stood up shakily, using a luggage cart for support. *I am going to escape. Just up the steps to freedom.*

Keeping his head low, he looked around for Kosoko. *That man is diabolic.* The other hostages sprinted by him shrieking. *Kosoko must have been gunned down in the shootout. We're free.* He joined the cluster of embassy staffers attempting to push their way onto the plane. Sheer terror drove them forward.

"Move in an orderly fashion. Remain calm," shouted a voice from inside the aircraft.

Joseph had seen this type of situation before, especially with these people. It was every man for himself. Men cared little for women and children. They fought a bitter battle to get on board. Joseph had no problem shouldering his way onto the plane. *No sir, there is no way I am going to be left behind here.*

Apparently, everyone else had the same idea. As he squeezed through the doors, a steely-eyed, gray-haired man grabbed his arm.

"Are you a doctor?" he shouted as people pushed onto the plane and exhaustedly found seats.

Oh God, more people who needed medical attention. Did it ever end? "I, uh, yes," he mumbled.

The man was stern. "Where are the CIA officers? Are they alive?" he asked.

Joseph hadn't checked their pulses, but he was pretty sure they were dead. He was tired of everyone shoving him around, demanding answers.

"Dead. The last time I saw them they had their guts torn out," Joseph snarled.

"We can't just leave them," he said in Joseph's face.

"They are dead, and we will be too if you let those people on this plane," Joseph shouted back.

The man didn't react to his outburst. "Sit here," he said, pushing Joseph into a first class window seat.

Joseph peered out the window. The dead were following them up the stairs, climbing the steps up to the open aircraft door.

"They must not be allowed onboard. They're infected with a deadly disease," he yelled at the man who had pushed him into his seat. The gray-haired man nodded to his partner, a very large blond man, who stepped out onto the platform.

"Get back," he yelled, a hammer striking an anvil. He shoved a big foot into the face of the first infected person climbing the steps. The infected toppled into the others, causing a domino effect down the stairs. He quickly stepped back inside the plane and helped a flight attendant close the door.

"What's wrong with them? They're mad," he said to the older man.

"I don't know, but I'm sure he does." He pointed at Joseph.

End Time

The giant man plopped down next to Joseph, his shoulders taking up all the available shared space.

"Don't worry, friend, we'll get you home safe," he said, speaking with an accent.

Who are these guys? Some sort of Special Forces? A pounding sound on the aircraft door brought him back to reality. A mass of people stood at the door, and as the plane slowly rolled forward out of the hanger, the pounding stopped. Joseph exhaled. He hadn't realized he was holding his breath.

The PA system crackled as the captain spoke. "Hello everyone, this is Captain Richards speaking. It appears that the airport is in the process of shutting down, but there is no way we are staying here. We have clearance from the US government to do what is necessary to leave the country. This situation is very unusual, but not unexpected given the chain of events. It's our pleasure to be here today to give you your freedom ride. We're going to have some bumps here as we take off, so keep those seat belts fastened. Drinks are on the house today." A couple of cheers went up, but nobody seemed to be interested in the free cocktails.

The captain wasted no time, abruptly throwing the throttle and thundering down the runway. Gaining speed, it finally lifted off into the air.

Joseph's ears popped and he sat staring at the television screen blankly, his eyes unfocused. His gut pain still hid in his stomach, probably an ulcer, but it seemed somewhat calmer, as though it were masked and waiting to re-emerge. *With everything I've seen in the last few days: disease, death and destruction; humanity at its worst, will I ever be the same? Home will be a good thing.* He rested his eyes, letting his head fall back on his headrest. He was only allowed a moment of respite.

When Joseph cracked open his eyes, the gray haired man who had pushed him into the seat stood expectantly in front of him. *Oh, what does he want now? A glass of alcohol would have been nice.*

"I am Agent Wheeler. You are a Doctor?"

"I am Dr. Jackowski." He fumbled for his glasses resting on the center console. Agent Wheeler came into focus, a stout soldierly looking gentleman.

"My fellow agents and I were sent to make sure you make it home safe. We'll hand you off to another security detail when we arrive at McCone Airport. I was told there was a team of doctors at the embassy. Where are the other doctors?" He looked concerned.

Joseph shook his head, pushing his glasses up the bridge of his nose. "They're missing or dead. I'm the only one left from the embassy."

Agent Wheeler coughed a bit. "Okay. What was wrong with those people outside?" he asked, squatting down next to Joseph.

Joseph rubbed his eyes. "I don't know. Some sort of mutated virus. It puts people in a hyper-aggressive state, making them extremely violent and unresponsive to intervention. So violent, in fact, that they'll attack and consume the flesh of their victims afterward. I was researching the disease in a remote village when the outbreak spiraled out of control." He left out the part about them already being dead maybe it would be easier for the agent to swallow.

The agent gave him a blank stare.

"Have you seen ever seen a zombie film?" Joseph added. It was the only way to get his point across in layman's terms.

Agent Wheeler smirked. "You mean like the classic, *Night of the Living*

Dead? Been awhile since I've seen that one."

"Something like that. If anyone's bitten, restrain them immediately. The gestation period seems to be getting shorter and shorter. The first infected persons took almost a week to turn. Now, it seems that it takes only a matter of minutes, but it may vary based on a host of factors."

Joseph watched Wheeler's face for a reaction. His words didn't seem to faze the man. It was as if Joseph had simply told him the sky was blue.

"We'll make sure you get home safe so you can figure this out. We have an entire team strategically placed on board this aircraft to make sure that happens. Jarl here is very good at what he does. He is a premier protection specialist, and he'll watch over you while you get some rest, doctor."

Joseph glanced over at the large man over-lapping into his seat. *He is quite a big fellow. Probably can hold his own. I'm not sure he could save me from a horde of the infected, but Wheeler does seem rather confident.* He became downtrodden the more he thought about it. *A lot of good it did Master Sergeant Snow. We are going to need more than muscle and brawn to defeat this virus.*

"Thank you," Joseph said, reclining back in his chair. *Can anyone protect me from this virus? Can I protect them from the virus? Is it not my job to research and control outbreaks?* As of right now, he was failing that job pretty handedly. He tried to push the thought out of his head as the after-effects of adrenaline dump knocked him unconscious.

STEELE
Somewhere over the Atlantic

The takeoff was shaky, rough air rattling the cabin. Turbulence didn't affect Steele in the slightest. There were a lot worse things than a little turbulence out there. His fellow passengers seemed to think otherwise, the former hostages bawled as the plane rose in the air and broke through the clouds, but the pilot soon found a smooth patch of air and everything leveled out. The people around him clapped while others cried tears of relief. Even Steele felt a bit better knowing they weren't getting shot at on the plane. He relaxed a bit. They were headed back home to the good old US of A.

The embassy staff had rushed onto the plane in such a panic. Many moving all the way to the back of the aircraft. He hadn't received any feedback on details of this situation, but they were flying, so he assumed it was good.

Steele was proud he could offer these people a safe escort home. The flight was more full now because the passengers that had traveled over from the United States never departed the aircraft. Nobody came to get them. So they were obligated to stay on board. *Odd.* But Steele supposed that it was better to go back to the U.S. then be stuck in the DRC for an unknown length of time. Combined with the gunfire from outside the aircraft, Steele was convinced they didn't mind staying on the plane.

Steele did notice a few locals were interspersed with the embassy staffers. Not an outright concern, however, they most likely were not supposed to be on board the aircraft. They would have to let Customs and Immigration figure that part out, and hopefully they would be allowed asylum. He wouldn't worry about it unless things got nasty with one of them.

The number of injured hostages concerned him as well. *No doctors to be found. I wonder if Wheeler has kept them up front?* Luckily, an embassy nurse with short brown hair bounced from patient to patient assisting in making her colleagues more comfortable. She spent most of her time attending a heavyset female about five rows ahead of Steele. The woman's head, wrapped in bandages, lolled around her headrest in pain, an icepack lying across her forehead. The nurse and the flight attendants strapped an oxygen tank to her, and Steele could see her shoulders heaving up and down as she struggled to breathe. *She probably doesn't want to inhale the stale recycled air. I don't blame her, last time I traveled this far, I had to put lip balm on and eye drops in every four hours to deal with the desert-like conditions of air travel.*

Hours passed by and satisfied with his surroundings he glanced down at his phone for a moment. *Shit, I was supposed to call Gwen. Surely, she would understand.* Now he would feel guilty for the rest of the mission as she most certainly waited in anticipation for his phone call. A curse shattered his self-chastisement.

"What the hell?" the nurse screeched.

Steele sat up straight in his seat, slipping his phone back into his pocket. He peered down the aisle and saw the nurse holding her arm to her chest. She pushed the injured woman away with her other hand.

"Stay away from me. That fucking hurt."

Steele glanced over at Mauser, who had perked up at this new sound of distress. Mauser gave him a hand signal: a closed fist meant sit tight, while an open palm indicated that action was needed.

A couple of flight attendants raced down the aisle toward the nurse and patient. Steele showed him an open palm and tapped his arm with two fingers, indicating a fight in progress involving two individuals. As a special protection detail, anything out of the ordinary was to be closely scrutinized.

Steele checked his six and the passengers around him before peeling himself out of his seat and rolling away from the unfolding scene to the rear galley of the plane. He met Mauser there.

Mauser stepped up beside him and spoke in a low voice.

"What's going on over there?"

The flight attendants now wrestled with the sick lady, trying to keep her in her seat. The sick heavyset woman bucked violently. "You think it's a ruse to draw us out?" Mauser asked.

"Nah. You think that sick morbidly obese staffer is playing for the bad guys like some sort of double agent?" Steele asked.

"Let's take care of it before people freak out. Show off a little physical prowess for Crystal, see if we can make her *layover* a special one."

"Jesus, you're a horn dog."

A man sitting in the back row watched the scuffle carefully from his seat. The flight attendants had the woman's arms pinned, but she strained her neck outwards, trying to bite them as if she were possessed by the devil. The lady writhed in the grasp of the two older women. It was go time.

Crouching low, he moved fast up the aisle, converging on the fighting party. Better to play the concerned passenger until he had to out himself. He reached down, grabbing the woman's hand and throwing his weight into an arm bar from behind. The woman's head slammed into the seat in front of her and she growled under his weight.

Mauser watched his back. Standard contact cover protocol.

The woman was much stronger than she looked. She squirmed and wiggled under his grasp, and he soon felt his hold sliding on her slick clammy skin. He weighed more than two hundred pounds and had immense strength; there was no way this lady should be evading him for an instant. Her other arm broke free and she yanked his shirt toward her. Then another man was there, forcing her head down.

"I'm a Diplomatic Security Agent," he hissed.

The man was average all around, but Steele appreciated his intervention. The agent held the woman tightly from behind her seat.

"Thanks," Steele grunted.

"Nixon's the name," he replied as they struggled to gain control of the woman.

"Ma'am, remain calm," Steele shouted. Quietly, he said: "I am a federal law enforcement official. Please cooperate."

The woman showed no acknowledgement of his authority continuing to jerk her head spasmodically, trying to extricate herself.

"Let's see if we can get her cuffed up," Steele grunted at Nixon, as more calls for help sprung up a few rows ahead of them.

Steele glimpsed forward. *Now what? Am I wrong? Is this a ruse? Is some terrorist going to jump out of his seat and try to slit my throat?*

He refocused, the woman still squirming beneath him. "Ma'am, remain calm," he yelled again with no effect.

Steele squinted his vision impeded by the low light of the cabin. Two people scuffled in the seats. A middle-aged male staffer had driven himself against the skin of the aircraft, trying to escape the short haired nurse. She clawed through his shirt, her nails raking skin from his chest.

"Please stop," the man cried out, trying to keep the nurse away from him. He tried to shove her away, but she persistently dug at him like a crazed dog.

"Mauser, will you check that out?"

Nixon gawked at Steele, his eyes wide. "We have to get back. These people are infected. They'll kill us if you don't shoot them."

Steele stared at him as though he were batshit crazy. *What the hell is wrong with this guy?*

"What do you mean?" Steele asked assertively as the woman continued to struggle in his grasp. *Just give up and quit already.* She would never escape them on this plane.

"No place to go lady. So you might as well give up." His words had zero effect.

Nixon retreated backwards releasing the woman. "If an infected person bites you, you're toast, man. My partner was bitten in Kinshasa, and let's just say the end result was bad for the both of us."

Steele continued to eyeball Nixon. "What do you mean *bitten*?" It sounded to him like Nixon referenced a diseased animal. Precious seconds ticked away as he contemplated whether or not he should trust the man.

Is this guy for real? I have no idea if this guy is a federal agent. He fit the description and had put the right restraining hold on the woman, but he also sounded crazy. Steele's gut told him the man told the truth. "Mauser, stay back. They're sick," he shouted.

Mauser helped Steele and they zip tied her and hauled the woman up, using her restrained arms as leverage. Together they dragged her to the back of the aircraft. Steele kept a hand on her neck as they walked her forward to stop her twisting her head from side to side. Passengers leaned away from the aisle as he pushed her forward. They acted as if she had the plague. People covered their mouths, shying away in fear.

He set the lady face down in the rear galley, as gently as possible. *Gotta keep the lawyers happy.* She flapped about like a fish out of water. Crystal covered her mouth, cowering in the corner.

Steele put a knee into the center of her back. "Ma'am, I have to control you until you stop trying to bite us. Can somebody get me something to gag her with? Crystal, you got any duct tape?"

She nodded, rummaging through a galley cabinet.

Mauser hopped on his cell phone, radioing the team up front.

The cabin spiraled out of control. Steele turned his body to see the rest of the passengers. The nurse leapt on another man, who watched in horror as the carnage unfolded.

"Somebody stop her," screeched a woman. Enraged cries carried through the cabin.

Tuning them out, he rounded on Nixon.

"What is all this 'infected' talk about? Are these people sick?" Steele asked angrily. If it was an airborne illness like tuberculosis Steele most likely already had it, in more ways than one.

Nixon balked. "Listen, you don't know what's going on here. These infected people are incredibly dangerous. You have to shoot them in the head or they won't stop trying to kill us until we're all dead," said Nixon, who paled like he'd seen a ghost.

This guy's gone off the deep end. "Dude, you're fucking crazy." He felt as though he had been thrown into the loony bin.

"Mauser, what's the word from the front?"

Mauser looked back, cell phone held to his ear. "Wheeler wants us to use extreme caution when dealing with these people. He said the ones that are infected are highly contagious, and they spread the disease through oral transmission."

"Infected? How do we know they're infected? Oral transmission? He means biting?"

Mauser smiled. "No idea, but they don't look like the kissing type."

"See. She's infected," Nixon said, pointing at the woman. Her head turned to the side revealing dead white eyes while her mouth curved in a wicked snarl.

"That's how this all started. The virus makes them cannibals," Nixon said, closing his mouth when Steele glared at him.

So everybody's lost it. Either that or Nixon was telling the truth. Did that mean he was telling the truth about shooting the infected people in the head?

"Come over here and restrain her."

Nixon hesitated. "You should shoot her."

"Fucking restrain her."

Nixon took Steele's place. *How the hell am I supposed to get control of this situation?*

Mauser and Steele drew their SIG Sauer P226s, their tactical badges out. The badges swung on chains, resting at the center of their chests like superhero emblems. They moved up to the lavatories, taking stock of the cabin.

The cabin descended into utter chaos. Bloodcurdling screams buffeted the agents. The nurse rose up from behind a seat. Vital red liquid ran down her mouth in a seamless blanket of crimson to her fingertips. Her eyes were dull lacking pigment in the irises, instead a milky hue clouded them. She looked like she belonged on the set of a horror film not on a flight into the United States. She ambled toward them letting out a low moan.

"Ma'am, stay back. Put your hands on your head and turn around. Do it now," Mauser commanded.

The nurse did not show any comprehension that Mauser gave her direct orders. Ten rows away, she used seats to stabilize herself as she propelled forward to the agents, reaching out with bloodstained fingers.

"Is she drunk?" Mauser asked.

"If she's drunk, she's the most messed up drunk person I've ever seen," Steele replied.

Mauser moved his gun into the low ready.

"I can't do it." Mauser holstered up and slung out his baton with a fluid sliding motion. Cha-chink.

"You actually carry that thing?"

"I knew I'd get to use it someday." Mauser widened his stance and squared his shoulders moving into a striking position. Twirling the metal baton, he held it near his ear, ready to strike downward.

The baton was formidable as an intermediate weapon. The sound alone could scare somebody enough to comply with an agent's commands.

"Stay back," he yelled. He performed an overhand strike to the woman's upper arm.

Mauser stepped into his backhand swing targeting her other arm, a non-lethal hit zone. She took the blow like a practice dummy, showing neither pain or annoyance. Unfazed by the strike, she took a wild swipe at Mauser's face. Dodging backwards, he wielded the baton into the woman's upper thigh with a loud thwack. She collapsed in a heap.

"Stay down," he screamed at her. Aggression was a key component of compliance. The more aggressive the better until the situation was under control. She rotated her head up slowly, blood running down her lips.

The nurse crawled to her feet, and with a burst of sudden speed, she lunged for him.

Mauser swung downward at her arms and was rewarded with a loud crack.

Damn. Mauser had a lawsuit coming his way.

He had snapped her forearm like a twig. Her arm bent at ninety degree angle lacking the structure to maintain uniformity. Eerily, she emitted no cry of pain, as if it never happened.

"Jesus," Steele cussed. He watched helplessly from the back galley. There was no protocol for a situation like this. The woman was impervious to any sort of physical trauma.

Passengers ran down the other aisle. *Shit.*

Steele addressed them, "Keep your hands on your heads. Move slowly." The people huddled against one another in the back galley.

"Shoot them! Shoot them! They are killing everyone," mumbled a man, pointing down the aisle.

Steele was stuck in limbo. Too much happened all at once, and they were losing control. *I'm not sure we ever had control.* He verged on Jeff Cooper's Combat Mindset code red – the zone in which he would have to take someone's life – and if he wasn't careful he would blast past code red and hit code black, in which he would probably die, frozen in fear, frozen in death.

Steele began losing his auditory abilities as Nixon continued to struggle with the restrained lady on the ground. Muffled cries for help tumbled from side to side in Steele's head.

The man in the galley kept pointing down the aisle and screaming, and Mauser went down as the nurse tackled him to the ground, his gun still holstered. Before his back impacted the airplane aisle carpet, the crazed woman pounced upon him. Mashing her teeth, she drove her face close to his. Blood and saliva dripped from her mouth onto Mauser's face. Steele just watched in indecisive horror.

Mauser got his baton up across her neck, pushing her away from his face. "What the fuck, lady?"

Her throat crunched inward, the muscles of her neck the only thing keeping her head attached to her body. Red fingernails met his cheek, her unbroken arm tearing at his face over and over.

"Steele, help," Mauser barely forced out.

Like a power surge, everything came back. Steele changed his mindset to action. It was time to move with direct purpose. Commands flowed from him like a practiced script.

"Help him. Hold her down," he yelled. He lined up his sights on the woman's forehead. A cake shot from less than three yards.

Is this the right decision? Should I take this woman's life? She has already grievously assaulted other people. She attacked Mauser, but she doesn't have a weapon. If someone with an infectious disease bites you, is that not an assault with a deadly weapon? A million other thoughts raced through his mind second-guessing his plan of attack.

"Shoot her!" Nixon yelled from behind. "Shoot her!"

There was no time to think. He pressed the trigger evenly, not knowing when the gun would go off, but certain that it would. A trigger press must be smooth and never overly fast. *Slow is smooth, smooth is fast*, he repeated in his mind over and over.

He had probably shot more than twenty thousand rounds during his career as a counterterrorism agent. These shots had been discharged during multiple scenarios, under varying levels of stress, and during the Tactical Pistol Assessments, as well as Close Quarters Combat Carbine Qualifications for which the CT agents had the highest qualifying standard for federal law enforcement. Other organizations argued that technically they weren't regular law enforcement so they shouldn't count, but they had badges. They had sworn oaths. The difference being that their mission was highly specialized for the law enforcement community and was blended with the military, making them highly effective, tactically speaking.

Due to their high standards and willingness to go hot, counterterrorism agents had been labeled wild gunslingers. They were willing to attempt shots from just about anywhere with extreme prejudice and definitive accuracy. But when one had to engage a bad guy through a sea of heads, he knew he couldn't afford to miss. Steele almost never missed in target practice. Most of the other agents had engaged threats in the field, but Steele had never been put into that situation. This time it was for real. Life and death were mere centimeters underneath the pad of his fingertip.

The woman's brains blew out the back of her head. Mauser looked shocked as he wrestled with a lighter, now partially headless corpse. He tossed her off him and bounded upright back to his partner, gun drawn.

Steele had just killed another human being. He would have to answer to the scrutiny of the courts for his action, and to the woman's family as to whether or not he had made a mistake. If deemed a mistake, it would haunt him and his family for the rest of their lives. Even if it wasn't a mistake, he could still be bankrupt by savvy defense lawyers, an all to common occurrence.

He physically shook it off. Thinking too much about one's actions could cause hesitation when making future decisions, so he tried to push it out of his mind. *Move forward with the mission.*

Technically, since he wasn't a doctor, he couldn't pronounce a person dead, but with the top part of her head no longer in existence, he was pretty sure.

"She tried to bite my face," Mauser stated in disbelief. "Seriously bro, this is fucked up." Mauser scanned the rear of the aircraft.

High-pitched ding-dongs jingled as Mauser's phone went off, interspersed with the screams of passengers. In the darkness, Steele couldn't identify clear targets to engage. It was a shadowy nightmare.

"Flight attendant, hit the lights," he shouted at Crystal, who cowered in the corner. She nodded, tapping a screen on the wall. Nothing happened.

"Nothing's working. The captain must have it locked," she said frantically pressing buttons over and over.

"It's okay," Steele said. He tried not to think about what was happening out there.

"That was Wheeler. He said they've secured the subject, and he wants us to move up to provide support. He said to leave everyone else behind, and to grab Andrea on the way."

"Why? Where's Andrea?" Steele asked urgently.

"I don't know, but she's not with them."

Steele felt a spike of adrenaline in his chest. He hoped she was safe, but he feared the worst. "We can't just leave these people here alone. They'll get torn apart."

Mauser's face strained. "I know, bro. We need everyone to calm the fuck down," Mauser said, waving his hands in their direction.

A crowd of people had congregated in the back galley including a big Congolese soldier with blood covered hands. This was a tactical nightmare for the two counterterrorism agents.

Mauser spoke loudly: "We need everyone to follow us, single file, up the aisle to the front. We'll be safe there."

He glanced over at Steele, who nodded. "We got this." They weren't going to let people die. It was inherently built in them to protect.

"I'll take rear security," Mauser said.

"You would," Steele said with a small smile, showing a spark of confidence that he wasn't feeling. "I'll lead the way."

Steele stepped in front of the group and shouted over to Mauser, "Moving."

"Move," Mauser replied, acknowledging his request to begin tactical movement.

Steele surged forward. He would have much rather been 'nuts to butts' with Mauser in a two-man stack, but the people in between them prevented appropriate tactics. A 'stack' was an operating term that law enforcement and military units use to tactically assault and clear rooms and buildings, predominately in urban close-quarter combat settings. The stack allows the best 360-degree coverage of an area and provides for as many guns as possible to be pointed down range at any given time. Ideally, they would have loved to form a stack, but nothing about this situation was ideal.

They both shouted, "Hands up, heads down," as they moved forward. Compliance was out the window, but this way the passengers wouldn't jump them thinking they were terrorists. The lights flickered in the cabin but remained off. It felt like a horrible haunted house, only its evil patrons were real.

Steele pulled his flashlight from his waistband shining it left and right. He flashed it intermittently so it would be difficult for anyone to zero in on his location.

"Please help," someone called out.

"No, please no. Get away," shouted another.

Steele kept moving forward. He tuned the calls for help and the moans of the dead out of his head.

Steele stepped over a body in the aisle. The mangled corpse stared up at him with glassy eyes. "Body," he called out to Mauser as he stepped over it. They moved quickly to the first bulkhead.

Quickly, he checked his corners and a hand pulled him toward the wall surprising him. A portly, bearded man in a bloodied suit leaned forward, trying to bite Steele's neck. Steele rammed an elbow into the man's throat, an instinctual reaction.

With a sickening grind, the man's head slammed back into the wall but held on to Steele's arm, pulling him closer to his face. A low growl gargled from its gore-covered mouth, its pale white eyes staring through Steele.

His feet sliding backward, Steele strained with all his might to keep the man wedged in the corner. A dark shadow blurred past Steele's head, a black hand ramming a knife up into the fiend's neck dangerously close to Steele. Taking a step back, the fiend dropped to the ground. Steele eyed the tall Congolese soldier warily. He bent down wiping the blade on the fallen foe.

"Thank you. Where did you get that?" Steele wiped blood from his face.

The man looked up baring white teeth in the dark at Steele. "I am a soldier. We must hurry. More come."

Steele's heart rate skyrocketed after his close encounter. The people crowded in the mid galley and Mauser shoved his way forward.

"You okay?" Mauser shouted eying the soldier for a moment.

Steele nodded, breathing heavy. Adrenaline pumped through his system.

End Time

Stress caused some people to break down and quit, while others lost focus and freaked out, but for Steele, it made decision making clear. He performed best under pressure.

"Let's keep moving," Steele called out.

The small group made its way through the rest of economy plus to business class. As they cautiously walked forward, Steele peered left and right, scanning the cabin for Agent Carling. *She has to be here somewhere.* Several bodies were slumped over in their seats, while others were in their death throes. *Where the hell is she?*

Heel to toe. Heel to toe. He 'Groucho walked' toward the front of the aircraft to keep his shooting platform steady. They called it the Groucho walk because it closely resembled Groucho Marx's comedic walk from fifties films.

Two human forms reached out for him up ahead. "Police! Stay back," he instructed.

The people did not stop. He lined up his three-dot tritium night sights. They created a flat sight picture across the front of his gun and the shambling forms blurred out of focus.

Pop-pop. Pop. *Two to the body, one to the head.* He could hear his firearms instructor repeating the phrase over and over. It was also called the three-shot technique or the Mozambique Drill after a mercenary discovered its effectiveness in the Mozambican War of Independence.

The two forms fell to the ground and ceased all movement. In many situations, it was the only way to be sure an enemy combatant was eliminated from the fight. Even then you couldn't be totally sure. The two to the body was to slow the target and to ensure that high-percentage shots and pain were going down range. The one to the head was supposed to put a stop to any nerve sending from the 'computer' – the brain – to the rest of the body. Even a person with two gaping holes in their chest could fire a few rounds back or, worse, detonate a bomb.

When aiming for a headshot, Steele aimed for the Fatal T Zone or an instant kill shot. The Fatal T Zone covers an area from the eyes down through the nose and wraps all the way around the skull. It is called the 'Fatal T' to reflect the shape the nose makes with the brow line. If punctured or shot, this area will in most cases terminate the enemy's ability to continue any operations.

"Argh," a man crawled over the middle aisle of seats reaching for them. Mauser silenced him with a few rounds to his left, laying the man low.

Steele fumbled upon Agent Carling in her business class seat. Her eyes were glazed over and her head reclined back against her headrest. She looked as if she were taking a nap except for a gaping bite wound exposed her esophagus and the main arteries in her neck. Her face was pale and her clothes were soaked with her own blood.

Fuck. Steele checked her pulse, but there was nothing. *Can't help her now.* Steele searched Andrea's body for her firearm. He found it and ripped it from her shoulder holster before shoving it into his belt.

Steele continued his steady platform movement to the first class cabin. When he ripped the curtain back, he almost took a round to the face from Jarl, who loomed in the aisle like a giant shadow of death.

"Freya's cunt, Steele. Say something. I almost shot you," Jarl said, waving them forward with a meaty paw.

Steele hesitated. "We've got some passengers with us."

"Move to us," Wheeler said from the front row seats. They had taken up a defensive position around the primary asset. A nerdy looking long haired man crouched near the skin of the aircraft next to Wheeler's leg, making him look like an odd damsel in distress.

Bounding his way passed Jarl to the front galley, Steele led the passengers with Mauser to safety. Two flight attendants and a couple of passengers poked their heads out from behind the galley, terrified.

"Andrea's dead. Somebody ripped her throat out," Steele snarled in disgust as he passed Jarl. *He would kill the rat bastard when he found him.*

"Damn it," Wheeler spat; as he pushed the asset ahead of him into the galley, Jarl closed the gap, sealing them off from the rest of the plane with his body.

Steele exhaled. They had made it to the aircraft front. It was safe for now, but it was only a matter of time before the infected people from the back made their way forward in a search for new victims. Nowhere to run to on a plane.

"Everyone's freaking out back there. We had to shoot multiple hostiles," Steele said, airing his frustration.

"Terrorists?" Wheeler asked almost as if he were excited.

"No, I don't think so. They seemed to be just regular people from the embassy gone mad."

The scrawny man with glasses stepped close. Steele gave him a hard look. *Who's this guy?*

"This sounds like the same outbreak we were dealing with in the DRC. It's as I feared; someone must have been infected in the embassy group. We should have screened them for infection before they boarded. We must self-quarantine when we land. Not one sick passenger must get off this plane."

The conversation blew Steele's mind. "Yeah, I keep hearing about this infection. What the hell is wrong with these people? And who the fuck are you?" Steele shouted, pointing a finger at the man, his anger rising. Steele wanted to punch this smart guy in the face.

"This is our protectee, Dr. Jackowski," Wheeler said, trying to calm Steele with a hand on his shoulder.

The doctor looked a bit squeamish under Steele's hard gaze. "I think it's a viral strain mutated from Monkeypox. People that contract it display similar symptoms, with a few exceptions. One is that conventional medicine has little or no effect on the patients. Two, the other more alarming problem is, after the patients die, they 'reanimate' and proceed to devour the living with little regard for anything except to spread the virus."

The what and the what? Steele brushed over what the doctor had said. "What's he trying to say?" Steele asked Wheeler.

Wheeler frowned. "Doctor, will a bite from these things kill us?"

"Precisely, Agent Wheeler. And as crazy as it sounds, after they die, they come back to life as a mindless cannibal."

This guy is a quack. Steele could only shake his head in disbelief that this guy might actually be right.

Wheeler called over to the other agents. "Shoot anyone who comes through those curtains."

"Copy that, boss," Jarl said.

"Got it," Mauser called back from the other aisle.

End Time

Dr. Jackowski looked back at Steele and Wheeler. "It should be noted that massive brain trauma seems to give them what I am terming *secunda mortem*, or second death." Dr. Jackowski eyed Steele with intelligent gray eyes almost as if he dared Steele to disagree.

"So you mean to tell me these people are *dead*? And we have to put a bullet through their heads to keep them from ripping out our guts? Like zombies?" He was beginning to feel like maybe he was the crazy one.

The doctor blinked. "In most rudimentary of terms, yes."

"Jesus tap dancing Christ. Can we get some lights on in here? I can't see shit," Steele swore.

Wheeler picked up the air phone and spoke to the Captain. The lights flickered on.

"Thank you," Steele said aloud to everyone.

"All right, guys, we've got priority into McCone. I've requested everybody and their mothers to meet us when we land, including the Center for Disease Control. We've got to hold tight and not let anyone near the subject until we land," Wheeler called out.

Jarl fired a few rounds from his position. The gunshots reverberated through the cabin.

"He's not going down," Jarl screamed over his shoulder.

"Aim for their heads," Wheeler called back. More gunshots went off from Mauser's side. Stopping when Steele was sufficiently deaf.

"Steele, bump up to the edge of first class, I want some space," Wheeler commanded. Steele nodded, surging forward with his weapon pointed downrange.

Steele couldn't have imagined a situation any worse than their current one.

Maybe we should have left the lights off, he thought as he eyed the bodies and blood.

This is going to be a long couple of hours.

KOSOKO
Somewhere over the Atlantic

Sweat flowed down Kosoko's face making him feel like he had been caught outside during the rainy season. His breath came out in haggard wheezes. It felt as though his chest was literally closing up from the inside out. He hugged himself, his muscles shaking uncontrollably. His heart pounded, heavy and rapid like a cannon struggling to keep going. Concentration evaded him, skirting him on the edges, but nothing would stop him now.

Kosoko's calf throbbed where Ajani had betrayed him. Even now he could feel the pain making its way up his leg and into his torso. It was like a black mamba forcing its way through his veins. Time was not on his side, he knew that much. Revenge was all that remained for him. *Nothing matters except that I rain pain down upon them. Not long now and I will be one of the cursed.*

He felt the long dagger wedged up the sleeve of his coat with a sweaty palm. Quietly, he leaned on the wall, watching the doctor and the American officers. Helping the bearded one had earned some of their trust. *It will allow for an opportunity.* The front galley held a few passengers, not enough to get in his way. They sat covering their heads with their arms, terrified of their own colleagues and friends, whimpering.

Cowards. What did they know of suffering? Had they ever been without food for weeks on end? Had they ever seen men blown to pieces? Had they ever heard the cries of dying children? This suffering was momentary; a flash of suffering compared to an entire lifetime of it. Soon this suffering would be over.

The moans of the monsters called forward from the next cabin. Kosoko would join their ranks soon. Dongola Miso. The boogeyman. That gave him some peace of mind. He hoped he would continue to haunt these people after he passed. It was as if he were given two chances to plague them, and that gave him great joy. Turbulence vibrated the cabin. People braced themselves on the walls and countertops of the galley. Carts, cabinets and coffee pots rattled in response.

The only man between him and the doctor was this puny, gray-haired man. The others called him Wheeler. Apparently, he was their leader. He carried himself in a cocky manner, a man who had the natural respect of others, but that didn't matter as Kosoko had dealt with his kind before. In his country, these men - the righteous - were the first to go so that the corrupt government officials and military members could keep lining their pockets.

He thinks he stands for something. He will fall for those beliefs. When this Wheeler turns away, I will cut his throat and finish the doctor off. Then I will take his gun and execute the other American scum. After that, little else mattered. I must be fast and quiet.

The cabin swayed in the rough air, and the gray-haired Wheeler reached forward to steady himself in the bulkhead doorway. *Perfect. Now.*

Without hesitation Kosoko leapt forward like a cheetah, sliding the dagger from his sleeve. Wheeler spun into Kosoko's arching knife thrust as if he were driven by some sixth sense, throwing both forearms into Kosoko's blocking his strike, losing his handgun in the process. Pain shot through his arm on impact.

A second later, an elbow struck Kosoko in the nose, rocking his head backwards. Pain fired through the nerve endings into his skull, adding further to the throbbing in his head. Only pure anger drove him forward.

This man is quick, and its so hard to concentrate. Wheeler grasped his knife hand like an iron vice. The warrior drove the knife to his side, keeping both Kosoko and the knife near the flank of his body. *I cannot let him control me.*

"*Rarrr*," Kosoko growled throwing his knife hand across his body, bringing the smaller man with it. They switched positions and Kosoko slammed him into the wall, pinning him. He placed his other hand on the knife and brought it upward toward Wheeler's face.

Technique and skill could only get a significantly smaller opponent so far. Kosoko's superior size and strength over the smaller officer would soon prevail. The blade inched closer to the policeman, who knew the tip of the pain was coming. Kosoko could see it in his eyes: he knew and accepted it. *You are out of options little man.*

"Embrace your death," Kosoko uttered.

The knife sunk gratingly into his chest, piercing him through. Blood spurted free as Kosoko withdrew the blade with a wicked twist. The man grunted as Kosoko flung him to the side.

Kosoko faced the doctor, a vile grin spreading across his face. All he saw now was red.

"Please, someone help," shouted Joseph as he applied pressure to Wheeler's chest.

Kosoko laughed at Joseph's feeble attempts to save the fatally wounded man as he closed in for the kill.

"He's dead. No one can help him, but you could have helped Ajani. I told you if you didn't help my son, I would kill you."

He snatched Joseph up by his shaggy mop like a sacrificial lamb.

"Arrgghhh," Joseph cried, clawing at Kosoko's hand. Kosoko felt nothing. Joseph's fingernails were mere pinpricks compared to his immense internal struggle to stay whole.

"I will see you in Hell," Kosoko said, drawing back his dagger to strike.

Bam. Bam. Bam.

Shooting between his legs while his lifeblood leaked out, Wheeler unleashed three rounds, each of which exploded into Kosoko's chest. Each blast felt like a hundred-pound weight hitting him and sticking. He staggered backwards reaching out for something to break his fall and collapsed near the cockpit door.

The pain erupted everywhere and it was too hard to breathe. He hacked, trying to get air into his lungs. Pulling his hand away from his chest, sticky bittersweet liquid covered his fingers. Every time he wheezed air, more blood flowed. Soon the coppery taste of blood filled his throat, spilling onto his face. He was drowning in his own blood. He sucked in air as hard as he could, but he couldn't draw enough in. *That stupid little man. He should have been dead.*

As his eyes dimmed, a younger, bearded man, looked down at him. *Is it my precious Ajani? Has he come to see his father to the next world like all good sons should do?* After a painful moment staring up in hope, any thought of redemption dissipated. *The man I saved earlier. I couldn't save Ajani, but I saved him.*

"I guess I shouldn't expect you to return the favor," he spat, spraying the man with blood. "I'll come back for you." He was sure of it. *I will rise again. Dig no grave for Kosoko.*

"No. No, you won't. You'll burn in Hell," the young man said.

"Finish it," Kosoko growled grasping for his blade. The last thing he saw was the muzzle flash of a gun.

GWEN
Red Cross Headquarters, Washington, D.C.

Gwen sat inside the Disaster Operations Center at the Red Cross headquarters in the heart of D.C. when the first news reports of the U.S. Embassy's capture in Kinshasa broke.

"We have confirmation from State Department officials that all United States Embassy personnel have been evacuated, and the Ambassador is accounted for," the newswoman reported with a nod. Gwen was thankful that everyone was safe. *We live in turbulent times.*

A blinking icon drew her to her inbox, indicating an incoming message. She clicked it. *Riots across London. Prime Minister recalls Portsmouth Flotilla up the Thames. The Tyne, Severn, and Mersey: River class patrol vessels provide support.* It felt like the world was imploding. All of the incoming news from Africa made her anxious about Mark. *He is resilient. He will be fine. He is probably lounging on some beach somewhere, concocting some ridiculous story about chasing bad guys and saving the world,* she reassured herself.

Her job at the Disaster Operations Center was to match victims' needs with the relevant resources as quickly as was feasible. The Center's primary purpose was to monitor the latest humanitarian crisis so the Red Cross could deploy resources accordingly. She would much rather have been out in the field, but everyone had to pay their dues before they were allowed to run a disaster relief operation.

From her desk, she watched four large monitors as the main news stations flashed the headlines. It was as if they were out to prove her wrong about the ease of

End Time

Mark's mission. Shaky homemade footage showed people running in the streets.

Gwen tried not to think about the perilous situation. Taking a deep breath, she forced herself to stare back at her computer screen. The sky blue desktop with little yellow folders could only hold her attention for about three seconds. Staying busy was paramount to stifling her worry, so she wouldn't dwell on the danger her loved ones were in. She reminded herself that people needed her help. *Sitting and stewing about the danger my boyfriend is in isn't helping anyone.*

Averting her eyes, she avoided eye contact as Cory from accounting walked past her desk. Per usual, he dressed in a preppy uniform of designer clothes unnecessary for their work environment. Gwen was always surprised that he didn't carry around a compact so he could admire himself wherever he went. He tarried in front of her computer, slowing down as if he were internally debating something. *Time to look busy.* She typed nonsense on her keyboard hoping her ploy would work.

Keeping her head down, he stood watching her over the top of her computer before he spoke. *Eww. Creepy.*

"You seen Michelle?" he asked, checking his phone. *You would think he would make eye contact considering how often he watches me from across the room. I'd put money he is using the camera app, it is about time for his daily work selfie.*

"No, I think she called in sick. Some sort of flu, but knowing her, she's probably too hungover from last night's happy hour at The Hoof and Plow."

Cory bent down, a little too close for comfort, but she tolerated it.

"Say, did you see this crazy video online? These fascist cops totally shoot some homeless guy who's eating another guy," he said, shoving his phone near Gwen's face.

"Gross, Cory. Please, I don't want to see that." He gave her a dismissive shrug.

"I guess it was bath salts or something, but they could have just shot the guy in the leg," he said, standing up. Gwen had read somewhere that bath salts, a common name for a designer recreational drug, could in fact make people do crazy things.

"Evan and Amy are gone today, too. Must be something going around. Say, you want to grab a drink or maybe some sushi after work? Love the necklace, by the way. Are those pearls real?" He gave her a white-toothed half smile.

Gwen knew this was coming. His real motive in asking about Michelle was so he could segue into a proposition for a date. This guy had a lot of nerve, and was relentless with his pursuit of her. She was pretty sure that if she switched jobs, he would have one at the same place within a week.

She gave him a look of contempt. "Thank you, Cory, but you know I have a boyfriend. And even if I didn't, I wouldn't date someone from the office. And yes, the pearls are real. They were a gift from Mark for my birthday," Gwen said, turning back to her computer with a large sigh. *Take a hint, buddy.*

Cory held his hands up defensively. "Don't shoot, all right. It was only a friendly invitation. No need to get all crazy acting like I asked you to marry me."

So, now I'm the fool for thinking that the coworker, who has asked me out a handful of times, wasn't asking me out on a date. She just wanted this conversation to end so she could go about her business, regardless if it meant worrying about Mark.

"I am declining on dinner," she said in a curt tone.

Cory checked his nails, grooming his cuticles. "How is 'Captain America,' anyway?" he said with a haughty smile.

"He is fine," she said, grinding her teeth. Her politeness stretched to the limit. Cory had been insistent that either Mark was a fabrication or some sort of bum, because Gwen had never brought him out to a work function due to his frequent deployment schedule. All she had told him was that he worked for the government, and that only seemed to make Cory's imagination run even wilder.

"Gwen. You need a guy who's around. Someone you can spend time with everyday. Somebody who chooses you over their work. Even if it's not me, you could do better. I know how his kind operate, they are inherently cheaters." He walked away not a moment too soon.

Gwen shook her head as he left. *How can I get any work done with his constant harassment?* His words made her think though. It wasn't that Mark didn't have his faults, but he was a good man. His loyalty was not in question. *Cory did have a point, about him being gone all the time. It would be nice to have him around more.* Gwen continued typing her report in disgust. Cory sickened her with his arrogance and his presumption that she had no choice in the matter of who she dated. It was as if Cory were waiting his turn in a long line of established suitors. To her it sounded like he suffered from symptoms plaguing beta males. They always hovered about when Mark wasn't around, trying to force their way into her life. She didn't want someone to trick her into liking them; she wanted somebody who was genuine, not a self-involved jerk.

Gwen had always been too nice. She didn't want to discourage men from reaching out by ruining their lives through rejection, but she also wanted them to leave her alone when she wasn't interested. Men never understood anything. If an attractive woman talked to some guy, he immediately thought he was going to get laid. *Seriously, could there be a more adolescent line of thought?*

After every sentence she typed, she felt herself being drawn back to the television screens. She couldn't keep her eyes away from it. Her report would never be finished.

One news station had reported it as a terrorist attack, and demanded the President to make a statement. It seemed that any incident would be thrown in the President's face. She knew Steele felt differently about him, but she liked the guy. The plight of regular American people seemed to be his focus. Having met him a few times through her work, she was partial toward him.

She scanned the office properly for the first time. *How is this place supposed to function only half-staffed? Where is everybody? They can't all be hung over from last night.* Sirens blared as emergency vehicles drove past the building like the President himself going somewhere in a hurry.

The disturbing footage of a large truck ramming the embassy gates shocked her. People ran into the embassy compound. *Oh my God.* A tingling feeling rippled down her spine. *This is going to get much, much worse.*

A rival news station reported a 'Breaking News' story from New York. Some sort of protest was happening in Times Square and the police were skirmishing with protesters.

The footage was jumbled at first. The camera bounced up and quickly panned across the iconic giant advertisement boards and the scrolling stock tickers as it zeroed in on the protest. *Looks more like a riot.*

A shirtless man with blood running down his face grappled with a NYPD officer. *Looks like some Occupiers getting out of hand again.* The rioters mesmerized Gwen, but she snapped out of her news-induced trance as her boss called her into her office. She walked over to Kim's office unable to remove her eyes from the talking heads.

Settling in a chair, she clasped her hands on her lap. Her supervisor, Kim Smith, was the Director of Relief Operations and gave Gwen a pleasant smile. Pictures of her and various people she had helped adorned every inch of her office.

"Gwen, how 'bout you head home early tonight? We will be needing you to deploy to one of these crisis zones in the next few days."

Gwen frowned. She had heard of a few issues, but was unsure as to the magnitude. "How many relief operations are we talking about?"

"Well," Kim said, skimming through a stack of papers. "It looks like we're having some big problems across Africa and the Middle East. Some sort of flu is overloading the limited medical infrastructure of almost the entire region."

"Like Ebola?"

Kim shook her head, flipping through papers. "I don't know. It says in here somewhere. All of our incoming information has been relatively vague, but they will need assistance. Scientists are projecting a high infection rate."

"I just want to be prepared for anything."

Kim smiled. "You are on top of things. We're going to need good people on the ground to determine the severity of these situations, and what resources we need to help the afflicted. So get your affairs in order, because we'll need you TDY, ASAP. Your division's down a few folks due to illness, so you'll be heading up the team to Guinea."

Gwen beamed. Finally she could get her hands dirty in the field. "Thank you, Kim. I'll prep my bags for deployment immediately." *They've been prepped for months.* Gwen could hardly stop herself from wringing her hands together in glee. Not that she would wish a disaster upon anyone, but she desperately wanted to be on the front lines against human suffering.

"We'll get ahold of you tomorrow with the flight details. Oh, and Gwen, keep up the good work out there. It is so nice to see someone with so much vigor and life still left in them."

Gwen was beside herself with excitement. She practically sprinted out of the office. She bustled her way to the Foggy Bottom Metro station elated.

She trooped awkwardly down a perpetually broken escalator to the lower level of the crowded Metro station. *Might as well just call them metal stairs.* Her heels clopped loudly on the steel-grated steps as she tiptoed gingerly down the escalator. A man brushed by her on her right-hand side hacking a lung onto her shoulder. She was appalled, but he was impervious to her look of disdain.

When she reached the bottom, the station was packed as if there were a Nationals home game that night. She called her dad first as she navigated her way toward the turnstiles.

"Yes, I am taking the metro. Yes, my car is fine." Her father would never understand the merits of commuting via anything except a car. He would also never understand why she would want to live in a large city. She was beginning to question whether there may be a nugget of truth in his rantings somewhere.

The mass of people were a herd of cattle moving sluggishly toward the turnstiles. Her fellow patrons' proximity to her made her claustrophobically hot.

End Time

Trying her best to not sweat in her crisp newly dry cleaned suit, she stood on her toes to see what the hold-up was. Unable to see over the people around her, she gave up trying to figure out the reasons for her delay.

"Of course it'll be safe, Dad," she lied. It wouldn't be a deployment if she wasn't in at least some danger. Whether it was disease, famine, insurrection, or hostile governments, there was always something that made the deployments a challenge. Just the way she liked it, a little danger made her feel alive. Getting impatient, she fished inside her purse for her Metro pass so, at the very least, she would be ready to scan her way through.

The sound of yelling drew her interest away from her father's play by play rendition of his day. The police had a couple of suspects handcuffed on the ground. They appeared homeless, garbed in soiled raggedy clothing. It wouldn't be a day in the District without its fair share of homeless. She passed them keeping a safe distance.

Locating her Metro pass, she scanned her way onto the platform. She politely squeezed into a train car filled to maximum capacity with D.C. denizens, the pleasures of a perpetual rush hour. An older gentleman was nice enough to give her his seat as she dialed her sister Becky. Her parents divorced when she was six, and she had always cared for her younger sister.

"Hi Becky, how was school?"

"Meh, those little brats are running me into the ground, but its a job. I'm running by the daycare right now to get Haley."

"I got a deployment," Gwen said ecstatic.

"Wow, that's great. How exciting to leave the city to go to a place without running water. When do you leave?"

"As soon as possible. Its some sort of disease outbreak in Africa. Isn't that great?" she exclaimed.

"Huh, yeah. I am happy for you. I think you are crazy, but everybody has their thing."

"Listen Becky. I didn't badger you when you took up roller derby or decided to date Rory." Becky audibly sighed on the other end.

"You finished? That reminds me. I almost forgot to tell you." Every conversation with her sister eventually led to a discussion on the latest small town gossip.

"They found Old Man Waverly out wandering in the cornfields the other day. Deputies had to bring him in after he attacked them. They got him up in county lockup. They say he's got something wrong with his brain making him crazy."

Gwen would never let go of her love for small Midwest town life, but she had always been driven to make a global impact. As she grew older, who won the county fair became less and less a part of her identity. Daylight disappeared ahead announcing an upcoming tunnel.

"That doesn't surprise me. He's always been a little off. I'll talk to you later. I'm about to lose service. Just wanted to share the good news. Give Haley a kiss for me and tell her she is one of my favorite people of all time," Gwen said, hanging up.

The train rocketed forward at full throttle, zipping through the dark tunnels. After a few stops, darkness gave way to bright light. The Metro had crossed the D.C. city limits into Arlington, Virginia. Once the Orange Line train reached Virginia, it traveled above ground, more or less mirroring Interstate 66. Office buildings and apartments whipped by.

Casually she glanced at the traffic on Interstate 66, thanking God she wasn't wasting her time stuck in that. It was one of the most traffic-ridden highways in the country and, per usual, it resembled a parking lot. On a good day, it could take more than an hour to travel fifteen miles.

The District of Columbia had recently overtaken Los Angeles as the city with the worst traffic in the country. It was surprising that a city of nine million people had less congestion than a city boasting a fraction of the population at just under a million, especially given that it was the nation's capital, where updated and efficient infrastructure was expected. Expected and rarely seen.

The Metro train rolled to a stop. Bored by her lack of forward progress she watched the people on the highway. A swarthy man in expensive jeans and a tight-fitting T-shirt exited his BMW and gestured wildly at another driver, who walked toward him. They became entangled and the fight dragged them both to the ground.

I will have to tell Mark I saw a fight on the highway. She tried to catch a picture of it on her phone, but the train lurched forward again before she could take the shot. Nothing really surprised her in this region. The people were so much more pretentious than in the Midwest, as though they thought being rude was a constitutional right.

Her phone rang and she tentatively picked up her mother's call. *Becky must have ratted me out.* Keeping this a secret from her mother would have been ideal, until she was about to leave the country.

Her mother blazed on the other end, complaining about how Gwen never visited and that she never called. The train continued its single linear motion, causing people hanging on to the handrails to sway back and forth like palm trees. *Thank God.* The Metro train sailed past the Interstate 66 traffic.

She had been tuning out most of what her mom said.

"I can handle myself. I know the rest of the world isn't like Iowa. You know this is why I live here in D.C., so I can help."

The train ground to a halt with a screech of the brakes. Gwen slid forward in her seat, almost losing her phone in the process. *Jesus, who is driving this thing?*

Peering out the window, she looked for a source of stoppage. *God damn it.* They were stuck on the tracks somewhere between Dunn Loring and West Falls Church. *So close, yet so far from Vienna.*

"Mom, hold on. Let me call you back."

"What is it honey? Is everything okay. I saw on the news."

"Everything is fine. I'll call you later." That woman would never stop worrying.

The lights flickered and sputtered out as the power disappeared from the Metro car. It wasn't a big deal, it happened all the time. At least, she thought it did. The power on the Metro line was sometimes shut off, and the cars would be turned off while they repaired the line. However, the city usually did Metro maintenance during the night rather than during the day for precisely this reason.

Thirty long minutes passed. The car sat dark and the air conditioning stayed off. Gwen was furious. *Figures, I would get stuck on the metro the one time I get let out early.*

Take seventy-five D.C. Metro goers, people impatient at the best of times, and lock them inside a Metro car toward the final days of summer with no air conditioning and prepare for congressional legislation.

Cell phones were out and the complaints were coming in. "I'm calling my lawyer. This is ridiculous," said a businesswoman in the seat across from Gwen. Gwen agreed, but then again, relying on public transportation meant they were at the whims of the public system. Gwen took to social media leaving a status update. *Out of work early. Stuck on Metro. #DCproblems.*

"They can't just keep us in here," complained a man in a suit with an ID card dangling around his neck.

"No shit. I was supposed to pick my daughter from daycare fifteen minutes ago," another man said, checking his watch.

No announcements were mumbled from the driver, adding more uncertainty to the metro riders' dilemma. The decibels inside the train car grew louder and louder as people cursed the transport system, Congress and the President for their predicament. Gwen rested her chin on her hands, completely over the Metro, D.C. and its citizenry alike. She would welcome the deployment with no running water, limited culinary options and sick people, as long as it got her out of here.

A couple of men near the sliding doors started to search for a way to open them. These were people after her own heart. She could not sit there and wait for a Metro or government official to rescue her from the train car. It was time to take actions into her own hands. She got up and squeezed past the other commuters, making her way toward the exit. *I am getting out of here, even if I have to walk.*

The situation reminded her of the 'Snowpocalypse' of 2011. The traffic had deadlocked and stopped as over twenty-four inches blanketed the D.C. Metro region. People left their cars stranded on the highway, walking to side streets to be picked up by friends and family.

People exited the car in front of her and were jumping down onto the tracks. *That's exactly what I want to do.* She wriggled her fingers into the sliding train doors and pried the doors apart from the middle.

"A little help?" she said to the two men that were hunting for a release lever.

The two men in business suits, probably former military by the looks of their closely cut hair, gripped the sliding doors on either side. She strained her arms and back. *Damn, this door is heavy.*

"Come on guys, put some back into it," she grunted. The men laughed a bit and pushed it harder.

She strained again, and a pair of hands shot through the space, wrenching it open from the outside. With a roll, the train doors shifted apart. Eager hands cupped her armpits as she jumped down onto the tracks. She stared upward at a tall black police officer in full tactical gear. Sweat drenched his face, and he had the wide-eyed look of someone who was clearly under a tremendous amount of stress.

"I need everyone to move quickly to the next Metro station. Walk down the tracks and stay to the right. The tracks are offline," he said in a low voice. He gestured in a westerly direction with his gloved hand. "Hurry," he urged.

Gwen turned and shielded her eyes in the direction of the District. She could make out the hazy outlines of people down the tracks, heat quivering as it rose up from the ground. *There must be another train out. The whole metro system must be down. Thousands of people could be stranded.*

"Ma'am, you've got to keep moving. NOW," he said, his voice rising to a shout.

End Time

"Okay," she said, feeling a bit admonished. *Dang, what's this guy's deal?* She walked at a brisk pace towards the next station, turning every so often to see the growing mass of people gaining on her.

After five minutes of crunching through the gravel lined tracks, a man sprinted past her, holding a briefcase above his head. Then another.

"Wait, why are you running?" she called out. The man didn't even turn to acknowledge her question. *What's wrong with these people?*

More and more people ran by her until she found herself caught up in the running. The hard gravel packed train track made it difficult to maneuver in her two-inch spike heels. Afraid she would turn her ankle, she kicked up her heels one at a time.

She jogged alongside a man. "Excuse me, sir? What's going on?" Sweat stained his collar.

"Some sort of riot. A lynch mob more like. They are ripping people apart back there. Haven't you been watching the news?" he said, breathing heavily.

"Oh my God, why?" she stammered.

He waved her off. "Stay away from me," he picked up his pace and ran faster away from her.

A mob? Why in the hell would there be a mob on the train tracks? It angered her to have to sit and wait on the metro, but this was ridiculous.

Every step, made her more fearful. People ran on the highway abandoning their cars. *Who is doing this? What is happening?* Her mind ran circles of dire scenarios. Gunfire boomed in the distance, adding to her angst. Sirens sang away further down the road. A helicopter circled above them. A man climbed the Metro fence in an effort to get onto the tracks. So many things were happening at once, she could hardly take it all in. Nails, rocks and glass littered the tracks, and she spent almost as much time dodging those as she did half-running.

Mark and she had discussed the necessity of fending for oneself in disaster scenarios, but she never thought of it as real. After all, when she went to a disaster, she helped people.

An elderly woman, probably in her sixties and wearing a visor with an American flag T-shirt, toppled over in front of her. *Tourist.* The crowd diverted around her without stopping. Grown men in business suits ran by without a second glance.

Mark's voice screamed in her head to run. Gwen stopped anyway, ignoring him. *Had these people no hearts?* Gripping the woman's hands, she pulled her to her feet. She was heavier than she looked.

"It's going to be okay," Gwen reassured her.

"Thank you so much. What's happening? Some men attacked my husband, and he told me to run. I'll never visit D.C. again," the lady stammered.

"I don't know, but we have to keep moving," Gwen said, wrapping an arm around the woman to help her walk.

"I'm so scared. Is he all right? I can't leave him," she cried, turning back to search for her husband. Gwen ushered her forward with a hand on her back.

"We'll talk to the police at the next station," Gwen said, trying to comfort her. She moved as swiftly as she could, but the older woman slowed her down.

The pack of metro riders dissipated in front of them as they escaped up the tracks. Gwen chanced a glance behind her. The crowd of rioters had closed the gap.

End Time

She didn't care to find out what they were upset about. After a few minutes struggling forward, she finally saw her oasis: a large concrete building with a long platform running alongside the tracks.

"There," she pointed. "The platform."

Sweat drenched her gray pantsuit, creating dark patches under her armpits and around her collar. *Great, I'm going to have to get this thing dry cleaned again.*

The humidity had to be up over a hundred degrees, and there was no shade out in the middle of the Metro rail.

"Just a little further," Gwen said to the dazed woman, although she really said it to reassure herself that this would all be over soon.

The woman stopped and pointed down the tracks, forcing Gwen to stop with her. "Well, there he is."

"There who is?" Gwen asked, easing the woman forward step by step.

"I see him down the tracks there. He's wearing a T-shirt just like mine. We are on a tour from Ohio."

Gwen shaded her eyes. A large, older man lumbered forward in a group of people. A crimson coating covered his hands and face.

"I think I see him. Let's wait for him in the shade of the platform," Gwen said, still edging the woman forward worriedly. She did not want to meet him or any of his friends.

She was so distracted by the pack of people gaining on them, that she didn't notice the man in dirty khakis stumbling from the platform. Dragging his foot behind him, his office ID badge still hung from its Virginia Tech lanyard. His foot bent sideways collecting gravel as it dug uselessly into the earth. Blood ran down the side of his face as though he had fallen head first onto the pavement. His eyes were pale. Before she could do anything, he reached out as though he knew the old woman and seized her arm, wrenching her from Gwen's grasp with a battered hand.

"Hey, what the hell are you doing?" Gwen yelled in alarm.

The man continued to scuffle with the woman.

"Please stop," the woman cried out as the man clumsily pulled her to the ground.

Gwen gawked in awe for seconds as the man took the old woman down. On his knees, he pinned her arm down and ripped a huge chunk of shirt and flesh with his teeth, jerking his head backwards.

Blood sprayed through the air. "Wha-?" Gwen uttered. She could not wrap her mind around what was happening, aside from the fact that it was bad.

Chewing with pleasure, the man tore into her American flag T-shirt digging his hands into her stomach.

"Oh my fucking God."

Gwen's response was a reaction to pure terror. She ran forward planting a foot into the man's face. Blood, saliva and flesh flew from his mouth as he fell backward, his security badge slapping the concrete.

"Stay away from her," she hollered. Hoisting the woman up, she half-carried, half-dragged the bleeding woman to the platform.

The woman held her stomach, blood oozing from between her fingers. "It hurts. It hurts," she sobbed.

"It'll be okay," Gwen said, practically shoving her up the ladder onto the platform.

End Time

At the top of the ladder, Gwen and the woman collapsed. The woman gasped for air suddenly going into shock. Hundreds of people still made their way toward them.

She pulled her phone from her purse and dialed 911, applying pressure to the wound with her free hand. Nothing happened. Cell phones were almost always obsolete during natural or man-made disasters, because the network is overwhelmed by the sheer volume of callers. She cursed everyone.

"Stay with me," Gwen said to the woman, whose eyes were starting to glaze over. The woman needed emergency care fast. Gwen dropped the phone in her cleavage putting both hands on the woman's stomach, trying to halt the flow of blood with pressure.

"Somebody, please," she cried out up the Metro stairs. Blood escaped from beneath her hands. "Please," she mumbled again. *No one is coming to help.*

She checked the woman's pulse. Dimly holding on. As she did, a bloodied man in a police uniform pulled himself up onto the platform.

The officer from the train didn't even look at her as he jogged toward the exit.

"Help us," Gwen cried out.

He faced her and let out a growl. Lunging at her, he pulled her upward, gripping her shoulders like his hands were made of iron.

"Lady, get out of here now. People are killing each other," he said, shaking her. "Run, goddammit."

Isn't his job to serve and protect the public? He should be administering first aid and contacting medical first responders. Gwen would get him back on track.

She would make him see that his duty carried importance. People needed him to take charge.

"But this lady's dying. A man attacked her. Look," she said, pointing a finger toward the woman. "See. She's getting up." The anomaly of the dying woman on her feet did not register in Gwen's mind.

Distracted the officer eyed the woman. A pair of gory hands wrapped their fingers around his ankles, and his eyes bulged out as he toppled forward, knocking Gwen backward. She managed to fall onto her backside, a jolt of pain reverberating through her spine.

"Shit," he exclaimed. His firearm spun out of his grasp, clattering onto the concrete. He rolled off his stomach kicking out at the snarling faces of dozens of disgusting gore-covered people. More hands dragged him to the edge and pulled him off the platform onto the tracks below. He reached for Gwen as he went over the edge and his screams punctured the air as they butchered him.

Covering her mouth, she scooted across the slick platform. She only stopped when her back slammed into the concrete wall. The old woman shuffled for her, reaching out an old speckled hand.

"Join us," she seemed to say, but it came out as an eerie moan.

STEELE
Somewhere over the Atlantic

"What are his vitals?" Dr. Jackowski asked Steele.

"His pulse is weakening. Respiration is low," Steele said as he applied pressure to Wheeler's chest wound with a white towel that rapidly turned red. He was bleeding out so fast; faster than Steele ever thought a person could. Blood had drenched Wheeler's clothes and pooled in the notch of his neck.

"Is the wound making a hissing noise?" Jackowski asked.

Steele removed the towel and listened hovering his ear close to the hole in Wheeler's chest.

"Yes." Steele replaced the towel pushing down hard on Wheeler.

"Damn it. He may have a punctured lung."

That soldier had helped me earlier. Why would he betray us now? I should have disarmed him. There might be more onboard. Sleepers. Securing Wheeler's handgun and the soldier's blade in the back of his pants, he felt like a walking arsenal.

"Mauser, you got that chest seal?" Steele shouted through the first class cabin. A chest seal would keep air from escaping the hole in his chest which may lead to a collapsed lung.

"It's in the front pocket of my bag in economy," Mauser shouted back, handgun in the high ready.

Steele had to make a game-time decision. "If we don't stop the bleeding, he's gonna die before we hit the ground."

Gunshots rang out from the aisle opposite them. Crazed passengers were climbing over the drink cart in front of Jarl. He physically shoved them back with a hand the size of a Christmas ham.

Jarl called out: "Down to my last mag." He threw a former Marine guard, still wearing a bloodied combat uniform, into the skin of the aircraft with one hand. He used the other to shove the muzzle of his gun point blank into the man's mouth.

The infected guard attempted to bite him with inhuman ferocity, mouth gnawing the slide of his gun. Jarl's hand engulfed the man's neck holding him in place on the wall. Spraying the soldier's brains into the cabin wall, he let the body drop into a first class pod.

"Why don't you take a seat?" he said to the corpse.

More infected crawled over the makeshift barrier. The lack of coordination harried their assault.

Steele's heartbeat thundered in his chest. *This is it.* He knew people he cared about were going to live and die based on the decisions he made. Gulping he steeled his nerves.

"Jarl, hold your side. Take these mags." He tossed Jarl extra magazines, and he snagged them out of mid-air, shoving them into his waistband. "Mauser, take Nixon and get the med kit. I'll cover your side." He was choosing to send his best friend into the jaws of death. Wheeler looked up with fevered eyes. He was fading fast. *No time for second guessing.*

"Steele," Wheeler breathed and then turned his head to the side unconscious.

With an icy stare, Steele called over to the only flight attendant who was not in shock. "Crystal, we need to get on the ground now. Call the Captain and tell him we're dying out here."

Her lip quivered with fear, but she nodded and stepped tentatively over the terrorist's body, as if she expected him to reach up and grab her. She picked up the galley phone.

Steele stood up, drawing his handgun from its holster. "Mauser, moving to you."

"Move." Steele stacked close to Mauser's back. He glowered over his partner's shoulder at the chaos unfolding in business class. Blood and gore blanketed the seats and aisle, and legs stuck out of the mid galley. The legs twitched and disappeared. *Jesus Christ.*

A few people in business class were still buckled into their seats, squirming against their seatbelts. *Where the hell was Andrea's body?* He shuddered at the thought of his teammate being one of these monsters.

Steele kept scanning with his eyes. A pile of bodies lay in front of the beverage cart on the other side. Jarl's lethal contribution to the mission; it would take an army of these things to bring him down.

Lead and smoke hung heavy in the air filling his lungs, making it harder to breathe. Combined with the stink of death, it made him want to gag.

It was like non-lethal simulation training, when the team had to wear thick helmets. The instructors had scratched the clear eye protection to impede vision, and after a few minutes of breathing inside the confined space they naturally fogged up. Anything to throw you off your game.

To add to the discomfort, the instructors would block the masks' air holes to restrict airflow, making the scenario even more stressful. The higher the heart rate is allowed to climb, the quicker the degradation of a person's fine motor skills, trigger control, complex movements such as dialing a cell phone and complex demands such as reading a paper. This decline in skills can be accompanied by auditory exclusion, tunnel vision and freezing up, all of which can get a person killed in a force on force situation.

Steele gestured to Nixon. "I need you to watch his back. If we don't get the med supplies, even more people are going to die. Do you understand? Here's Wheeler's piece."

Nixon took the blood-covered weapon and looked it over. He press-checked the slide to make sure it had a round in the chamber. It was imperative to know the status of one's weapon. If you pulled the trigger and it went click, that might just be the last thing you heard.

"Here's an extra mag," Steele said, handing him one of Wheeler's secondary magazines.

Nixon shoved it into his belt. "Thanks. We'll be back in a jiffy," Nixon said with a little smirk, as though he didn't believe it.

"Don't take too long, now. We have a plane to land," Steele said.

They switched positions and Nixon stacked up on Mauser. "I'm up." Squeezing Mauser's shoulder, he gave a physical indicator that he was ready to move any time Mauser did.

In a tactical stack, if the team, whether a two-man or larger team, became too spread out, it would leave lapses in sector coverage, increasing the risk of danger for the team. The more people in the stack, the less coverage individuals would be responsible for, but communication would become more difficult and even more important.

The two moved rapidly through business class to economy. Speed was a key tactical element, creating confusion amongst the enemy. Steele firmly stepped into place in the aisle and resumed his watch on aircraft right.

He calmed himself with a deep breath, trying to get his heart rate under control. Keeping his heart rate steady was paramount to his success. Countless hours in the gym doing high-intensity interval training with weights and the treadmill gave Steele that edge.

The flight attendant called from the front: "Captain says we got thirty minutes before we land."

"Copy that," he responded while maintaining his coverage of the cabin.

What a cluster fuck. The FBI Hostage and Rescue Teams better be ready to meet us when we land because this is one hell of a shit show we got ourselves tangled in. He gripped his handgun and took aim at a woman groaning as she crawled over a row of seats.

GWEN
Dunn Loring Metro Station, VA

Gwen pushed herself upright against the cool concrete wall. The old woman ground her teeth together as she got close. They locked arms wrestling for a moment. The elderly woman's hands felt stronger than they should as if she may have been undergoing some sort of anabolic steroid therapy.

"Get away from me," Gwen shrieked. She brushed the old woman to the side, knocking her to the concrete and instantly feeling guilty. She had just beat an old woman to the ground, an old woman in need of her help, probably somebody's grandma. *Hopefully, no one captured that act of kindness on camera.* The woman awkwardly tried to stand, slipping in her own blood and collapsing on the slick platform.

It was like the whole world had gone insane, and Gwen was stuck in the middle. She needed to get out of here.

Taking the steps two at a time, she bolted up the stairs to the Dunn Loring Metro station.

"Sorry," she called back at the woman. It was just too much. She hardly noticed the bloodstained handprints that covered the thick walls like a finger painting project gone seriously wrong.

She stumbled over the remains of people that looked as though they had been attacked by a pack of wild dogs. Bite marks covered their faces and necks, while dark pools of blood outlined the bodies, reminding her of twisted 'blood angels.'

End Time

The smell was horrid as she got closer to the bodies, and she involuntarily choked up the chicken salad she had for lunch. Hot bile spewed forth from her lips, splashing around her ankles. Her throat burned. Her eyes watered. Holding her nose, she pressed forward.

Where are the authorities? Didn't they have task forces for this kind of thing? She kept moving. Lackadaisically, she made her way toward the exit turnstiles, fumbling in her purse for her Metro card. *I can never find the dumb thing.*

Gory handprints streaked down the outside of the glass security booth, the door was cracked open a bit, but nobody was inside.

Do I need to scan my way out? Screw this, I'm out of here. Gwen hopped the turnstile and made a beeline for the parking lot. *Maybe the 46 line buses are still running.* With a furtive glance behind her, she ran.

Near the exit, police cruisers blocked her path, their lights swirling blue. Beyond them the parking lot sprawled in disarray with half the cars sitting empty or abandoned. A pile-up of vehicles near the south entrance blocked any escape to the highway which left only the north entrance.

A bus lay on its side, smoke rising up from its engine. She gasped and her hand involuntarily covered her mouth. The level of destruction shocked her system.

"Dear God," she breathed. She punched 9-11 into her phone again. The busy tone mocked her, rubbing it in beep after beep.

Like a moth, she instinctively fluttered her way toward the flashing police lights. Somehow they seemed to ease her nerves; the promise of succor in times of need. At the same time, they seemed to warn of danger ahead.

She ignored her mind screaming danger, and jogged toward the navy and gray Fairfax County police cruisers. Slapping the hood of the car with her hands, "Hey, anyone there?" she called out. She circled the car. The passenger door stood ajar, but no officers were present. She stuck her head inside the squad car.

"Anyone?" she muttered, scanning the area for any sign of assistance. Blood covered the sidewalk leading away from the vehicle in the direction of the bushes. She sat down in the passenger seat, and grabbed the radio pressing down on the mic.

"Hello, we need help. I'm at the Dunn Loring Metro Station. Anyone there, over."

"This is Dispatch. This is a secure channel. Verify your identity."

"I'm in a cop car at the Metro stop. There aren't any police here."

"We are going to need you--," the dispatcher was cut off.

Thump. Thump. Thump. Directly behind her head the protective glass reverberated under violent impact. Her stomach flittered a cloud of butterflies. She carefully turned her head to the backseat.

Inches from her face, snarled a man. Repeatedly, he rammed his head into the hard plastic window separating the front from the backseats. Blood ran down his shaved head and goatee, covering his leather biker vest.

She slowly backed up as he continued to use his head as a battering ram, against the squad car. The front of his head dented inwards as he did irreversible damage to his skull, oblivious to the pain.

Gwen stepped away cautiously from the cruiser and headed into the commuter lot. People milled about the south exit ramp leading onto Virginia Interstate 66, while a number of others walked unhurriedly around the parked cars.

End Time

They meandered through the cars, appearing not to know which way to go.

Someone had to help her. *Just a ride to her house or away from here. Maybe she could borrow a car.* She would never consider it stealing. The owner would understand it was an emergency.

If she could get home safely, she would grab her emergency go pack, and get out of town. She would take Mark's SUV. He had carpooled with Mauser. That would work. Drive to the hills of West Virginia, and wait for the authorities to straighten this out. Most likely, the Red Cross would insist she deploy back into D.C., but only in a safe zone.

Her thoughts quickly turned to Mark. He would be coming home later today. *Thank God! He would know what to do. Wait. If McCone was anything like this, then he would be in immediate danger. I must warn him, but only after I am safe. That's how he would want it.*

Fueled by survival, she walked briskly toward a neighborhood of townhouses nearby. The townhouses seemed like the safest bet. Each townhouse sat three stories high with a garage, and were all painted off-white. Subdivisions seemed to spring up overnight in this area. *Surely someone can give me a ride from there.*

Her head instinctively scanned from right to left overtly searching for danger. Mark had taught her simple situational awareness techniques, but at this point there was no need to be discreet. She felt like a meerkat, tall and alert.

When she got into the parking lot she crouched as she moved, using the cars as cover, trying not to draw too much attention to herself. She rounded outside the mess of cars blocking her way through to the townhouses. A maze of carnage and twisted metal sprawled out before her, with people she didn't trust wandering the wreckage. The most convenient way through had the most suspicious-looking people. *Right or left? Or chance it up the middle with the people.* Her whole body shook. *Which way to go? Which way to go?*

A low female voice called to her: "Psst, hey you. Over here."

In between two cars crouched a dark-haired young woman in her twenties wearing jeans and a loose-laced flowery blouse. She gave Gwen a little wave, trying not to draw too much attention to herself.

Hurrying, she hustled over to the woman, stepping over broken glass and metal from accidents in the lot before crouching down beside her. *Her pants better not rip.* Her suit pants were most definitely not made for any kind of athletic activity. *Fuck it*, she thought. *I can just buy new ones when this is over.*

The other woman peered cautiously over the hood of the car that concealed her. Relieved to find someone else alive, who wasn't trying to kill her, Gwen put her back to the car.

"Jesus, I am glad to find someone like you."

The young woman eyed Gwen up and down. "So you aren't one of them, are you? I suppose not, or you would have tried to bite me by now. Ha." She gave Gwen a sheepish smile. Gwen thought most guys would have called her cute, but not necessarily pretty.

Gwen stuttered, "No, no… I'm just trying to get out of here. My car's at the Vienna Metro and everything's going insane. I've seen a policeman murdered and a woman eaten alive, and I just want to get out of here."

The young woman peeped back over the car again. "I know," she whispered. "Crazies have been crawling all over this parking lot. They killed," she stopped as if she were going to cry.

Moaning grew louder from the lot. The young woman's brown eyes went wide, and Gwen held her breath. She put a shaky finger to her lips.

A man in a filthy black business suit knocked into the car they hid behind. He groaned a low ominous call. Using the car as a crutch, the man gazed around and continued his morose shuffle elsewhere.

Gwen exhaled heavily. She grasped the young lady's hands giving them a squeeze. The young woman brushed tears from her eyes on her shoulder.

"I *would* help you, but there's one problem," she said, sniffling.

"What's that?" Gwen asked urgently in a hushed whisper.

"My car's over there." She gestured toward a green Jeep Wrangler a few rows away. Several bloodied Metro workers in orange vests stood around it. They lumbered as if they were bored, sauntering between the cars.

"I tried to get to it earlier, but they chased me away until they came across a guy thrown from his car."

The young woman closed her eyes for a moment, reliving the terror. Her voice shook. "He couldn't even walk. And they just ripped him apart, blood all over the place. He screamed and screamed. I was so scared. I didn't know what to do."

"It's going to be ok, but I need you to hold it together for me. My name's Gwen," she said, giving the girl her best assertive smile. "We're going to get out of here."

Gwen wasn't sure she believed herself at this point, but it seemed to calm the young woman a bit.

"I'm Lindsay," she said, sniffing back her tears.

Gwen knew she had to formulate a plan, and fast, before the wrong person found them.

STEELE
Washington-McCone International Airport, VA

Steele maintained his coverage in a heightened state of alertness, ignoring the knot of muscles cramping in between his shoulder blades. *Hurry up, Mauser.* Keeping his weapon in the high ready, for what felt like hours, exhausted him. Regardless, his body leaned forward, ever the aggressor, ready to strike hard at anything that presented an ounce of resistance.

His silent vigil was broken by Mauser's hoarse voice. "Mauser coming up."

"Move," Steele responded in relief.

Mauser hustled up to the front with his backpack strapped to him. He tossed Steele another pack, which had been attached to his front. "Found these. Thought they might be useful."

Throwing his black daypack over his shoulders, he tightened the straps to ensure a secure fit.

"Nixon?" Steele asked. Mauser shook his head, negative.

Steele would have time to consider the man's sacrifice later. "Hurry, Wheeler needs help," Steele said, maintaining his post.

Mauser nodded and jogged up to the front galley. He would help apply the chest seal and decompression needle to Wheeler's wound, hoping that their team leader had not already lost too much blood and watch for signs of tension pneumothorax.

Wheeler is one tough son of a bitch. Steele took his eyes off the cabin for a moment, watching Mauser perform first aid beside the doctor. Remembering his tactics, he rotated himself 180-degrees, so he could see the front of the plane as well as the back.

Unlocking the secure door, Captain Richards walked out into the galley. "Dear God. Is he going to be okay?" he asked, grimacing at the dead terrorist and at Wheeler. "Just keep whoever did this away from the cockpit. We're landing in five. We have limited runway space and because of the headwind we're low on fuel. We've only got one shot at this."

"How's he doing, doc?"

Dr. Jackowski handed Mauser's a long tube and pointed at Wheeler. "Get that NPA tube in his nose. If we get him to a hospital, I think he'll make it. He's lost a lot of blood, but the chest seal is keeping him alive," he said with a determined smile.

The Captain nodded. "Good luck, gentleman," he said, ducking back into the cockpit, the door slightly ajar. The pilot's task was laid clearly before him: land the plane in one piece and keep his living passengers alive.

Steele leaned over a first class pod and slid open a window shade. Bright light pierced the cabin. *We've dropped below ten thousand feet.* The checkered landscape of Virginia farmland covered the ground like a patchwork quilt of greens, browns, and grays. *That means we are getting close to the airport.* Closer in, the farmland gave way to wooded suburbs and the concrete slab of runways belonging to the Washington-McCone International Airport. Longer crisscrossing runways for international travel, ran perpendicular to shorter ones, and a tower overlooked all a domineering flying saucer on a spire. It was the largest airport in the National Capital Region. Smoke rose up from the end of one of the runways.

"What's going on down there? I see smoke," Steele shouted.

Captain Richards turned, yelling over his shoulder. "Someone put a round through our radio. We've had no contact with air traffic control for some time."

NORAD should have scrambled the fighter jets by now. For better or for worse, the jets scrambled by the North American Aerospace Defense Command should intercept the incoming plane, but no 'flyboys' escorted them home.

Steele remembered one of his instructors always harping on about fighter jets. *Your only backup at thirty-five thousand feet is an F-15. No pressure or anything.* If something was wrong, they should be escorting the flight in. Steele refocused on the task at hand. His job was to get the doctor safely on the ground. *As long as I do that, everyone else can pick up the slack and deal with the fucking psychos, or infected, or cannibals or whatever the hell they were.*

The plane dipped and descended rapidly, dropping toward Washington-McCone International Airport. He locked his feet in the bulkhead and braced himself for impact. *God, I hope it's not a real impact or I'll fly through the front windshield of the plane. And that's after I bounce off the front galley, the cockpit door and in between the pilots, leaving me in little pieces all over the ground. That's what happens when you crash at 150mph standing up.*

A few bodies rolled forward as the plane descended, bouncing from seat to seat like a sickening trapeze of death. Finally they got stuck, bent into various inhuman positions. Blood ran from their lacerations, twisted broken bones and bite marks.

Steele glanced over at Jarl. He didn't even need to brace himself; he simply deposited his girth in the bulkhead door jam.

Jarl gave him a thumb's up with a mighty, blood-soaked grin showing through his beard. "Boar tusk," Jarl said loudly.

"Boar tusk," Steele shouted back. It gave him energy. *I am not alone. Bring on the pain. They would have one hell of a story for Chip when they got back to the office.*

As the slight G-forces pulled on the plane. The carts in the aisles rolled backward over the bodies that had fallen in front of it. The finish line was in sight, and he couldn't have asked for a better team when things went bad. However, he dreaded the phone call to Andrea's parents explaining why she wasn't coming home.

The plane hit the ground, almost knocking Steele off his feet. Fallen bodies of the infected and the dead somersaulted toward the back of the plane finishing in a mangled heap of limbs.

The pilot threw open the flaps and applied the brakes. The bodies and the dead now slid toward Steele. Gradually, they stopped as the plane slowed.

Some bodies still writhed in their seats. The simple task of 'lifting the metal buckle,' shown in the safety video before every flight, now seemed an impossible task. Arms flailed around, searching for new victims. *Why don't they just undo their belts and attack?*

The plane slowed and pulled into an empty runway lot. *Where is Captain Richards taking us?*

Steele ducked his head and looked out of either side of the aircraft to see which part of the airport they had parked in. They were about as far away from a terminal as they could possibly be. This particular section put them on the other side of two runways, across from Terminal D. The plane ground to a halt. They had made it and in one piece. Eerie seconds passed while they waited. *Reinforcements should be here any minute.*

Captain Richards came back through the cockpit door. "We've called Air Traffic Control four times on our personal phones, but haven't received a response. We should have emergency personnel waiting for us."

Steele gazed out the first class window again. There were no flashing lights, no hostage rescue teams and no people in sight. That was not right. *Where is the cavalry?*

His job was to ensure the VIP was kept in one piece. Once they reached the ground, the place should have been teeming with backup from the Division, FBI, local officers and paramedics. *What the fuck is going on?*

Steele turned on his cell phone and called Operations. A busy signal answered him. *What the fuck, Mika? Always calling me to do stuff, but you never pick up when I need you. He was probably paying for a pizza.*

He stared at his phone in confusion. This had never happened before. *I don't want to be on this God-forsaken plane with these cannibalistic assholes any longer. On top of that, I need to get the doctor to the handoff team.*

His mind raced. "We've got to get outta here. We're low on ammo and I don't know how many more bad guys are back there. We need to evacuate now."

Captain Richards didn't hesitate. "I agree. Let's get those emergency slides going. We'll make our way to the terminal on foot."

Nobody needed more encouragement than that to get off the death trap of a plane.

"Wait, we cannot allow the infected passengers off of here," Joseph demanded, raising his hands in the air.

"We are leaving now. We don't get paid enough to deal with this shit. Somebody else can quarantine these crazies."

"But it could be catastrophic. An epidemic. Even a pandemic of global proportions."

"Not my problem. Crystal, let's do this."

Crystal grabbed the red emergency handles and pulled them down hard. With a loud whoosh the emergency door blew open and an inflatable plastic slide shot out, leading diagonally away from the plane to the ground.

Mauser jumped first, holding his pack in front of him and shooting down the slide. He took up a kneeling position at the bottom, his weapon drawn, searching for threats.

Steele covered Jarl's retreat to the bulkhead, keeping potential threats ahead of them while the surviving passengers, flight crew and the doctor jumped down the slide, exiting the plane. Steele's jaw dropped as lifeless forms rose up throughout the plane, a puppet master playing his entire entourage. Mangled and abused, bloodied and battered, none of it mattered, they stood all the same. Dead eyes stared his way. They preached doom. *Dear God.*

Steele gritted his teeth and yelled to Jarl, "Exiting now." *We'll meet again.* He didn't know how true his thoughts would be.

"Exit," Jarl said in a gruff voice.

Steele leapt onto the slide and grunted. The slide was much harder than it appeared. Jarl was only a step behind him.

The air outside the plane was smoky, and alarms signaled in the distance. A few planes were parked at their gates. Something was amiss. He shook off his gut

instinct. Cautiously, they moved forward in a determined manner. The airport

sprawled before them. Their refuge sat in plain sight. *The easiest day was yesterday.*

GWEN
Dunn Loring Metro Station, VA

Can't turn back now, Gwen thought, as she ran to the middle of the commuter lot waving her hands in the air like she didn't care. She began to rethink her plan as gravel and rocks dug painfully into her feet while she navigated the car-filled lot. *These crazies better be slow, because I sure as hell am not going to be fast like this. Even after I trained in those minimalist shoes.*

On her tip toes, she could just see her target, a green 2012 Jeep Wrangler. The two Metro workers near Lindsay's Jeep were overweight and definitely infected. Blood caked over their neon orange vests, and the worker on the left had a grisly, jagged stump with a protruding bone where his arm should have been. *I suppose I don't look much better in my destroyed suit.*

More infected bodies milled around to the right of the vehicles. These men and women must have been on some sort of tour, judging by their matching D.C. T-shirts; the kind people tended to buy from street vendors down by the Smithsonian museums.

One of the tourists appeared normal until he turned his head to face her, exposing a fleshy flap of an ear with puncture wounds from a bite. The woman next to him moaned loudly, reaching a hand out toward Gwen. Blood and gore decorated the front of her shirt, painting the cartoon caricature of Washington D.C. a dark red. She had bites all up and down her forearms, as if she had attempted to protect her face from attack. Gwen gutted herself up. *Stay strong.*

"Over here," she croaked, her confidence waning. Her voice gave away how she felt. Scared and alone.

"Over here," she mustered.

Her voice drew their attention not unlike she hailed an old friend. The woman started her awkward gait toward Gwen, and the others hastily followed suit. They moved with a herd mentality. A clan of ravenous cannibals desiring only one thing, her flesh.

Here we go. Just have to lead them away from the car long enough for Lindsay to get in, spin around and pick me up. Provided that Lindsay does her part and the group of tourists doesn't murder her. Provided that these dozen or so people aren't fast enough to catch me. Provided that I don't twist an ankle and get eaten alive.

The possibilities were endless, and if this didn't work she would be in a world of pain, literally. She tried not to think about the bad alternatives, but they hovered over her like a dark swarm of bees.

Complexity in a situation like this was the devil. She knew the acronym KISS: Keep It Simple, Stupid. Complex plans almost never worked out as they should. After looking over at the group of infected tourists, she thanked the gods for fatty fast food and sugary super-sized drinks.

The infected lumbered to her at a dragging pace. They resembled a group of late-night bar-goers, making their way for the nearest greasy burger joint. Holding her place in the open, she allowed all of them time to locate her. From all around her they moaned and reached for her, traversing the lot in an effort to reach her. *I have to get them all coming my way or Lindsay will never make it.*

The infected closed in faster than she expected, an ever forward moving force, and she was forced to jog ahead of them in the direction of the parking garage near the south exit. She led them past the place where Lindsay hid and gave her a nod as she passed.

"Keep it coming," she hollered back over her shoulder. She wanted all their attention on her. Not on Lindsay who needed to sneak back to her car.

Weaving in and out of the abandoned cars, she slammed doors as she passed them, creating even more noise. They funneled down the lane she created taking the path of least resistance. *Lazy bastards. Thank God they are lazy bastards.* Her bare feet pounded the pavement painfully every rock, pebble and piece of glass causing her to grimace and tip toe. Mostly, she tried to dodge the broken glass, but avoiding all of the treacherous pieces was impossible.

"Shit," she swore as a shard dug in deep into the pad of her foot. She jumped on one foot like a human pogo stick, rubbing the green glass off her sole with the palm of her hand. She chanced a glance back. The infected had closed, as she struggled with her feet. Their faces were emotionless and gore-stained as if they neither enjoyed nor despised the chase.

"Come on, you sons of bitches. I'm right here," she jeered at them. Not one of them called back. They simply drudged ahead with an inhuman tenacity. Diluted white eyes followed her. *Come with us*, they seemed to say while uttering nothing at all. It made her skin crawl. *After all, it is human nature to respond to the communications of another, isn't it?*

Her heart thundered threatening to burst from her chest. The combination of fear and exercise had driven her into a state of near frenzy. People were trying to eat her alive, and barefoot she tried to escape, like some B rate horror film.

End Time

I can only keep this up for a little while. Every dumb marathon and 10k race seemed so important at the time. I had no idea I trained for this.

She spun backward, backpedaling for a few strides. The taillights of the Jeep flicked on across the lot, bright orange illuminations of hope.

"Yesssss," she said out loud. *Lindsay made it. Just a little further.*

Gwen darted close to a parking garage, a large four story square. *Maybe I could hide in there?* Hesitating, she slowed up, momentary indecision stealing vital seconds from her. The idea evaporated as a flood of corrupted people emerged from the inside. The garage entrance angled in such a way, that the murderous people would pop out ahead of her directly in her path, cutting her safe distance a little too short. *They are going to be too close.*

Pointing herself away from the entrance, she tried to create some space away from the new comers. Something had drawn their unwanted attention, and she didn't want to be around when they caught up to her.

Bloodied business suits, tattered T-shirt clad college students and entire families surged forward. Most were slow and one man crawled, but the ones that looked more athletic were fast enough to make her panic. *Holy shit.* Gwen picked up the pace. She felt every piece of glass, stone, and metal that hammered into her feet, but adrenaline drove her onward, accented by fear of being eaten alive.

Come on, Lindsay. The mass hobbled about twenty yards behind her, but a determined defense contractor, who had the gaunt look of a triathlete, along with a couple of younger college students in George Mason University gear, were within five yards. Their heavy moaning defiled her, as though they were excited by the proximity of fresh meat.

Don't look back. Don't look back. She repeated to herself, but she had to, and immediately regretted it. *It was that odd quirk about being in danger, you always wanted to know how close you were to harm's way.*

The whites of their eyes unnerved her; they were inhuman lacking a soul. Gwen felt as though she moved in slow motion, and her assailants were tireless. She lived a nightmare while she was awake. The glass biting the bottom of her feet felt like mere pinpricks in her temporarily lucid state, but she knew from her bloody footprints across the pavement that she would require medical attention.

She must keep going. Her lungs burned and a ball of pain had built up in her side as if she were rupturing a tumor.

Where the hell is Lindsay? A small copse of birch trees lined the section between the commuter lot and the residential areas. She made for it. It was survival. Lindsay hadn't come, and she had no other option than to run for it. *Cross this street. Through those trees to those houses.* Her foot caught and everything slowed down as if the Earth stopped rotating.

She floated through the air. *That's funny, I should still be running. My feet should be pounding the pavement, but they aren't.* Gray concrete leapt for her head. She flailed her arms attempting to catch herself before she crashed into the pavement with a crack.

Stars exploded in her head as she bounced off the concrete. Immediately, she was disoriented. Gwen knew she was supposed to be moving, but she couldn't remember why. Crawling in a semi-conscious state, survival chemicals fueled her muscles and organs. It took years to sit up.

Everything continued to echo until she faintly heard them coming; the

End Time

heavy tread of clumsy footwear on the pavement; the low groans voiced their desperate pleas for her flesh. Exhausted, she let her head back down on the ground and brought her hands up to her skull. *That was odd. Why are my hands red?* She let them fall down onto her chest. *The sky is the most beautiful shade of blue.* As she faded out of consciousness, her vision filled with the ugly disgusting faces of the others.

STEELE
Washington-McCone International Airport, VA

The remainder of the counterterrorism team formed a tactical diamond with Jarl at the point and Steele and Mauser on the flanks, the other survivors clustered in the middle. Only a handful of the flight crew and embassy staff remained. Under better tactical conditions they would have someone pulling rear security, but in their dire case, the agents on the flanks took turns checking their rear. Each agent had his gun in the high ready, each warily watching his responsible sector.

Where are the good guys? Steele's vision blurred and his head ached from lack of sleep and the subsequent adrenaline dump. He was alert but tired, an excited exhaustion. He felt giddy, almost drunk, and even if he were to close his eyes his body would jerk itself awake with involuntary muscle spasms. Having told his body to stay awake for so long, it would no longer respond when he told it to go to sleep.

They marched to the terminal, allowing the Boeing 777 to shrink behind them. Dark, acidic smoke hung low, polluting the air with burning jet fuel. After about a hundred yards, Steele called them to a halt. He pulled his work phone from his front pocket. He ignored the stench and scrolled through the numbers in his phone. Finding himself awkwardly using his phone and gun, he holstered up.

His mind was not operating at peak efficiency. *Tighten it up Steele. Mistakes happen when you are tired and lose focus.* He found Ops and tapped the number. It immediately began to ring. *Finally going to get someone on the horn.*

The dial tone simply rang and rang, a never-ending buzz. Then there was an insulting click. "Hell-o," a female robot voice echoed. "This is an emergency broadcast." It was as if she were excited by the prospect of an emergency. "The Operations Center is currently experiencing technical difficulties. Please contact your supervisor for further assistance. Thank you. Ba-Bye." Click. End of transmission.

Seriously? That robot bitch. There was never a time when Operations went unstaffed; twenty-four hours a day, seven days a week, three hundred and sixty-five days a year, all holidays went covered as a support unit for agents in the field. I need assistance to hand off the 'package' and get Wheeler to the hospital, but no one had even bothered to send a bus to pick us up.

His mind struggled to wrap itself around the conundrum. *This can mean only one of two things: no one knows we are here, which is impossible because we just landed a triple seven at an airport, or they aren't capable of sending anyone to help, also impossible considering the fact that we just shot half an airplane full of ravenous disease-ridden people.* Both were clearly unfathomable. The National Capital Region was known to have some of the highest numbers of law enforcement officers in the country – over twenty thousand - and they couldn't seem to spare a couple of local PD officers to assist them. Steele stood in shock for a moment.

"Agent Steele," Dr. Jackowski addressed him.

"Not now, doc," he said, dismissing the doctor with a wave.

"That plane must be quarantined. No one must be allowed to leave it." *This guy is always blathering on about some quarantine.*

Steele's wild eyes pierced through Dr. Jackowski. He must have looked like a barbarian with a full beard, blood covered clothes and a weapon stuck through his waistband. "Joseph, I can call you that, yes?"

The scrawny doctor nodded.

"I have to get you to another security detail, get my colleague to the hospital and get ahold of my supervisors so I can tell them my team just shot a bunch of people, most of them Americans, on board an international aircraft. I sure as hell ain't getting the fuck back on that plane without more bullets, more guys, and a fucking hazmat suit."

Joseph looked as though he had been struck, but he persisted. "No, Agent Steele, I don't think *you* understand. I have clearly dictated the magnitude of this situation multiple times now, yet you, a man in a position of authority, God knows how, refuse to address it."

Steele's mouth closed tight. He didn't want to hear Joseph's words but he listened anyway, angered by the doctor's demands.

"If this disease spreads into the United States, we could be looking at a pandemic of epic proportions." Joseph looked stalwart in his conviction, pissing Steele off even more.

The man continued like a man with a stick jabbing a bear through its cage. "Like wipe out the dinosaurs. Extinct. Adios. Blamo."

Steele had enough of Joseph's mouth. Grabbing Joseph by the scruff of his neck, he shrunk away in Steele's grasp. "We can't do everything. Get back in line," Steele said, releasing the man.

Joseph pursed his lips as if to say something more, but held his tongue and nodded.

Steele knew Joseph was right. There could even be people left alive on board, but he couldn't swallow it whole.

"We're going to Terminal D. To get help," he said with a harsh glance at

Joseph. Steele out-faced him. "Let's move, NOW."

The group made painfully slow progress across the tarmac.

Planes sat idle at their gates seemingly abandoned. Only one taxied down the runway. A black, orange and yellow German flagged plane screamed into the air, lifting off only to hook to the left and go up in a fiery smoke as it barrel-rolled into the tree line surrounding the airport. The impact threw out explosive shockwaves.

"Holy shit," Mauser said, eying the smoke. "Did you guys see that?"

"Couldn't miss it. Let's hurry. Keep moving toward the terminal. We'll get on a landline and hook up with the airport authority to get help for those people." He spoke with a certainty he didn't have. *One manageable step at a time.*

Just a little further and he could go home to Gwen and his nice soft bed. At least he hoped he could. Then he would have to write a million reports. The office would probably have him filling out paperwork for months. Court dates. Lawyers. Statements. Memos. An endless headache of scrutiny. Normally, he would have dreaded the experience more than the action of doing the work, but he didn't even care at this point as long as this was all over soon.

"We got two coming out of the building. Hands are clear," Jarl called from the front of the diamond. He tracked them with his handgun much too far away for a good shot.

Steele broke formation, trying to wave them down.

"We need your help," Steele called out, brandishing his badge at them. They headed right in his direction. *Finally, somebody who can help us.* When they were about twenty feet away, he saw the markings of violence on their bodies, blue baggage handling jump suits torn asunder as if someone had taken a chainsaw to them.

"Stop there. No further," growled Steele, fumbling for his gun still in his pants.

The sound of his voice seemed to quicken their pace. They reached out, their fingers spread, trying to seize him.

"Stop now," he shouted, tripping backward as he tried to create space between himself and the two men. Not having time to get back up, Steele stayed on his back in a ground fighting position. He kicked out his heel hammering the first man's knee, bursting it back. The man collapsed and Steele crab-crawled rearward.

Jarl's shadow blurred past him, closing the distance between him and the other crazed man. With one meaty paw, he hammer-fisted the top of the man's skull. The force behind the downward strike was incredible. The baggage handler dropped, a puppet with its strings cut. It reminded Steele of the academy, when Jarl had knocked out an instructor with a single blow to the head. It had been a very short training session.

Jarl bent down and gave Steele a hand up.

"Thanks, bud," Steele said.

Eyes running away from him, Jarl manhandled Steele back to the ground, lunging forward with his booted foot. The crawling baggage claim worker's head exploded like a watermelon struck by a sledgehammer, guts splattering the ground.

"They're acting just like the crazies on the plane," he yelled at Steele.

Steele wasn't used to getting tossed around, even if it was by a giant friend. Clambering upright, he was a little shaken by the turn of events.

"Let's get in the building and get somebody on the horn who knows what's going on," Mauser said, watching the building tensely.

Steele had more than that on his mind. *The plane wasn't an isolated incident. This is happening here. We're screwed.* It would only be a matter of time before they ran out of bullets and were eaten alive.

Distant sirens brought him back. With his hand Steele shaded his eyes. Blue lights spun inside black SUVs that sped down the runway. He sighed deeply. *Finally, the cavalry comes galloping up to save the day as if they were on the wild frontier.*

"Our relief," he said to no one in particular. The haggard group let go an exhausted cheer. With his support hand, Steele felt for his tactical badge, it hung at the center of his chest on a black chain. He wouldn't die here; allies were on their way.

From around his neck he ripped off his tactical badge. The last thing he needed was some gung-ho, high-speed operator trying to be a hero and shooting him and his guys in a blue-on-blue scenario; an agent-on-agent crime of mistaken identity. It wasn't uncommon when dealing with plain-clothed military or law enforcement. Often in a violent scenario, law enforcement would zero in on threats - the gun - and, through visual exclusion and tunnel vision, fail to see the badge hanging from around the other officer's neck. High above his head he held the badge along with his gun. *They always look at the hands, because hands are where threats came from.*

The convoy of black SUVs became larger and larger, accelerating toward the small group. *These bastards better not run us over.* The vehicles screeched to a halt, forming a semi-circle around the survivors. Doors burst outward and men in black tactical gear wearing M50 CBRN protective gas masks pointed guns at them from behind open doors. Steele's initial assessment was at least ten plus CQB assault rifles pointed in their direction. *No cover. No concealment. Not very good odds. These must be the saviors we've been waiting for.*

"Drop the guns and turn around," boomed a voice from behind the center vehicle's door.

Steele kept his hands up. "We're Division agents who have been escorting this doctor back from Africa. There was some sort of disease outbreak on the plane and most of the passengers are dead. We need medical attention."

A tense silence filled the air. Steele gestured with a thumb behind him. "We need help. Do you have any EMTs with you?"

Nothing. *If these assholes shoot me, I'm gonna be so pissed.*

"Drop your guns and kneel with your hands on your heads." Steele was disgusted. After all his team had been through, these federal goons were going to treat him and his team like common criminals.

He considered the people behind him. *Once we give up our weapons, there is no guarantee we will get them back. It is part of the process.* The warm wind whipped off the concrete tarmac and ruffled his tactical striped button-down. Weariness cut him to the bone. From experience, he knew that dark bags hung low beneath his eyes, and as he glanced down at his clothes, he realized he was covered in shit, piss, blood and who knows what else. *I must look like them. The dead on the plane.* Squeezing his eyes shut, he tried to focus. He was almost surprised they hadn't just shot him already.

But what can we do? We are at their mercy and isn't this the mission? Retrieve the staffers and protect the doctor; the guy the government needed so badly.

End Time

Three of them had already died for it. Wheeler needed medical assistance immediately. This was no time for having a dick-measuring contest.

He slowly bent down, setting his SIG and badge down on the concrete. "Everyone do as they say."

He lowered himself onto the tarmac and rested his hands on his head, interlacing his fingers, feeling the grime and sweat that caked his skin. Exhaustion set in through his chest and arms from holding his weapon at the high ready for so long. Slumping forward, he let his knees grind painfully into the hot, weathered concrete.

People shuffled around behind him as the tired group quietly complied with the unnamed agents. As soon as the last person knelt in a position of disadvantage, the black-geared agents surged upon the survivors. Thick boots kicked their guns out of reach, and rifles pointed in their faces.

"You realize that's taxpayers' money you're scratching the fuck up," Mauser scolded an agent who walked past him.

"Shut up, you," the gorilla responded, giving Mauser a boot to the stomach. Mauser bent over, wheezing.

"Same team, assholes," Steele said, his hands still folded on top of his head. The handoff team simply ignored him, too focused or too arrogant to care.

One of the agents held a picture up against each of their faces. When he got to the doctor, he stopped.

"It's him," the ogre grunted, putting a hand on his earpiece. "We have the package."

Two agents grabbed Joseph by his elbows, hauling him to his feet. Another grabbed his bag.

"Wait," Joseph pleaded.

They hauled Joseph away and shoved him into the back of the unmarked SUV. *Really? This is how the handoff was going down. This is definitely going in my report, but I'm not sure anyone will care.*

"Can we get up now?" Steele called out to the speedily retreating agents. His only response was the slamming of car doors. "Where are the paramedics?" he shouted.

Engines revving, the vehicles made sharp U-turns and sped back down the runway.

The SUVs shrank smaller and smaller and faded away all together. Everything seemed so far away from the middle of the tarmac. The terminal buildings rising up like some mythical mountain range. It was like being on an island in a vast ocean of concrete runways.

Steele collected his handgun, inspecting it for scratches and finding a deep gouge running along one side of his slide. He rubbed the groove with his thumb. *That would never come out. A reminder of the time he was disrespected.*

"Who are those fucks?" Jarl asked. His English always became more broken and his accent more pronounced when he was tired or had a few too many beers.

"I assume they're the handoff team, or we're as good as fired," Steele said, looking up at his hulking colleague. "They hung us out to dry, too. Didn't even call the paramedics."

He ripped out his phone and dialed Operations again. Busy. Then he dialed his boss. Busy. Then he dialed 911. Busy. *What the hell, man?*

End Time

At this point, they should have had upper management calling for their badges and guns for shooting civilians, even if it was justified; even if the bad guys were eating the other passengers.

Steele was still trying to get his head around all the virus talk the doctor had been babbling. Secunda mortem; it sounded like a drink you get at the swim up bar at a Mexican resort. *Could there already have been a widespread outbreak in the United States?*

The virus couldn't be connected to the phone outage in Operations. There is no way it could have spread so fast; it just isn't possible. But things are bad, and no one is responding.

"What do we do now?" Captain Richards queried.

"Where should we go?" asked Mauser.

Steele simply didn't know any more. Everything that was supposed to be wasn't. Desperate faces stared back at him, but he ignored them and dialed a number on his phone.

Gwen. Oh God, was she all right? The woman who made him a better man. Checking his recent calls, he scrolled to her name and hit dial. *Please pick up, honey.* Silence. *Please get through. Please get through.* A low ringing buzzed through his phone.

"Yes," he exclaimed. He had gotten through. The phone buzzed and buzzed, but no one picked up. *Damn it Gwen.* The dead line battered his worn spirit. *What now?* He squatted down in exhaustion, anger and frustration. Heat rose from the tarmac in wavy lines. *We are alone. The whole thing is FUBARed: fucked up beyond all recognition and we are in the middle.*

"I'm not going to stand around here while junior makes personal phone calls," the copilot said, hands on hips. Steele gave him a dirty look.

"Feel free to do whatever you want," Steele said, standing upright. He had no problem smacking this guy in the face. The copilot stood upright raising his chin, a posturing move to seem taller, but if he were a fighter, he would have tucked his chin down lower.

Mauser drew Steele back from the edge. "We've got some people coming toward us." He pointed to the edge of the terminal. A group of people half-walk, half-stumbled toward them. There was no strategy to their approach.

"Look at em'," Mauser said in disbelief.

"Just like the infected on the airplane," Steele barely got out.

The pack was led by a man in a Steelers jersey who's head hung limply to the side as if the tendons in his neck had been severed, but he continued to move along with the others as if he were going to a game.

Steele slipped his tactical badge back around his neck. *I am still a federal agent, and I have a responsibility to the public. I have to get these people to safety, one step at a time. They would work this all out later. Compartmentalize.*

"Everybody up. We've got to make our way to the terminal," Steele said. People groaned. There was no time for dissent.

"Nobody's coming to get us; we're on our own. Let's move to the terminal and find help."

"Finally," the copilot said, but Steele ignored him. He could have 'words' with him later.

"Good, let's move. Stay quiet. We don't want to draw any more attention than we have to," Steele said, wiping his brow. The beard he wore made it hotter than normal, and the heat was uncharacteristically high for September. He bounded forward. *You can rest when you're dead. Or can you?* He was too tired to ponder the thought.

JOSEPH
Chantilly, VA

Starfishing in the backseat of the SUV, Joseph held on for dear life. The SUV flew through an open gate, taking the on ramp to the highway too fast. Shifting hard to the left, the vehicle clung to road with what felt like two wheels. His head whipped back and forth. *This guy is a mad man.*

"Slow down, Jake," the passenger agent said.

"I can't see shit in this mask."

The driver ripped off his mask. "I hate wearing those things."

"Protocol states that we must wear the mask while dealing with potential infected persons."

"Screw protocol, Mike. He ain't infected," Agent Jake said. They each gave him untrusting glances.

Joseph adjusted his glasses, trying to compose himself.

"I'm not infected. I would have already turned at the current mutation rate." The agents said nothing.

"Why did you leave the other team?" *We just left them standing there. Who could know their fate now? The two men on the runway were infected.* Praying wasn't his thing, but he made a silent prayer to God in case he had been wrong.

"Excuse me." Neither of the agents acknowledged his voice. He waited a second and plunged in. "Excuse me, what's happening? Are there sick people here in the U.S.? Has the outbreak struck here already?"

The chisel-jawed Agent Mike in the passenger seat turned his face to the side, eying Joseph. "You're on a need to know basis. You'll be briefed upon arrival."

He faced back to the front.

These guys were hopeless, but Joseph didn't need them or a briefing to answer his question. The signs were everywhere.

The convoy sped down the highway; just slow enough to avoid the other traffic. The traffic was ungodly. Cars honked and people shook fists at one another. People rushed to leave the area. *It is already happening. People are panicking.*

Then he saw them. They moved without grace or conformity, and stumbled from car to car, slapping windows with gore-covered fists.

Joseph pulled his safety belt around his waist, clicking it closed. Traveling upward of 50mph, as fast as possible in the congestion, the g-ride avoided other traffic but the flashing lights of the lead SUV had little impact on the passing civilians. People tried to wave them down, but the government vehicles flew on by black, sleek and unfeeling.

The driver swerved into the grassy median to get around the people at the side of the road, causing Joseph to bounce around the back seat. They huddled over a body, tearing meat from its torso. Joseph grabbed the handhold and closed his eyes.

The infection was here in the United States; that was clear. His eyes shot open. The village of Kombarka did not contain the original virus or 'patient zero.' He glanced over at his satchel. His dirt-covered, bloodstained bag holding thumb drives, his computer and blood samples that men had sacrificed themselves to obtain were mostly irrelevant. His importance in this fight was quickly diminishing.

He wondered if the government knew. *They have to know. It is happening all around them.* It would be best to keep his mouth shut. Although his satchel contained plenty of information on the disease, the information would no longer be groundbreaking.

I must have a use. Maybe I am the only doctor with any firsthand knowledge of the virus? I could be the go-to expert to decode the disease. In a scramble like this? Me, be the lead? I am just a researcher, not a conquering hero.

The SUV veered again. Joseph set his head back in his seat, feeling queasy. He had made it this far, and he knew he was still alive for a reason. If it wasn't for divine purposes, maybe it was for secular ones.

Taking a deep breath, he collected his thoughts. The virus had a much faster gestation period than he had originally perceived. People must be expiring and reanimating under an hour, depending on the location of the bite on the body. The turn rate onboard the aircraft was so much faster that the mutation must be accelerating. The idea was more terrifying than even he could imagine.

Estimating from the time he had first seen the infected people in Kombarka, to the time he saw them rise up from the dead, to the time the DRC collapsed, he strained his mind. It couldn't have been more than a few days before the DRC's collapse, and the DRC only had a few major urban centers. Once the disease hit Kinshasa the government had quickly been pushed under by waves of the infected.

There hadn't been enough time to experiment with any of the infected to understand whether they retained their memory or other basic skills. He was torn on the issue, but then he wasn't there to make ethical decisions. *If they retained their memory, they were still human. On the other hand, if they retained no memory, what was there to save? Could they even be considered human?*

Every organism had basic needs. Viruses contained genetic material, both replicated and evolved. Organisms from the animal kingdom had more complex

basic needs, air and water usually being the most important. Food coming secondary

but necessary. Shelter was a 'need,' but it wasn't strictly necessary.

People were more complex still. Sharing the same needs as animals, people

also needed shelter and social interaction. The infected persons operated at the most

basic of microbial levels, having diminished human needs. Once a person became

infected, they seemed to be driven by the need to feed or 'fuel' themselves and

procreate. But they weren't procreating in the traditional human sense. They

replicated themselves using the microbial trend; by spreading the virus to new hosts.

They transmitted the microbial data held in the saliva or blood into the new host,

enabling the virus to inject the new DNA into the host's cells.

On a molecular level, the virus was breeding continuously. If they were only

biting to spread the disease, it would make sense for the infected person to bite a

potential host and move to the next potential host. Therefore, he could infer that the

infected must acquire some energy transfer from the consumption of human flesh. Or

it could be a byproduct, side effect or symptom of the disease, much like rabies. Take

the host away and it could force the infected to either eat other animals or to face

starvation. Maybe they would eat each other. He speculated that this would not be

the case, but he didn't know.

A man stepped into the road. He waved his hands over his head, trying to

flag down the speeding vehicle.

"Look," Joseph shouted, pointing forward.

"Shit," the driver cursed. He turned the wheel hard. The SUV swerved and

clipped the man, slamming Joseph's head against the tinted glass window. It was a painful reminder of the horror of the situation. The vehicle threw the man to the side like dirty laundry, and the driver struggled to straighten it out.

Joseph thought back to Agent Reliford's attack. Reliford had retained much of his impressive strength and speed during his assault on Bowali, while the weakened villagers were still slow and debilitated from the illness that had wreaked havoc on their bodies.

The agent had exhibited no recognition or sympathy for the man he once knew. Joseph would have to make notes about that in his research. They needed more time and more experimentation on the infected to find out whether any of his assumptions were true.

Given all of these facts, his aircraft must not have been the first to transport the infected to the United States. Considering the number of large cities combined with the landmass of the United States, the U.S. probably had less than a month before the entire nation was overrun. Combined with international travel from other countries, the infection could potentially spread even quicker. The infection would spread slower in rural areas, but it would still spread, creeping anywhere a person could go.

Had the government known anything at all? Was I even supposed to come out alive? The thought made him a little more suspicious of his new acquaintances.

There were too many questions and not enough time. As if to accentuate the fact, they passed four police officers that were beating a man with nightsticks. It spread so fast. They needed to warn people to stay inside, avoid the infected and stockpile food. Hospitals needed to be prepped for safely treating infected people. Police and military needed to be briefed to deal with mass evacuation and safe handling of infected persons. *Anything. Whatever emergency plan the government had, it needed to activate now.*

"When did you first see the infection here?"

The agents exchanged a look. "Sir, no more questions please until we reach the facility," Agent Jake said.

Joseph shook his head. Zero help from these goons.

"But off the record, the first Zulu I saw was three days ago," he said.

Zulu? "What does Zulu mean?"

"It's what we call them. Zombies."

The passenger agent stared ahead, not acknowledging his partner.

"Thank you," Joseph said.

"For what?" Agent Jake said.

Joseph nodded. The conversation had never happened.

This was very bad. Mentally, he envisioned a map of the United States with D.C. and other East Coast cities on which small red dots represented infection. As the weeks went by the dots grew in diameter, with wider and wider circles spreading across the country until the U.S. was one big blood-red outline.

He squeezed his eyes shut. *Oh God.* This disease could have the same dramatic effects smallpox, influenza, bubonic plague and other diseases had had upon Native American populations during the first European contacts. Except those had killed ninety percent of indigenous people over hundreds of years, and those who had died stayed dead. And when the Europeans had first interacted with the Native Americans, people weren't living nearly as close together.

He had to stop the microbe or there would be no world left. He needed to be updated on what was happening elsewhere.

A new sense of urgency took hold of him. The two agents sat in silence as they drove.

"Where are we going?"

Agent Jake turned his head halfway toward Joseph. "A secure location," he said, taking the car into a ditch and gunning it, causing the turf to fly up from the grassy center median.

They flew by cars that were stuck in traffic. Nowhere would be secure for long if they couldn't come up with a way to combat the virus. *These guys have no idea*, thought Joseph.

"How much longer before we get there?"

"We're thirty minutes out. People will be wanting to talk to you when we arrive," Agent Mike said.

Joseph folded his arms across his chest, sulking down in his seat a little.

"I bet they will," he murmured under his breath. He closed his eyes, shutting out the chaos that zipped past him. Feeling sick to his stomach, his mouth started to water. He wasn't sure if he was getting carsick or if it was simply a bodily response to envisioning the impending doom of mankind.

NIXON
Washington-McCone International Airport, VA

Agent Nixon lay in the back galley of the plane. His head pushed painfully on a metal beverage cart, secured in place with a red clip. Bright red blood pumped from his veins with every beat of his heart. The deep bites covering his body burned like fire. He lifted himself into an almost upright position. Pain shot through his limbs like a thousand knives sticking him. Bodies of the deceased and infected lay around him in a pile of disgusting carnage.

He struggled to push the remains of a Foreign Service Officer he knew from Kinshasa off his chest. *Was her name Kalyn? Putting thoughts together is like fumbling through a dense fog. Breathing is hard. No matter now.* The FSO's eyes looked like a doll's; lifeless and open, seeing but not.

When the plane engaged its final landing sequence, many of the dead had been pulled backwards by the G-force, causing the bodies to tumble, slide or roll into the rear galley. He had tried to cover himself as they all started toward the galley, but he couldn't stop the tortured bodies from landing on him. He was a mere child swiping at falling rocks. Sharp pain plagued his legs, but he was unable to pinpoint the source as if his legs were broken into tiny pieces.

Every movement was a monumental task. Picking his head up, he tried to see his legs. A young woman, her throat chewed out, looked up at him. He couldn't say she had made eye contact, but they had made a connection on some sort of animalistic level. *Hunter and prey?*

Flesh hung loosely from her neck, exposing her pink ringed trachea and damaged vital arteries. Her pale white eyes stared blankly, with no recognition that he was either human or alive. She chewed noisily through her macabre face. A chain hung around her neck and a shiny gold shield dangled from it. *That…is familiar. I… should know what it is.*

"Argghh," he managed to put out instead.

She cocked her head to the side like an inquisitive dog and bent back down close to his body, but all he felt was pain. Exhausted, he laid his head back down.

Acid rose in his throat and he turned to the left and spat. A frothy, reddish globule spattered onto what remained of the upper half of a male flight attendant. His lower half gone.

Agent Nixon thought about his partner, Agent Reliford. He had shot Reliford in the head as he tore apart their interpreter. *Who…for me?*

Soon he would join his stiff comrade. He had known he was a goner the second he was hauled into one of the lavatories. *Bastard…must have…taking a shit.*

The monster's pants had been down around his ankles and, if Nixon hadn't been within arm's reach, the half-naked man wouldn't have been able to bite him or even pursue him. He probably would have just tripped and fallen.

Nixon had pushed the bathroom assailant down, the man's pants easily tripping him. But it was already too late; he had been bitten. He had cursed himself for not having been more careful. *Just too…many infected.*

He had told Mauser to leave him to hold off as many of these damn things as possible. The bodies of six infected lay about him as testament to his sacrifice.

Things were getting hazy. *This is it.* A reddish hue surrounded his peripherals, giving him a fiery tunnel vision. His blood boiled in his veins, but oddly enough he felt as though he were getting better. He embraced the painlessness. It had to be the virus. Nixon wanted to laugh, and he wanted to die. Instead, he gave out a pathetic, bloody cough.

He tried to finger the gun that lay at his side, slick with blood. *Is that...my blood? I must have...one...bullet.*

The handgun felt like it weighed a thousand pounds in his hand, but he hefted it anyway, straining to point it as close to his left temple as he could. *One... effort...peace.* His finger shook as it depressed the trigger. Centimeter by painful centimeter it moved rearwards. Click. *Damn...would...have been...nice...to die.*

Nixon pulled himself upright. Wobbling a bit, he realized something wasn't right with his legs. His entire vision was now a red blur. Hunger penetrated his entire form, the only thing driving him forward.

A female stood up next to him. They ignored each other. *Not prey.* Having surrendered himself to the virus, Nixon had no control left over his limbs. The thing dropped from his grasp, falling with a loud thud as it hit the body of food. *No need for that. It would just get in the way.*

Stumbling down the aisle of the plane, he dragged his non-functioning leg behind him. *That didn't matter. There is no more pain. Only the need to feed. Feed. Feed.* The hunger dominated him. When he reached food, he would stop and eat. He would never be full with the endless hunger that plagued him.

Not knowing why, he needed to feed desperately. It was as if it had always been inside of him, a part of his DNA, but he only just realized it. Falling, he dug his hands into the food that lay in the aisle. He ate his fill, stuffing it into his mouth. He would have kept eating, but loud noises nagged him from outside. Like the siren's call, he was drawn to them. Some of the others rose up and followed him out the plane door.

He pulled himself outside into the daylight. The man formerly known as Agent Nixon twisted his head left to right, listening for the sound of prey. His milky white eyes looked up at the sky. His tattered, gore-covered clothes rippled in the warm breeze that he would never acknowledge was there. Warm or cold, he felt neither. The man that was once Agent Nixon cared not if it was even possible for him to care anymore. The only thing he knew was that there was more prey up ahead. *Prey always made noise. Let the feeding frenzy begin. FEED.*

STEELE
Washington-McCone International Airport, VA

Steele's group neared the terminal, a dark gray building, three stories high with long windows running down its sides for air travelers to see the taxiing airplanes.

A big pedestrian vehicle, unique to McCone, called a mobile lounge, sat connected to the side of the building like a loading dock. The vehicle was large, old and ugly, and Steele had ridden in one more times than he could count. As a frequent traveler, Steele hated the thing. The people, the musty smell, the way the driver took corners, the way peoples' bags toppled over, the times when people wouldn't create space to fit others on board; his complaints were endless.

Steele regularly found himself smashed up inside of a mobile lounge with scores of other jet-lagged travelers trying to not fall over. It was as if the airport wanted you to have just one more miserably claustrophobic experience just after you escaped the confines of the last miserable experience: the aircraft. Lazily, the airport would only send one mobile lounge to pick up incoming flights, forcing the passengers to wait and then travel in the most uncomfortable fashion possible.

He exchanged looks with Mauser.

"Are you thinking what I'm thinking?" Mauser asked, circling the base of the vehicle.

"You know I hate these things," Steele said, kicking one of the giant five-foot tractor tires with his boot, finding the mover sturdy.

Mauser chuckled. "Funny thing is, this bastard machine might just be our ticket out of here."

Since the early sixties, Washington-McCone International Airport had used the latest technology of large 'mobile lounges' to transport people from the main terminal to the outer terminals and aircraft. McCone had yet to complete its rail system maintaining its mobile lounge transportation system for most of the airport.

"Can you believe they still use these things?" Steele asked.

"I don't get it either. Give me a hand."

The passenger cabin stood far enough off the ground that Mauser would need a boost to lift himself up to the long rectangle seating area lined with windows. A sophisticated hydraulic system would raise the cabin from its driving position to the docking position in order to connect with a terminal building.

"Let's get Mauser up there to see if this thing's operational," Steele said in a low voice to Jarl. They hoisted him up.

Mauser peered over the lip of the floor. When they dropped him back down he described a grisly scene.

"By the doors that connect the mover to the terminal there are two people: a cute blonde in a sundress; and a douche in ripped jeans and a T-shirt," he said.

"Infected?" Steele asked, but he already knew the answer.

"Does eating people count?" Mauser said.

"Yes."

"They're eating, quite loudly, what appears to be the remains of the driver, Alan," Mauser said.

"They got Alan?" Jarl said angrily, clenching a fist. Jarl had befriended the plump older driver on their frequent trips together.

"Sorry, buddy. I say we waste 'em," Mauser said.

"Mauser, you know what to do. And do it quick. We're drawing some unwanted attention." Steele pointed to the edge of the terminal. The crowd had followed their movements and was on its way.

"No worries," Mauser said, flinging open his out-the-front blade with the push of a button.

Jarl and Steele helped him back up to the ledge and Mauser disappeared as he crouched low. They heard a scuffle and the thuds of two bodies hitting the floor. A minute later, Mauser's familiar face leaned over the ledge.

"Good to go," he announced with a thumbs up.

An emergency ladder was lowered down to Steele, who helped the other survivors up. The remainder of the group scampered up into the people mover while Jarl covered them.

The carnage in the cabin was prolific. Bloody bits and pieces covered most of the space designed for about one hundred passengers, soaking into the mover's maroon-carpeted floor, making it squish beneath their feet.

"People must have fled on here trying to escape," Steele said at a whisper.

"Doesn't look like it worked."

"Shhh. You hear that." Mauser's eyes went wide.

Something dragged itself along the tile floor of the terminal, scraping as it went.

"The doors are open," Steele breathed. They both bolted for the connecting terminal doors, but Steele was a step ahead. He slammed it closed with a bang, leaning his back against it, while the ugly disfigured faces of the infected appeared above. They snarled and clawed at the glass.

"Hurry up," Steele said with his back pushed against the door. Mauser strained driving his legs into the door. The weight of the infected forced it open a crack. A stained hand stuck through grasping for Steele. He shoved his back into it again hard, crunching the door closed. "I'll cover the door. Help Jarl," he grunted. Mauser nodded sprinting to the other end of the vehicle.

Without Mauser's help he fought a losing battle, Steele watched helplessly as he was driven forward. Spreading his back wide, he squatted low and thrust into the door. It closed, but only for a moment.

On the other end of the mobile lounge, Mauser bear hugged Wheeler inside. He could feel the weight as more people pushed against the door. His tendons stretched to the point of snapping, his muscles were beyond their capacity. The infected bellowed into his ear, a deep gnar forcing Steele to turn his head away. *I can't hold this much longer.* He readied himself to spring forward and begin shooting the last of his bullets.

"Mauser, I can't hold it." The other survivors just watched his losing battle in horror. He gave the infected inch by inch. Much more and they would wedge themselves in the begrudged space and it would be over.

Mauser vaulted into the driver's compartment. "I'll take it from here Alan," he said morbidly. With a rattle of its large diesel engine, Mauser ignited the people mover and it roared to life. "I always wondered what it would be like to drive one of these things," Mauser yelled over his shoulder.

Jarl barreled forward leaning his weight on the door. From their elevated viewpoint into the terminal lobby, a great mob of the infected marched in their direction.

"We won't be able to hold," Jarl growled.

Mauser hit the gas, ripping them away from the terminal but failing to remove the lounge's overhanging attachment. Steele fell to the side, his counter pressure gone, grabbing a gooey seat to help himself up. Mauser rocked them free.

A long elastic overhang extended like an accordion and collapsed, banging into the mover.

"I guess I was supposed to retract that thing before driving," Mauser laughed.

Some of the survivors cried out, as they were jostled around, grasping for handrails. Mauser pulled the lounge to the side of a building where other mobile lounges sat. Great ancient beasts sitting dormant like an elephant graveyard. *Maybe they could blend in. Hide for a while and take a break. Wait until someone came to help. They all needed a break.*

The survivors huddled almost on top of one another in the relatively unblemished corner section of the vehicle. The rest of the mobile lounge was a mess. Blood doused the long panoramic windows in modern paint-like streaks. Half-consumed bodies lay on the floor strewn out amongst an air traveler's intestines and unclaimed limbs. A man in fatigues, probably an active duty soldier, sat slumped in his seat. His neck bent at a strange angle and his eyes were wide open. He stared indifferently, his eyes seeming to follow Steele's every move.

The agents however were offered no respite. As long as these people were under their protection they couldn't rest.

Mauser spun around in the driver's seat, covering his nose. "Look at all the bodies."

"We have to dump them," Steele said, feeling queasy as he stared at someone's lone leg. Keeping diseased bodies on board would be detrimental to both their physical and mental health, in particular having to stare at the remains of other victims.

Steele pushed open the sliding doors. "Looks like we attracted some visitors below," he said in disgust. The dead had already found them. *So much for hiding.*

"We should shoot the crazies," Jarl bellowed, "not feed them."

"We can't shoot them all. Help me or don't, but they can't stay here," Steele said. Jarl scratched at his beard, lost in thought, but he followed suit.

"I don't like this," Jarl said, but he hoisted a body onto his shoulder anyway.

Led by Steele, the agents dumped the dead bodies out the doors of the mover. It devastated them psychologically. It was one thing to deal with the action of taking someone's life who posed an imminent threat to yourself and the public. Steele had been prepared to live with that action. Even worse was to see your friends slain, but also in the realm of possibility. But it was entirely off the charts, to toss and inadvertently feed dead bodies to diseased people who fed upon them like starving men.

The infected gathered eagerly, awaiting the bodies like goldfish clustering around scattered bread in a pond.

"You're just going to let those things eat them?" an Asian female State Department Officer asked.

"Yes," Steele grunted, as he and Mauser swung a body out the doors. It landed on the pavement with a loud thud.

"You can't do that. It's… It's inhumane," the female staffer said.

Steele set down a woman's legs, her sundress twisted oddly. The light flowered garment a reminder of the summer. A piece of human flesh hanging from her mouth betrayed her. Her once pleasant appearance tarnished by violence. *Summer is at an end.*

He walked over to the State Department Officer and pointed a bloody finger at her. "You're right. It *is* inhumane. It's one of the most depraved acts I can think of. But do you know what the alternative is? Have you thought about what would happen if we left the bodies in here?" he demanded.

Her chin tilted upward. "No, but there has to be a better way," she snapped.

Steele didn't have time for her politically correct bullshit. "The alternative is to leave these people in here and have them get back up and eat us. Or maybe it'll spread to us through the air. Maybe we'll catch something else altogether from the bodies. Let alone the fact they stink already. No, there's nothing nice about this, but it's going to happen, so get used to it and take a seat, sweetheart."

The woman sat down with a "humph."

"If you don't like it, you can get out," Steele said, pointing to the door. She shot him daggers with her eyes. *That should shut her up for a minute.*

Does she think I enjoy feeding infected cannibals with the bodies of the deceased? Does she think I want it like this? Does she think I get pleasure out of it? I am no monster. I would much rather be sitting on a beach somewhere with an ice-cold beer, but sometimes you didn't have a choice. The cards were dealt, and you played with what you had. All the while, hoping that you could scrape together a win.

When they were done lobbing the bodies out of the mover, Steele tried to ignore the hapless, noisy feast on human flesh that was taking place below. *They are no longer human.* Steele watched people in the terminal - more of the infected - pounding on the glass doors in an attempt to break out.

Night fell over the people mover and the survivors sat in silence. Crystal made the only noise rummaging through someone's luggage. Steele was too tired to care if she scored some new clothes.

"What are you doing?" Mauser asked her in a hushed tone.

"Put this on tough guy," she laughed throwing a lacy shirt his direction.

Mauser's eyes darted back and forth and Steele was sure he was probably blushing.

"Ah. You're into some kinky kinda stuff," Mauser said spreading it across his chest.

"Yeah do it," Steele echoed softly. Crystal giggled a bit.

"Found one for you Mark," she tossed Steele a night gown.

"I don't know what to say. I can't say I'm a fan."

"Its for the seats, goofballs," she said smiling.

"Ohh. Gotcha," Steele said. "Thought you were going to do it," he said to Mauser, nudging him.

"Me too."

They wiped down the seats, windows, and handrails making the lounge a little bit more hospitable. Plopping onto the floor, Steele tried to dodge a bloodstain. He leaned against the seat back and closed his eyes, the first rest he had had in over twenty-four hours. He dozed for a time, but as much as he wanted to sleep he couldn't drift off.

His mind raced, images flashing up one after another. The woman he had killed. Gwen. The infected. The doctor. The survivors. His parents. His friends from work. Andrea. His body kept involuntarily shaking him back awake, as if it knew its preservation depended on his alertness.

Unable to find peace, he checked his watch and studied the infected below. The monsters had finished their unholy meal, and hundreds of hands reached for the living in the mobile lounge. They shuffled in place each undead person staring expectantly. A sorrowful tune of pain and suffering emitted from their morbid lips.

Steele turned away from his undaunted single minded foes. *We are in a tight spot. No help. No relief in sight. We're going to have to gut this one out.* Mauser sat in the driver's seat, his head resting on the steering wheel. Jarl sat on a bench and gazed out the window, his large arms crossed, looking every inch the predator of men. He waited for the go-ahead to rip apart the enemy below them. Regular men wouldn't stand a chance against him. But these were no longer men.

Steele clicked the circular button near the bottom of his phone, illuminating a picture of Gwen and him on a cruise. He pressed the white speech bubble and a new screen sprung open. Steele ran his thumb over the screen, dragging it downward over and over. Her last message said, *"I love you. Be safe."* He pulled the screen down again. Nothing changed. *"I love you. Be safe." I'm coming back for you,* he thought.

His mind ran circles. *She could be anywhere, or she could be dead. No. She can't be dead. I have to get back to her.* He had always promised her that nothing would stand in the way of him getting back to her. Nothing. If he had to crawl out of the pits of hell itself, he would do it.

He had known that she was the one as soon as he met her. He remembered thinking, *this girl needs someone like me in her life*. When she had pulled him close for their first kiss, it had felt like stars colliding. He knew that when feelings like that were real, they created a true and inseparable bond.

Lost in his thoughts Steele scratched at his beard, removing flaked blood. The sooner he delivered the civilians to safety, the sooner he could go find Gwen. Stalking over to the driver's compartment, he patted a woman's shoulder as he passed. He was trying to keep it level for the survivors. People needed a shepherd in times of crisis, and although he had always thought of himself as one, it wasn't until now that he really knew what it was to be one.

They didn't know how bad this was yet, and obviously some portion of the government still operated. But they weren't active in McCone. Maybe McCone was compromised; maybe it was under some sort of quarantine. That meant there could be secure areas nearby where he could seek help for their wounded.

He knelt by Wheeler, who laid on his back, skin dangerously pallid. Steele gently planted two fingers on his carotid artery. His skin cold and clammy to the touch, but a faint pulse still remained.

"Hang in there, you tough old bastard," Steele said under his breath.

Steele continued to the driver's compartment, placing a hand on Mauser's shoulder. "You all right, man?"

Mauser slowly sat up, blinking and staring around, wide-eyed. "What?" he wiped his mouth. "Just tired."

Steele exhaled loudly. "Hang in there. How many rounds you got left?"

Mauser ejected the magazine from his handgun. "Just eight, man."

Steele knew Mauser could see they were in a tight spot. "Say, you wanna make a trade?" Steele asked his friend. Mauser narrowed his eyes wary of some sort of trick.

"What ya' got?" he said cautiously.

Steele rummaged around in his pockets pulling out a spare mag. "I'll trade you twelve hollow point rounds for a chew," Steele said, placing the mag in his hand.

Mauser grinned from ear to ear, pulling out a green tin from his pocket. Holding the tin in between his thumb and middle finger, he whipped his hand letting his index finger slap the outside of the can. After packing the small granules to one side, he opened the tin with a twist. Steele preferred natural flavor, but wintergreen long cut would do in a pinch.

"It's a deal," Mauser said with a tired smile, shoving the full mag in his pocket. Steele took a wad of the grainy tobacco from the tin between his forefingers and his thumb, and placed the chew into the bottom-left corner of his lip. He could feel the surge of nicotine and other chemicals enter his blood stream.

"Thanks bro, you're a lifesaver," Mauser said.

"Don't say I never hooked you up," Steele said, spitting onto the floor.

Steele didn't 'chew' on the regular. *If I am going to stay awake any longer, I'm going to need it.* Nauseousness lurked behind its invigoration. Mauser threw some into his mouth, losing some onto the front of his shirt. He wiped the black granules onto the floor.

Opening a side window in the driver's compartment, he spat down onto the infected below. He was rewarded with a chorus of moans. "How do you like that?"

he hollered down toward them. He turned toward Steele. Dark circles hung beneath his eyes, making him seem older than he was.

"I'm not sure anyone is coming for us," Mauser said. He patted the steering wheel. "But this thing can handle just about anything. We could just drive out of here."

"How long's it been since we landed?" Steele asked him.

"About four hours," he said with a glance at his big watch face.

"I'm afraid to see what it looks like out there, but I think you're right. Nobody's coming," Steele replied. "Let's get everyone together and talk about our options."

Steele clapped his hands quietly. "Everybody listen up," he said.

Scared, eager eyes stared back at him. He stood in front of them. There was no point being nervous now. He was in charge whether he wanted to be or not. *Isn't this what I wanted: a chance to prove myself?* That thought made butterflies bounce even faster, along with fear of not living up to his own lofty standards.

How does one empathize with the terror we have been through? Is it too soon? I'm no psychiatrist. What could you possibly say to someone who just saw their friends and family eaten alive?

Wheeler would have known what to do. He would have known exactly what to do. He eyed the survivors, another pang of butterflies filling his stomach and subsiding.

"For those of you who don't know me, I'm Agent Steele. Here with me are Agent Mauser, Agent Thorfinson and Agent Wheeler, who is incapacitated at the moment. We've tried to contact the local police and paramedics, but we haven't been able to get through to them yet." He spit chew on the floor growing confidence with every word.

The staffer, who had been giving Steele hell earlier, lifted her head promptly. Her eyes bored into him, judging him like he was prized cattle on display. "Why can't we go into the terminal? I'm sure there's help inside, or at least a bathroom."

"I'm sorry. What can I call you?" Steele said, taking a seat across from her.

"I'm Foreign Service Officer Kim. I'm the embassy lead for financial aid programs to the DRC," she said with some pomp. "What kind of agents are you guys? Like FBI or CIA?" she asked.

Steele smiled briefly. "Neither. We're part of the Counterterrorism Division. Just think of us as your guardian angels."

"Well, I've never heard of that organization," she said, crossing her arms.

Steele grinned. "Good, FSO Kim. That's just the way we prefer it. If you don't know we're there, it's a good day for everyone. And as to your question earlier, we know that there are infected inside, and we have no idea if we can get help. As far as I can tell, the outbreak on our plane has already struck here. And it's bad," Steele said, stroking his beard.

She glared at him, unbelieving. Steele knew FSO Kim would be the death of him. She needed everything spelled out to her, questioning his every move. It was infuriating.

"How do you know?" she asked.

"Frankly, Ms. Kim, we can't tell. For our country's sake, I hope we are in a quarantine zone so at least we would know rescue is on the way."

He jabbed his index finger at the terminal doors. An infected man with his scalp hanging loosely to one side ground his face against the glass, while others crowded around him.

"I know this. Those people right there are infected, and they mean to do us harm. So we're not going in there. If the virus were airborne, we would already be infected because of the airplane's air recirculation system. We also know that the disease makes them fearless with a taste for human." Mauser chuckled from behind.

"Those were our friends on the plane," a man in a blazer said angered sitting upright.

"I lost colleagues as well. So don't think for a moment that I enjoy discussing the intricacies of our assailants," Steele said. He gave Mauser a backward glance. *A little less crass next time.* The agents would often use humor as a morbid coping tool. Something that many people would never understand.

FSO Kim sat back arms still folded under her chest. "How do we know its not airborne?"

At this rate, Steele would tug the beard off his face. They questioned everything he said. *Can't they just accept my answers and move on? Wheeler would have had them eating out of the palm of his hand by now.*

"Let's just call it an educated guess," he said, pausing while he let that sink in. "Body shots only appear to slow them down. Headshots will stop them. I wish the doctor were here to explain some of the science."

As the representative speaker for the airline crew, Captain Richards spoke up. "What about the guys who grabbed the doctor? Why didn't they help us?"

That is a sore subject. Being left for dead by the other agents, was a definite low point in his day. A betrayal by men who were on the 'same team' would be something that he never forgot. Steele didn't know why they had been left behind, but any reason was a bad reason.

"Your guess is as good as mine. It seemed to me they were getting the hell out of here, no questions asked."

Disappointment filled their faces, but no one objected.

"We're gonna stay put until we hear something from somebody. I suggest you get some rest. I have some protein bars in my bag."

Steele never left for a mission without a significant supply of protein bars, tuna packs, nuts and other high-protein foods. He had traveled enough to be cautious of the airline food. "We'll update you when we have new information." Steele left them to their own thoughts and joined Mauser in the front.

"Nice speech. Anything else you don't know?"

"I know nothing except what I can see, and right now, that ain't much," Steele said. "Can you get the radio working?"

Mauser flipped some switches in the side of the compartment and a static filled radio sprang to life. "I'll mess with it here and see if we can pick something up."

Steele's own internal dilemma preoccupied his mind. "As soon as we get these people to safety, I'm out. Mission accomplished," Steele said. "Got to get home."

Mauser nodded, watching him. He understood why Steele needed to get home.

Steele hit redial on his phone again, only to hear the busy tone. He gazed at the smartphone in distress, taking in Gwen's caller ID picture, which lit up the background of the screen.

"Ah, man. I'm sure she's fine. You two will be back in each other's arms before you know it. I got your six."

"Yeah, I know," Steele mumbled.

Having someone's six meant that you covered his six o'clock position or his back; someone's most vulnerable position. *That's all well and good*, thought Steele, but his gut told him things were going to get much worse.

The hours ticked on, and night descended upon them. The radio spewed static and, after an hour of messing with it, Mauser eventually turned it down. The remaining CT agents took turns standing watch as the moans of the dead rose up from beneath them like an ungodly choir. The survivors dozed in and out of fevered consciousness.

Steele took the middle watch. Performing a magazine exchange, he situated the half-full mag into his magazine pouch, and slid the full one into his gun. They were never geared up for a war. As undercover agents in the field, they carried just enough rounds per person to put some serious damage down-range quickly. Unless they were deployed to a combat zone, they would never suit up like a SWAT team or a Special Operations unit. They couldn't realistically carry around hundreds of rounds of ammunition or the heavy weapons needed for an extended combat situation. *Give me a long gun, hell, give me just some more ammo, and this would be a totally different scenario.*

He glanced down at the mass of people gathered below. In the dark, their constant movements made them look like a sea of maggots: shuffling forms of death; always eating, never resting. Their ranks swelled as mangled, charred corpses from the crashed flight added to their horde. Helicopters thundered past them above. *We're alive down here*, he thought, silently shouting for their help.

After an hour of nothing, the monotony of his watch was suddenly broken.

Buzzzzzzzz. Beep. Beep. The radio lit up, abruptly coming to life. "This is MWAA police, you guys all right? Anybody there? Over."

Steele leapt over to the radio in the driver's compartment.

Mauser beat him to it. He held down the radio microphone key. "Ah, yeah, we're alive in here. This is Agent Mauser speaking. To whom am I speaking? Over."

Ten tense seconds passed, and they held their breath.

The radio crackled. "This is Officer Summerdyke. We're in a utility shed on the far side of the airstrip 0-9-L. Can you make it to us? Over."

Steele exchanged looks with Mauser.

"Yeah, we should be able to. What's in the shed?" Mauser said.

"It goes underground. Over." The radio fell silent.

"Excellent, we'll be over in a few," Mauser said, glancing at Steele, who nodded his approval.

"Just keep it down. Last time we checked, there were a few of them near the door on the surface," Summerdyke said.

"Copy that, we're on the move."

Mauser threw the mover into reverse jolting everyone awake, and steered for the edge of the tarmac. Driving around the airport could have been a slow process if the airport was active. The vehicle rumbled down the middle of the runway the only mobile vehicle in sight.

"What's going on?" Jarl yelled, reaching up to grab a handrail.

"MWAA is in a shed," Steele yelled, holding onto the side of the driver's compartment.

"What are they doing in there?"

"Probably hiding," Steele called back. "Something that we're going to do too." The mobile lounge mushed the infected under its massive tires, swaying.

"Wahoo," Mauser shouted. "Take that you stupid fuckers," he called out in glee.

To their right, the runway lights glowed yellow and blue in the night signaling a safe place to land, but no planes glided in. *The skies aren't the problem,* he thought. Mauser circled the runways, backtracking twice in an attempt to locate the utility shed.

On their third pass around the airport, Steele began to think they had been duped. He scanned the darkness looking for something that looked like a shed. "You see that? There," he said, pointing at the beacon. "That must be it." A single light flicked on and off in the distance.

"Get ready to disembark. Jarl, you and me are on bad guy duty. Everyone else make for the building."

"Good to go," Jarl called back.

"Incoming," Mauser yelled. A moment later Steele found himself sitting on the lounge bench. The mobile lounge rocked back and forth as Mauser crushed the infected people below.

"Got 'em," Mauser called back, spitting tobacco out the window.

Steele used a handrail to pull himself upright. "Don't fuck up our only mode of transportation, please."

"Oh, come on, man. Gotta have a little fun with it."

Mauser slammed on the brakes, almost crashing into the concrete shed near the side of a runway. Tall trees stood like dark sentinels behind the little brick of a building. Acres of forest surrounded the airport, and a great deal of wildlife could be found residing within the grounds.

The building was a simple, windowless structure with a couple of antennae on top and a large steel door. The light revealed six infected people crowding close to the door. As one they faced the mobile lounge.

"We're here," Mauser called back, a huge ball of chew protruding from his lip.

Steele jumped down from the mover, crouching into a roll to absorb the impact. He immediately scanned his surroundings, using his flashlight to light up the trees, left and right. A large shadow landed behind him, marking the arrival of Jarl.

Their flashlights were out in an over-under flashlight-gun grip. This was the most accurate grip if the flashlight wasn't attached to the gun, but it still wasn't as accurate as a standard two-handed grip, because only one hand was gripping the weapon while the other held the flashlight. However, by pushing the backs of their hands together it created a semi-steady platform that was more accurate than shooting with one hand.

Steele pressed the button on his tactical light shining it in the faces of the dead. Gore splattered faces snarled at him in the night, and he unleashed a deadly barrage of single, well-aimed headshots in quick succession, driving his hips from threat to threat.

One of the ugly bastards got within a yard of Steele, baring blackened teeth. Steele disintegrated the back of his skull with a shot through the Fatal T. In a matter of seconds, the infected were loudly vanquished.

Steele and Jarl sprinted to the door and Steele placed a heavy hand down on the flat handle. The door rattled mocking them, and didn't open. Steele pushed and pulled harder, but nothing happened. *The stinking thing is locked. This has to be the right utility shed.*

He looked around. There was nothing remotely like it in sight. *Could there be another shed?* Steele frantically pulled on the door. Unable to produce any results he turned to Jarl.

"You want to take a swing at it?" he asked. The giant huffed as he gripped the door and pulled. Nothing.

This is bad. They could shoot the hinges, but that would leave the shed exposed. The other survivors had already started helping each other down from the mobile lounge and were huddling around the door.

"Hurry up," FSO Kim said.

"I can hear them coming," Crystal hushed, looking over her shoulder. Their white eyes were wide with fright in the night.

Jarl hammered on the door with a closed fist. More of the infected emerged from the shadows as if the devil were spawning them himself. Closing in, their survival decreased with each spent bullet and each fleeting second.

A single infected man covered in black blood with dead eyes rounded the side of the utility building. Steele saw him, but couldn't move fast enough.

"Watch out," Steele managed to sputter, but the infected pounced on a bewildered Captain Richards. Steele pushed the copilot out of the way as he scrambled toward the Captain.

The force of the encounter took the Captain to the ground like a wrestling match. The cannibalistic man's teeth tore into Richards' arms as he tried to prevent him from mauling his face. A person's natural inclination was to protect the face and neck. Now, it didn't matter where you were bitten. It only matters that you had been defiled.

Steele moved within a few yards of the struggle. "Push his head up," he shouted flashlight illuminating the bloodied attacker.

Richards must have heard him, because he shoved both arms up, raising its body away from his. The infected's ugly, disfigured head swerved back and forth as it tried to reach more of the pilot's flesh.

Steele fired his handgun pulverizing the assailant's nose, ending its miserable second life. Confused the pilot stared at his arms.

"Oh no, oh no," Richards cried out, turning in Steele's direction for help. Dark stains seeped through his white pilot shirt corrupting his once professional appearance.

Mournful moans announced the arrival of more infected. Steele ripped a shot over Richards head dropping an infected into a heap of flesh and guts. Seconds stood between them being overrun. He grabbed the pilot by the back of the shirt and pulled him up.

"You know we can't let you down there. You're infected," Steele said.

The Captain's eyes panicked, the blood draining from his face. "No. I can't be. I feel fine," he said, nodding his head as if to convince himself.

Steele shook the man hard.

"This only ends in one way," Steele said, gripping his handgun. *I don't want to shoot him. I don't want to waste a bullet better left for the dead.* Slowly, the realization of his impending doom crossed the man's face.

"I can't be," Captain Richards started. He wiped the blood from his arms repeatedly as if it would stop the infection racing through his veins.

"Save us."

The Captain's wide brown pupils stared back, clutching his arms. "I'll do what I can. I'll draw them away," he said, shaking but regaining his dutiful composure.

The Captain turned and yelled, "Over here. Over here. Come and get it, you filthy bastards." He ran into the darkness of the night, and that was the last they saw of him.

Mauser cut the engine and hopped down. Jarl still banged away at the reinforced steel door with his shoulder. The moans of the dead surrounded them like wolves howling in the night. *The Captain bought us a few seconds.* The frontrunners of the hideous dead materialized in the dim light.

Steele began a controlled backpedal, picking off the closest of the infected, always keeping his enemy in front of him. His back smacked into the wall of the shed. *Back against the wall. Literally.* He was trying to conserve his ammo, but did it matter if he died with a full mag in his pouch. Mauser was next to him, unleashing a hail of bullets into the infected. The shouts of the survivors echoed in the background, sheep mewing in the face of the wolf.

Jarl pounded away on the door, his large fist beating into the metal. He hesitated momentarily, as an elderly black man wearing an airline cap, poked his head through the door.

"Keep it down, we know you're here," the man said, opening the door a crack. Jarl forearmed the man inside, and the survivors piled in.

Steele and Mauser brought up the rear and slammed the door behind them. Steele took a deep breath, his heart thumping away after his latest brush with death. *Safety.*

He took a step away from the door as he heard the infected bodies ramming it. Wham. Wham. Wham. Wham. The door reverberated in response to each new assault. It grew louder as more and more people threw themselves against it. Fingernails screeched down the metal, worse than a chalkboard, repeatedly clawing the door. The harsh noise pierced their ears, undergoing an attack that would never cease. Steele's gun stayed trained on the door, muscles tense.

"Holy shit," Mauser cursed, bending over at the waist breathing hard.

"That was close." *I wouldn't be surprised if I pissed myself.*

The stairwell was dark, and knowing that something wanted to kill them a mere few feet away gnawed at his courage. With a shaky hand, Steele grabbed the cold metal handle making sure it was locked.

Following the old man down three flights of stairs, the noise of the infected slowly faded. The old man rapped three times before a woman in her sixties answered. She had a grandmotherly look to her, almost as though she were inviting the kids in for Christmas Day.

"Thank God," she said, ushering them inside worriedly. Bright lights blinded them.

JOSEPH
Mount Eden Emergency Operations Facility, VA

A dingy yellow and navy blue carpet covered the conference room floor. It sprawled from wall to wall beneath equally outdated desks that looked as though they had been installed under the Ford Administration. Joseph's mind drifted everywhere apart from the congressional panel that sat in front of him. He inspected the carpet with his eyes, amazed that the government had made the effort to install it so far underground.

Joseph felt as though he was on some sort of display at the zoo. Congressional representatives and military generals peered down at him seemingly curious and disgusted by him at the same time, looks of practiced skeptical scrutiny written across their faces. It was as if they expected him to throw his feces or do some amazing trick at the same time. He probably seemed very common to them in his borrowed striped button-down and khakis. A single ID card dangled around his neck, it being the only thing that made him stand out from any of the other bureaucrats. The purple card gave him access to the medical lab which was strictly off limits for almost everyone, even the VIPs.

A chubby congressman with a long fleshy nose and jowls that jiggled as he spoke leaned forward as he questioned Joseph. The problem was, Joseph didn't have the answers to the congressman's questions. He needed more time to test his theories, and to isolate and eliminate speculation of which this man would never understand. So instead of pleading his case, he stared at the carpet.

"What research and analysis have you collected on the virus that has led to the evacuation and quarantine of most of the East Coast?" the congressman asked, narrowing his eyes. "Need I remind you that you were brought here under a special order from the President because of your *expertise* on the virus?"

Even during a pandemic of this magnitude, it seemed Congress was actively searching for somebody to blame all the death and destruction on. *How could they blame a naturally occurring virus on anyone?* This pandemic couldn't be blamed on a political party or a presidential policy. It was a microbe that couldn't be seen with the naked eye that reanimated people either after it killed them or after someone carrying the disease killed them.

Joseph's eyes glazed over as he blandly reiterated what he already knew about the virus. It was all very scientific, which did not impress the Congressional representatives. They wanted black and white answers; right and wrong. Reactive policy making at its best.

They were working hard to place the blame anywhere they could to distance themselves from any sort of repercussions. If there was ever a time when they needed to come together, it was now. Democrat or Republican, people needed to rally. So many American lives were at stake. This is the time where it matters. Their actions could save or kill the world.

Joseph reiterated his story in layman's terms. He felt as though he had to justify his existence and his presence in the protected underground bunker.

"After the negative response of the patients to common treatments, I became aware that I potentially monitored a new virus in the village of Kombarka. I never imagined that it would mutate as fast as it did and incur such violent symptoms in the patients before and after death. Upon arrival in the United States, I found that the virus had already struck. After that, I only have a marginal degree of confidence in the quality of research material that I presumably acquired from the original outbreak."

"You only have a marginal degree of confidence?" the Congressman asked. "I don't think this is a time of marginal degrees of anything."

Flashes of the horrid screams of passengers under assault onboard the plane echoed in Joseph's ears. Sweat beaded on his forehead. His stomach roiled as though he was about to vomit. Images of the infected chewing sickeningly upon the living flashed across his mind. He gulped bile back down his throat.

A balding military officer with three stars on his green suited shoulders interrupted. "So the only way to kill these *people* is shots to the head?"

Joseph acknowledged him by giving the only scientific answer he could think of. "Yes," he said averting his eyes.

Gazing upwards, he realized he received blank stares from across the panel. He tried to dumb down his approach. "Yes, that is most likely the case, but you should really be asking the counterterrorism agents who did all the shooting on the aircraft, or your men in the field."

Wiping his brow, he tried to ease his stomach as it rocked and rolled. More testing would need to be done to ensure this was the only way to 'put down' an infected person. He couldn't fault the General; it was probably the only way any of the human race could survive. The General was working with what he knew: efficient, effective and pinpoint violence.

"Are you okay, Dr. Jackowski?" an older female congresswoman in a dark green business suit asked, peering at him over her glasses.

Joseph placed a shaky hand around his glass of water and took a sip. The water tasted tepid and stale, over-chlorinated and flat like someone really wanted clean water. She continued to glower at him from her elevated desk, a slight look of disapproval on her face.

"I'm okay, ma'am," he mumbled.

"Then we'll continue. Please let me get this straight," she said, pausing for effect. Pushing her thumb and forefingers together, she accented each point with a fist shake. "You're saying that you cannot *treat* people with this disease? You're advocating that we *kill* sick Americans? You're advocating for the United States government to *murder* its own citizens?" She pursed her lips, awaiting a response.

Joseph didn't know whether it constituted murder if they were already dead. "Ma'am, I am uncertain of the legalities surrounding the termination of infected populations. However, isolation of healthy populations from infected populations is paramount, because even according to your reports we cannot seem to stop the spread of the disease."

She leaned over to an aide, whispering something into his ear. "First, I completely disagree with your prognosis. Americans have nothing to fear from this treatable 'virus'," she said. *What would I know? I'm only a CDC virologist.*

"Second," she said, holding up two fingers. She glanced down at whatever she was reading.

Joseph peeked timidly over his shoulder. *Is this being recorded?*

"We need to enact the Emergency National Health Act now more than ever. We're expecting a survivable infection rate of more than 90%, according to my experts' best estimates."

End Time

I wonder who her experts were? It would be nice to confer with these people.

"People need access to healthcare now, more than ever." She enunciated clearly, making sure her comments were recorded accurately.

Joseph knew she must be massaging her hands underneath the table in triumph. *How could she wish someone ill so that they were reliant upon the government for aid? To her, Americans would have to rely on the public system if they wanted to be cured.* He wanted to vomit more than ever. *She had no idea what this virus was doing to people. The violence was unimaginable. She only knew that it provided her with a scary reactive opportunity to enact her policies while she sat smugly behind a desk, safe in a deep underground bunker surrounded by soldiers willing to fight and die for her.* He sat back in his seat.

If she had been listening earlier, she would have known that the problem with the disease was its reanimation of the dead, which in turn catalyzed the spread the disease. Providing that it simply just killed people, there would only need to be a cleanup. It would be a nightmare, and would most likely cripple the global economy, if not sending it into total collapse. Horrifying in itself, but at least it would have been easier to contain like the Spanish Flu in 1918 except with casualty rates off the charts, ten to fifteen times higher.

'Easier' was an understatement, thought Joseph. Even if it were possible to produce a cure, he doubted whether he could administer it quickly enough to stop the disease from taking over the human host.

The officials should be thankful that the infected almost immediately lost humanity's most developed human ability: cognitive reasoning. If the infected managed to coordinate their attacks instead of relying on sheer numbers and violence to spread the disease, Joseph was sure that humanity would already be a footnote in Earth's long historical timeline.

As much as Joseph hated to side with the knuckle draggers, he thought the General had the only reasonable idea. Killing the infected Americans was a disturbing strategy, but it was the only plausible containment method he could come up with at that time. An idea which horrified Joseph.

Joseph wondered if he could manipulate the virus in a short enough time to create a vaccine. It was possible to manipulate the flu vaccine on a yearly basis. The base components of the vaccine were already there, they just needed to tweak it to treat the most aggressive strains of influenza for the season. He knew he could potentially save many soldiers' and civilians' lives if he could. *The task is monumental. How can I ever do this? I should be in the lab not sitting here.* He worked with a good team of doctors, but the instructions coming down from the government were unsurprisingly muddled at best.

The parties were split over whether to treat people with the disease or, on a harsher scale, to quarantine and eliminate those who were already infected. Everyone's first response was: "How do we make our loved ones better?" Half the time the researchers were being asked to develop some sort of cure for the infected, and the rest of the time they were being asked for a vaccine to protect the uninfected from transmission.

You can't cure death. People just couldn't come to grips that their loved ones, who were still stumbling around, were already gone. Some simply refused to believe that these people were dead. Joseph reviewed his notes while the panel members argued amongst themselves.

The General suddenly pounded his fist into the table. "We need more troops and the executive order to go-ahead and execute the infected. I hardly have a doctor from here to Maine, because they've all been infected and shot while trying to treat the other infected. This is a Code Black situation. Extreme measures are justified for the continued existence of the nation," he shouted.

Fleshy Nose shook with rage. "I will not be responsible for the military - operating on U.S. soil, by the way - executing sick Americans. There'll be a national rebellion."

Green Suit chimed in. "If people found out the military was executing their sick loved ones, they would never trust the government again. Our careers would be over. The latest polls say the people want a cure." She humphed as if to say the discussion was over.

The latest polls? Who is she polling, the bunker?

Joseph adjusted his glasses, eying the panel. Even if it were possible to successfully 'cure' a person with the disease, they would still be clinically dead. As for the second part of the equation, no one had explained how they could round up the entire Eastern seaboard for administration, especially while the infected were trying to kill them.

Containment of the disease was almost as impossible a task. According to his limited reports, much of D.C. had been overrun with the infected, as well as most other major city centers over the East Coast. More cities across the interior of the United States were also beginning to show the initial signs of an uncontrollable pandemic. It didn't seem likely that it would remain that way for long.

It was hard getting through to a Congress who were still thinking about re-election campaigns when this all blew over. This was one problem they couldn't shift to the next Congress or generation.

"There won't be anyone left for the next election," Joseph said as he stood up. The indecisiveness of these *leaders* had driven him to a state he had never been in. Wide-eyed, they gaped back at him.

"Excuse me, Dr. Jackowski?" the female representative said.

"I said, there won't be anyone left for the next election."

"That is preposterous," Fleshy Nose jiggled. "There is no way it could spread that fast."

Joseph didn't care what they thought. He continued onward anyway. "Yes it can and it is. We will all be dead or infected if we don't start eliminating the diseased persons now."

There, he had said it. He had spelled it out clearly for them. "In my professional experience, I may be able to work on a vaccine, but I can't do that if we are overrun."

The General nodded his head in affirmation. "Just as I thought," he said, pointing a stubby finger at Joseph.

"Nonsense," Fleshy Nose yelled. He gripped paperwork as if it were Joseph's neck.

"You are dismissed doctor," Green Suit commanded.

Joseph stood trembling and collected his folder of paperwork. For the time being, he hid safe underground, but he wondered how long that would last.

STEELE
Washington-McCone International Airport, VA

Another heavy steel door clanged shut behind Steele. The tall steel-girded ceilings of a giant warehouse greeted them. Boxes were stacked all the way to the ceiling resting on large metal shelving units, marked with food labels, beverages and commercial merchandise. A large section of the boxes in the middle had been cleared away, revealing a mix of air travelers, airline employees and police officers sitting in hopeless despair.

The elder woman immediately tended to Wheeler's wounds by checking his bandages.

"He's not sick, is he?" she asked with sudden seriousness, as if her natural inclinations were overshadowed by her logic. She took a step back.

"No, ma'am," Steele replied. "He was stabbed when we were flying in."

Studying him for a few moments, a sad gaze fell over her weathered face; a face that had seen too much sun in her younger years.

"Mary's my name. I retired from nursing about ten years ago. I was trying to go to Florida when all this madness began. I'll do what I can," she said with a determined voice, her hands moving with practiced efficiency.

Steele sighed. "Thank you, Mary."

"He don't look so hot, does he?" the man with the ball cap said, removing his hat and rubbing his baldpate.

"He saved a very important man's life," Steele said, glaring. *I hope that shaggy haired jerk was worth saving.*

"I meant no disrespect. Hope he gets better. The name's Eddie."

Eddie placed a worn, callused hand in Steele's. "I'm an aircraft mechanic," he said, shaking his head as he spoke. "I saw a couple of the other guys huddled around one of our supervisors on the ground. Thought he'd had a heart attack or somethin'. When I got close, they came charging after me all covered in guts and moaning. I wasn't gonna wait around to see what they were doin'. I ran as fast as I could to the nearest utility shed. Those guys pounded on the door for an hour before they moved along."

Steele nodded. He understood the man's fear and unknowing.

"I understand," Steele said. He was eager to talk to Officer Summerdyke and take stock of their situation. "Where are the locals?"

"Local what, son?"

"Local police. Officer Summerdyke's the one who contacted us."

"Oh, the cops. They're over there," Eddie said, gesturing to a side room door.

The flight survivors quickly found places to rest and made small talk with the other people. It always amazed Steele that the presence of other people could ease the suffering of a traumatic event. He'd seen people come together in the aftermath of the Boston Marathon bombings when his team rapidly deployed to track the terrorists.

Just being with one another helped them. They were not alone. A husband and wife sat with their heads together whispering. A gate agent hugged Crystal and they held each other with tears in their eyes. Steele was thankful he didn't have to babysit anyone for the moment.

As Steele walked, he thought about his people. *Mauser is here safe, but what about my family? What about Gwen? She has to be safe. I will it; there are no other options. I will drive out of here tomorrow, and when I arrive she will be safe at home making no-bake cookies, like this shit had never happened. Creamy chocolate, peanut butter, oats, honey and her.*

His stomach growled loudly to remind him that it required sustenance. Apparently it had teamed up with his head to nag him into some sort of restful compliance. It was a struggle to focus on any one thing. He was far past the point where coffee could bring him back to life.

Gwen had been working at the Red Cross Headquarters in downtown D.C. *Wait, did she go in today? What day was it?* He took a deep breath and rubbed his bloodshot eyes. Disorientation plagued him.

A short, stocky police officer with a buzz cut emerged from a side room. Wearing a McCone Washington Airport Authority police uniform, he carried himself with an edge of confidence as if he erred on the side of cockiness. His thumbs were looped through his gun belt like a frontier gunslinger.

"I'm Officer Summerdyke." He gestured to a portly officer sitting with the other survivors, "And that's Officer Jenkins."

Steele could only imagine how haggard he must look. "I'm Counterterrorism Agent Steele and over yonder is Agent Mauser and Agent Thorfinson. Agent Wheeler is the one who's all banged up," Steele said, pointing at the agents behind him in turn.

"So where are we?"

"This is warehouse C3, one of the many storerooms for the businesses in

McCone. Piled high with enough supplies to last us through Armageddon." He looked at Steele for approval.

"I can see that. Not a bad place to be. Where's the bar? I need a drink after the day we had," Steele said with a laugh.

"I hear ya' brother. This whole thing's been a shit show."

"Has there been no response? No attempt to clear the airport?"

Summerdyke shook his thick neck. "Follow me. I will show you."

Steele obeyed. *This is more than a shit show. This could be the final shitty act.* He followed Summerdyke into the next room. Immediately, he became enthralled with the newscast that flashed images of vicious violence. It occupied the wall of a break room complete with a fridge and microwave.

"This is a break room for the warehouse employees. It's better than the closet we have for a lounge." He laughed, but Steele ignored him.

Videos of police fighting on the white steps leading up to the pristine columns of the Capitol building dragged across the screen. Flood spotlights shadowed the police as they locked in a deadly struggle with hundreds of infected. Steele was captivated with the footage. The video cut back to the news anchor.

"Has it been like this for long?" Steele asked, unable to tear his eyes away.

"About eight hours since we've been down here."

A handsome, gray-haired news anchor explained: "The images you're about to see are so graphic they had to be cleared by the studio director to be broadcasted today. We felt that people would not believe the gravity of the situation unless we showed them these truly unspeakable acts of violence." His lips formed a thin, grave line and the broadcast went to the footage in the field.

End Time

The video footage was choppy, as though the cameraman was running. The camera jostled around as he scampered past bodies in the street. It was hard to tell with the shaky camera work. Somebody screamed in the background.

The voice of the reporter sounded off. "Hurry," he said in a muffled voice. "Are you getting this, Kyle?" he said louder.

"I'm trying," the cameraman said hurriedly.

The camera straightened out. 'Washington D.C. Violence, 1000s killed' lined the bottom of the broadcast in bold font. The city was a war zone making Fallujah look like an amusement park. The cameraman wobbled the camera as he threw it up onto his shoulder, but managed to steady the film to show the countless bodies that lay unmoving in the streets. Panicked people sprinted in front of the camera. Others fell upon the fallen. They moved with an unnatural gait, like the infected persons on the aircraft.

"That guy's infected, and so is he," Steele said, pointing at the screen.

"I was thinking they didn't look right. Like they're drunk, maybe, or under the influence?" Summerdyke said.

"Exactly. They move clumsily, but I'll tell you something: they are strong. You have to aim for the head, not center mass. It was the only way we could take any of them down. We wasted a lot of ammo on center mass."

Summerdyke folded his arms across his chest. "Damn, that can be a tough shot."

Steele frowned. Without practice, headshots could be difficult; even more so under pressure, especially when traditional military and law enforcement principles were to shoot for center mass. His training had made it seem effortless, and over time he had forgotten about its difficulty for less experienced shooters.

"Just hit 'em in the head," he said and continued to watch.

A businessman in a suit and tie ran up to another man, who had the scraggily chaotic appearance of a homeless person, and shot him in the head. He was running again before the body hit the ground. No one stopped him or gave him a second glance; the chaos just continued to unfold.

The camera panned to the left to show the iconic image of the White House: the green lawn, flowers out front and semi-circle drive leading to the front door. Steele half expected to see the President waving to the crowd before he entered his house, except the iron gate that surrounded the President's home had been reinforced with razor wire. Secret Service agents stood with FN P90s in the low ready. The camera cut to the reporter.

"I am Nathan Bartholomew for WUSB and for those of you just joining us, I am embedded here with a determined line of D.C. Metropolitan Police officers and Uniformed Division Secret Service. As you can see, they are dressed in full riot gear attempting to hold back an *overwhelming* group of D.C. citizens."

The cameraman panned out to the officers, who fought with a determined ferocity, sticks swinging widely, shields to the front, as they attempted to beat the citizens of the capital back.

Steele choked up as he watched his brothers in blue - literally a thin blue line - attempting to use riot control tactics on people who he knew felt no pain, fear or regard for human life. One officer struck an infected man in the collarbone with his long wooden riot control stick, shattering it through in a single strike, but the man kept clawing at the officer, body slumped and mangled. They slammed riot sticks into the bodies, but the people pressed forward unfazed by the police.

"As you may have seen over the course of the day, the mass of people protesting has grown a great deal. We have not been able to find anyone to comment on why this violent demonstration has sparked. The people are attacking the officers with an unheard of blind rage. Wait, something is happening," he said, turning holding a hand to his earpiece. The camera twisted back to the police.

Steele knew it was coming. The crowd would outlast the officers. *You're only as strong as your weakest link*, he thought. As if to echo his thoughts, an officer was driven onto his back. His stick flew from his grasp. Attempting to crawl to the safety of his fellow officers, four of the infected dragged him into the mass of people.

The officer reached back in a struggle to save himself, his face a portrait of agony. Blood sprayed across clear shields. He disappeared; piled under countless bodies.

The gap filled with the broken bodies of the infected and the shield wall crumbled. The riot officers were overcome one by one until the remainder broke and ran.

"Kyle we have to run," the reporter shouted. Battered bloodied bodies reached out for the camera. The cameraman froze stiff in fear.

"Kyle?" the reporter squeaked. Screams permeated the television, and the camera crashed onto the ground falling on its side. The cameraman's lifeless eyes above his bearded face stared blankly into the camera lens. Filthy feet marched passed the screen.

An officer tried to make it over the tall iron fence, but was pulled down by a bloodied fellow officer in riot gear. Half a dozen of the infected tore him limb from limb. Gunshots went from singular to full auto within seconds before the cameraman's eyes turned pale and he disappeared from in front of the lens. The footage cut back to the news station and a pallid news anchor.

"Our hearts go out to Kyle McCarthy and Nathan Bartholomew's families. Wait. We are getting something," he said, nodding to someone off screen. His eyes widened. "I'm not sure this is correct. Frank can you confirm this?" The anchor looked past the camera at his producer shuffling his papers.

"This is serious?"

"It's real. Report it." Someone called from the back.

"The White House has been overrun. It is our understanding that the President has been removed to a remote; secure location before this horrific event took place. Our hearts go out to the dedicated men and women who have fallen in this senseless act of violence." The anchor gulped before he continued.

"Congressional representatives have told us they are being moved to secure facilities until order can be restored in the nation's capital. The President is calling this a state of emergency. I'm being reminded by the authorities to tell everyone to stay inside your homes, bolt your doors and restrain anyone who has been bitten. That is correct. I am being told that this deadly disease is transmitted through a human bite. The authorities are working hard to regain control of New York, Atlanta and Washington D.C., but cannot respond efficiently to events when the streets are congested with traffic. I repeat, avoid 'infected persons' at all costs."

Summerdyke muted the talking head. "Where'd you guys come in from?" He tossed Steele a sports drink from the fridge.

End Time

Steele cracked it open and took a gulp, the wash of electrolytes replenishing his system, making him feel slightly better. "We were on a flight from Kinshasa. About halfway through a sick passenger began attacking everyone. It wasn't long before most of the plane was infected. It made them extremely violent; we barely made it off the plane after we landed. We were expecting the cavalry, but I guess you guys had enough on your plate," Steele said, screwing the cap back on the drink.

Officer Summerdyke grimaced, leaning against a table folding thick forearms across his chest. "You could say that. Officer Jenkins and I were patrolling the A-C terminal train when things got bad in the airport. Someone must have had it coming off of some flight. We led the people from our train car onto the tracks here. I know all the nooks and crannies of the airport. Actually, from the tracks we can access multiple storage areas, including the loading dock."

The situation sounded bad to Steele, but things could be worse. They could be trapped on the surface. He surveyed the surroundings. "This is a pretty secure setup."

Summerdyke shrugged. "Even if those things got onto the tracks it's like a big fatal funnel, and there's no way they could beat down one of these doors."

Steele nodded. "Remember, forget center mass, aim for the head. You have any extra ammo, and maybe some food? I could use some. Me and my guys are running low."

"We got plenty of food, but to get more ammo we would have to make it all the way to our armory in the main terminal. It's possible, but we haven't done it yet. We also haven't heard anything from our supervisors, so our plan is to sit tight until this blows over."

Steele hadn't heard from any of his supervisors either. Not having a clear direction or report station was the first problem in any disaster response.

"We appreciate your help. We'll spend the night and head out tomorrow. There are the plane survivors and the injured man who we can't take with us."

Officer Summerdyke held up his hand, "Say no more. Leave them with us, and we'll take care of them the best we can."

Steele extended his hand in gratitude. He had found a kindred spirit in the fellow officer. "Thank you. Wheeler's a tough old bastard, but I think if we take him with us he'll die."

Summerdyke led him back outside.

"You can crash anywhere you like. We've got some extra blankets over there. Brand new with the presidential seal right on them. They're souvenirs, but they'll keep you warm. I'll keep you posted on any important events."

Steele took a seat next to Mauser in front of a stack of boxes that read 'Washington Monument T-shirts.' They sat without saying a word, enjoying the relative silence and peace of the underground warehouse. Steele felt all of the fatigue and heaviness from the past couple of days weighing down on him. He was sore. His body felt as though he had run three marathons without stopping, combined with being hit by a car.

Steele broke the silence. "Remember when we deployed to Berlin and met those hot Russian chicks?"

Mauser smiled, staring off into space. "Of course, we were out all night. Could hardly stay awake the next day. Wheeler was so pissed I could practically see the steam coming out of his ears."

"Man, that was fun," Steele said.

Mauser's smile turned downward, "Well, it ain't over yet."

Steele sat in silence, lost in his own thoughts. Uncertain of what the future held for the men.

"You got any of that chew left?" Steele asked.

"Here you go. Last one."

Steele smiled faintly and placed the chew in his lip. "Thanks," he said. Enjoying the burning sensation, he spat some into his empty drink bottle.

"I'm leaving tomorrow. I'll understand if you want to stay. It's safe here."

Mauser glared at him from the side angrily. "You think I'd miss the ride of a lifetime during the zombie apocalypse?" He shook his head.

"I guess they are, aren't they? Zombies. I always envisioned it differently. Unlimited ammo, taking on the hordes from an elevated position. Rifle in one hand, hot chick clinging to the other."

Mauser laughed. "Don't matter. I'm with you to the end, brother. Besides, maybe you can still have your unlimited ammo shootout against a bunch of undead cannibals. We just have to make it back to the house."

Steele grinned. "So you are telling me there is a chance." He had never doubted that Mauser would come with him, but he had to give him the option. For a logical person, it would have made sense to stay in the underground warehouse, but Mauser didn't see things that way. Mauser saw sticking with his pals, regardless of safety, as more important than self-preservation.

"Tomorrow, we go." Steele leaned his head back, hoping the realm of sleep held less horror than the realm of the walking dead.

GWEN
Dunn Loring Metro Station, VA

Shadows danced around Gwen. Her vision obscured as if she were enveloped by a thick fog. Her mind was stuffed cotton unable to recall her impending danger. She frantically struck out attempting to impede her attackers' progress. It was one of the tenets she had learned from her and Steele's Krav Maga lessons: use everything in your power to win.

Muffled yelling penetrated her brain, and a python wrapped tightly around her torso squeezing her. The assailant's hot breath steamed onto the side of her neck. She screamed in frustration, but couldn't extract her body from its constriction.

A familiar voice hushed her. "Shh. It's okay. It's us."

Gwen's vision sharpened slightly revealing a long brown haired woman. "Lindsay?" She reached out hesitantly for her new friend. Lindsay gave her a worried smile from the driver's seat. She shifted gears.

"It's me. You scared us there. You've been in and out all night."

Lindsay swerved the Jeep around an abandoned vehicle in the center of a residential street. "You went head first into that curb," she said, not taking her eyes off the road.

The burly arms restraining her seemed hesitant to release her. It was as if they dared not let go, for fear of never holding her again. Gwen checked herself for further injury running her hands over her arms and legs. Her head pounded with pain in rhythm with her heart.

"I think we should take you to a hospital," Lindsay said.

End Time

Gwen bowed her head as she reached up, gingerly touching the lump where her head had run into the pavement and lost. She was still confused as to what had happened.

Lindsay almost rolled the Jeep as she took a suburban street corner too fast, her tires sliding.

"No. I think hospitals are a bad idea," Gwen said, holding her head in her hands.

"If you say so."

"I'll be fine. I just feel like I'm going to be sick."

"I want you to meet somebody," Lindsay continued, gesturing toward the back seat. "This is Ahmed. We owe him."

Gwen twisted in her seat, offering a limp hand to the stranger in the back, still cradling her throbbing head. He took her hand in his. He radiated warmth. "It's nice to meet you, Ahmed. What happened?"

"Well," Lindsay responded. "There's no doubt in my mind that Ahmed was an All-Conference baseball player in college."

Gwen turned again to get a better peek at Ahmed, who appeared to be in his mid-twenties. He was a handsome man of Middle Eastern descent. About average height, he had an almost entirely shaved head. He had large, muscular arms and wore a tight-fitting T-shirt with a gold chain dangling outside. Twirling a gore-covered baseball bat, he made small circles with it between his legs.

Smiling shyly, he spoke. "The pleasure is all mine. I was hiding in a car when I saw you sprinting away from those ghouls. I tried to wave you over, but you bit it on the curb and those assholes were gaining on you. I couldn't let them catch you. I only held them off long enough until, thankfully, Lindsay came driving through the middle."

"How did I get in here?"

"It's not like you're heavy. I just picked you up and threw you in, and we took off," he said as if tossing another person was easy.

Lindsay grabbed Gwen's hand. "Don't let him underplay his part. When I drove up, he stood over you, bashing in the head of every crazy within ten feet. He must have killed at least eight or nine before I got there. He's a hero."

Gwen sat amazed. These people had gone out of their way and risked their lives to save her when the most prudent course of action would have been to leave her as food for the dead. Her head was still foggy. *At least a mild concussion.*

"I can't thank you enough. I owe you both my life," she said earnestly. Red bricked town homes zipped by. "Where are we going?"

Lindsay downshifted, slowing the car to a steady roll. She gripped the steering wheel with white knuckles.

"I don't know where to go," Lindsay said.

Gwen shook her head. "Just give me a minute," she said trying to think. She gazed out the window. The neighborhood of townhouses around them seemed deserted. Garage doors closed and lights off. In the breaking daylight, an Indian family strapped suitcases to the top of their minivan. They eyed the Jeep suspiciously as the trio drove on.

Further down the street they passed a father and his teenage son feeding on what appeared to be the mother in their driveway. A half-packed BMW crossover stood with its doors open. The pair looked up at the Jeep with milky white eyes, dark red blood running down their lips. Soon they lost interest in the car, and returned to tearing at the woman's ribcage. The image made Gwen want to puke her brains out. It was that or her head; she couldn't tell which.

"What in the world is happening out there?" Gwen murmured to herself. Neither of her companions responded to her as if they were unwilling or unable to answer. Lindsay watched straight ahead, as if she didn't acknowledge the gratuitous violence around her it would just go away.

"I just moved here a month ago from Tampa," Lindsay said. "I'm not even done unpacking yet. I wish I hadn't now. Never move for a man," she said with a nervous laugh.

"Men are an unreasonable necessity," Gwen said, trying to hold the vomit back in her throat. "Ahmed?"

"I live by myself in a big apartment building down in Arlington. I don't think it's a great idea to go back there. Besides, I don't have anything particularly useful aside from this bat," Ahmed said, laughing at himself. "Got plenty of booze and supplements," he followed as an afterthought.

Gwen knew the best option would be her home. At the very least the house held plenty of food, supplies, and guns, Mark made sure of that. "I want you both to come to my townhouse. We can stay holed up in there until the military gets this straightened out. We have plenty of supplies. My boyfriend's a counterterrorism agent. He should be home any time now."

Lindsay sighed and Ahmed was quiet, but they both seemed relieved at the idea of sticking together. Any reason to stay together was a good one.

"Have you heard anything from your boyfriend?" Lindsay asked.

"No, but he'll be back any time now," Gwen said assuredly.

"Are you sure?" Ahmed asked. Gwen had never contemplated the fact that Mark might be in any sort of serious danger.

"Of course I'm sure," she said with a little less confidence. *He better get his hairy ass back home in one piece.*

"No offense, Gwen, but it is pretty bad out here. Have you spoken with him?" Lindsay said.

"Well, no. But he should be traveling back from Africa any time now."

"I heard on the radio that's where this thing started. A disease," Ahmed said. It had been in her face the whole time. All the requests for aid. The crippling disasters abroad. *They all couldn't be related to this madness?*

"It's of no matter. He is a big boy and can take care of himself." *At least I hope so. He promised he would come back. Was that not a promise he could actually keep? Was it just some foolish lover's promise, whispered as a sweet nothing in the night? Was it truly the lie that they told themselves, so they could go about their daily lives in peace, ignoring reality? The fact remains, agents in his line of work died in 'training accidents' all the time.* Her heart sank as fear set in. *No, he would be back. He has to come back.*

"Now, we just need to figure out the least-known route to get there," she said. She pulled out her phone, clicking the map icon. A map of the area appeared, marked with a blue dot to show their location. *At least GPS still worked.*

She quickly scrolled back through her emails. There was an email from her sister and her father, but nothing from Mark. Her sister and her niece were safe. Apparently, nothing had gone on there yet. The local school had closed and the hospitals were on high alert, but no one seemed to know if the reports coming from the East Coast were fact or fiction.

She hammered out a quick email:

Becky, I'm safe. Waiting for Mark. Get to Grandpa's farm right away. Don't let anyone sick near you. Keep the dogs out front.

Love Always Gwen

It was time for Gwen to get home. She clicked her volume down so she didn't have to listen to her phone's electronic voice.

She pointed toward the next street. "Turn left up here onto Merryfield Road."

STEELE
Washington-McCone International Airport, VA

Steele awoke with a start. *Where am I?* Many a night in the field, he had

come to, so tired from his travels that he couldn't remember where he laid his head.

He blinked repeatedly, trying to recognize some part of his surroundings. Steel

girders lined the ceiling. Unopened boxes stacked upon one another rose to the

ceiling like a real life game of Tetris. People around him slumbered fitfully,

breathing, and snoring. Mauser lay nearby sprawled out, Crystal lying on one of his

arms in a ball. He relaxed a little as he realized he was in the warehouse underneath

McCone.

His eyes slowly adjusted to the light. The Trijicon night sights of his pistol

glowed pale green in the dark. He reached for it, finding the course sandpaper grip

tape along the handle of the weapon soothing. The fit felt perfect like the weapon and

man were made for one another. *There are many like you, but you are mine.*

A scratching noise came from the corner. *What is that?* He pointed his SIG

Sauer P226 in the direction of the sound, his night sights forming a straight green

line in the dark. He quietly shifted into a crouch. Scrape. Scrape. Scrape. Step after

step he approached, silently stalking the offending noise.

Tiptoeing over bodies, he crept until the azure steel door loomed ahead.

Leading to the surface, it was an even gloomier shadow in the darkness. Hesitantly,

he turned his ear to the door listening. His ear hovered an inch from its cool surface.

Something scratched along the other side. *I will probably regret this.*

Gradually he slid the large deadbolt free of its confines. Its soft metal faintly rasped along the door. *Must be fast. If things go bad, I can use the crowned bezel of the taclight to crack a skull.* He took a deep breath. Gun in the high ready, he pulled the door hard. Flicking on his tactical light, he shined it into the stairwell illuminating the darkness with 500-lumens. He checked his corners, casting bright LED light into the left and then the right. Then up the stairs. Nothing moved. A heavy silence hung in the air as if it were waiting for him to breathe. He exhaled slowly, realizing that he too had been waiting to breathe.

Utterly thankful that a horde of dead bodies hadn't pushed him down to the floor as they flooded into the room, he wiped his brow. Scratch. Scratch. Steele jumped as he saw a rat scampering straight for him.

"Jesus," he cursed, regaining his composure. Something pink stuck out of either end of its mouth. Steele contemplated shooting the rodent, but decided a kick would suffice. It squealed as it flew through the air, dropping its treasure, and scrambled into the warehouse. Steele turned to watch it run into the darkness.

Steele lit up the object the rodent had left behind and recognized it, as a long pale finger. A gold band decorated the base of the finger. Steele stepped back inside the warehouse, gently latching the door.

He checked his watch and almost ran into Mauser.

"Everything all right?"

"Yeah. Just some rats in the stairwell. One had a finger in its mouth."

Mauser looked unsurprised. "We live in a dead zone, where eaters of the dead reign supreme."

"I've got to check my phone. Its 0800 and we should start getting ready," Steele said and Mauser nodded. The break room was the only place in the underground warehouse where Steele received a single bar of service on his work phone. Reception was spotty at best. He wanted to smash his personal phone for failing him in his time of need, but held off, maybe it would come in use later.

Steele plopped down at a table and messed with his phone. His inbox had been flooded with a host of emails from headquarters, revealing the general breakdown of the Division. It started with an email to 'Please Check Open Source reporting about protests.' 'Airport operations have ceased in all major cities.' *Nobody is coming home on commercial airlines.*

'Please stay at your designated rally points until further contact is made from your Operations staff.' Teams scattered throughout the world would find themselves in various safe houses or US consulates stranded until further notice.

'Personnel that are inside CONUS are to report for duty at the nearest Field Office.' Teams that were in the Continental United States were to report to the nearest field office in their area of operations (AO). Nothing from the Washington Field Office. He wondered how many of his colleagues were still alive.

They had undergone a great deal of training, which made them tough agents in the field. At the same time, most of the agents had probably been at the focal point of any transiting outbreaks. Others would be responding with alternate federal agencies in overt tactical teams. The rest that were scattered across the globe with little to no intelligence wouldn't have known what to look for or how to stop the disease as it spread. The death toll within their ranks must be dramatically high. He tried not to worry about his brothers and sisters in arms. They would have to take care of themselves, just as he had done. *Nothing from WFO. His field office must be out of commission. Perhaps they could eventually reach the Baltimore Field Office.*

End Time

His government phone buzzed indicating another email from headquarters. 'ATTN: Infected persons are extremely dangerous avoid contact.' *Thanks, a little late to the ball now aren't we? But if the emails are going out, some aspect of the Counterterrorism Division must be up and running somewhere.*

Gwen had better have made it out of D.C. before all this shit went down. He would make sure she was safe and deal with the repercussions from work later. If this was as bad as he thought, he didn't think they would be calling any time soon.

With Summerdyke's help, he called together the two intermingled groups of survivors. They numbered twenty-two in total. He explained the situation, and that he meant to set out to find Gwen. Heading into an area most likely infested with diseased, cannibalistic people to find his girlfriend didn't have the group's broad range of support. As Steele listened to himself explaining his plan, it also sounded pretty outlandish to him. *Did you expect everyone to raise their hands for a chance to die? Shouldn't have bothered.*

It was reminiscent of a horror film when the imprudent yet well-intentioned jock declares he will go out into the dark forest alone in order to 'get help.' It was always a death sentence, but Steele had no choice. This was something he had to do. He wondered if that was how the brave yet foolish characters of horror films felt. *If I don't go, I will never be able to live with myself. Dead either way.*

"I can't promise your well-being, but this is something I *have* to do. We have a large vehicle and we can take anyone who wants to go. We'll leave here in thirty minutes. Thank you for your hospitality."

People talked in hushed tones to themselves, and one by one they walked back to their makeshift beds. Crystal ran up and hugged him, wiping away the tears in her eyes.

"Keep him safe. He owes me a date," she said, sniffling. She ran to Mauser, wrapping her arms around him. Mauser held her hands and leaned in close, whispering in her ear causing her to smile a bit.

The others moved away from Steele and his team as though they were already dead and rising. They would rather stay burrowed underground like hedgehogs than risk their own necks escaping. He expected no more and no less. These people were safe. Outside was a violent whirlwind of chaos.

To Steele's surprise, the copilot lingered after everyone had disappeared. The older man crossed his arms on his chest appearing uncomfortable. Steele rose an eyebrow at the man.

"Copilot Gordon. Is there something I can help you with?" *Like a slap to the face.* The copilot shifted on his feet.

"I just wanted to say thanks. Thanks for getting us here. Never thought I'd be so excited to stay overnight at an airport."

"I know the feeling, but I only did what I was supposed to do. No different than you landing the plane."

"I know. Just wanted to say thanks." He extended a hand to Steele. Steele took his hand.

"Good luck out there." The copilot walked away. *People surprise you everyday.*

Steele checked his pack. *The gear is secure.* He press-checked his handgun to ensure he had a round chambered, and felt for his mag carrier touching the top of his easily accessible extra mag. *Weapon manipulation is the difference between the living and the dead.*

His final preparation before submitting himself back to the world of the dead was saying his goodbye to Wheeler. He officially opted to leave a man behind, and the odds were against them seeing each other again.

Wheeler's corner make-shift cot was dark. It tore him up to see his senior colleague lying unmoving and incapacitated, torso partially covered with a blanket. He watched his mentor for a moment. It seemed as if his chest didn't rise at all. His skin was pallid with his eyes closed. A large bandage sealed his chest wound, and a small needle stuck out of the white gauze. Wheeler knocked on death's door. *Do not give up the good fight brother.* Steele knelt down, taking his mentor's hand. It was cool to the touch.

"Hang in there, Boss Man. I've got to leave you here, but I'll see you when this is all over." *God willing.*

Wheeler's eyes flickered open and his lips moved, but his mumblings were too faint to be heard. His heavy lids drooped down and his eyes closed again. Steele gave his hand a squeeze and stood up to leave. He brushed a tear from his eye and made quick time for the door. *Too much of a liability in the field*, he told himself.

Steele tossed his pack over his shoulder and made a beeline for the reinforced door, nodding to Jarl and Mauser, who fell in line.

"Wait, wait," someone called from behind. Steele stopped. He was surprised to see Eddie in his greasy coveralls and a baseball cap, with a tool belt around his waist, hurrying after them.

Steele couldn't help but smile. This man wore his tools with pride. FSO Kim followed Eddie eying them with calculating eyes.

"Hi there. I was wondering if you had room for me to ride with ya?" Eddie said.

"We sure do," Steele said without hesitation. Steele had no right to refuse the man a ride, and who knew when they might need someone familiar with the mechanical arts.

"Thank you. I got some family in West Virginia, and if you head that way, which I assume you will, maybe you can drop me off."

"We will be headed that way, west at least. We would appreciate your help. Perhaps you know something about the mobile lounge maintenance?" Steele said, impressed by the man's insight.

"I sure do, son. I would be happy to help out," Eddie said with a smile and a handshake.

FSO Kim could hardly wait for Eddie to move out of her way. "Agent Steele, I'm going with you."

Steele was a bit taken back by her sudden interest in his team. "We will do our best to protect you and get you to a safe place. You have my word."

"It's not that. You do think quite highly of yourself, don't you?"

His jaw dropped a bit. He was confident, but not overly optimistic in their present situation.

"Don't bother to answer that. However, your team does seem a bit more highly trained than the security personnel down here," she gave a rearward glance at portly Officer Jenkins. "I could never stay down here. Besides, I am sure things will be better outside the airport," she said, flipping her hair out of her face to settle the issue.

Steele gave Mauser a sideways glance. He had a shit eating grin on his face.

"Okay. I will give you a moment to gather your belongings."

"That won't be necessary, I am ready." She over talked him and gave him a hard handshake.

She smiled triumphantly. *What just happened? Does she think that she is somehow in charge?* It was likely she waited to jump all over him as soon as he went to make the next decision; a constant hounding until he didn't know up from down, right from left. Feeling a few new gray hairs sprouting in anticipation, he took a deep breath. If the infected didn't kill him, surely she would.

The path he led them down most certainly meant death, but *he* had no choice. He couldn't sit back and wait knowing Gwen was still out there. If they wanted to follow him through hell, so be it. None of these people had to come with him; this was all voluntary. Regardless, the burden of responsibility weighed down on his shoulders like an Atlas stone.

GWEN
Fairfax, VA

Lindsay allowed the Jeep to roll to a stop, its brakes grating slightly. *Please don't attract any of them.* A green sign read Bircham Rd. Gwen squinted at a mangled mess of cars crowding the intersection. It looked as though the accident had started with a minor fender bender, but had extended outward as other cars had tried to drive around and became entangled with each other.

An SUV had wrapped itself around an oak tree. Its hood scrunched up like an inchworm, and the windshield spiderwebbed. Pieces of wreckage lay strewn about. The driver flailed inside pressed up against an inflated air bag. Struggle as he might, he couldn't extract himself. Gwen's first instinct was to rush over and help, but a large tree branch emerging from the center of the man's chest revealed he was one of the undead. *Not everything that moved was alive.*

Another road blocked. "We can make it on foot. Plenty of daylight." *Jesus, it's only a few blocks. Surely we can walk it.* Her thoughts brought on a serious case of doubt.

"Those guys from the gas station are still back there," Ahmed said, peeping out the back window.

It seemed that the more they drove around the more the dead tried to follow them. Most gave up and wandered toward easier prey, but those assholes from the gas station were persistent.

"See if there's a way round," she said to Lindsay, who knuckled the steering wheel. *As long as we keep moving we seem to be okay.*

End Time

Lindsay edged the Jeep up over a sidewalk trying to take it around the wreckage. A combination of trees and cars stopped them from going any further. Gwen simply didn't know what to do; she had never heard of anything like this before in history.

"We're only a few blocks from where I live. If we lay low and stay quiet, I think we can make it without running into any of those things," she said quickly.

Gwen glanced over at Lindsay, who visibly blanched. Ahmed didn't say a word. "Guys, we have food and guns at my house, so we'll be safe. We can't drive around forever, because those people keep chasing us. We need a safe place to hide. We can leave the Jeep here, and if we can't make it through we can circle our way back and get out of here."

Over her shoulder, she peered at Ahmed, who had an odd look in his eye. She couldn't quite put her finger on it.

He flashed a smile. "I'm in. We should move fast though, before those guys catch up," he said with cautious glance over his shoulder.

Lindsay scowled blowing hair out of her face.

"Lindsay, please. We'll be safer. I promise." *I have no idea if it will be safer.*

"I don't want to go out there with those monsters. I've seen what they do to you. We should stay in the car." Tears welled in Lindsay's eyes.

Trying to comfort, Gwen rubbed Lindsay's shoulder. It was tense, a fearful knot of anxiety. Time to put some of her psychology classes from college to work. All those student loans had to pay off at some point.

"You can stay here, but I think we'd be better off together. You know, watch each other's backs, right? Just like the Metro. We're a great team. Ahmed and I need you, and you need us."

Ahmed caught on. "I agree. Let's stick together. We'll come right back if it's too dangerous," he said, leaning in from the backseat in between the women.

She would never have let Lindsay stay there by herself, but it would be better if she could persuade her to want to go.

"I can't fight," Lindsay muttered.

Gwen half smiled. "Ahmed and I will protect you. I promise." *I will try*, she thought, *will that even be good enough?*

"That's right. None of them will even get close," Ahmed reaffirmed, showing her is baseball bat.

After a minute of silence, Lindsay sniffled. "Okay. But if it gets scary, I'm coming back to the car," she said.

"We all will," Gwen assured her.

They exited the vehicle and quietly closed the doors, trying not to make a sound. The three of them trudged their way down the street toward the cul-de-sac that held her townhouse. Every row was broken up into six townhouse blocks along each side of the street. The houses had been built during the eighties, and each had two stories. They were quiet, quaint and secluded, each with a small driveway. Trees ran along the backs of the houses blocking them from the main road. It could have been just a regular day in the neighborhood, or maybe a holiday weekend since only about half the cars were parked in front of their respective homes.

The group stalked down the middle of the street. A minivan sat running in a driveway, the doors open, blood dripping from the door handle into a widening pool on the ground. They passed holding their breath, not daring to peek in. Gwen led the way, their little party huddling together for safety. Ahmed held his baseball bat close to his chest. They made a desperate party. If anyone had noticed them from the townhouses, they weren't letting on.

Three houses away from Gwen's, Ahmed touched her on the shoulder and pointed ahead with his baseball bat. They scrambled behind a parked crossover and squatted down. Lindsay's teeth rattled.

"What is it?" Lindsay whispered.

Gwen peered out from behind the car. Two cartoon clad small children were outside. It was Timmy and Jessica, Gwen's next-door neighbors, aged nine and ten. *Please let them be okay.*

She watched them closely. They seemed to be dancing around something on the ground straw colored ringleted hair bouncing on their shoulders. Every few moments they would release a high-pitched mewing. *Are they crying? Are they hurt?* They bent down tugging on a form on the ground. *They must need help. If I can't bring myself to help the most vulnerable in society, who am I? I have a responsibility to aid them.*

She stood up, hesitantly, brushing dirt off her suit. *Better to not resemble one of the infected if they need our help.* Ahmed caught her by the sleeve, pulling her back down with an iron grip.

"What's your problem?" she asked, shaking his hand free.

His dark eyes bore into hers like black drills. Holding her gaze he mouthed, "No." *What has gotten into him?*

"They're children, for God's sake," she whispered.

Ahmed closed his eyes slowly. "Not any more," he breathed.

That can't be. She looked back at the children scrutinizing them.

They dug relentlessly at something on the ground. Gwen realized they weren't crying for help; they were eating. Blood covered their little hands, faces and their pajamas, as though they had turned while taking a nap. The outline of a yellow-haired corpse lay motionless. *That must be Jill.*

Gwen's heart dropped. She had babysat them on various occasions when their parents enjoyed a night out on the town. She wondered if their father Henry was around. He worked at the Pentagon as a defense contractor, so maybe he was still alive.

If they didn't want to address the issue of infected children, which Gwen didn't know if she had the stomach to do, they would have to find another way. Gwen shuddered at the thought.

It would take an extra few minutes, but they could make their way around the back of the house and go in through the basement. "We've got to go around," she said in hushed tones.

Both Ahmed and Lindsay acknowledged her with a nod.

The infected children didn't look up from their gore-splattered feast as the trio backtracked to the other side of the street. They hugged the backyard fences until Gwen came upon one that was familiar. Each wooden fence came up to eight feet, providing reasonable privacy from the outside.

Gwen unlatched the gate, as quiet as possible, and they went inside. Her hand shook as she closed the fence. Taking a moment to relax, her heartbeat slowed down a little. *We are on the home stretch.*

Their feet crunched through a section of brown grass that Mauser had killed in a weed eradication project gone wrong. In utter contrast, an attractive garden sat on either side of the yard, filled with perennials that covered the fence, while a beautiful hydrangea bush grew in the corner. A sliding glass door led to Mauser's room in the basement.

Whew. She sighed a breath of relief. *We made it.* Gwen tugged at the sliding door. Nothing moved. She pulled at it again. This time it moved slightly, but only enough to let her know it was locked.

At that moment, they heard the footsteps and the moans. The rustling movement of a mass of people approaching their direction in haste. Thump. Lindsay shrieked covering her mouth. The whole fence shuddered on impact.

"How did they find us?" Lindsay mouthed. Ahmed looked panicked, but he immediately took up a wide stance facing backward.

"Gwen, we need to get inside now," he called over his shoulder.

The moaning of more infected echoed off the backs of the townhouses. The wood bent inwards as another body fell into the fence. Gwen felt frantically for her purse. No purse hung in its normal place by her side. *I must have lost it when I fell.*

"Shit. Shit. Shit," she said, trying to remember where they had hidden the spare key. She wildly flipped over rocks in the garden. *It had to be under one of these things.*

The fence rattled as they tried to breach it.

"I don't have a key," she screamed at Ahmed.

"Hurry Gwen," he hissed.

Dirt caked her fingers as she clawed the black garden earth in a desperate effort to find the key. *Fuck it.* She wrapped her fingers around a softball-sized rock and chucked it through the middle of the sliding door. The glass bursted inward. *Mauser would understand.*

They hurried inside as the fence gave way under the weight of the bodies. The infected toppled over each other, becoming an entangled mess of limbs.

Gwen ran straight into the laundry room and grabbed Steele's Mossberg 500 breach barrel shotgun that he kept slung on a rack. She grabbed the gun, pumping it quickly to ensure that it was loaded.

She faced the disfigured, walking corpses of her neighbors as they staggered into the basement. Janine from across the street didn't even flinch as her sleeve caught on the broken glass, cutting right through the flesh and muscle of her arm. More blood-covered bodies marched inside the fence with dead white stares and gaping open mouths.

"Lindsay, there's a revolver in that case over there," she hollered, before taking up a firing stance, wide but not too wide, and prepared to unleash a barrage of gunfire in the direction of the unwanted newcomers.

Pulling the trigger, she pointed the shotgun at the assailants without using the single bead sight. A slug to the chest put down what was once their nosey neighbor, Mr. Wilson. His face had been gnawed at, exposing his jawbone and teeth. She reloaded by pumping the handgrip up and down. Boom. Another police slug hit what remained of Mrs. Andrews in the face, effectively halting her forward progress. She was missing an arm and looked almost comical with her hair still in curlers. *Won't need to worry about her seventies hairdo now.*

Gwen jerked the trigger and took off an infected jogger's leg collapsing the man. He crawled toward her, his leg a bony, sinewy mess of tendon and flesh. Janine reached for Gwen swiping red fingernails inches from her face, a gaping hole in her chest. Gwen rotated her hips, thrusting the gun like a spear into Janine's skull. A sickening crack rewarded Gwen as the breach barrel punched through Janine's head like parchment paper. Janine toppled downward, the hole where Gwen had rammed her filling with blood. She doubted that was the barrel's intended purpose, but it had done the trick. Janine didn't get up again.

Gwen was thankful Mark had taken her to the range and let her shoot the shotgun before, otherwise the sound and recoil might have surprised her out of shooting it more than once. The sound was deafening and the recoil kicked her shoulder like a mule. Fire erupted from the front of the serrated barrel each time she shot. She kept firing until she ran out of ammo.

All the infected were down and chalky gun smoke had taken their place. Lindsay crouched in the corner covering her ears.

Ahmed walked over to Mr. Wilson, who was beginning to sit up despite his shredded upper torso. He hammered his skull with an overhead swing. Ahmed dispatched the jogger and several others with the same technique, which seemed to do the trick. Gwen's neighbors failed to rise again.

When he had finished, he gave Gwen a quick smile. "Damn, girl, you just rocked those things."

She smiled back, her adrenaline levels beginning to drop and the relief of surviving the encounter ebbing through her. "You should see me Bachata," she said, sweeping her hair out of her face.

Ahmed pierced her with his dark eyes. She ignored him and reached down to grab a handful of shotgun shells. One by one she slid them into the bottom of the gun.

JOSEPH
Mount Eden Emergency Operations Facility, VA

Joseph strolled to the elevators hands in his pockets. The Bottomside of Mount Eden was a dry and claustrophobic dungeon that Joseph called home. The bunker had been built in the late sixties as a fallout shelter for the President and Congress in case of a nuclear strike from the Soviet Union. It could hold over a thousand people for six months without Topside support. Underground reservoirs, ventilation and air recirculation systems ensured the compound's self-sufficiency. And Joseph actively sought to leave the protective labyrinth. He needed a breath of fresh air after his meeting with the *Special* Committee.

A soldier in full combat gear waved him into the elevator, which shuddered as it sped to the surface. Joseph stepped out into a foyer, which could have been the lobby of a office building or hotel except for the two-foot-thick steel doors encasing the entrance to the elevator.

The faint sound of helicopters thundered as they flew back and forth from supply runs or combat missions into Northern Virginia. The high and tight held up a hand making him wait.

"Private, front and center." A young military man hustled forward tucking in his shirt, helmet in hand.

"You are on *escort* duty." The young soldier's eyes dropped as if he were being punished.

"Do I really need an escort?" Joseph inquired.

The older grizzled soldier hardly batted an eye at Joseph.

"Orders are orders. You go outside. You get an escort." *Was there no privacy in this place?*

The young soldier followed him outside, casually holding his rifle downward. The bright sun blinded Joseph, and he shaded his eyes. It wasn't too hot, but it wasn't cool either, a perfect end of the summer weather.

Joseph had never been aware that Mount Eden even existed. Trying to hide such a huge facility on top of a thickly wooded mountain seemed silly to him. Very supervillainesque, with a boring government twist, plain white and gray warehouse style buildings covered the mountaintop.

"Do you know anything about this place?" Joseph asked his shadow guard.

"Never been here in my life 'til now, but Sarge said this is some sort of 'go-to' facility for FEMA and other Feds if their D.C. facilities were ever compromised."

Our current predicament is a little worse than compromised.

"Do you mind?" the soldier asked, lighting a cigarette. Joseph didn't respond. The soldier spoke out the side of his mouth, the other holding his cigarette in place. "I guess there's a bunch of underground facilities in the Washington area that hold government agencies so they can still operate in the case of a disaster." Joseph nodded. He had seen a show on television about it.

"They call it continuity of government, but they don't tell me shit. Just go here, hump there, and shoot them. We got a brigade of the 82nd Airborne flown in, the 12th Aviation Battalion and stragglers from the 3rd Infantry. The Old Guard had a rough time of it being so close to the city and tasked with bringing out all those officials."

Joseph nodded. All the military jargon meant little to him. Helicopters landed and took off every few minutes. Large trucks unloaded supplies and men raced back and forth. A host of buildings decorated the Topside: dormitories, cafeterias, training venues and office buildings. Now most were being utilized by the military.

Organized chaos, Joseph thought. He deliberately quickened his pace away from the military encampment, stopping at a hodgepodge of tents and shelters. *No uniformity.*

The soldier stepped next to him in a leisurely fashion, as if they were old friends at a cookout.

"Refugees?" Joseph asked, but he already knew the answer.

"Yup." The soldier pushed his combat helmet upward revealing his forehead. "At first the refugees were told they couldn't enter the secure zone, but that quickly changed when the people outside caused more problems than they would have if they'd been inside the fences," the soldier said, tossing his cigarette butt. "There are over five hundred acres up here and only two access points." He eyed a family heating food in boiling water huddled around a small burner.

Joseph thought about asking the soldier's name, but decided a name exchange might be a bad idea. He didn't have a great track record given the demise of his last chaperones.

The young soldier pointed to a large tent guarded by masked soldiers with rifles. "See that over there. That's the duty nobody wants. We call it the 'Old Rochambeau.'"

"Why is that? Never mind, I don't want to know."

The young soldier smiled. "Cause anybody would much rather get a swift kick in the nuts than man the screening tent. You got to get up close and personal with potential Biters."

"I see." *Screening the civilians could be a very dangerous duty. Best left to the general practitioners.*

"After a thorough screening, the people are allowed to set up camp in any of the abandoned areas or open areas of the facility, provided it hasn't been designated mission essential." The fence was covered with razor wire, and, near the entrance, large concrete barricades were in place at intervals to slow approaching vehicles.

Joseph made eye contact with a little girl, who stared at him from outside the facility, awaiting clearance to enter the compound. She clung to her mother with one hand, and held a dirty torn teddy bear in the other. Staring vacantly, much like the infected, her eyes unclouded by the virus.

"Say, you're a doctor, right?" the soldier said. *Damn.*

"Yes." He dreaded the next questions, the ones that always came.

"Have you come up with a cure? You see, my daughter back home is sick."

Joseph cut him off. "Please, private whatever-your-name-is, I came up here to get away from all that. I don't have a cure, and I don't have anything to help you or your daughter." Joseph turned away.

The man stood silent for a moment. "It's Private Gordon, sir," and the soldier's mouth clamped shut. *Why do they always tell me their names?*

"I'm going back to the Bottomside," Joseph said.

The soldier didn't say anything; he simply followed a few steps behind. Joseph didn't look back as he quickly processed through the screening area and a soldier escorted him back inside the bunker.

The elevators led him back down four floors. Upon stepping out into the fluorescent light, he could take one of three corridors. One led to the Congressional chamber and news-broadcasting center. The last place he wanted to go back to.

Attached to the Congressional chamber, were the VIP dormitories and cafeteria. He wouldn't had even known they existed, but he had taken a few meals with an energetic young Representative Baker from Indiana. Incredibly, the Congressman was interested in doing something about it while they still had time.

The second corridor led to the regular dormitory, where everyone, who was not important, rotated sleep in what appeared to be naval shipping bunks. It wasn't time for his sleep shift so he couldn't go back there. It also had a larger, blander cafeteria, but no pictures of founding fathers adorned the plain walls. Next to the general cafeteria were standard showering facilities. Joseph had been relieved to see that the stalls had curtains, or he would have had to wear his boxers while bathing. *The alternative was most uncivilized.*

The third corridor led to some offices, storage rooms, and a medical lab that the scientists had commandeered. This was the only place where he truly felt comfortable.

He flashed his badge at a couple of towering Army soldiers, who held short rifles across their chests. Waving him through to the lab, they hardly glanced down at his badge. They were probably more concerned about him running ravenously down the hall like a rabid dog, hell bent on ripping their throats out than the color of his badge.

Joseph worked on into the night, skipping dinner with his colleagues. Time was running out; he needed to come up with something fast. Dozing off at his computer, he awoke to the pinging sound of a new email. *No doubt another horrible news update.*

'Los Angeles closes hospitals.' The number of cases on the West Coast had skyrocketed, and the hospitals were turning away bite victims. *It's only a matter of time now.* He scrolled through his emails to distract himself.

The computer mouse squeaked as he rolled through his inbox. He had to use an ancient machine from 2001 that was slower than his grandmother because only government computers were allowed in the building. *Your grandmother is probably dead.* He pushed the thoughts from his head. Squeak. Squeak. *Nothing important here. Wait.*

He paused, double-clicking on an email he had received a few weeks earlier from a former CDC colleague in Chicago. It read 'Can you believe this? Monkeypox cases reported in city.'

The sent date was two weeks earlier. He checked the date again. Two weeks and a day. *Why haven't I seen this earlier?* He supposed it could have slipped past him when he was in the field. He hurried to print the email. *This could be the missing piece.* He pounded the mouse trying to expedite the print speed, and ran from the room.

STEELE
Chantilly, VA

The mobile lounge's speedometer hovered at a steady 25mph. Mauser slowing it to weave the unwieldy behemoth in and out of abandoned traffic on Route 50. This road was normally gridlocked with people on their morning commute. Now abandoned vehicles sat gridlocked, not moving at all. The mobile lounge shifted to the left or right as it flattened an infected person or rolled over miscellaneous car wreckage.

Mauser sped up the mobile lounge and a body thudded as he crushed another infected. With an evil grin, he shouted: "Old lady, that's five points." Wrestling the steering wheel, the lounge swerved to the left.

"Ooo, hot blonde, that's ten points." The mover didn't acknowledge her existence as she bounced off the side of its thick wheel tread.

Steele ignored him, and watched the road grimly. His gut burned with worry and doubt. Steele had been listening to his friend's morbid game for around fifteen minutes, and wasn't helping. "Mauser, shut the fuck up and drive." *Did he not understand what was at stake?*

"Come on, man. Lighten up."

"I'm serious. Don't you see what's happening out there? Our community is fucked," Steele said. Mauser stiffened and sat in silence. "Just drive," Steele said, shaking his head. *This is not a game. This is real. People are dying, and I have to find Gwen before it's too late. I won't rest until she is in my arms again. I won't rest.*

Mauser piped up in front. "I know exactly what's going on. If its the last thing I do, I will get you back to her. I care about her too."

Steele felt a pang of guilt for admonishing his friend. *I know we are on the same team.*

They lumbered past a strip mall, red-shingled storefronts with white lettering above. "People are on the roof," Jarl reported gruffly, pointing out the window. Living souls waved their arms above their heads trying to track them down.

Steele made eye contact with Jarl.

"Should we stop?" Mauser chimed in.

"No," Steele said. He pointed ahead. It was as if everyone was trying to prevent him from reaching her.

His tactical badge swung back and forth around his neck, a constant reminder of his duty to the public; a duty that he elected to disregard. He stared down at the gold badge. *What does it mean to serve and protect when society consumed itself? What does it mean to defend the Constitution and the United States against all enemies foreign and domestic when the people of the United States itself were the enemy?* He tucked the badge under his shirt. For better or worse, his decision was made. It was a decision that he would have to live with.

Mauser slowed down as they approached a pileup at the intersection of VA Route 50 and Bircham Road. "Can you get around it?" Steele asked.

"I don't think so," Mauser replied.

The engine idled for a minute, and they scanned the area looking for some way to improve their position. Groups of the infected navigated around the abandoned vehicles. Steele had good 360-degree vision through the mobile lounge's long, wide windows.

The infected were drawn to the lounge like moths to a flame. They closed in on the vehicle all while the engine sang a lonely diesel tune.

A man in his fifties darted out of a car to the left, swinging his arm to get their attention. He held a young boy in the other. They were haggard and dirty, as though they had been sleeping in their car.

"You want me pick them up?" Jarl called from the rear. He pushed open the folding doors with a big hand.

There was just enough space between the father and the infected that he might make it. He yelled as he ran: "Wait! Wait for us!"

Steele ignored the call for aid. He pointed to a small gap in the pileup with some smaller vehicles. "Get some speed and drive through there," he said without a backward glance.

Mauser looked up at him and back at Jarl, concern spreading over his face. "What about that guy and the kid?" he asked. The yelling grew louder.

"Help us. Don't leave," the man shouted.

"He's probably infected anyway. Leave him," Steele said firmly to Mauser.

"That guy has a kid, for Christ's sake. Tell me you're not serious?" Mauser glowered.

"Agent Steele, they need help," FSO Kim said.

Steele fingered the handle of his gun. *I promised myself I would do anything to get back to her. I promised her that I would never let anything happen to her.* "Mauser, drive this fucking thing before I lose it."

Mauser gave Steele one last chance to change his mind, glaring at him in disbelief.

"This is on your head."

"Fine. Just go."

Mauser gunned it and the lounge lurched ahead, rolling up and over the cars in the intersection. Steele could hear the cries of the man and his son as the infected brought them down like a pack of feral animals. The cries for help were replaced by the crunching of metal beneath the giant vehicle.

The man's screams pulled at Steele's heartstrings, but it was the child's high-pitched bawling for his father as he was ripped apart that burrowed deep into his mind. Shoving his unrelenting thoughts to the back of his head, he tried to justify what he had done.

What if the time it takes to pick them up leads to the death of my loved ones? Haven't I done enough to help everyone else? I have risked my life, time and time again for the doctor, the flight crew, my teammates and the survivors sitting within this mobile lounge. Isn't it my right to protect my family and friends from harm? When does my watch over the public end? Does my watch end if there is no one to take my post? How can I do my job knowing that my loved ones are in immediate danger?

Rolling forward, they passed abandoned vehicles in the residential street, and within minutes the mover turned onto his cul-de-sac. Everyone sat in silence. No one commented on what had just taken place, too stunned to utter a word. Steele was also sure they probably hated him for it. Mauser acted pissed, but he didn't care. He was so close, he could taste it.

"Drive," he commanded. Mauser put the mobile lounge right onto their front lawn. The thick tire treads tore through the green grass, leaving dark, churned earth in its place. Steele couldn't care less. His landlord probably wandered the streets hunting for someone to infect.

Their brown front door swung ajar, hanging off one of its hinges. Blood covered the entrance like an ancient Passover. *No.* Life as he knew it crumbled around him. He stared at the door to his townhouse, not quite believing what he saw was the truth. His heart sank; any remaining hope dying inside him.

"NO, NO, NO," Steele screamed as his frustration boiled over into blind rage. *I had willed her to be alive. This isn't happening.* He shoved his way through the mobile lounge's folding doors, jumping from the vehicle before Mauser could lower the hydraulics.

A shooting pain bounced up his knee as he landed. Ignoring the injury, he ripped his SIG Sauer P226 from his front waist holster as he ran toward the townhouse. No tactics were used in his approach. He ran through the doorway of his home, stepping over the fallen body of a swarthy man as he hurried to get inside.

Steele failed to check any corners as he rushed. Blood covered the living room that had seemed so cozy in the past. Gratuitous amounts of blood coated the walls and ceiling reminding him of an overdone haunted house.

Jesus fucking Christ, he thought as he slipped in a puddle of blood on the hardwood floor. *There's blood everywhere,* his mind raced skipping from thought to thought. His sofa, the TV, even the lamps were varnished with the coppery liquid.

Gripping the handrails on his stairs, he looked upward. Pictures on the walls tilted cockeyed as if some prankster had thought it funny to turn them all sideways with a filthy hand. An infected body lay sprawled on the steps. She vaguely resembled his neighbor, a nurse at the nearby Inova Fairfax Hospital. Most of her head was missing from what appeared to be a shotgun slug to the head. The scrubs were the only thing that gave her away; there just wasn't much else to go on. A faint sickly fruit odor hung around her making him want to gag.

"Gwen," he half yelled, half whispered. He spit the bad taste from his mouth.

A creak on the floorboards alerted him to an inhabitance on the top floor, and he took the steps in twos. The door to his bedroom was latched shut. *Please be in the bedroom. Please be in the bedroom.*

"Gwen baby," he said at the door. Nothing. Silence. He rested his head on the doorframe as he slowly twisted the doorknob. It was locked and he could hear something move on the other side.

"Gwen?" he whispered. "Gwen open the door, it's me." No acknowledgement echoed from the other side. *She must be inside.*

Leaning back, the door splintered under the assault of a ferocious front kick. A rancid stench lashed at his nose as he charged inside. Precious seconds dripped by as he waited for his eyes to adjust to the darkness of the room. The ominous presence of something lurking inside came over him and his eyes, led by his ears, were drawn to an infected man hunched over in the corner. It was clear by its jerking movements that it was feeding. With a slow turn of his head it briefly acknowledged Steele's existence, a mouthful of human meat hanging loosely from his lips.

Twisting its body, the infected exposed the form of a woman. She lay proned out, limbs lifeless at her sides. Steele raged. "Stay away from her," he growled, lining up a shot through the creature's temporal lobe.

He refused to believe this thing had once been human. No human could possibly be capable of such a depraved act. Letting his momentum take him straight into the fiend, he slammed the handle of his handgun into the thing's head, again and again. Gore splattered the walls, the carpet and the pictures he had taken with Gwen from their trip to St. Lucia. Unrelenting he pounded his gun into its face until the arms of his fellow agents lifted him up and away from the beast. He kicked out one last time in blind hate, as reality set in.

"It's okay. It's not her," Mauser whispered in his ear. His words fell on deaf ears.

Deep down, he knew it was her. Much of her body had been consumed, her clothes now a ragged mess of slippery insides. Her silver diamond necklace she received for their anniversary lay wrapped around her hand as if she held it as she was attacked. *She was here and now was gone.*

Steele stopped resisting his colleagues and they set him down. If he had driven faster, fought harder, done anything differently, she would still be alive. His sequence of actions mocked him. It blew apart his whole belief system like a grenade dropped on his whole shit covered cake of a life. He would have to live knowing he had lost his most important battle. *Anything except this.* A thousand painful deaths were preferable to this.

Sitting in a heap, he stared forward. His hands stroked her blood-soaked hair, now a reddish-golden hue. The others cleared the house and secured it, but he didn't care. He had failed to protect the one person he had loved above all others. Tears ran down his cheeks as he held her remains, rocking back and forth. *It wasn't supposed to be like this.*

After what seemed like an eternity of grief, but was only a few minutes,

Mauser squatted down beside him, putting a hand on his knee.

"Mark. We don't know if that is her. It could have been anybody." Steele knew she was gone, and he hated that his friend would lie to him about it.

"Leave me here," he said solemnly, his chin hanging down to his chest and Gwen's remains draped across his lap.

Mauser gaped at him. "You can't be serious. You'll die." Steele didn't care if he died, because he was already dead inside. He didn't respond to his best friend. "Come on we have to go before we get trapped. She could still be out there," Mauser said, giving Steele's leg a shake.

Dejected, he knew his fate. He couldn't go on knowing her light had been extinguished. He broke eye contact with his friend, ashamed of his weakness.

Mauser frowned. "You aren't done until I say you're done, asshole," Mauser snarled. He gripped the front of Steele's shirt and slapped him hard across the face.

Spittle flew from Steele's mouth, and snot ran down his nose, his cheek stinging with fire. He made no move to defend himself. Mauser slapped him again.

"Now buck up. We need you out there. Our team needs you and, as much as I hate to say it, I need you." Mauser looked at him desperately, trying to read his eyes, searching for any will that might be left in his squad mate, his friend, his brother.

Steele stared at him blankly.

Fire blazed in Mauser's eyes. "You know what? Fuck you, man. I thought you were made of tougher shit than this. You got us all the way here just to give the fuck up *now*? If you want to die here, be my guest, but I won't sit here and rot with you." He released Steele, letting him fall against the bedroom wall.

Mauser stopped near the door and shook his head in disgust. "It's not safe here. They'll come for you and kill you."

Steele didn't respond. *Why should I go on? Where was it written that I have to live if I have no reason to live? The infected will probably sniff me out and tear me apart just like that little boy and his father. I deserve death for letting innocents die on my watch.*

"Go to Hell," Mauser called back at him. *Already there.* Mauser went back downstairs with a dismissive wave. People argued down below, but he didn't care. He had brought them far enough.

Jarl checked on him. He held a light weight Daniel Defense AR-15 carbine with red dot sights with a thirty-round mag locked in. Years ago, Mauser had three carbines built specifically for this type of end time scenario. One of their spare tactical vests covered Jarl's torso, with six more mags hanging from it. Jarl looked every inch a warrior: fierce, hard and wary.

Jarl gazed down at him, an old pagan god judging the worthiness of the prostrated man below him. After a moment, he bent down, taking a silver chain from around his neck. A small metal hammer hung from its lowest point, the pendant so worn it appeared as an upside down T.

"This is, Mjölnir, symbol of Thor, Norse god of thunder," Jarl said, holding the chain out in front of Steele. "In the Dark Ages, my people were forced to convert to Christianity. In secret, we still worshipped the old gods. You have been a good friend and a strong warrior. You have a long fight still ahead of you, and Valhalla will be your reward. I will see you at Ragnarok." Smiling he resembled more of a bear than a man, and he draped the chain around Steele's neck, patting his friend's shoulder. "Die well," he whispered, steel in his eyes, and he left Steele alone.

Steele looked up, tears in his eyes, and then laid his head back down. He had once been a warrior, a public servant and a rock in the winds of chaos. Now only his shell remained: no heart, no will and no life to live.

Downstairs the movement ceased, and the engine revved up, grew faint, disappearing altogether. Steele had resigned himself to his dire fate. For although he yet breathed, he had joined the dead.

JOSEPH
Mount Eden Emergency Operations Facility, VA

Joseph ran as fast as he could through the drab halls to the employee sleeping quarters. His shoes slapped the tile, and he gripped a corner wall to catch himself before he shoved open the dormitory doors. Too many people were crammed into the small space, making the air hot and stifled. People lay in single bunks in various states of sleep, or, if they were like Joseph, various states of insomnia.

It reminded him of an old black-and-white submarine film. The sailors were all packed inside a small metal tube, sweating and trying to scrape out some sort of life while any mistake could bring thousands of pounds of water pressure crashing down upon them. A mere oversight effectively turning the ship into a piece of crumpled metal. The Mount Eden facility was little more than a thinly plated U-boat, but instead of water destroying them, three hundred thousand diseased people awaited their chance. Even a single infected unleashed among them could enlist the whole bunker into the ranks of the dead. Joseph shuddered at the thought.

In the dark, he stumbled over someone's backpack as he made his way to Dr. Williams' bunk. They slept in rotations, much like being on a ship, and had been assigned bunks to share with two other people. He searched high and low from bunk to bunk for an old man with a ridiculous snow-white mustache.

Dr. Williams was the Deputy Director for Infectious Diseases at the CDC. He had been giving a presentation to Congress on bioterrorism when he got trapped in the D.C. area due to the outbreak of the virus. As a leading expert in the field of infectious diseases, his word sparkled like gold. He was shuttled to the Mount Eden facility immediately.

As a disease surveillance specialist, Joseph was far below him in the hierarchy of the organization. *Dr. Williams was probably squinting through microscopes while I was running around in diapers.* None of that really mattered now that their science team could be one of the only things standing between the human race and total extinction.

Joseph discovered the old man lying on his side in a bunk. He gently shook his shoulder. *I don't want to startle the old buzzard; he might croak with too much excitement.* Dr. Williams opened his eyes and gasped, recognizing Joseph's face. A small man with white, thinning hair, his upper lip was adorned with a wispy mustache that was usually reserved for cowboys and fine gentlemen from the Victorian Era. Slowly, he sat up in his bunk and put on his glasses.

"Joseph, it can't possibly be time to switch sleep rotations. What's wrong?"

Joseph could hardly contain himself. "Dr. Williams, sorry for waking you, but I just came across some information you have to see."

Dr. Williams took his time getting out of the bunk, as old men tend to do when they wake up in the morning.

"Read this email," Joseph insisted, pushing a paper into Dr. Williams hands.

"It can wait until we get to the lab," Dr. Williams corrected, stretching his back. Joseph wanted to run back to the lab, so excited he could hardly stand it, but was forced to walk slowly beside the old doctor. He bounced from foot to foot until they finally reached his computer. The old doctor tenderly sat down at Joseph's desk adjusting his glasses.

"It was sent two weeks ago from a former classmate of mine from the

University of North Carolina."

The old doctor skimmed the email. The look on the elder man's face didn't change. His eyes moved back and forth as he digested the information. *Had he read it? This could be the biggest piece of the puzzle they'd found yet.*

Finishing his digestion of the material, he took off his glasses and rubbed his eyes. "Dr. Jackowski, this email is speculative at best. It is not worth a further second of our time."

Joseph's eyes bulged out of his head. *What? He cannot be serious.*

"Sir, with all due respect, this could possibly be patient zero; our needle in a haystack the size of New York. If we could get our hands on a live strain of the infantile virus we could produce a vaccine. We could save millions of lives and give ourselves a fighting chance."

Joseph shoved the printout of the email into Dr. Williams' hands. He coughed impatiently, glancing at the email again. "We don't even know if this is the same virus," he said, pointing at the print out. "See right here. While the patient exhibited violent tendencies as well as fever-like symptoms, Dr. Anderson mentions nothing of the reanimation of the patient, or any other information that would lead me to believe that this is anything other than common rabies or typhoid fever. When severely dehydrated or hallucinating during a fever-like state, patients can exhibit all these phenomena. In fact, it also says that the patient recovered from his condition, which is clearly not a possibility for the people outside this facility."

While it might seem like a stretch, this was hardly something that could be passed over. At the very least it deserved a thorough investigation. How could a man of this genius, a man of such caliber, not see the connection? It had so much potential Joseph could taste it.

The report stated that the patient had been to Africa.

Dr. Williams continued: "I don't want you pursuing this false hope while we're working here. It will distract you from your important research into finding a cure. There are many lives at stake here, and I need everyone on the same page." He stood up and put a hand on Joseph's shoulder.

Joseph leaned back. He wanted to strangle this old fool. *You can't cure this disease,* he thought. *You could only hope to contain it.*

"You should get some rest, Joseph. By God we all need it," Dr. Williams said, turning to leave.

"You know, you're absolutely right. I shouldn't waste our time on such a foolhardy patient case. I just need some sleep," Joseph said convincingly. Inside he boiled in anger.

Dr. Williams looked him up and down, his eyes weighing the truthfulness of his words. "When we cure this, Joseph, we'll be the saviors of mankind. We'll win Nobel Prizes for sure." The old man's eyes twinkled with ambition.

"Now get some rest." He patted Joseph on the shoulder again, an action Joseph was starting to despise - and he left the small research room.

Joseph leered his blank computer screen, his mind racing. Time was short; he had to get this right. Determined to pursue his lead, he hoped no one found out. Even if they did find out he wasn't sure he would care. His fingers hammered away at the dusty keyboard.

STEELE
Fairfax, VA

Steele slept. He slept like there was no tomorrow, because for him there was no tomorrow. Having lost all sense of honor, duty and resolve, he sat crumpled in a pile of his own filth. He had no one left: no friends, no love, and he figured his family was most likely gone as well. But none of that mattered; they were all going to die anyway.

Thoughts of her flowed through his mind as waves fall onto a beach. Her smile, her emerald green eyes, and her sun-touched hair all rolled seamlessly into one. When he awoke, he didn't know how long he had been there. Photos of Gwen stared down from the wall, dried blood covering the frames. Her smile accused him of her death. Her cheerful eyes blamed him for her torture. Every frame simultaneously reminded him of his past life and his current state of misery.

The blood caked on his skin dried into a crusty, flaky mess. It itched his skin, but he endured it. The distinct and putrid smell of decomposition settled upon the body of the infected and Gwen. Flies buzzed around the room, accelerating the process. They landed on his face and arms, biting him, but Steele refused to brush them away. He dozed in and out of consciousness, plagued by feverish dreams of Gwen and the infected.

Sometime that afternoon as the sun shone in underneath the shades, he could hear movement downstairs. Gwen's body lay draped across this lap. They would die together like a tragic Shakespearian couple. He gazed at her brutalized face. It twitched in the dim light of the bedroom. *Is she still alive?*

He thought back to when he had shot his first deer as a child; how he imagined it was still breathing long after it had passed into the spirit world. As his father taught him how to field dress a deer, the buck's eyes followed him. Steele couldn't escape its glassy gaze as if the former forest king judged him for partaking in its expiration.

Taking a dirty hand, he swept her sticky hair out of her face. *She seems whiter than normal.* The wiggling continued, and he felt sick as he discovered maggots eating through her flesh. He picked at them, brushing them off her face, but the more he brushed the more he discovered.

"Damn it, Gwen," he whispered to her. "Why didn't you wait for me? I'm so sorry. I should have come to you faster," he stammered, tears of anger growing in the corners of his eyes. He gently set her body down next to him. Side by side until they die.

Footsteps resounded from the living room. They creeped and creaked on his hardwood floors, a deranged shuffling of infected feet. *So they have finally sniffed me out. Well, at least it would be over soon and I can be at peace. Maybe my friends will shoot me in the head after I turn. Mauser has a good shot; it would be fitting if he did it. Aim true, old friend.*

He wondered if there was a heaven, or if it was an endless darkness after death; a sense of fading into nothing. *Maybe I will reincarnate into someone or something else, or perhaps I will go to Valhalla to fight all day and feast all night. The funny thing about people is that everyone thinks they know, but nobody actually does. Even the ones who think there is nothing afterwards can't prove it. The only ones who know death, are the ones who have already passed, and the dead share no secrets.*

People throughout the ages have made up countless different answers to reassure themselves that life wasn't finite, but that is the only sure thing about life, that it eventually comes to an end. No matter how long you eked out an existence, you would meet the same fate as everyone before you, death.

Could this be the resurrection of the dead that the Bible spoke about? That's pretty twisted if that's what I've been singing and praying about at church all these years. Soon I will find out who's right or wrong. Or perhaps I will just cease, learning nothing, and the mystery will die with yet another insignificant human being.

Stairs groaned, a warning call of an aging house, and alerted him of the imminent arrival of the intruders. Steele closed his eyes and lay still. There was no use struggling now. The hobbled footsteps entered the room and stopped. He waited for the searing pain of a ravenous human bite. Their canines would rip through his docile flesh.

Nothing.

A hushed whisper broke the tense air. "Mark...?"

Steele slowly opened his eyes. Gwen's apparition stood six feet away from him, pointing his breach-barreled Mossberg directly at his head.

Wow, there is a God. And he is cruel. Steele felt he must have really messed up in life pretty bad to deserve this kind of ending.

"Is he one of them?" came a voice from the back. A man who looked suspect to Steele moved forward, his baseball bat ready to bash his head in.

"Wait!" she exclaimed.

The darker complected man stopped his forward progress, holding his bat high behind his head. His dark eyes were wide.

Shadowy Gwen passed him and used the serrated barrel of her gun to lift his forehead. Cold steel bit into his skin, and it shocked him like a cattle prod.

The steel is real. I can feel the steel.

He locked his eyes with her angelic face, "Gwen..." he croaked, his throat raw after days without water.

Kneeling down, she took his gore-covered head in her hands, and kissed him. She kissed him repeatedly, all over his face.

Suddenly realizing what she had done, she jerked her body away. "Are you bitten?" she asked.

"No," was all he could muster in a gargled voice. He reached his arms around her. They felt heavy, like they were made with lead, but she felt warm and soft and real. *This is real. She's really here.*

Tears of joy fell from his eyes, and her chest heaved as she gripped him tight. *They were together once again. The world might be ending, but at least we are together. Isn't that all I could ask for? To be with my true love while the world as we know it took a Titanic dip?*

Gwen and her companion helped Steele to his feet. He was incredibly dehydrated, and they led him down the stairs.

Furtively, she peeked out the window while the man with the bat raided the pantry. He shoved canned goods of all descriptions into his backpack.

Gwen called back softly, "We should move now while the coast is clear."

"I'm hurrying." He picked up his pack and put a strong arm around Steele, basically lifting him by himself. They dragged him out the door into the sunlight.

After being in the shaded room for so long, the bright light stung Steele's eyes, but he didn't complain. The threesome limped their way over to a townhouse across the street. Closing the door, she bolted it gently as if she dared not make a sound. They slid a couch back into place, barricading the door. Steele leaned on the wall, exhausted from his meager effort. A woman with dark brown hair came into the living room holding a .38 Special snubnosed revolver.

"Is he bit?" she asked.

Gwen held a finger to her scowling lips, and helped him down onto an old, weathered sofa. "Lindsay, this is my boyfriend, Mark."

"He looks like hell. Where did you find him?" Lindsay said.

"We found him over at my place when we were searching for supplies. Get me some water and bandages, hurry."

She stayed up with Steele all night tending his wounds. The next morning, he awoke and she was gone. Fear of her absence sent him into a fight or flight mode, but the sight of her belongings on the nightstand calmed him.

He crawled out of bed, and stretched his legs. Spare bed sheets covered the upper floor windows, preventing anyone or anything from seeing in. He inched a sheet back to get a view outside. A few people lumbered on the street. *Bastards are out there in my neighborhood.*

He let the sheet fall back in place. *I must be in old man Benson's place.* Benson had been a widower recluse, only coming out of his house at odd times. Steele had always wondered what the inside of his place was like.

Based on the appearance of the guest room, Benson must have been an avid comic book collector. *This is what he was doing. I wonder where he has all his video games stashed?* The bookshelves were lined with hundreds of comics and graphic novels. Large framed posters of superheroes and other science fiction movies adorned the walls. The room was topped off with a three-foot model of the Millennium Falcon, which hung from the ceiling. Steele laughed to himself. *When did the old man have time for a wife?*

Gwen came in with two cups of coffee. Steele wondered how long the electricity supply would last before it blew out. It had to be only a matter of time before the grid collapsed without human intervention. He smiled broadly, exposing crow's feet around his eyes that only appeared when he was truly happy. Gwen had his favorite shotgun slung across her back. There was nothing sexier than a woman with a gun.

"How did you end up here?" he asked, sipping the hot dark brew he loved.

She smiled sadly. "It's a long story. It was awful, and I was terrified."

"I understand."

"I couldn't have made it without Ahmed and Lindsay," she said. "I'm lucky we all found each other."

He thought about the friends he had lost: Mauser, Jarl and Wheeler. With no idea whether they were alive or dead, he feared the worst.

Steele sat up as Gwen recounted her journey from Foggy Bottom to Fairfax, and took his turn taking care of her. He inspected her bruised and lacerated feet and finding no major damage he bandaged them with gentle care.

"Ow," she said as he rubbed ointment on the bottom of her foot.

"You will live," he said with a smile. He shook his head in wonderment at her resilience. He knew what he was capable of, but throughout his struggle he had relied on firearms and brute force to win the day. She, on the other hand, had run, fought and snuck her way home.

"How did we miss you when we first came in?" he interjected.

"We were in here hiding. We didn't want to out ourselves in case you meant us harm," she said. "We just weren't sure what was going on."

"Who was the dead woman in our room?" he asked. Her blonde hair waved back and forth in a tactical ponytail.

"I don't know. She must have been a looter or something, because I left that necklace on the dresser when I went to work the other day. I wore my pearls the day the outbreak started." The pearls had vanished from her attire.

He shook his head. "I honestly thought you were dead," he said, emotion rising in his voice. He looked down, uncomfortable at his display of feelings. It wasn't common that he made himself emotionally vulnerable. "Mauser and Jarl were with me, and I quit on them."

She took his hand. Warmth radiated from her. "We've all been through a lot, baby. No one blames you for anything. You made it all the way here, and now we're together again." Sticking out her bottom lip she smiled at him.

Steele averted his gaze. "People died because of me. I chose not to help them, and they died," he said, picking up his tactical badge from the bedside table next to him. It felt heavy to him as if it repelled him. He didn't know if he still wanted it. He didn't know if he deserved to carry it. He felt a thousand times its weight in shame. His fingers examined it, running them over the large shield with U.S. Counterterrorism Division scrawled on the front, and over the emblazoned seal of the federal government raised up in gold. Blood had filled the grooves from top to bottom, making the American bald eagle a mixture of gold and dark red. *Am I defender of the weak when I let them die? How can I ever wear this again knowing I failed them?*

Gwen sat beside him, knowing his thoughts were weighing him down. "You saved many people, and you did what you had to do to get back home. You can't save everyone. You aren't superhuman."

I could have saved the father and son. I could have done more.

"I'm scared, Mark. Where do we go now?" she asked.

So am I.

He looked directly at her. "I don't know."

"What are we going to do?" she rested her coffee on her lap.

What options do we have?

"I don't know," he responded again.

An uncertainty filled the room, creating an air of uneasiness between them. He didn't have all the answers. *How can she expect me to always know what to do?* His brow clouded over with the stress and confusion of not knowing the best path to take, not seeing any suitable path at all.

"We need you to get us out of here," she stammered. Tears welled up in her eyes, her lip trembling. "I need you. Those people downstairs need you. You can keep us safe."

Can I? He inwardly doubted himself.

He focused his eyes on her, taking her in. She had always given him something to believe in. She represented the good in people; a compassion and empathy for others. She spread the warmth of her goodwill to him. The world needed them.

This compassion could only thrive if men like him protected it, shielded it from the refuse of society, and stood the lonely watch in the night, facing the evil and turning their backs to the good in the process. *How long can you face the evil before you mirror it?*

She leaned in, her eyes dropping tears as he embraced her. "Shh, we're going to be fine. I promise," he whispered in her ear. *I hope.*

"I, I was so scared. All these people were trying to kill us and I shot Janine and Mr. Wilson, and Timmy and Jessica were turned," she said, struggling to get the words out.

He held her, letting her overwhelming emotions release from the spot in her soul where it had been repressed. She always tempered his wariness with compassion. He gave her the tools to protect while she engendered in him the necessity to compromise. Her words drove out in him the protecting instinct of the sheepdog; the will to fight for those who could not defend themselves against the wolves in the night. He had betrayed that trust to protect. *Is there a way back?*

The world was changing. He had to make tough decisions to survive, but he would have to live with the decisions he made. As much as he wanted to, he couldn't crawl into a shell and hide away with her. *Hiding away isn't the right thing to do. But how can we balance survival and justice?*

He released her and put his head in his hands. Even if he brought about just a little order and justice it would temper some of the chaos and maybe give people some hope. Gwen leaned back on the bed, and sat in the corner of the room watching him.

Glistening eyes watched him, and her arms wrapped tightly around her knees, pulled up close to her chest. Some people had the need to bring order to chaos. It was ingrained in Steele, even the chaos couldn't change it.

Steele ground his thumb into the grooves of his badge and rubbed hard on the metal, chipping the blood off with his fingernail. Pain perforated in his fingertip as he pushed down harder to remove the blood from the deepest grooves. *As clean as I can get it, but it will always be stained.* He would have to live with that. He put the badge around his neck and tucked it into his undershirt, if only to keep it out of the way.

It belonged with him; he knew that now. It was a part of him that would never die. *People need me, and I will do my best to help them. It is the only way. I have to do my duty and stand up for what is right. Those who stand for nothing, fall for anything.*

MAUSER
Northern Virginia countryside

The people mover chugged along, black diesel smoke pumping out of the top exhaust pipe. The behemoth hadn't run into any obstacle it couldn't traverse, except fuel; its lifeblood; the only thing it couldn't live without. The fuel gauge needle wavered near half a tank. *We should be able to make it.*

They had filled it up to the max. It was unsurprising to Mauser that the hulking train-car on giant wheels took more than a hundred gallons of diesel. Jarl and Eddie had acted as lookouts while he fed the diesel-starved machine at a small countryside convenience store that doubled as a gas station.

Mauser laughed to himself when he remembered the look on the gas station owner's face when Jarl had given him his government credit card and told him to charge the three hundred and fifty dollar bill on it.

"I, uh, cash only," the owner had said. Jarl had flashed the owner his badge and brandished his carbine, and the man had suddenly thought better of it. Jarl had grinned through his blond beard and grabbed a big bag of beef jerky on the way out.

"Keep the change," Jarl said, leaving his government card behind. Their bosses would have flipped if they had known what they had been charging to the G-Card. Jarl would have been handed at least a week 'on the beach'; an agent term for a seven-day suspension.

Turning the mobile lounge sharply, he struck an infected man and crushed him beneath his vehicle. It made him feel a little better. All the drama surrounding Steele made him want to scream in frustration, and mowing down some of the infected eased his pain. He tried to push his anger toward Steele from his mind, but it lingered, nagging at him. The guilt hid just beneath the surface, torturing him about abandoning his close friend. He couldn't will the man to live or fight to live in this madness. *How can I expect that of anyone?*

Mauser tried to come to terms with his decision by rationalizing it as his way of granting his best friend's last request: to be left alone to die; to join his dead lover in heaven. He grimaced as he thought about Gwen's mutilated corpse sitting up and tearing Steele apart while he simply sat there, love-stricken: an undead Tristan and Isolde. The idiocy of the whole situation disgusted him.

Twisting the steering wheel to the left, he avoided a mass of ensnared car wreckage. A few people struggled through the countryside, and signs of violence decorated their bodies, marking them as infected. He weaved in and out of traffic, finally deciding the grassy median was best for him. He had avoided major roadways like Interstate 66 and Route 50. The mobile lounge could roll over just about anything, but he didn't push it, driving around the larger pileups.

After hours of internal anguish, Mauser's guilt turned sour. Steele was such an idiot. *Screw him for quitting on us. Steele is just young. Just couldn't hack it. Lacked that mental fortitude. Must be some sort of generational gap. I can do this.* Mauser swung the mover around an abandoned vehicle on the roadway. *That's the first one I've seen in a few miles. Infection must not be as bad out here.* A glimmer of hope burned inside him, at the very least, the will to move on.

On a map, his route would seem erratic with no obvious purpose, but in reality, he was just avoiding any routes that went directly west. Cars littered the road outside Fairfax, abandoned by people attempting to flee. As people fled west, the infected were following suit.

Mauser figured it would only be a matter of time before the infected from the D.C. area arrived en masse, infecting anyone who got in their way. They would be a brood of jungle army ants consuming anything in their path. A scorched earth policy that applied only to humans. But for now, the infection was still light, and that was just the way he liked it.

Beautiful green rolling hills surrounded the more urban capital, where D.C.'s wealthy elite had taken up residence. He drove past mansions that sat atop acres of historic horse breeding farmland; prime real estate. Mauser could never have dreamt of residing there, not on his pittance of a salary. On the low end, the houses cost millions of dollars and on the high end, tens of millions. *I suppose I am getting the last laugh though. Without the warrior caste to keep them alive I wouldn't expect them to be around for long. Rich or not.*

Mauser realized that the funny thing about the disease was that it didn't matter how much money people had, what race or how old they were. Everyone was the same in the disease's eyes, a great viral equalizer. All you were was a cellular host for the transmission of the disease. If a person was unfortunate enough to be bitten, he or she would succumb to the virus and try to bite anyone who wasn't already an undead asshole. Mauser let out a gruff laugh at the irony. He might have figured they would eat each other, but so far they only seemed interested in him and the remainder of the living.

There had been only one place on his mind as all this went bad. A facility that was specifically designed to withstand a disaster of this magnitude. He had spoken about it with Jarl, who seemed to think it was a good idea. Jarl was the only family he had left. The only person in this group he could truly count on in a scrap and trust not to stab him in the back. He was a true warrior. *No way in hell he would quit on us.*

Somewhere between Fairfax and Aldie they stopped and picked up a young Hispanic family whose car had run out of gas. The Ramirez family sat quietly in the corner of the lounge, having only whispered a meager 'thank you' when Mauser and company stopped to pick them up. They seemed to have had a rough go of it. They were cautious about the agents and spoke to no one. *Probably think we are going to arrest them or something.*

Even if they had been prepared to talk, Mauser didn't speak Mexican. He paid them little regard because soon they would be out of his hair. That way he wouldn't have to carry the weight of their deaths on his conscience when they got themselves killed. Cautiously, he gave them a rearward glance. The mother clutched her infant to her chest, her timid dark eyes fearful. *The sooner we get our ass up there the better. I will not be held responsible for anything that happens to them.*

An inconspicuous reflective green sign that read Exit 37 took them to the foot of a wooded mountain. The Blue Ridge Mountains were much softer and rounder than its Rocky cousins in the West.

This is it. What if they don't let us in? Then we will deal with that when it comes. He turned the hulking vehicle down the two-lane road and it inclined rapidly.

The mobile lounge meandered slowly up the twisting two-laner, curving back and forth as if the road builders hadn't been able to decide which way they wanted it to go. The mobile lounge was a bit top heavy so taking the turns fast was not an option. However, at the same time, he edged the accelerator down with his foot afraid that if he slowed down too much the people mover would stall out. Rolling backward down a mountain surrounded by trees would not be ideal. No cars passed him on the other side of the road. *Is that a good or bad sign?* He decided it didn't matter, the die was cast.

Nice and easy, Lunchbox. That's what he had named the mobile lounge, because that's what they were sitting in: a human lunchbox. The Ramirez family would be tacos, Kim would be sweet and sour chicken, and Eddie would be slow-cooked BBQ ribs. Mauser would be a cheeseburger and Jarl a giant steak. The infected could take their pick should they crack them open.

He imagined everyone in the mover running around in their respective food costumes, which made him feel even hungrier. *Maybe I caught the virus? No. You're just hungry you stupid son of a bitch. What I wouldn't give for a big greasy cheeseburger with bacon and cheddar cheese right now. And a large side of salted French fries with chili and cheese sauce. Extra cheese sauce. Mmmm. When was the last time I ate something? Yesterday? The day before?* He couldn't remember.

"Jarl, you got any of that jerky left?" Mauser called back.

"Ate it all," he hollered to the front.

"Damn it," Mauser cursed. *Never mind. This place better be well supplied. Fingers crossed.*

Thick woods full of large maples and oaks covered with green leaves surrounded them on either side of the two-lane road. The trees covered the mountain like a thick fog blocking all lines of sight to what lay on the other side.

Only a few desolate houses and several small weathered summer cabins decorated the green landscape carving little alcoves of humanity inside the overgrown nature. A man in a red flannel shirt, sleeves rolled up, jeans and a baseball cap with a hunting rifle on his back, eyed them closely as he unloaded boxes from the bed of a pickup.

Virginia was an unusual animal. A few minutes from the rich aristocratic mansions were small country homes, and twenty minutes from there, brand new townhouse subdivisions. IT analysts to truck drivers they all lived here.

Mauser ignored the man with the hunting rifle. He didn't know if the man stared because he wasn't used to seeing new people in his area, or because Mauser drove a giant mobile lounge that looked like a NASA space lander. Most likely, he was suspicious because of the outbreak. Mauser didn't give zero shits what the man thought, as long as he didn't get in the way.

Mauser leaned forward on the wheel, trying to urge the mover forward by repositioning his weight. He could probably browbeat the man about being on official government duty, but he didn't know whether that would hold any sway. This guy probably had the news on non-stop making him suspicious of anyone new in his neighborhood.

The news could set off a national panic on a mere whim. An impending snowstorm sent everyone in the National Capital Region running to the store to clean out everything from food to ice salt.

Shit, practically every day there is the 'storm of the century' or 'protestors protest something,' or somebody is declared a hero. In today's world, everything is exceptional, sensational, shocking or downright amazing, which made everything they jabbered on about exactly the opposite: regular, normal and average. It is as if the news fed everyone a perpetual dose of clickbait, hoping that something it gave you is offending, hair-raising or galvanizing. Anything to keep you hooked on it for just a little bit longer.

How could people differentiate from the extraordinary and the norm? Maybe it was just a storm or a protest, or perhaps some unlucky sap stepped the wrong way when someone slung a round in his direction. Maybe being a hero was just somebody doing his or her job well. Does doing your job make you a hero? Possibly. No job description ever mentioned heroism in the list of desired skills and if it did, it lied to you. Being a hero isn't a skill. It is a selfless act in the face of danger.

The ironic part is that the news is probably right this time. Even a broken clock is right twice a day, and all hands point to end time. I just have to keep moving forward, he told himself. A tall, barb-wired top steel chain-link fence ran along the road, announcing that they had crested the mountain top and were close. *So close.*

Jarl clapped him on the shoulder, jolting him. "We made it," he said with a laugh.

"Not quite," Mauser said, pointing at the gate.

A platoon of brown and gray camouflaged soldiers at the entrance peered out over concrete barricades, their M4 carbines pointed at him. Behind them, a couple of High Mobility Multipurpose Wheeled Vehicles, or Humvees with .50 caliber machine guns swiveled, turrets pointed in their direction.

"They don't look too friendly," Jarl said.

"I'm banking on them not turning us into swiss cheese." Mauser inched the Lunchbox closer and closer. He only stopped the vehicle when a loud, booming voice sounded over a megaphone.

"Turn off your engine. Throw your weapons down. Step forward with your hands in the air."

That wasn't his favorite command to receive. He tensely eyed the soldiers with bloodshot eyes. Helmets and gas masks covered their faces. If he could see their eyes he would stare right into them, seeing who would turn away first like a dog in the wild. Flicking a lever, he let the hydraulics depressurize, bringing the mover closer to the ground. Even if he thought he could run through the barricade, those . 50s would have eaten through the mover, turning everyone into red mush.

Mauser turned in his chair and addressed his fellow Lunchbox contents: "We've arrived at a place of refuge. Follow the soldiers' commands and we'll be okay."

They stared at their new leader with dark weary eyes, scared and unconvinced.

"It'll be okay," he assured them, not feeling very confident. Everyone watched him as he stood up. "Follow me or stay here, but I'm going down there," he stated, pointing.

Hopping down, he held his hands high. Mauser knew the drill. *Always look for the hands. It's hard for someone to hurt you when you can see his or her hands.*

He knelt down, placing his hands on his head. *For better or for worse, we're here.* A sign that read Mount Eden FEMA Emergency Operations Facility stood nearby. He hoped it was for the better, as a soldier wearing a gas mask pointed an M4 carbine in his face.

"Are you *sick*?" he screamed at Mauser.

The sound of bile splattering the pavement made him cringe.

Fuck.

STEELE
Fairfax, VA

Shadows labored along the asphalt, illuminated by a streetlamp that flickered on the corner. From the second story it was the easiest way to watch the ragtag mob of bloodied, battered and disease infected people below.

The streetlamp faltered again, fighting to stay aglow. After a meek struggle to stay lit, it sputtered out, allowing the darkness to prevail. Steele could hardly see the bodies of his puppet-like former neighbors who were mere shades in the foreboding night. He let the bed sheet slide slowly back into place. For three days, he had done the same thing: sat and waited in the dark. Weariness washed over him becoming a permanent fixture of his physical state.

Steele patted his gear down. It had become a nasty habit, but he couldn't help it. The stress was wearing him thin, not to mention the fact that he was feeling a bit thin around the waist. As if to affirm that he was hungry, his stomach grumbled in complaint.

His nervous ritual would start by tapping the handle of his handgun, feeling the coarse sandpaper-like grip tape around the handle. Then he would feel for the mags he wore at his waist and run a lone finger down the head of his tactical tomahawk, a gift from a buddy who was in Afghanistan. It made an excellent addition to his combat kit as a close-quarters striking weapon.

The ritual would have been longer had he worn his tactical vest, which lay nearby covered with thirty round magazines, extra magazines for his SIG P226 and a tactical trauma pack. Alongside it was his AR-15 lightweight battle carbine, which he never let out of his sight. Gwen had the foresight to pilfer it from their ravaged townhouse. It had red dot sight, swivel swing, fore grip, iron sights and a tactical light offset on the rail. *I wonder if deep down Mauser knew that I would need it, or if I was just lucky he overlooked it.* Either way he was thankful for the long gun.

He peeked out the window again, trying to get an infected count using a single beam from the moon. Lights would have been nice, but he didn't want to hurt his night vision, and more importantly did not want to draw attention to the townhouse.

Forty. That was a dozen more than yesterday. The exact number he counted had been thirty-seven, but he assumed some were hidden or stuck somewhere out in the brush, in cars, or in the townhouses.

Everyday more and more of the infected reared their ugly heads. It was a bad omen. First, he didn't want to have to fight more than a few of them at a time. Second, if they wanted to escape, their window of opportunity closed with each new monster that roamed below.

He wanted to snicker at their stupidity, but that would lessen the severity of the situation and the lethality of the assailants. The way they would get hung up in bushes and trees or stuck against each other in doorways was idiotic. But he couldn't bring himself to laugh. As stupid as they were, they never rested. And they were relentless when they found someone to eat, suddenly moving with speed and purpose. *They don't have half a brain between them and they are beating us. They are more than beating us; they are driving us into extinction. Not just us, life itself is under assault. Shit, not even the neighborhood squirrels are safe.*

The day before he had silently cheered on a squirrel with no tail that he had nicknamed 'Stump' as a couple of the infected clumsily tried to catch it. He had to restrain himself from laughing out loud when one of the wretches reached out, lost his balance and fell face first into the pavement leaving part of his scalp on the concrete. Steele could almost have shouted for joy, that bastard. Stump had made one final dodge before scampering up a good-sized maple tree. The dead stared upward for a while, waiting for it to come down. In the silence of the townhouse, Steele had heard it mocking their foiled attack by chattering away from the safety of a branch. Not so dissimilar to Steele sitting up in the house. Except Steele didn't have the balls to mock them. Not like Stump. Eventually they lost interest and moved toward the next victim.

Lucky for him, they hadn't found his hiding spot. Steele could handle a small group of infected with his long gun, but questioned his capabilities for a larger group. Even if he could handle small groups of infected in killing zones, more would keep coming and eventually he would be overrun. This made stealth a much more palatable option.

Impatiently, he sat upstairs, waiting for a military unit or government agency to clear out his neighborhood. He hated waiting. Action was his mantra. He liked to be *doing*. Any kind of action was better than nothing. He read on his phone that elements of the Virginia National Guard and Maryland National Guard had been called in to help contain the chaos in Washington D.C., but it didn't seem to be going very well. He supposed that it was too little too late. Infected people who hadn't turned yet, had fled the city in droves during the initial outbreak Gwen had been caught up in.

Now it was more about preventing the horde from leaving D.C. in one giant mass, and the military was apparently on the losing side of that battle as well. A host of soldiers in ACUs with awkward gaits marched alongside civilians. *One big fucking happy family.* An infected soldier crossed the front lawn of Mr. Wilson's place, black blood covering the front of his uniform. It didn't seem as though they were getting the upper hand.

As if the outside situation wasn't bad enough, the other survivors were driving him crazy, adding to his anxiety. Lindsay seemed incapable of performing even the most menial of tasks, such as emptying the piss bucket out in the enclosed backyard. She also complained incessantly about the quality of the food.

Meanwhile, Ahmed seemed to undermine him at every turn. And Steele knew why; he wasn't a dimwit. It was clear that Ahmed had affections for Gwen and would do anything to wrestle her attention away from Steele. *What a douche. The world is ending, and all this meatball can think about is trying to steal my girl.*

Ahmed should hook up with Lindsay, he thought. *She is cute and single, or at least she is probably single by now.* To make matters worse, Gwen tolerated the man's lustful stares and questioning glances, as if Steele wasn't in the same damn room.

Just the day before, Steele had asked Ahmed to take a watch from the front bedroom window, and the guy had flat out ignored him until Gwen asked him to do it. They had some unspoken bond that Steele didn't understand.

Gwen had mentioned something about him saving her life, but that was no reason to outright ignore somebody, especially when their safety was at stake. *After all, I am a trained counterterrorism professional. I deserve a little respect.*

He lightly lifted the sheet, returning to his obsession with watching the dark street below. *Those dummies were still milling around out there. If the bottom floor had been barricaded better and I had more ammo, I could just sit up here sniping those suckers down.*

Gwen rolled over in bed rustling underneath the comforter. "Baby, come to bed. If they try to get in, we'll hear them," she whispered.

"No," he replied quietly. *I want to know it before they make it to the front door.* He motioned her up, gesturing for her to sit on the side of the bed with his hand.

"What is it?" she asked, her eyes suddenly wide in the dark.

"Everything's okay, but we can't stay here. It's only a matter of time before one of those stenches below catches wind of us, and a bunch of them break in here and tear us up."

"Jeez, I thought something was happening."

"No, but we should leave soon."

"I know. But where would we go?"

"Well, I was thinking," he said, taking her hand. "Remember when I went to a FEMA disaster response exercise at a secret facility?"

"Yeah, vaguely," she murmured.

"Well, it's called Mount Eden and it is up on a mountain not too far from here. It's probably twenty to thirty miles. We could probably hide up there and wait this out. I doubt there would be many infected there."

She looked at him clearly thinking. "That sounds like a good idea. Lindsay's Jeep should be just around the corner. We could use that."

Steele smiled. "That's exactly what I was thinking. I'll check it out in the morning."

He brought her in close and kissed her deeply. She smelled of ordinary soap. Her beauty supplies were left at their home, not a priority now, but she still managed to smell amazing to Steele. The fire between them that smoldered beneath the surface flared bright. He hoped they didn't make too much noise as they enjoyed each other's bodies. They didn't want to make any unwanted guests aware of their presence, but part of him hoped that Ahmed, at least, heard her moans of pleasure.

JOSEPH
Mount Eden Emergency Operations Facility, VA

Work on a cure with Dr. Williams had hit a dead end. The virus mutated at

such a high rate within the DNA code of the host's cells, that little working

knowledge could be acquired from their research. Isolation of the virus was near

impossible, and when the team was successful the host cells were destroyed or had

mutated beyond significance. It was as if armies of microbiological hijackers stole

and infected pure human DNA with every beat of the host's heart. Millions of

infected cells became billions in moments. This ruled out a common flu type

treatment that blocked the virus within the human penetrated cells from leaving and

infecting other cells. The virus replicated too fast to effectively use reverse RNA

transcription, targeting the viral proteins or introducing antisense molecules,

messenger RNA that attach themselves to the virus rendering it ineffective.

Working on such a doomed project, was crushing his will to go on.

Everything was pointing to the eradication of mankind. The only microbial ounce of

hope came from following up with his former classmate from Chicago.

He checked and rechecked his inbox every free moment he had. The refresh

bar slowly inched its way across the screen as it updated, as if the computer were

mocking him. The combination of government internet paired with ancient

computers was slowly driving him insane.

Joseph still hadn't received a response. *My friend is probably dead.* All of

this work was for nothing if they couldn't get a sample of the original virus from

patient zero.

The medical research team had been working with the data and blood samples Joseph had collected, but the data wasn't close enough to the original virus, making their manipulation of it less than optimal and extremely slow. There was still much that could be learned from studying his data from the DRC, but greater strides could have been made faster had they been able to pinpoint the original host with its original mutations.

Odds were that the original host was wandering some city with the rest of his infected friends feeding on the living or, worse still, decomposing with a bullet in his head from some overzealous redneck neighbor. This was an abysmal thought for Joseph. He realized the rednecks probably thought the zombie apocalypse was a bit of fun, giving them free reign to use all their guns and survival gear on the population at hand.

With the cities in the process of being overrun, who would be left to run the country or to inherit the Earth for that matter? Overall wearing denizens from the countryside? Billy Bob and Cindy Lou? They might be the only people who survived for any length of time, isolated from large populations. Joseph tried to push the thought of an America run by rural folk, banjos in one hand and shotguns in the other, out of his head.

Justifying a grant for research would be all but impossible with those folks and their guns in charge. *I understand the necessity for law enforcement and for the military to have guns, but why did everyone in the country seem to have them? Now that they need them to survive, I guess that issue has been put to bed.* Joseph needed to put a stop to the virus or no one would get to enjoy being the sole presiders over the nation.

End Time

Back to the problem. How can we ever identify the original viral host in a sea of infected? We have a chance if the host lives in relative isolation outside a city, but nothing matters if we don't know who to look for.

Joseph still thought he was onto something with his link to Chicago, although he knew there was only a slim chance it would lead anywhere. He needed to find out more about the Chicago Monkeypox outbreak before it was too late. Information was coming in too haphazardly.

Both Paris and London were in the process of being overrun, and most of Africa had gone dark. There hadn't been much hope for saving the African continent, anyway. According to Representative Baker, it didn't take much to topple governments that were already on shaky ground. Rep. Baker was totally convinced that this would be over in a few weeks once the U.S. military forces were fully mobilized. He told Joseph that the Pentagon had survived the initial D.C. collapse and that the President had been moved to an 'even more secure' facility farther west. Joseph fired off another email to his former classmate's personal email address. *If I'm lucky, he is still alive somewhere, and will respond.*

His head pounded. The yellow industrial lights seemed to smother Joseph. The combination of the fake light and the glow of the computer screen added to the claustrophobic feeling from living underground, all seemed to make it worse. The only cure seemed to be fresh air from above ground. He had spent too much time inside the lab for the day.

He flashed his badge wherever he needed to in order to leave the Bottomside. He stepped into the elevator, which had only two buttons: floor zero and floor minus one. He punched zero. The elevator rattled as it made the four-story ride to the surface.

He stepped out of his steel encasing into a large antechamber that resembled the lobby of a hotel. A couple of soldiers sat behind a desk and a couple more stood nearby, their rifles slung leisurely downward. He nodded to the soldiers behind the desk awaiting his escort. No one moved to shadow him. *No escort today?* As much as he disliked being babysat, it was kind of nice to have someone to talk to.

"Is Pvt. Gordon around? He's my usual escort."

The soldier's face darkened.

"Don't know him. No more escorts unless specifically sanctioned."

Joseph stood for a moment dumbfounded. It struck him that the Private's absence could mean the man was dead. *Nah, he's just off the clock.* Alone, he stepped outside.

The sudden nighttime breeze burrowed into his skin. It invigorated him. It awakened him. He breathed the cool air in deeply. It was fresh, clean, unspoiled mountain air, and it made him feel human again. He resisted the primal urge to howl at the moon as he tipped his head backwards toward the sky.

The night sky appeared fuller on the mountaintop. It was as though he were somehow closer to the stars; tiny twinkling pinpricks of heaven peering down on the world. He closed his eyes, breathing in the peace, only to have his tranquility shattered by the thudding of helicopter blades. The blades cut the solitude with each swirl. Huge military floodlights, placed in intervals around the facility, defiled his stargazing. The occasional crack of a sniper rifle from the guard towers sounded off, picking off one of the infected from an elevated position. It sickeningly reminded him of a prison or, worse, a World War Two concentration camp, except here the guards looked outward. While seemingly one with nature, humans were indisputably separate. Humans were born of nature, but reveled in destroying it for the 'greater good.' He tried to remember that his solace came from this camp, while he merely existed in the bunker below.

He felt relatively safe at the Mount Eden facility; safer than those on the other side of the fence, at least. He walked aimlessly around a small shantytown of D.C. citizens who had found the place as a safe haven. Hands in his pockets, he stood and people-watched. He took some comfort in knowing that others were near. Tents had been set up for the survivors as well as portable bathing and lavatory facilities that looked like mobile homes.

This isn't going to work too well in the winter. Three more months and these people would be cold. Very cold.

Two men shouldered past him in a hurry, startling him.

"Watch it, buddy," one of them said as he passed.

The doctor glanced back. They were vaguely familiar: a very large man along with a shorter, reddish-haired man in tactical gear. Joseph supposed anyone would seem shorter next to the gigantic man.

"Excuse me. Do I know you?" he called after them, yearning for a bit of human interaction.

The shorter of the two turned around. "What do you want?" Recognition lit up in the man's face. He crossed his tattooed arms. "Dr. Jackowski, glad to see you made it." His comment oozed with venom.

Joseph tried to ignore the stabbing comment and answered: "Agent Mauser, I believe, and Agent Thorfinson. It's a pleasure seeing you both. Are Agents Steele and Wheeler here as well?" He would never forget the agents from the Kinshasa flight.

Agent Mauser's face darkened at his reference to the other agents.

"I guess not," Joseph mumbled to himself, searching for words that would excuse him from the uncomfortable conversation.

"Yeah, they didn't make it," Agent Mauser said, pointing a finger at him. "No thanks to you and your black-suited cronies who left us out there to die." Joseph felt a pang of guilt in his gut.

"You know if I'd had a choice I would have taken you with me," he said. "I would have taken all the survivors. I was as much a hostage as anything else."

Mauser spit at his feet and stalked off.

Agent Thorfinson seemed a little more sympathetic, a thin smile pushing up through his bushy blond beard. "We're working on the camp's security detail. They needed people with law enforcement experience, so they asked us to head up a team that keeps order among the civilians. It's not bad. I'd rather be out fighting."

The doctor nodded, happy that both men didn't despise him. "Well, I'm glad you and Agent Mauser are safe. Sorry to hear about the loss of your teammates. They seemed like good men."

Agent Thorfinson's stony face reclaimed its normal hardened look. "Death comes for us all. Some sooner than others. It's how you embrace his final hug that defines you," he trailed off, thinking about his friends. "I'd better get back to rounds with Mauser."

"Yes, of course. Be careful," Joseph replied.

A gunshot rang out from one of the towers, reminding him of the desperate nature of their situation. Rat-a-tat-tat, a machine gun rippled. It was getting worse. The last time he had been on the Topside he had heard only one gunshot in his short foray. Now they went off every few minutes. And it would get worse every day.

He made his way back to the secure underground facility. He immediately walked back to the medical research lab and began his next test. Time was a luxury he couldn't afford to waste in this battle.

STEELE
Fairfax, VA

Steele rose before dawn. He already had the reconnaissance mission to the Jeep planned out in his mind. He rolled out of bed, threw on his tactical pants and ritually checked his gear.

Gwen stirred as he draped his tactical vest over his thick shoulders, a bit leaner than normal. "Why so early?" she asked.

"We have to use the light to our advantage," he said. He knew she didn't really expect a response. She was just slowing him down because she didn't want him to go.

Stepping softly, he went into the next room and gave Ahmed a slight kick with his boot. "Get up, it's time to check the Jeep."

Ahmed's eyes opened a crack, dark orbs peering forth.

Steele gave him another slightly harder tap with his foot. "Get up. We have to go while it's still dark."

"I'll be down in a minute," Ahmed said, yawning.

Steele tiptoed down the stairs and waited. He checked his magazines and slapped a mag on the palm of his hand to ensure that the rounds were seated properly. Ten minutes passed and no Ahmed. Then, another five. The sun breached the horizon, spilling light across the chaos of Northern Virginia.

"Ahmed, we have to do this now," Steele called up the stairs in a hushed tone.

A minute later Ahmed, Gwen and Lindsay came down the steps. *Jesus,*

End Time

Ahmed.

"Ahmed, it's supposed to be you and me," Steele said, looking at the two women, who were dressed for war. He didn't trust Ahmed as far as he could throw him, but it was better than bringing Gwen into certain danger, or Lindsay for that matter. If he brought Lindsay, he would probably end up having to carry her the entire time. Steele wasn't ready to risk getting everyone out of the relative safety of the house only to find out that the Jeep was gone or disabled or surrounded by a horde of infected. Ahmed could show him where the Jeep had been abandoned, and that way he wouldn't have to take Gwen.

Gwen crossed her arms in obvious distaste at the idea of not being included in the expedition outside the house. Defiance settled across her features. "I'm going."

Ahmed casually held his bat across his shoulder blades as he stood with his sable eyes fixed on Steele, a smirk settling on his face. Steele could practically read his thoughts. *Can't even keep your woman under control.*

"I'm going if she's going," Lindsay said, arms folded across her chest in imitation of Gwen, her ponytail bobbing up and down. *Holy shit, these people.*

"No. Only Ahmed and I," Steele said. He wasn't going to budge on this. He had lost Gwen once, and he wasn't about to risk losing her again. She would just have to deal with it. Besides, he wanted to see Ahmed in action.

Ahmed had made it this far, so he had to be willing to fight, but Steele had yet to see firsthand exactly what he had to offer. *Perhaps we may be better off without him?* Steele deeply desired the foray outside to be low-key. They already risked a lot by potentially compromising their hiding place. Brief flashes of infected pushing through the barricaded door, and rushing up the steps as he frantically shot into their faces crossed his mind. *We can't afford it.*

"We want to go with you guys. We don't want to be left alone," Gwen argued, the most front and center of his problems.

"Do you think I want to go out there alone? Do you think I want to leave you?" he said a little too loud. She shook her head, no, taken aback.

"Of course not. But it's easier to sneak with two people as opposed to four, and I need you two to get packs and food ready in case we have to leave in a hurry. Just help me, please. Don't second-guess it. Just help."

Gwen punched through him with her green eyes, pulling her arm free. She could tell that he wasn't testing her womanhood.

"I'm not testing your will to fight. I just need you to stay safe. If I spend the whole time worrying about you, I am ten times more likely to get killed myself." She started to say something and then stopped, lips tight.

Steele took a deep breath. He didn't want to lose it on them, but the stress drove down on him from every angle.

"Lindsay and I will stay, but I swear to God, Mark, if you're not back in twenty minutes, I'll come looking for you. Don't think for a second I won't," she said.

Steele sighed in relief. "Okay. We'll be back soon. Promise," he said, eyes kissing her. "Come on Ahmed, let's go. We're already behind schedule." Ahmed raised his eyebrows and followed him.

Steele and Ahmed moved into the basement, the women following them down the creaky steps. They went over the plan one last time. It was nice and simple: find the Jeep or, if there was no Jeep, find another vehicle to drive. *We have to do this. Not having an exit strategy is a death sentence.* At the least, they needed to acquire a vehicle outside of the wreckage that blocked the cul-du-sac. *Otherwise we will be hoofing it. More like running it.*

"Remember the plan," Steele said, eying everyone. Steele press-checked his SIG Sauer P226 and slid it back into his cross draw vest holster. It would remain holstered unless he got into a real tight spot.

Ahmed hefted his baseball bat, giving it a few trial swings, as if he were getting ready to take a turn in the batter's box. *Better be good with that thing,* Steele thought, pushing all distractions from his mind. He pushed out Gwen, Lindsay, and Ahmed, allowing him to bring his mind into focus. It was a focus technique he always did before entering a known hostile region.

He calmed his heartbeat with controlled tactical breathing. He breathed in for four, held it in for four and breathed out for four. *I am ready.* His mind was level. His mind was sharp. His mind was the tip of his spear. *I will be quick and I will be deadly.*

Steele challenged Ahmed with his ocean blue eyes. "Let me know if you can't keep up," he said, hazing his companion.

Ahmed's dark gaze never left Steele's. Instead, he gave the agent a wry smile and a wink. "I'm sure that won't be a problem."

Steele gave Gwen a nod. *I'll be back one way or another.* He quietly stepped out of the basement door into the small fence-enclosed backyard. Despite his breathing technique his heart jumped a bit in his chest. Faint moaning drifted through the air. The infected roamed nearby, but not close.

Steele cracked the gate a little so he could see better. The hinges squeaked loudly, causing butterflies to rise in his stomach. *Nothing.* He pulled the door open with more force, checking his corners. Nothing lurked to the left and nothing creeped to the right.

He gave Ahmed a quick backward glance and moved on the double to the tree line that ran along the back of the townhouses. He could hear Ahmed's footsteps softly striding behind him. For the most part, he seemed relatively adept at moving with stealth. *Pretty good for a guy with no training. I wonder how far I would have made it without any combat training? Best not to consider that scenario.*

Focus. Don't look. See. Steele slowed to a halt as they neared the edge of the tree line. He crouched down, making himself a smaller target. This was an instinctive action for those in the tactical world, but he didn't know how useful it would be against these relentless enemies, who followed none of the rules he followed.

A large space separated the blocks of townhouses, and two of the infected milled near the corner of the townhouse. In the other direction, a larger gathering of the shambling infected roamed the cul-de-sac. It was as though they knew that somewhere in the neighborhood victims awaited their sentencing.

Steele would have preferred to use hand signals with Ahmed, but settled for whispering instead. "There are two over there at our two o'clock, and it looks like there's a small pack in the street at our nine o'clock. Let's take the two out. Then we'll work our way back around to the street. From there on out, it's your lead."

Ahmed gripped the handle of his bat tightly. "You lead the way, hero," he sniped at Steele.

Steele snorted at that. "Just don't get yourself killed," he said, loosening his tactical tomahawk hanging from his belt.

He emerged from the tree line, crouching at a trot, his tomahawk in the low ready striking position. He covered the distance at a run, but something gave him away as he ran. *My footsteps? Shit.* The infected turned around awkwardly when Steele closed within five yards, a dirty ugly man missing part of his jaw. The unwarranted announcement of his arrival forced him to speed up.

The tomahawk whistled as he swung a wide, arcing strike with the cleaving end. Whatever life inhabited its body, disappeared from its milky white eyes, as the hawk sunk deep into the brain cavity.

The second infected, a jogger wearing her expensive running shoes, short shorts and ragged marathon T-shirt, spun around, reaching for Steele. He shoved her backward to give himself space to pull his hawk free. She toppled into the side of the house and fell onto the grass, giving him valuable extra seconds.

He kicked his foot into the man's chest to gain leverage. The man's skull reluctantly relinquished his hawk with a spray of brain fluid.

The infected woman pulled herself upright, shoulder sagging downward, blood oozing from the corners of her mouth like she had eaten a handful of berries. Her unkept brown hair stuck out every which way. She growled while lunging for him, and unable to load his swing he used a backhanded strike with the spike end of the tomahawk. The hawk bored deep into her temple with a sickening smack and he sent the former jogger to her maker, or wherever it was they went the second time.

Steele heaved on the hawk with all his might. Stuck in deep, her head twisted at a funny angle, but it wouldn't budge free. Her vertebrae ground together as he pulled with all his might. *Damn thing. I am going to rip her head off if I continue on like this.*

"Ooooow," reverberated in his eardrum. *Danger close.* Tucking in his chin, he looked over his shoulder to see a heavy blur bearing down on him. All he could do was turn into it as he braced for impact. The force of the impact took him in reverse and a morbidly obese woman with pieces of skin hanging from her face like drapes drove him into the wall of a townhouse. Her flowered muumuu tangled with his harness as she latched onto him, bringing him in close for a wicked wide-mouthed bite.

Steele reeled rearward. The veins in her face were black and varicose and her neck swollen beyond recognition. The stench of her breath caused him to stumble, and he tripped over the jogger's body.

Her bloated body came crashing down on top of him, forcing the air from his chest. "Jesus Christ, you weigh a…ton," he grunted, avoiding her snapping teeth. Everything happened so fast. *I must get my hands free.* Shifting his head side to side to avoid her bite.

Steele did what came naturally as most people do in a fight. He threw his arms up into her body like an offensive lineman. His hands were met with soft, squishy flesh that enveloped them. He was strong, but the woman was huge and he could only push her so far as she struggled against him. Her head craned, drawing closer and closer to his. Black spittle oozed out of her mouth, the flesh hanging from her face overlaying onto his like a dead fish. She clawed at him as she scrambled to reach him.

"Fuck. Ahmed. Help," he called out, half-yelling, half-whispering as he struggled to keep the distance between himself and the obese infected. Attracting her allies, was a certain death sentence. He threw his hand back, grasping for his tomahawk. If he didn't change his position fast, he would be on the losing end of this exchange.

He threw his knees up between her body and his to create space. She wrapped fat, stubby fingers around his leg and bit down on his knee. He never felt it. Throwing her weight to the side, he rolled his body on top. Grabbing her throat, he barely kept her head controlled.

She snarled, going berserk in his grasp, Steele struggled to stay balanced on top of her disgusting rodeo. With his free hand he ripped his dagger from its tactical harness and slammed it up through the soft under part of her jaw into her brain. The one-time competitive eater finally lay still.

Steele bounded up, putting his back against the townhouse as he scanned for more threats. His chest heaved. Adrenaline coursed through his veins; he was in fight mode. No army of infected marched down on him. He relaxed a centimeter, the void filling with anger.

God damn it, Ahmed. A little help would have been nice. He exhaled, beginning to temper his breathing. He snatched his tomahawk off the ground as Ahmed made his way over to him. Steele shot ice daggers with his eyes as he scrutinized Ahmed.

"We'll have words when this is over. Take me to the car," Steele said, resisting the temptation to cut him down with the hawk.

I could kill him now and the other two would be none the wiser. No, that isn't right. There is too much at stake. I will deal with this asshole later. Pain shot up his leg. *What's wrong with my leg?*

Ahmed gaped at Steele. "Did you get bit?"

Bit? Of course not. "Fuck you, man," Steele said. He didn't think he had been bitten. He started patting himself down. Arms, good. Chest and neck, good.

"No, your leg," Ahmed pointed down at his tactical pants bat wavering.

Steele tilted his head down. A black, bloody hole through his pant leg met him. It must have happened when he created space. Gingerly he felt through the torn fabric. He pulled his hand away, as if stung, his heartbeat going a mile a minute. Blackish bloody wetness covered his fingers.

Slowly, he looked up at Ahmed. Ahmed stared back, hesitantly taking a step away from him. They both knew what a bite meant. Certain death. "You've been bit, haven't you?" he said, brandishing his baseball bat behind his back.

"No, I haven't," Steele said a little unconvincingly. *I couldn't have been bitten. Not like this.* His throbbing knee pounded otherwise.

"Stay back you fucker," Steele said, eying Ahmed. *There is no way I am going to let this asshole put me down like a wounded animal and then let him go back and get the girl.*

Ahmed held his bat ready, dark eyes waiting for an opportunity. Steele drew his SIG Sauer in a quarter-second maneuver keeping it close to his chest. "I don't give a shit. I'll take you with me. Stay away from me while I figure this out."

His eyes never left Ahmed, and he felt the skin of his leg through his pants. It burned like hell. *She really did bite me, didn't she?*

The muscles in Ahmed's shoulders and arms tensed as if he were about to strike first. Steele continued to examine his skin with his hand while keeping an eye and his gun trained on Ahmed. *I wonder how fast he can swing that thing? No way he can hit me before I get a round off, but if he swings first, I have to react to his movement putting me on the losing end of that exchange. If I can get my arm up in time, maybe he would only daze me and break my arm.*

His hand combed the skin of his leg. *Wetness, sticky slobber, and skin. Intact skin.*

"I'm good, man. She just tore my pants. And thanks for the help asshole," Steele said, standing up and holstering his dagger and handgun. Ahmed held his bat between them still unsure of Steele. "I see the road over there. It's your turn to lead."

Ahmed gave him a cautious nod.

"Don't think this is over," Steele said behind him.

That was a little too close. This guy is going to get me killed out here. He wondered if that was what Ahmed had planned all along. *Wouldn't it be convenient if I was bitten and Ahmed had to take care of me while they were away from Gwen. Ahmed hadn't even lifted a finger while that crazed bitch almost mauled me to death.*

Steele stalked behind him. Keeping his head scanning as close to 360 degrees as possible. When they rounded the other side of the townhouses, they saw the compacted remains of several automobiles that had tried to escape the area. Infected bodies bumbled around them.

"I don't see it," Steele said.

Ahmed waved him forward. They used a large tree as a barrier to shield themselves from the infected near the wreckage. Steele kept checking his six o'clock, making sure no one snuck up on them.

"There," Ahmed said, pointing. The dark green Jeep sat intact.

"Good. Let's get back," Steele said.

They quietly retraced their steps to the townhouse. Steele's knee crackled where the lady had bitten him, or tried to. He hobbled into the house after Ahmed, ensuring that the fence was secure, only to be confronted by the unhappy faces of Gwen and Lindsay. The expressions of the two women said they had been gone too long.

Gwen's look changed to concern when she saw his blood-covered harness and pants, but Steele didn't care. "I'm fine," he said, replacing the barricade before turning on Ahmed.

Steele stepped up an inch away from Ahmed's face and slammed a finger into his chest. "Dude, what the fuck was that out there? You almost got me killed."

Ahmed pushed his chest into Steele's finger.

He sneered as he spoke. "I didn't want to draw more of them in. Besides, you handled yourself just fine."

The final straw had been drawn. This guy had been ogling his girl for the last few days, undermining him at every turn, and now he had sat back while Steele almost had his face chewed off. *Some people just needed a good old fashion ass whooping to straighten them out*, he thought, feeling happy to oblige the man in his correctional therapy.

Steele swung a wild haymaker. Not a characteristic strike considering his training, but his blood boiled in his veins. A punch that he immediately regretted throwing on emotion alone.

Ahmed anticipated the strike and ducked low, bringing a forearm up to block the blow. He led with an uppercut, catching Steele on the chin, and followed with a cross to Steele's nose.

Steele staggered back, using a bookcase to catch his fall. His hand leapt to his nose as the blood flowed freely. He stared down at the blood covering his hands, wide-eyed.

"Steele we can talk this out, right?" Ahmed asked, showing open palms and smiling.

Steele narrowed his eyes. *The nerve of this prick.* He knew Ahmed was strong, but he hadn't thought he would be as well-versed in martial arts. Underestimating his opponent in his rage, he admonished himself for his stupid mistake.

Gwen's voice driveled in the background, telling them to stop. Steele completely ignored her. *She knew nothing.*

"Stay out of the way," he barked, not taking his eyes off Ahmed flinging his blood onto the floor.

Steele feigned a jab and a crossover, allowing Ahmed to block them away with minimal effort. During the exchange, Steele moved close enough to catch Ahmed with an elbow to his eye. Ahmed tried to back away and cover his face, but Steele dropped himself to waist level and took him down with a double-leg takedown.

Steele picked him up off the ground. Raising Ahmed over his head, he slammed him down hard, causing his head to bounce off the hardwood floor upon impact.

The slam-dazed Ahmed gave Steele a starry-eyed look, but Steele wasn't waiting to see if he submitted. He scampered into a full mount, straddling Ahmed's hips.

Punches rained down on Ahmed, as he feebly tried to cover his head. One, two, three times Steele connected with Ahmed's face, each hit punished him. Ahmed's eyes danced back and forth not knowing which way to go, his body telling him to keep breathing and fighting, not understanding that he should have been knocked out.

Fighting to survive was an involuntary action. Steele wrapped his fingers around Ahmed's neck and squeezed. *Fuck this guy. He tried to get me killed.* With his other hand, Steele reached up to his harness where his dagger lay sheathed.

Ahmed pushed his face away with two hands, not having seen Steele rip the dagger free. The blade hovered next to Steele's body, waiting ready as he prepared to strike. A moment later, someone grabbed Steele's arm and someone else grabbed his neck. Knowing it to be Gwen and Lindsay, he didn't resist as they pulled him away.

"What the hell are you doing?" shouted Gwen, her face floated surreally above him clouded in anger. "What were you going to do, kill him? A federal agent was going to kill somebody because he was pissed off. Get your shit together."

Across the room, Lindsay wiped blood off Ahmed's face. He looked distraught, his cheek and lips swelling up from the beating.

Steele sheathed his knife. In a few days it would only be his pride that hurt, if they made it that far. "Gwen, you don't know what happened out there. He tried to get me killed."

Why won't she believe me? Why is she taking sides against me? Isn't it clear that Ahmed is the bad guy here?

Gwen shook her head. "Pull it together," she repeated.

"An infected lady almost bit me," Steele said, hearing the whine in his voice. *My shit is just fine, thank you very much.* He stood up, his face still flushed

from the fight. He stared at the rest of them; his eyes still wild. "Be ready to go at

dawn. If you don't want to come with me, you're more than welcome to stay here."

GWEN
Fairfax, VA

Gwen had a fitful night's sleep. She tossed and turned, never really falling into a restful slumber. Mark had been distant with her since the fight. She snuggled deeper into her blanket, searching for comfort and finding only the distinctive musty scent of an elderly person's closet.

Something rustled through the bushes near the front of the house fumbling along the walls. She held her breath, listening intently. *Is it the wind or something more sinister?* The rustling moved along. She couldn't help but hold her breath every time one of them came near the house, scratching the vinyl siding with filthy evil hands. The departure of the dead allowed her to focus on her true problem: Mark.

Gwen's brow creased as she lay there. She couldn't put her finger on Mark's problem. *There is no way Ahmed would have tried to get Mark killed. Why would he do something like that, when he had gone out of his way to save her?*

Mark had been insistent that Ahmed hadn't helped him when the infected people attacked. She asked him again and again what had happened and he had simply repeated that he knew what he saw. He was utterly convinced. She had known Mark for a long time and he wouldn't lie about something like that, but he had drawn a knife on Ahmed. *A knife.*

Mark had been trained to take a life, but she knew him as a reasonable man who used reason and logic as much as his emotions. Mark had almost killed Ahmed. A half-second quicker and he would have slit Ahmed's throat. *Could he do that to me? No, he never would.* He had never shown any outward aggression toward her in their relationship, but she knew violence lurked underneath his stoic surface. *As are men, perpetually closer to their distant primal relatives.*

Mark frayed at the edges. She was sure of it. *I have to help him somehow.* Oddly enough, he probably needed to get to a safer place even more than the rest of them. He stood guard most nights, constantly watching the infected that roamed the neighborhood. Dark circles set in beneath his eyes, and his facial features were fixed in a perpetual glower, as if he were pissed off at the world and everyone in it. His temper flared at the slightest provocation.

Gwen rolled over in bed searching for a cool spot, and glanced over at his side. No hairy chested man lay there. He was up again. A shadow sat near the wall in the dark, a rifle across his lap and gear stuck out from his vest in the dim light. Even in the dark, she could tell that he was awake, his head resting on the wall. *He needs a place where he can shut down, cool the engines and turn off the higher state of readiness, or he would snap and hurt someone, or worse.* Gwen fell back into a restless sleep. She rose before dawn and checked the power on her phone. The display read twelve percent. She switched plugs. No lightening bolt popped up across the top of her phone. *Power's out.*

Gwen gave Mark a break from his vigil, taking up watch by the top floor window. The things outside were hideous to look at, so she checked her email instead. Department stores, flower shops, fitness gear and home goods were all apparently having sales. *No you're not. You don't exist anymore.*

She scrolled through her email, clicking on one from Becky. Her sister was at the farm, where everything was fine. The flyover states were unaffected, as of now.

Gwen opened the sheet a crack and snapped a picture of the undead below. The photo turned out blurry as the creatures were too far away. It failed to accurately depict the mutilated walking corpses below. They looked like ordinary people in the streets, despite the fact they were missing arms, legs, organs and souls.

She wasn't a particularly religious person, but it made her wonder if they had souls or if they were just empty bodies, human husks. *Did they remember who they were? Were they mindless or did some grandiose master drive them? Were they spawns of the devil, as a religious expert on the news had suggested? I wonder if the 'infected,' can be fixed. Mark is insistent that they can't be, but maybe he isn't giving it enough of a chance. Hopefully, Mount Eden will have electricity up and running, so I can stay in contact with my family.* The situation was hard enough as it was.

The clock in the bedroom blinked 9:07 which meant the power in the townhouse had been out for twelve hours. They weren't using lights for fear of attracting the infected, but their phones were running out of battery, draining in fact.

The thought of being cut off from the social media world was a terrifying reality for anyone who was left alive. The internet had been taken over by people posting and publishing on their loved ones' walls, pages and platforms. Her friend Heather kept writing on her husband's personal page: "Please come home, Tony. The kids miss you."

All the messages were similar: people trying to reach their loved ones, people searching for answers, people grasping for life. Day after day, fewer and fewer of these people were finding those things.

People's last days could be counted down by following their social feeds. She cried when she saw that her friend Patrick had left a farewell post on his page: "I can't take the sounds of Rose being ill in the next room. I'm going to get help. Love you all. Patrick."

That had been his final post. No other posts lined his page. *Your last status update while you were with the world of the living.* She wondered what her final post would say, or if anyone would be around to read it.

Some people were sending out useful information: stay quiet; kill the infected with headshots or blunt trauma to the skull; barricade your house; infected loved ones are dead; no lights; stay on the top floor; grab any weapon you can get hold of and fight; get out of town; use the back roads; make sure you have enough water.

For every helpful post there were a twice as many bad ones filled with fatal information: the infected are just sick; take them to the local hospital; treat them with antibiotics; if bitten, stick with the group; the Army is on its way; use high-percentage body shots; you only need a week of supplies; the infected cannot see flashlights; the infected are repelled by loud music. Unfortunately, these posts would be self-correcting errors. For some folk it was probably more terrifying to be without internet than to have their friends, family, neighbors and strangers trying to kill them.

Mark came back up the stairs and started shoving items into his pack. They switched places. Someone always had to have eyes on the front of the house. The door was barricaded, but no one was sure how long it would hold up under pressure.

Gwen packed in silence. She had taken a picture from their townhouse of the two of them and Mark's family on a trip to Beaver Island, Michigan. She placed it in Mark's pack. Hopefully, it would remind him why he fought. People depended on him.

The group needed him to survive; he had the weapons training that could help keep them alive. On a personal level, she needed Mark to remember what it was to be in love, to be happy, to be human. She knew he hardened himself so that he didn't have to come to terms with all the death and destruction he witnessed and partook in.

Gwen had tried to do the same but, while she let herself cry at night and talk quietly about the deaths of her friends, he kept it all inside. He would just lie there bottling all his anger, sadness and pain; internalizing his problems. He bore the deaths of the people under his watch personally, and she knew that it ate him alive inside.

She took it upon herself to help him remain the man he once was, and in doing so, she hoped to keep part of her humanity intact. Together they would maintain in each other the small parts of a normal life. They owed it to one another.

Gwen punched a small pink pill from a dispenser, the last one in her cycle of birth control. She had been awaiting her new prescription in the mail, but when the D.C. outbreak occurred the mail carriers had been among the first to be attacked as the disease spread. Those who were outside in the community, going door to door, were basically facing a death sentence much like most first responders.

Her birth control had never arrived, and she knew she would have to get more from somewhere. Mount Eden might have some, but she doubted it. Gwen knew that she and Mark would have children someday. It had always been a part of their plan after they were married. *How could we bring a child into this disaster of a world?* It would be like feeding her newborn to the wolves.

She didn't know why, but they had made love every night since they had been reunited. Maybe it was the stress of survival that drove them to live their days like everyday were their last, or maybe it was just to dull the pain long enough to fall asleep. Not that she minded the nightly ravishing.

Gwen's pulse quickened at the thought of Mark's hands all over her, and her neck burned with embarrassment at her carnal thoughts, although only the two of them were in the room.

"Why are you all red?" he whispered and her cheeks burned at the sound of his voice.

"Nothing."

"Are you sick?"

"No."

He looked back out the window satisfied that she was okay as if she were some sort of soldier.

"It was about last night and the night before."

He gave a sly glance at Gwen. "Oh," he mouthed. Then he chuckled softly, cracking the first smile she had seen from him in days.

"Why are you laughing?" she said in mock anger.

"No reason," he smirked.

"There's something I have to tell you," she said.

His face hardened and she immediately wished she hadn't said anything. "What is it?" he asked, running a hand through his beard.

She looked down at her empty birth control package. "Nothing. I love you," she whispered.

He gave a faint smile. "Love you too. We're going to be okay," he said, his eyes betraying his own doubt.

It wasn't the right time for that conversation. Mark had so much on his plate that finding out she was out of birth control might push him over the edge. She finished shoving the rest of her belongings into her hiking pack: hiking clothes, batteries, a flashlight, shotgun slugs, food and medicine. She strapped Mark's machete to the outside.

She hoisted her pack onto her back and slung her pistol grip shotgun around her body. She was as ready as she would ever be. She put on her bravest, most confident smile for him. "I'm ready."

Mark hoisted his pack onto his shoulders, checking the status of his weapon. "Let's roll."

It isn't during the shit people went through that they decide to quit; it is during the periods of relaxation, Gwen concluded. The idea of leaving the house terrified her, but it felt good to be on the move. She wanted to be doing something instead of waiting to die.

They gathered in the basement, and Mark made sure they were ready. He inspected everyone's gear. Ahmed eyed her over his shoulder as Steele checked his pack. She broke eye contact focusing on Lindsay. The woman looked like she was about to cry.

"We are going to be okay. We just have to make it to the car."

Lindsay smiled weakly. "I guess." Gwen returned her smile.

"Mark will get us there." He looked at her, tightening a strap on Lindsay's pack.

"We are up. Everyone stay close and quiet."

End Time

Quietly, they funneled outside. Everyone waiting tensely while he knelt on the ground, commencing the first part of their escape. He wedged a flimsy red stick into the ground and, with a flick of his thumb; he sparked up a lighter holding it to the fuse. The rocket screeched overhead to the other end of the cul-de-sac with a loud pop. Mark repeated the process three more times and launched several old bottle rockets into the middle of the cul-de-sac. Apparently, old man Benson was even more of a kid than they had thought, as Mark had discovered a stash of fireworks in his workshop.

Everyone held their breath while Ahmed looked over the fence. "They're hurrying over to the other side of the street," he said with a grin.

"I'll go up front with Gwen and Lindsay in the middle. I want Ahmed to take the rear." He hoisted his AR-15 in front of his chest.

"Remember, if things get bad, make a run for it. No one looks back," he said, staring right at Gwen.

"I know," she mumbled. She locked eyes with him. She knew the plan. *I won't leave him. No matter what he wants.*

Mark went over it again and again until she wished he would stop talking about it. *Does he think I'm an idiot?* The whole thing was easy enough.

With a cautious look backward, Mark pushed open the fence gate. He set out at a brisk walk along the tree line, scanning back and forth with his rifle in the high ready. She found herself breathing hard without much exertion.

Mark waved them hastily on to the ground his flat palm pumping downward. A group of infected plodded past toward the townhouse. Gwen held her breath, hoping not to be noticed. Moaning, they were close enough for Gwen to catch a whiff of their putrid stink. Her breath tightened in her chest, her heart pounding. The infected wore a variety of ripped hoodies and purple letter jackets. *Looks like the stoners and jocks have finally united.*

As soon as they were out of earshot, Gwen quietly stood up. She copied Mark's high ready position with her shotgun, making sure she was not about to flag Mark in the back as she scanned for incoming threats. She swept her shotgun left and right searching for the infected, taking in too much scenery and almost running into Mark.

He gave her a sidelong glare. "Fist means stop," he reprimanded her, pulling her aside when he saw how flustered she became.

Her heart dropped when she looked over his shoulder at the Jeep. Infected milled around it as if they had been waiting for them.

"It's as if they knew we were coming here," she stammered.

"It's okay. We'll kill those ones by the car quick. As soon as they're down, run for the Jeep. I'll take the three on the far side and you take the two closest to us." He gave her a small smirk. *How is he smiling at a time like this? What could possess someone to show such indifference under stress?*

"Try not to hit the car." he said with a nod, resting the stock of the carbine on his shoulder. His eyebrows crinkled as he aimed in.

She nodded and set her mouth flat. Then her nerves kicked in, immediately making her palms sweaty, and the shotgun feel heavy in her arms. A butterfly explosion went off in her stomach instead of the gun. She could see the two infected, but they appeared fuzzy now. Hazy outlines of people she was about to shoot.

"Off your mark," he said, taking a knee. "You two get ready to run. As soon as we shoot, more are going to come fast." He spoke in a harsh whisper eyes on his sights.

Gwen brought the shotgun up, firmly fixing the butt of the gun to the front of her shoulder muscle. She allowed her armpit to support the bottom of the stock, just as Mark had taught her. Lining up the small shotgun sight bead on the infected closest to her, she took a deep breath.

The infected looked like a regular woman wearing jeans and a sweatshirt; probably a stay-at-home mom with a husband, kids, a dog and a house. Aside from the huge gaping hole in her neck, which had started to turn black with corruption, she could have been normal. Gore stained her sweatshirt and she exhibited the classic dead white eyes.

Gwen hesitated for a moment, trying to zero in on the woman's head. Her hands shook violently. She couldn't seem to line up the bead to the woman's forehead. The gun wavered back and forth in a small sideways figure eight. *What's wrong with me?* The lady turned, seeing her. She shuffled toward Gwen. *Shit.*

"Gwen, shoot. Now," Mark whispered.

His prompt snapped her back into survival mode and she unloaded a slug toward the woman.

"Direct hit," she said. The woman's head rocketed backward as the slug removed the majority of her head. The infected faced them, alerted to their presence. Ugly faces growled in the prospect of killing the newcomers. Echoes from Mark's staccato gun shots kicked off followed by barks from her shotgun. She hadn't even realized she was running until she stood near the car door.

Gwen yanked the door open and Lindsay crawled into the back as if she had been cattle prodded. Mark leaned over the hood of the car watching the edge of the townhouses as Gwen thrust the keys into the Jeep's ignition. Pop, pop, pop, his rifle sounded off. Bodies toppled over brains ejected from their skulls.

The key turned, but the engine lay dormant. *Are you kidding me?* Gwen panicked. She kept turning the key over and over, the engine clicking each time. Lindsay rapidly talked over her shoulder like a rabbit on crack, pointing at the dashboard.

Mark's voice echoed from the outside. "Get this thing going."

Stop yelling at me. I'm trying.

She turned the key again. Click. Click. She sat baffled, staring at the ignition as she tried to figure out why the car wouldn't start. *Battery? Starter?* She had done the entire rudimentary process like she had done thousands of times before. *Take key. Place key in ignition vertically. Turn key. Then the car starts. But it's not working.*

She looked up. A wall of infected bodies rounded the corner of the townhouses, moving through the abandoned vehicles that blocked the road. Mark leaned over the hood of the Jeep. Using it to stabilize his rifle, he blasted away at the closest infected. His rifle fired rapidly as he transitioned targets, but not fast enough. Bodies fell without getting up again, but more were making their way to the stalled car. He shouted, his face snarling in anger as he ripped off more shots.

Oh shit, oh shit, ran through her mind. She didn't realize that the car had finally started until she felt Mark shaking her shoulders.

"Drive, drive," he screamed into her ear.

A body slammed onto the hood, crawling onto the windshield with its teeth bared. She threw the Jeep into reverse while Mark leaned out the window with his sidearm popping away. The body slid off the hood of the Jeep.

Making a U-turn, she floored it over the median onto Route 50 launching everyone momentarily into the air. She straightened it out avoiding debris.

No one said a word for fifteen minutes. Mark reloaded his weapons with fresh mags while Ahmed supplied him with more ammo for his exhausted ones. He clinked brass on brass as he loaded his magazines. She turned on the radio, hoping for something to break the tension, but all they heard was the incessant repetition of emergency broadcasts.

JOSEPH
Mount Eden Underground Bunker, VA

An email sat open on Joseph's screen. His wait was over. He gobbled up the words on the page like a starving man at a feast.

Joseph,

It's good to hear you're safe. My family and I are up in Wisconsin at our family cabin. Nearest town is Oshkosh. Rusty well water and an outhouse, but it's away from the cities. We have zero cell phone reception and spotty internet access, glad I had that installed a few years ago, but I know that I made the right decision to leave Chicago. Military quarantine, hospitals being overrun, the deaths of thousands. My home hospital, Chicago Sacred Heart looks like Kamdesh...all but destroyed.

Chicago looked worse than war zone as the military tried to quarantine the city, not letting anyone leave. Joseph was relieved Anderson had taken the initiative to escape. Things were quickly going from bad to worse there. But that wasn't the part Joseph was interested in. He read on.

On August 27th I treated a Mr. Thompson, who was exhibiting unusual symptoms. He had been hospitalized at Chicago Sacred Heart while he passed through O'Hare from Washington-McCone. He had a fever, rash covering his torso, severe diarrhea, insomnia and a swelling of lymph nodes. He had been pulled off a plane after collapsing on the jet bridge.

End Time

Soon after he was hospitalized, he had his first violent outburst that we witnessed. One of our RNs was bitten during this episode. She was later hospitalized with similar symptoms. I do not know her current status. After we restrained the patient, he became relatively lucid again, saying that he didn't recall his previous behavior. We notified the police and held him for treatment overnight. The RN declined to press charges.

At this point, I remembered you were in the DRC studying the Monkeypox virus. This case sounded right up your alley, although I don't think in the end that it was Monkeypox. He responded well to a strong anti-viral medicinal cocktail, and he had no more violent outbursts under our care.

We released him to his family the next day. With more space, I would have kept him longer for observation, but you know how it is.

You're lucky I can still log in to the hospital database from my computer. You know this is confidential information and that I am violating HIPAA, but if it helps I am sure it is justified. His address is:

1523 Shuttlecock Ln.,

Grand Haven, MI 49563.

Stay safe,

Dr. Ian Anderson

The first email hadn't been a hoax. Dr. Anderson had treated a patient with Monkeypox-like symptoms almost two weeks before the outbreak Joseph had investigated in the DRC.

One sentence stuck out in Joseph's mind: "With treatment, the patient had gotten significantly better and had been sent home."

Sent home? That definitely wasn't consistent with his current understanding of the disease. But maybe if the virus was weak enough, or in its newly crossed-over mutation from animal infection to human form, the host could have remained alive or the virus could have remained in a dormant state. It was possible with an anti-viral treatment. This Mr. Thompson might be the only thing standing between the United States and total infection if it wasn't already too late.

He hammered out a quick thank you and printed out the email containing Mr. Thompson's address. Now all he needed to do was get somebody to take him there before it was too late.

Joseph didn't even bother presenting his newfound discovery to Dr. Williams. He already knew the doctor would scoff at the notion that there was a patient zero in the United States.

He beelined for the congressional quarters in the underground facility. A few armed soldiers sprinted past him toward the elevator exit. Joseph ignored them intent on his mission. He pushed through large glass doors to the congressional wing. A sign on the wall read congressional sleeping quarters and he went that way. He stepped into a nicer version of his dormitories with individualized sections. On his tiptoes, he tried to find Representative Baker. Everyone seemed to be going somewhere or in the process of leaving. He found the representative hunched over his personal bunk packing his bags.

"Steve, I was wondering if I could talk to you for a minute," Joseph asked, feeling uneasy as the man haphazardly shoved clothes in a bag.

Rep. Baker gave him a shifty look and continued to stuff a pair of khaki pants into a suitcase. He sharpened up with a politician's smile. "Sure thing, Joseph. Have you come up with anything yet on the research front?" he said, continuing to focus on his packing.

"Well, I came across some important information. And Dr. Williams has been less than helpful in ensuring that it's used properly."

He turned away from his task, giving him a practiced look of thoughtfulness. "What have you got there?"

He reached up and took the paper from Joseph's hand, skimming the document. "Well, well, yes, hmm, I see. I think what you have here is important, and I'd like to take this to the Special Committee on Virus Eradication for you."

This is not the time for a committee. This is the time for action.

"Sir, with all due respect, action needs to be taken now. We don't have time for a discussion on this matter. If this truly is patient zero - the first human infected as the disease passed from animal to human - we *must* find him." The representative eyed him, visibly gulping.

Joseph had his attention. It was now or never. "This may be our only chance to find a vaccine to fight this disease. We need to send in the Army or somebody to pick this guy up alive so we can get the purest form of the antibodies."

Representative Baker stared up at him, taking account of Joseph's serious demeanor. He rubbed his smooth jaw and said: "I'm sorry, Joseph. It's not really my decision, and our resources are stretched too thin to go around chasing one guy who may not be patient zero. Have you watched the news lately?"

Joseph shook his head. Admittedly, he hadn't been watching any of the less than comforting news reports. He had fallen in line with the rest of the research scientists who played to Dr. Williams' every whim.

A solemnness fell over the Congressman. "We're in full retreat. We've completely lost LA, Seattle and San Diego, on top of the cities on the East Coast. The Pentagon will fall any day now and Chicago is all but overrun. The military's on the brink. We couldn't even get our troops back from overseas fast enough. Most of our forces got bogged down fighting overwhelming populations of the infected before they knew what they were dealing with. Hell, CENTCOM and AFRICOM are eradicated, and that's where most of our deployed active duty troops were. Sure, pockets held out here and there, but no help is coming. It's too late. I'd suggest you hide here and hope that no dead find their way into this facility. Either that or make your way to the West."

Joseph knew the situation would get bad, but this exceeded his predictions. *How could this have happened so fast? Would mankind disappear into the annals of history without a gasp or a sputter?*

"This makes this patient all the more important, then," Joseph said, forcing the paper back into the Congressman's hands.

Rep. Baker read the email thoughtfully. His brown eyes met Joseph's. He sniffed heavily through his nose. "The President's aide is a friend of mine. We went to law school together. I'll forward this to him and he'll make sure the President sees it. Maybe we can get a team in there to pick this guy up. It's the best I can do," he said with a weary smile.

Joseph relaxed. "Thank you. If this pans out, you might get to be President one day, provided we aren't dead already," he said halfheartedly.

The Congressman flashed a white smile. "I'll expect your vote and some campaign contributions when the time comes."

Fat chance.

GWEN
Mount Eden Emergency Operations Facility, VA

At midday, Gwen and her small group reached the Mount Eden Emergency Operations Facility. By this time, Gwen had the emergency broadcast seared into her brain: "This is an emergency broadcast for the National Capital Region. This is not a test. Authorities request that you stay inside your homes. Help is on the way. Please avoid contact with the sick persons. This is not a test."

Gwen and her friends had done the exact opposite, and this was the only reason they were still alive. That and Mark. Mark had slain more than fifty of the infected by the time they reached the facility. She marveled at his explosive violence, and was a little terrified that he could just destroy them with such indifference.

Mark was reluctant to give up his weaponry when they arrived, but he was too tired to put up much of a fight. They surrendered their weapons to the soldiers at the gate and were promptly escorted to a medical tent for quarantine.

A military doctor wearing a HAZMAT suit inspected all of them under the watchful eye of a soldier, also in a HAZMAT suit while pointing a M4 at their heads. After a thorough probing, the doctor had deemed them 'not infected,' and they were allowed to join the rest of the civilians who had made the pilgrimage to Mount Eden.

"Lavatories are over there. Civilian camp is there. Stay away from those buildings there," a soldier muffled, with a mask-covered face.

They stumbled into the refugee camp in a daze. People were scattered haphazardly around and they eyed the newcomers with apathy. Mark found them an open spot in a long disorganized row of tents.

"We're lucky we brought our own tent," Gwen said.

End Time

The alternative was a massive tent that housed the destitute, which already appeared to be filled to maximum capacity.

Gwen helped Mark set up their two-person tent. He cursed as he tried to line up a tent pole with the other side of the tent. She left him to his own cursing as an old couple waved at Gwen.

"Look, hun, more newbies," the old woman said.

The white haired couple camping next to them acted as though they were on vacation. They had every piece of gear imaginable: radios, lawn chairs, hats, pots and utility belts among many other items.

Gwen looked at her meager setup with a little bit of apprehension.

"I'll trade ya' some water purifying tablets for some AA batteries," the old woman said with a toothy smile.

"Let me see if we have any," Gwen said, rummaging in her pack.

"Harold just can't live without his disc players," the old woman said. An old man, presumably Harold sat with his headphones on in a lawn chair, white hair peaking out from underneath his wide brimmed safari hat.

Gwen dug through her bag and found a pair of batteries. She handed them over to the woman, who placed a small bottle of tablets into her hand.

The elderly woman smiled at Gwen. "Hear anything about the District?"

"I don't know. I was in D.C. over a week ago and haven't been back since. We just came in from Fairfax. It wasn't in very good shape. Lots of people there are infected," Gwen said somberly.

The white-haired woman nodded. "That's what we heard, too. Heard the Army's been takin' a beating out there. D.C.'s lost. But I hear the Pentagon's still holding out. There are hordes of them pounding on the outside of it, but our boys won't let them in. God bless our troops," she stared off into the distance.

Gwen wondered if she was all right. She looked over her shoulder and there was nothing of note to draw her gaze.

"My grandson's a Marine. He's over in Afghanistan right now. Should be back any day," she said with a sad smile. "We are so proud."

Gwen smiled back. "I'm glad to hear he's safe." She feared that he wasn't coming back.

Later that night, as they lay down in their new tent home, Mark told Gwen that he had spoken to some of the Army paratroopers stationed at Mount Eden, who had confirmed the old woman's story about the Pentagon.

"Generals, officers, grunts, contractors and staff have fought the good fight, but a single breach could end the most sophisticated professional armed forces headquarters in history. It hasn't fallen yet. Its survival hangs on the back of determined Americans," Mark said with a little pride.

"It's like the Alamo," Gwen said.

Mark frowned a bit. "Baby, everyone died at the Alamo," he said.

She felt little foolish. "Sorry, I was trying to be optimistic, you know, Remember the Alamo," she said softly.

He stripped off his shirt. Deep creases outlined his six-pack. It was well defined. *Too well defined.* He looked thin. An unhealthy thin.

"What's wrong?" he asked.

"Nothing. Lynn in the tent over there said the infected are moving even further west. There have been sightings in West Virginia and Pennsylvania."

"Doesn't surprise me," he said, resting his pistol nearby his head.

"They gave that back? I thought there were no guns in the civilian facility."

"Well, not exactly, but being a former Division agent does hold some clout." He gave her a mischievous grin.

What she really wanted to say was: *"How are we going to make it? How can we live like this?"*

Mark pulled her in close, wrapping a muscled arm around her. "Everything's going to be fine. We have to take this one day at a time. Do you hear me? One manageable task at a time. Eventually this will end."

She heard his words, and his sense of assurance made her feel a little better.

"I talked with the civilian camp manager. They could really use your help," he said.

She smiled, nestling into his body for warmth. Being involved in helping others was just what she needed to take her mind off of this terrible situation. She hugged him close. "That sounds great," she said into his shoulder. He smelled of the perfect blend of sweat and dirt.

"He asked you to meet with him first thing in the morning. I'm exhausted." It wasn't long before she could hear him breathing soundly. A sound she could recognize from anywhere. It seemed to beckon her into sleep like a masculine lullaby and soon she joined him.

The next morning she spoke with the distribution manager, Tim, a middle-aged balding bureaucrat. He put her in charge of managing care packages for new arrivals. The place was badly in need of organization. They had plenty of supplies, but getting the right supplies to the people that needed them was haphazard at best.

Once settled in, she set about directing her staff of one to tasks. She knew she could make the process of being homeless a little better for the refugees.

"Nathan, I need you to add blankets to all the incoming refugee packages, the nights are getting colder, along with the water bottles." She bent over to review a checklist. "Nathan?" she queried. Her volunteer assistant was nowhere to be found.

A big box slammed onto the table. "Nathan, please," she said, shifting her gaze away from the document.

A figure shadowed over her, his face blocked out by the sun.

"How can I-?" She failed to get the rest of her sentence out.

The man charged around the table and she was unable to resist him picking her up, and bear-hugging her tight. "Gwen, I never thought I'd see you again," he said.

Realization came over her in a rush. "Mauser! Jarl! Oh my God! You're alive."

She cried, Mauser cried, and she was pretty sure Jarl also shed a tear, maybe two.

Mauser and Jarl were like family. The Division agents had always kept to themselves in a tight-knit circle of friends.

"Mauser, not so tight," she chided. "I can't breathe."

He set her down and looked her over, inspecting her for mistreatment like an older brother. "I knew that wasn't you in the townhouse, I just knew it. I tried to tell Steele." He trailed off when he realized what he had said. His head bent forward in sorrow, worried he may have hurt her feelings by mentioning Mark.

She grabbed his hand. "He's alive. He got me and a few others here safely."

Mauser let out a wholehearted chuckle. "Well, I'll be damned. That bastard didn't quit, did he?"

Gwen beamed. "We found him half-dead at our place, but a little TLC fixed him up right," she said with a cool smile.

"I'll bet," Mauser replied with a wink.

"Well, where *is* that son of a goat?" Mauser asked, his mouth crinkling in a smile.

The pop, pop, pop of gunfire echoed in the distance. The sound of gunshots was an aspect of camp life that people were getting used to, but to which they could never really grow accustomed.

Mauser glanced over his shoulder with no real concern. "It gets more frequent every day. I'm not sure about it. It's just too big of a camp for us to secure."

Gwen pointed over her shoulder to where she and Mark had set up their tent.

"Well, I brought you a new recruit. He's over there in the orange and black tent getting some shut-eye."

Mauser looked in the distance mirth in his eye. "Perfect. Let's get his ass up, because I need some help."

They all marched over to the tent, and Gwen watched Mauser unceremoniously rip it open and pounce on Steele. A struggle ensued, and then laughter came forth.

Well, at least they're making up. Their friendship endured. Steele had told her about the harsh words that had been spoken between them as they parted ways. Not all things could be broken by this apocalyptic event; a part of the human spirit remained: friendship. She half-smiled at the sound of them talking. Things weren't as bad as they seemed.

STEELE
Mount Eden Emergency Operations Facility, VA

Three days dragged by on the wooded mountaintop. It had been thirteen days since Steele left the U.S. on a mission to the DRC and returned to a country in utter chaos. It numbed his mind how things could change so fast. It was as if they had somehow stepped into a parallel universe that only mirrored their own. Only in this alternate reality, the disease had spread like wildfire scarring the land and everyone in it. It left only disaster and violence in its wake, and society - along with the cumbersome government entities - had been gobbled up by legions of the dead in the blink of an eye.

Steele awoke before the yellow sun crested the horizon and rolled Gwen off his arm, regaining feeling as the pins and needles drifted away. He gazed at her gold hair, snarled from sleep like a lion's mane. He was proud of her. She contributed to the mission by aiding the stranded civilians here. It seemed to put her mind at ease and, in turn, put his mind at ease.

Steele stretched his arms above his head and rubbed his lower back. *The firm ground is supposed to help bad backs*, he thought. He never minded camping, but he also never thought he would view it as a luxury. Then again, anything on this side of the fence was a luxury. Life itself was a gold-plated pile of shit, but a luxury nonetheless.

He collected his long gun from the ground next to him. It had been returned to him by Mauser to support his law enforcement duties. He removed the magazine and looked inside. Brass-lined bullets lay side by side in the magazine. *Little messengers of death.* He shoved it back into the rifle. *Always know the status of your weapon.*

He threw his tactical vest over his thermal base layer, tightening a strap, and stepped outside, his breath fogging in the morning air. It would get warmer as the day went on. It wasn't the time of year yet when it stayed cold. The sheer amount of walking would ensure he was sweaty by the end of the day. Slinging his AR-15 around his neck and shoulder, he let it relax across his chest pointed toward the ground. They had offered him a military version, but he kept his own.

Mauser had enlisted him into the camp law enforcement forces. Not that he would have denied his friend's request for help given a choice. The military maintained control of the perimeter and their base, while the various mismatched law enforcement groups loosely prevented the civilian camp from imploding onto itself. The job he performed was similar to that of a regular patrol officer. It wasn't what he had trained for, and he quickly found out that the duty of settling petty disputes was not his forte. He would manage, knowing that he made a difference. The camp grew everyday as the amassing hordes of infected from D.C. pushed more refugees ahead of them onto the mountaintop.

He walked to a tent that served as a temporary detention center and command post for the refugee camp security teams. A group of new refugees stumbled in making the ever-growing sea of colored tents.

"Excuse me, sir. Where do we go?" a haggard elder man asked. *Is he old? Or has he been beaten into such a run down state?*

Steele pointed. "If I were you, I would set up away from the latrines, but not too close to the fences."

The man nodded, understanding his meaning. "This place was a bitch to find, but we just followed the direction of the helicopters."

Steele nodded and took his leave. Mount Eden was hidden away, and he suspected that people were not the only ones following the helicopters and military trucks. Word had gotten out that it was the only place to find safety in the area, so they kept coming. It didn't matter what walk of life they came from, they were all in the same leaky boat now.

A yellow and black bulldozer pushed dirt down the hill clearing trees in the process. A day prior, the military started clearing the tree line to increase their field of fire.

A group of men with picks and shovels marched through the front gate with an armed escort. Only three soldiers went with the workers. Hardly enough to protect them. Every morning they would go clean up the bodies from the night before, dumping them in shallow graves and torching the remains.

Valuable resources were being poured into camp defense and the cleanup of corpses instead of fighting the masses of undead flooding across the Key Bridge, Arlington Memorial Bridge, and the 14th Street Bridge into Virginia.

Steele continued his round through the camp toward the perimeter fence. He nodded to a man in a once-smart sports coat, now filthy and tattered. The man crouched over a small fire, heating water. The human apocalypse was the great equalizer of men. You were dead or trying to avoid it. Either way, they were all living on borrowed time.

Steele patrolled along the perimeter fence. It was a ritual he did every morning. He would prefer to be the hunter, but he wasn't sure what he was. He pushed on the standard chain-link fence and it bowed out. It was not a sturdy fence, having been designed to prevent easy access as opposed to physically blocking an attacker. A mass of infected could push through it. Steele tried not to think about it.

He gazed out at the retreating line of trees, green and lush, and then at the brown earth covering the ground from the forest to Mt. Eden. Open ground had been churned up making it appear like a World War One no-man's land.

From Steele's position, the land rolled moderately downhill and now had no obstacles. *That asshole facility director should have us digging some sort of trench, maybe a pit of stakes, to slow down the infected and prevent them from piling up on the fence. Then we would only have to focus on protecting the chokepoints, access gates up and down the mountain. This could be a fortress, impregnable, well supplied, and safe. This could be a bastion of hope. This could be a true Eden in a dead world.*

Steele had previously voiced his concerns to the facility director.

"This is a FEMA operations facility, not a medieval castle," the sniveling bureaucrat had told Steele.

"But you don't understand. These 'things' will come in the hundreds and thousands, and when they do-" Steele was cut off.

"Thank you for your input, but please leave facility management to the professionals," the facility director had said, moving on his way clipboard in hand. *This is like no disaster we've ever seen.*

It was only a matter of time. His sharp eyes caught sight of a figure as it emerged. His awkward gait exposed him as one of the infected. From a distance he looked as though he might once have been a farmer.

End Time

A sniper rifle cracked through the morning air and the infected man's shoulder ripped backward as if something pulled on him from behind. He staggered but didn't fall. He slogged forward, blackened coagulated blood running down his front. A second boom resounded and this time the man went down, his head turning into a red mist.

Steele cut up through the refugee camp and navigated his way up to the command tent, where Mauser and Jarl awaited his arrival.

"How'd you sleep?" Steele asked Jarl.

"No good. The gunfire keeps me awake."

Mauser handed Steele a cup of coffee, which he drank greedily. Instant joe or not, he welcomed the boost.

"Nothing much to report from the overnight team. Everyone's scared shitless out there," Mauser said. "Military brought in a couple of truckloads of MREs last night. Facility Director Douchebag, wants us to be there while they hand them out. He's nervous there will be another food run like the last time."

"Jarl and I will handle it," Steele said, looping his thumbs on his tactical vest.

"Make sure you give the camp a once over before you head up. We can let that little turd sweat it out a bit without us. Stay safe."

Most altercations broke out over the limited distribution of government-issued supplies, but the real reason Steele wanted to man the food distribution was so he could be close to Gwen. Mauser knew this and deferred to Steele, giving him the patrols near the civilian disaster response tents.

"Maybe you could borrow a box of MREs for our packs," Mauser added with a wink.

"Shouldn't be a problem."

Steele didn't see any harm in commandeering some loose supplies to make sure their 'Go packs' were well stocked. Steele and Mauser had stashed the packs and extra supplies near the vehicles in case one needed to high tail it out of the camp. It was a constant feeling of uneasiness, but it was better than being on the run, or at least that's what he told himself.

Steele made his rounds with Jarl, knowing that Gwen would already be prepping for the food distribution. He had to keep telling himself that they were safe, although he knew that simply wasn't true. *But what chance do we have on our own?*

They walked by a giant motor pool and waved at Eddie, who helped a military mechanic working a Humvee. The mobile lounge sat dark to the side like some ancient relic. It was one of the only areas in the compound that civilians had easy access to the military.

"How you doing, Eddie?"

The elderly black man waved at him and smiled. "Oh, ya' know. Just showin' these young Army brats how to fix up a Humvee with a little style." The old man laughed and did a dance move, spinning in a circle.

Steele chuckled and patted him on the shoulder. "Keep up the good work. I'll see you later at lunch."

He and Jarl continued their patrol of the camp. They rounded the shanties up near the civilian disaster response tent. It was a large green tent, probably on loan from the military surplus.

Many remaining federal employees, who were not considered 'essential' enough to be protected underground, had set up camp there. A sort of begging around the table of the bunker for the scraps of security. It was a general whirlwind of activity, with federal employees attempting to apply some sort of order and hierarchy to the situation. It seemed to give the civilians a little hope that someday things might get back to normal.

Steele knew better, but people had faith that the government may yet save them from death. Even he had a little hope.

A couple of armed soldiers stood nearby, faces flat. *Uneasy. Worn out. On edge. And grim.* It matched what he had seen and what he had been told by some of the military operators working out of the base. It would only be a matter of time before they asked him and the other law enforcement officers to supplement their ranks, leaving the camp even more poorly defended. Not that everything wasn't already spread too thin.

"The food is killing my stomach," Jarl grumbled.

"Don't like the four fingers of death, huh?" Steele laughed.

"I hate the processed food. Give me steak. Give me whole chickens. But no. They give me hotdogs in beans, and the shits."

Steele could see Gwen from where they stood. She smiled offering a man a bag of supplies. The old man nodded as if he were crying and she gave him a hug. She held so much empathy in her heart.

"I'll be back. Have to conduct some actions from the seat," Jarl joked.

"Careful in there," Steele laughed.

"Bah," Jarl barked back, walking away.

Steele continued his watch over Gwen. At least she was safe, that was all that mattered. Now that Steele had his allies around him, he had seen very little of Ahmed, and that was just the way he liked it. He didn't trust the bastard. Maybe he had found some work in the laundry facility or, better yet, cleaning the latrines. Steele laughed inwardly.

Bang, bang. Rapid gunshots interrupted his overwatch of Gwen, hair rising on the back of his neck. Steele turned around, squinting his eyes as he combed the tent village. Tents, tarps, shelters, cook fires, and lawn chairs decorated the landscape in a disorderly fashion. *That sounded close.* A stab of fear wound into his gut. *That sounded like it came from inside the camp.*

He gripped his pistol grip rifle handle a little tighter and walked quickly toward the gunshots, boots treading hard over the ground. It was his instinct to move toward a disaster that others ran from, like a sheepdog protecting its flock. Before the outbreak, he would have been moving, high-speed, weapon drawn to the sound, thinking there was an active shooter in progress. Now, it promised something so much worse.

A man in a sweatshirt and jeans shaded his eyes with a hand.

"What's going on?" he mumbled.

"Get your family back to the command tent," Steele said, fearing the worst and hoisting his long gun up to his shoulder.

Gunshots were heard all the time. No reason to think that anything was amiss. It had become a regular part of their lives, like car traffic on a busy city street. Everyone expected it and ignored it. *Why is my hair standing on end?*

Pop, pop, pop. This was different. The gunshots came rushed and frantic; the kind of shooting a scared person does. Steele picked up his pace, half-running to the gunshots, his active shooter training shining through his complacency for the sound of gunfire. People materialized from inside their tents. That was not a good sign.

It had been made crystal clear that any outbreak was to be extinguished with extreme prejudice, which meant there would be many needless deaths unless someone stopped it right away. He imagined one of the AH-64 Apache helicopters strafing the civilian camp with a 30 mm chain gun. *Must be quick.*

Steele's tactical badge bounced against his vest as he sprinted. He shouldered through people running his way. Shanties whipped past him, and he slowed as the screaming got louder, not wanting to run headlong into a shit storm.

Wailing pierced his ears. He modified his position and moved into the high ready, peering over his sights. He kept his stride as tight as he could shoot effectively. He scanned left and right searching the area for threats. He tracked two people racing toward him. He let his trigger finger rest easy upon the slim piece of metal. They sprinted for him and he slowly depressed the trigger backward, only holding when he saw the wide-eyed look of fear in their eyes. He let them run by, one of them clutching a baby. He scanned the area twenty to thirty yards ahead. *Where are the bad guys? Follow the screams.*

Sobs echoed from a nearby blue tent that had been ripped open with long, claw-like marks. Bloody handprints covered the plastic. Shadows danced inside. He leaned hard to the right, quickly sidestepping. Both eyes were wide open so he could pick up any threats from his peripheries, but he fixated on the forms inside.

To a person who didn't know better, what he viewed might have been two people locked in a lover's embrace, but this obviously was not the case. A form hunched over the body of an elderly man. The older man struggled, his hands feebly slapping at the other man's back. The man's eyes dimmed before Steele rattled off two rounds into the infected's head. The undead were inside the facility.

The infected, covered in mud, collapsed on top of the man. Steele didn't think twice as he gave the gasping elder a round to his eyebrow ridge, preventing him from rising up again.

Steele scanned the camp once again. No part of the village was uniform. No easy grid of streets and no fatal funnels. Tarps blew in the breeze and people darted back and forth. It was utter chaos and he was caught in the middle. He brought his rifle optic close to his eye and zeroed in on another man who hurried toward him. Wild eyes captured the man's face, but he was still human. The man raced past him, breathing heavily.

"The fence," he hissed at Steele as he passed.

His eyes ran along the long chain link fence, causing a lump to rise in his throat. A mass of the infected pushed their way through an ever widening hole. *How the fuck hadn't anyone seen this group moving up the mountain? We need reinforcements, NOW.*

A hundred yards ahead of him, as far as he could see, were mangled forms of gray skinned decaying bodies. Their necks were blotched with brown, puss-filled, lymph nodes the size of plums. Every wound imaginable surged forward at a determined pace, mixed in with the faces of new recruits from the camp.

Shit was breaking bad. He slowly moved backward, retracing his steps, taking on the leaders in the pack. He had no choice, but to give up ground to his overwhelming foe.

End Time

Trigger press after trigger press he brought them down before a .50 caliber M2A1 opened up from an elevated guard tower spraying death into the horde's flank. Bodies exploded as hot rounds buzzed through rotting flesh. Arms were removed from torsos, legs blown from bodies, and people who existed one minute ceased to be there the next.

"Get some, boys," Steele shouted, and he turned hastening his retreat further inward to the center of the facility while he was covered.

The soldier in the tower had probably saved Steele's life. Steele turned to deliver more fire as a tan Humvee rolled past him with a screech, lending its support of its M2 .50 caliber turret machine gun. The heavy rattle of multiple .50s dominated the air.

Steele couldn't hear a thing. He retreated before the mass of bodies, bounding ten yards, turning to sling off five or six rounds as he tried to create some distance between him and the undead. He was acutely aware that he didn't want to be mistaken for the infected and turned into red mush.

Three times he bounded backward before the Humvee was overrun. The horde swarmed around the truck too many to stop. The gunner spun in his turret unloading his M2 from side to side. The bodies slammed up onto the hood of the military vehicle, and the undead climbed over one another. The M2 went quiet, and in a matter of seconds the disfigured corpses dragged the gunner from the turret and dismembered him, shreds of flesh and clothing flying into the air. Steele knew his tactical retreat was at an end. He turned and ran.

A million things raced through his mind. *How many rounds do I have left? Where's Gwen? Where's Mauser and Jarl? What's the quickest way to get to the people mover? This is it. The gig is up.* Steele knew he needed to get to Gwen and escape. He ran straight for the civilian disaster management tent.

Pushing his way through a crowd, a man with an ID badge on his breast stepped in front of him.

"Stop sir. Where is your access card?" the bureaucrat said.

"Get out of my way," Steele shouted, shoving him to the ground without a second glance. People stared at him angrily, but he didn't care. He placed himself in front of Gwen, his chest heaving.

Gwen looked up at him from her table, startled. "I heard lots of gunfire. Is everything okay?"

She stared at him. Fear filled her eyes. Words couldn't articulate what was happening. Cold steel blue eyes told her the worst. She stood, and her hands involuntarily reached for her mouth. People in the tent pointed in the direction he had come from. He grabbed her by the hand, pulling her toward the garage that housed the vehicles. "I'll be back in a moment," she called back to her coworkers.

No you won't, he thought as he guided her toward the garage. Begrudgingly, she let herself be whisked away.

"We're being overrun," he said as they jogged to the garage, his hand leading her along.

"I'm not a child," she said from behind him, cursing under her breath. Steele ignored her and released his grip.

Mauser and Jarl were already inside, prepping the mobile lounge. The garage held two Humvees with open engines and missing tires like a chop shop. Eddie stood in the corner with a young private both their eyes wide.

"Eddie, is this thing ready to roll?" Steele asked.

Eddie removed his hat, and wiped his bald head with a hand.

"Yes, of course. I made sure of that. What is happening?"

Steele frowned grabbing a bag. "We have to go. Your friend too if he wants to live."

The young military mechanic stammered as indecision washed over him, "I, I, can't leave without orders."

Steele gave him a dirty look. "Private Bonds?" Steele asked eying his name tag. The young soldier nodded dumbly.

"Get in the mover, Pvt. Bonds, or you'll die here."

Bonds' mouth drooped slightly as if he couldn't believe what was happening. Fear radiated from him at the prospect of disobeying orders that had been drilled into him since the first day of basic training. "I'm not sure. Where is Sergeant Rice?" he said, looking even younger.

"Probably dead. I'm offering you life. Those outside only offer death. Don't waste my time private."

Bonds timidly looked down. "Okay. I'll go."

Steele barked a laugh. "If anybody asks, you can tell them I kidnapped you," he said, cupping his hands and hoisting the young man up into the mover.

Mauser looked like he had just woken up, his hair sticking out in random places. The darkness of the garage shadowed his features. "How bad?" he asked as they handed bags to Bonds.

"This place is toast. Time to saddle up."

They threw bags into the people mover. Jarl took up a defensive position near the garage opening, overlooking the edge of the civilian camp. More Humvees rolled by from the military camp, joining the fight. Jarl squeezed off a couple of rounds, leaning forward in a battle stance.

With everyone inside, Steele turned around. "You're up, big guy," he called back to Jarl.

Instead, Ahmed came flying around the corner with Lindsay. Ahmed gave Steele a foul scowl as he approached. Steele wasn't surprised. *Gwen has a big mouth. I am sure she is to thank for him being here.*

"Figures that you show up when shit starts to get ugly."

"I wouldn't be here if somebody did their job," Ahmed said, locking eyes with Steele. *The nerve of this guy.*

Steele gave his rival a callous gaze as they pushed Lindsay up.

"Ladies first," Steele mocked. He boosted Ahmed up. One of his heels swinging dangerously close to Steele's chin as he scampered into the cabin. *I'm sure that was on purpose.*

Jarl's firing picked up in the background. Then silence.

Steele glanced over his shoulder to see what the problem was, but it was too late. Jarl front kicked an infected backward. The diseased man collapsed on the ground with a snarl. Jarl shook his forearm like he had been stung as blood spurted from the wound.

"Jarl. No," Steele shouted heart sinking.

Jarl put a bullet into its skull.

Steele took three steps toward him, but Jarl shook his head in a silent 'no' and took off outside. The big man knew his fate.

"Fuck," Steele shouted. He climbed up into the people mover and Mauser rolled it out of the garage. Steele and the other survivors had a front row seat to the disaster unfolding within the camp. People panicked as they searched for cover within the FEMA buildings as the swarm of undead human locusts extinguished all life within the facility.

"Oh my God, Jarl," Gwen whispered.

Speechless, Steele's mouth hung open. Jarl marched directly for the infected mass, hundreds of the soulless trudging for him. He walked straight ahead at a steady pace. His long gun blared away. Mag after mag he exhausted until the last one dropped free of his gun. Jarl went forth to earn his place in Valhalla, where the brave live forever.

Devoid of bullets, Jarl tossed his gun into the grass. He had once told Steele that the gun was an impersonal weapon anyway. He much preferred to be close to his enemies when he dealt them their deathblows. His hands flexed at his sides, his back and shoulder muscles bursting from beneath his tactical vest.

Jarl swept up a sledgehammer that lay near a large tent post. It appeared small in his hands, like a regular hammer. He marched forward, downing an infected with a blow to the face.

All Steele could do was watch as if he had been transported back in time to the Battle of Stamford Bridge. They attacked Jarl without fear. Forerunners grabbed at him. He struck the first with a single forward thrust to the head and the second he punched, caving the man's skull in. They dropped like sacks of potatoes. The horde of infected ignored their fallen members and continued to reach for him with dead, rotting hands.

Steele held his breath, and they were upon Jarl like a swarm of bees. He swung his hammer mightily back and forth, every swing dealing a backbreaking blow. An infected tore into his arm, and he flexed his bicep knocking the offender off. Even more of the dead took his place biting at his arms and legs. They fell to his left and his right, the bodies piling up around him. He tossed them like an enraged grizzly bear attacked by a pack of dogs. This single man was holding hundreds at bay, like a hero from an ancient saga.

The mover remained where it was, idling. None of the survivors could take their eyes off the heroic battle until Gwen shouted, "Look!"

She pointed to the side of the camp, and the motive behind Jarl's struggle became clear. A man in a lab coat rushed a woman holding a child to their vehicle.

"Well I'll be damned. Never thought I'd see that weakling Dr. Jackowski again," Mauser said.

"What's that egghead doing out here?" Steele wondered out loud. The doctor had a visible limp, and he wouldn't make it to the vehicle unless some force kept the horde at bay.

"Can we reach them?" Steele asked. Lindsay balled, tears flowing freely from a seat nearby adding to the chaos.

"Not unless we want to get stuck. Look at that slope." *Getting down won't be the problem, but getting back out of the facility will.* They sat stalled between Jarl's war against the undead waiting for Dr. Jackowski, unable to move without him.

A low war cry erupted from Jarl's lips and penetrated the mover as he inflicted a massive blow to the skull of one of the infected, decimating it. His presence was confusing them. They stumbled and slipped over their fellow spawn trying to reach him.

An infected closed in on Dr. Jackowski and his companions. He seemed to smile with his chewed off lips exposing its gums and teeth. Dr. Jackowski looked over his shoulder. Fear plastered all over his face as he hobbled, driving the woman ahead of him.

Steele shoved open the lounge's front doors. He leaned out away from the doorway. His breath caught in his chest as he tried to stop the optics from involuntarily moving. The red dot briefly crossed Dr. Jackowski's face and settled momentarily on the infected's ugly one. Crack. The undead man's head kicked backward. Steele exhaled.

Steele lowered his rifle and turned toward Jarl, covered in gore and beginning to tire. He watched with a mixture of pride and grief wallowing in his gut as his friend, colleague and brother lost his grip on his weapon. It slipped from his hands and fell to the ground.

His fate sealed, he glanced back, knowing that these were his last moments on earth. Facing the jaws of death, he threw himself into the mass of bodies, and in a final act of valor drove many of them to the ground. More of the infected pushed in around him before he disappeared beneath hundreds of hands and teeth. He was gone. And in his place were a scrawny doctor and a woman with a baby.

Steele dropped to the floor, reaching down to help the woman, child and doctor up into the mobile lounge. *Your sacrifice has not been in vain, brother.*

"Thank you. Thank you so much," Dr. Jackowski said. He collapsed in a seat, chest heaving.

"All of a sudden they were pouring through the camp. We had nowhere to run, but I saw Jarl on the hill like a god send. So we ran for him," Dr. Jackowski managed between breaths.

"Lucky for you," Steele grunted. Unlucky for Jarl, he left out. The horde paraded in their direction, having acquired their next victims, and Steele had no doubt there were enough of them to tip it over and kill them all.

The infected swarmed the lounge's tires like a river of humanity around a mechanical rock. Hefting his rifle, Steele leaned over the side and fired into the tops of their heads. Many now wore the familiar faces of soldiers and civilians from the camp. Their identities stolen by undead kin.

Pop, pop, pop. He continued firing until his mag went dry, then he pushed the mag release and slammed another into the gun in its place. Each shot from his elevated position hit a target; he couldn't miss at this range with so many so crowded together. He stood about four feet above them, out of their reach, but they grasped for him anyway. Heads exploded, destroyed by his bullets, but it was as if he were shooting at an ocean. He nearly lost his grip on the mover as Mauser lurched the machine forward.

"Hang on," Mauser called out.

Steele slung his rifle onto his back and held on tight as they barreled forward, smashing through the front gate of the camp. No one tried to stop them. No one manned the gate. Either they fled or they were dead. The Mount Eden Emergency Operations Facility was being annihilated.

Gunfire rattled as they left, but they had no idea if anyone had survived. Mauser floored it away from the facility and down the other side of the mountain road, heading west.

End Time

The woman cried as she held her baby, whispering in Spanish, while Dr. Jackowski sat somber, lost in his own thoughts.

Mauser threw in a lipper and passed the tin back to Steele.

"Should have cleaned out the PX before we left," Mauser said. Steele gave him a faint smile. Mauser seemed unfazed by the camp's fall, or maybe he was too numb to feel anything at all.

Steele's heart raced, but every moment away from the horde made him feel slightly more at ease. Ahmed stared forward, eyes resting on Gwen. Lindsay sat cross-legged, rocking back and forth with her head in her hands.

Steele's hard gaze ran across the road ahead, searching for threats. Gwen took his hand in hers. It softened his demeanor, if only for a moment, as he looked at her hand in his. He would have done anything to keep it there, and he knew he would have to yet.

"We are safe now?" Gwen asked, looking up at him.

"I'm not sure if we will ever be safe again," he said quietly. *Can we ever trust any 'secure' place? If Eden can't shelter us, are we now condemned to live a wanderer's life? Where else could provide refuge from the dead?*

Expelled from Mount Eden, this was the world they now faced, and they drove straight into it. For in this new world, it was either keep moving or die with the rest.

Thank you for reading this book. I truly hope that you enjoyed what you've read. If you have a moment, I would greatly appreciate your review on Amazon. Cheers!
Facebook Page: https://www.facebook.com/DanielGreenebooks/

Never fear the End Times will continue...the second installment is in production.

For updates on new books and news from the author, please sign up at danielgreenebooks.com

A special thanks to http://www.joyofediting.co.uk/ for your excellent work. One can only imagine what this project may have looked like without your assistance.

A big shout out to Mike Tanoory for turning my ideas into images. Please see more of his work here: Tanoorystudios.com

And last but not the least, a special thanks to Kevin, Jen, Kathy and Mom for your honest feedback and for listening as I prattled on endlessly about the intricacies of the book.

Meet the Author

Daniel was born in the Midwest and grew up with a heavy dose of 80s action films. He has always had a passion for history, exercise and zombie apocalypse fiction. He is inspired by the fiction of George R. R. Martin, Robert Jordan, Bernard Cornwell and George Romero, who set the bar so high for excellence. If he isn't working on his next book, you can find him training his body for the impending rise of the undead. He now resides on the East Coast.

danielgreenebooks.com

Made in the USA
San Bernardino, CA
09 March 2016